Pinstripes

'Remember this, we will never put this behind us until we've dished out our just deserts. I don't particularly like you and you obviously don't like me, and well, I don't know about her but I expect she doesn't like either of us. But we have to unite and do this. We owe it to ourselves,' Clara looked at the two girls in front of her. Virginia and Ella looked like the worst kind of fighting partners anyone could have. She stood up. 'I'd like to propose a toast. To revenge. To avenging. To giving these people what they bloody well deserve.'

Also by Faith Bleasdale

Rubber Gloves or Jimmy Choos?

Pinstripes

Faith Bleasdale

FLAME

Hodder & Stoughton

First published in Great Britain in 2001
by Hodder and Stoughton
First published in paperback in 2001
by Hodder and Stoughton
A division of Hodder Headline

A Flame Paperback

10 9 8 7 6 5 4 3 2 1

A CIP catalogue record for this title
is available from the British Library.

ISBN 0 340 76817 7

Printed and bound in Great Britain by
Mackays of Chatham plc, Chatham, Kent

Hodder and Stoughton
A division of Hodder Headline
338 Euston Road
London NW1 3BH

For Thom whose courage and strength
is true inspiration. You are my hero

Big thanks to my wonderful family who have again surpassed themselves with support. I return that love.

Big thanks to my friends. You know who you are. You're the best.

Thank you to everyone who read my first book and especially those who emailed me with kind wonderful comments. I look forward to hearing your views on Pinstripes at faith@faithbleasdale.com and visit my website:
                 www.faithbleasdale.com

Thanks to my old work colleagues. Thank you for being nothing like any of the characters in the book.

Thank you to Shelley, Sara and Carolyn for all your hard work.

Finally thanks to Jonathan. For everything. You're still a top fellow.

Here's to all the Goodies. Down with all the baddies.

Prologue

In the nineteenth century, three partners founded investment bank Seymour Forbes Hunt. From a small investment house, it has become one of the major players not only in Europe but also in the rest of the world. Today, twenty-one managing directors run and own the company. Its successful partnership formula makes it an attractive company to work for which is reflected by the high standard of its personnel. The headquarters are in the heart of London's financial centre, the building is one of the oldest and most prestigious. It is a bank with a great history and a great future.

Excerpt from the official SFH publicity brochure.

Seymour Forbes Hunt is Britain's oldest investment bank and a British institution. At this time of recruitment, we are inviting you to participate in our success. As not only the oldest but also the most successful UK investment bank, we only pursue the best candidates to work with us. If you feel you wish to join us you must show us the commitment to the world of investment, the dedication and the intelligence we require. We in return will offer you a career with rewards that reflect our status. What we mean is that in return for the excellence that we demand, we offer an excellent package and unparalleled opportunities.

The SFH presentation to the Cambridge undergraduate class of 2000.

Again, we show that we are a fighting force in the world of investment. Our results this year not only outstrip those of last year but also show that we are on the right track with our policies and management. We are one of the best this country has to offer and we give unparalleled results to our partners and to our clients. All of us in this room may congratulate ourselves on the successful completion of another year. We not only show we can make money, but we show that we are the best at making money, which after all is what we are all here for.

Peter Seymour, SFH's Chairman's speech at the end of year managing directors' meeting.

As we see Seymour Forbes Hunt continuing to grow, we ask ourselves why it is so successful as a British investment bank. It shows an unblemished record in business and one that is hard to follow. A major force in this country if not the world, again we must congratulate the private partnership which makes this bank a British institution.

Gerald Barr, of the Financial Times, *reporting on the success of SFH.*

Flotation is always a temptation for a company that shows success. However, this temptation is still being resisted by successful investment bank Seymour Forbes Hunt. The chairman, Peter Seymour issued the following statement: 'Why change something that works so well? Not only is the ownership of our partnership based on merit and hard work, but also we have an incentive to staff that few other institutions can offer. The management know how to manage this business, and as they are also the shareholders, they have a strong interest in ensuring that clients and staff alike are given both excellence as a goal and a reward.' Thus, SFH enters the year 2001 with the goal of avoiding becoming a public company and continuing with its tried and tested partnership.'

Gerald Barr from the Financial Times, *on speculation that SFH may succumb to the pressure to go public.*

Interview for the graduate programme at SFH:
Interviewer: 'What does the City mean to you?'
Interviewee: 'Pinstripes and Porsches.'

PART ONE

Pinstripes and Porsches

Chapter One

'So, is it hard surviving in such a man's world?' Jim asked, grinning.

'No,' Ella Franke replied, through clenched teeth. She looked at the tall, dark-haired man standing in front of her and wondered why she kept paying this penance.

'But don't you feel guilty about the amount of money you earn? Look at the poverty in London, and you earning a fortune. It doesn't seem right somehow,' Jim riposted.

Ella's heart-rate was increasing. 'Don't you feel guilty about the torture you're putting me through at forty quid an hour? Give that to the starving millions.' She gasped for breath. She should have known better than to try to put a long sentence together, especially when she was this close to collapse.

Jim seemed to ignore her last statement. 'Are you happy? Really happy? I mean, I bet you have a great life — nice flat, lots of clothes, fast car and, of course, a personal trainer, all the status symbols a woman like you needs. But does any of that make you happy?'

Ella took a deep breath. Her worst fear on the treadmill was losing her footing. Another deep breath. She studied Jim, big, bulky and smug. The worst type of man. He felt that in his role of trainer he could play God with her life. She knew that his other clients let him, but she would not. Hence the hostility every time they met. Finally, she felt able to speak again. 'For fuck's sake, will you shut up? I am on a treadmill, not a couch, and you are supposed to be training me, not interviewing, counselling or annoying the hell out of me. If you feel compelled to make small-talk, please restrict it to, "Run faster," or "You're doing great."' Ella could feel herself overheating and the sweat pouring down her face was making her skin itch. She was exhausted.

Jim laughed. 'You, girl, crack me up. You're just so funny. Let's go faster.' And before Ella could retort he put the treadmill speed up even further and smugly watched her huff and puff her way through her final minute and a half.

Jim studied Ella closely. She was tall, black and thin. She had long legs, (which Jim often admired as he watched her run), a firm stomach and tiny boobs. Jim thought her boobs were the only things that let her down. Her thick black hair was cut into a shoulder-length bob. She had great hair. He quite fancied her, then he was just a man, and most men would, but her manner was something else. She was always aloof, uptight. She could be a real bitch. Most girls fell at his feet and Jim was pissed off that this one did not. That was why he enjoyed winding her up every Monday.

'Water,' Ella whispered, as the treadmill finally came to a halt. She felt as if she had been running for hours, not just ten minutes. She wondered again why she put herself through this. She gulped the water noisily, and tried to make a mental note not to be rude to Jim again.

'Sit-ups now. You're looking a bit tummyish this week.'

Ella realised as she looked at her flat stomach and lay down in the sit-up position that she truly hated Jim.

She had been training with him once a week for almost three years — forty pounds for an hour of pure hell. He was rude, arrogant and he treated Ella with disdain. Ella hated him, and only put up with him because that was another way she could fit in. She longed to tell him where to stick his 'positive mental attitude', but she couldn't and she didn't know why.

When Ella started work at SFH, she had been encouraged to take corporate membership of the posh gym by the horrific human-resources woman who seemed to take Ella under her wing. It had been she, too, who had encouraged Ella to use Jim. When Ella first started work, she had been so concerned to fit in that she took every suggestion on board and became the clichéd City type. She was more of a cliché than anyone else she knew: she had a trainer, she shopped at Gucci, she had a flat in the Docklands, she had a sports car, and she practically had 'City' tattooed on her forehead. And for her to continue in the job she loved, Ella felt that all these trappings were necessary so, hate him as she did, it looked as if Jim was here to stay. 'Oh, the things I do to keep my job,' Ella thought as Jim counted forty then told her that her exercise hell was finally over.

Ignoring his smile, she hissed goodbye and marched to the changing room.

It was full of the usual girls, those who were dedicated to looking after their bodies before work most mornings. Ella nodded curtly and took her towel out of her locker. As she peeled off her sweat-drenched shorts and T-shirt, she tried to justify being there. Five thirty in the morning, exercise for an hour, then in the office by seven. It was mad, she was mad. It wasn't even as if she enjoyed or, more to the point, needed it. Glancing at her body as she walked to the shower, she knew she didn't have an ounce of fat on her. Not like most of the girls in the gym, who had the Michelin Man's spare tyres on them. No, this was corporate sucking-up and Ella was not terribly pleased with herself for it.

As the lukewarm water covered her aching body, she tried not to think too much about Jim. Instead, she focused on the day ahead. A tingle of excitement ran through her as she thought about the previous week's trading. The market had been volatile and many people had lost money, wrong-guessing the direction of stock. Not Ella: every move she had made had been spot on and she had come out up. She was looking forward to that today, hoping that the same buzz would fill her and that the unexplainable instinct she seemed to have for the job didn't desert her. 'If only you could see me now, Sammy', she thought, and, for a minute, the sadness washed over her again.

She finished washing her hair, and prayed that her worries would be rinsed away along with the dirty shampoo. She knew that it would take more than prayers.

As she walked back to her locker the girls were gossiping. Again, they smiled at her, not quite knowing if they should. Ella smiled back but said nothing. She had never engaged in their chat, and they no longer tried to include her. She dried her hair, pulled her Armani pinstripe suit from her suit bag, put on a little makeup and as the other girls were still getting ready she said goodbye and left. Leaving the gym, she walked up the hill to the office, stopping only to buy her usual espresso from Coffee Republic. The excitement returned as she walked through the front door of Seymour Forbes Hunt, and she put everything, apart from making money, well and truly out of her mind.

As soon as her alarm clock buzzed at her Virginia Bateman jumped out of bed. She peeled off her pyjamas and walked the short distance to her tiny bathroom, pausing on the way to flick the switch on the kettle. She stood in the shower for exactly five minutes. As she stepped out, shivering at the cold, she picked a towel from the rail, then dried herself. She pulled her bathrobe from the hook on the door and put it on. Wrapping her hair in a second towel, she walked back into her living area and made herself a cup of tea, then reached over to put on the television and sat in her small armchair, sipping the tea and concentrating on the news. When she was finished the tea she went to the sink, washed her cup and left it on the draining-board. Her outfit for the day, a grey pinstripe trouser suit and crisp white shirt, was hanging on the front of her wardrobe waiting for her. She dressed, still watching the television, mentally noting anything said about the stock market. She turned away to dry her short hair, brushed it flat, and applied a little makeup: foundation, mascara and clear lip gloss. 'I look professional,' she said to herself in the mirror, when she was ready.

Virginia always looked professional and prided herself on it. She was quite tall, about five foot seven, and a size ten. She had mousy brown hair, grey eyes and unremarkable features. She always looked the part, and although devoid of glamour, she was not unattractive. The only unattractive part of Virginia was the continual scowl — this scowl that had become so much a part of her features, that it was now part of her.

She picked up the towels and her bathrobe and hung them up in the bathroom. Then she collected her coat, her handbag and her helmet, and left her bedsit.

Virginia lived near Maida Vale, right address, wrong flat. Wrong because it wasn't even a flat: it was a tiny studio apartment, which was called a studio because letting agents realised that 'studio' sounded more romantic and inviting than 'bedsit', which is exactly what it was. Although technically it wasn't because it had its own bathroom.

When Virginia had moved to London two years ago, she had shared a house with four other people, strangers. It had felt like a student house because they were so messy. She hated it and lasted only two months before the dirt got too much for her. It was then that she decided she needed to live on her own and the 'studio' was all she could afford. Renting a one-bedroom flat on her sec-retary's salary was out of the question. 'One day,' Virginia said to herself, as she did every day when she thought about her life.

As she walked down the street to where her scooter was parked the cold air blasted her. She smiled at it, as she did every day. Virginia loved her scooter, the freedom it gave her and the way she could get to work in a short time without suffering on the tube. It had been another sensible buy. She loved driving through London, with the wind in her face; it was the most invigorating way to begin the day.

She started it up and drove off into the quiet, dark streets. The roads were not busy and weaving in and out of the traffic encountered meant that she could get to work in no time at all. The drive to and from work was Virginia's favourite part of the day.

The street that held her usual parking bay was deserted and she left her scooter in its usual place. She removed her helmet, put her lock on the wheels and took the four-minute walk to her office.

Her heart skipped a beat, as it always did, when she saw the building. Although not particularly big, it was old, grand and commanding. She felt it must be the most beautiful office building in London. The Seymour Forbes Hunt sign glistened in the grey air. She paused briefly, as she did every morning, and asked for an opportunity. Anyone who saw the professional-looking girl standing in front of an office sign mouthing, 'Please give me a chance,' might have thought she was mad, but no one ever did.

Virginia loved SFH. It had been her first choice of bank to work at, and although she was unable to get the job she wanted, at least she had a job with the right company. Seymour Forbes Hunt was a British investment bank, and a British institution. She had read all about it before she left university. It had been founded in the late nineteenth century, and had remained a private partnership, shunning all attempts at takeover and flotation. The company was run by its twenty or so managing directors, who all owned part of it. Everyone who worked at SFH dreamt of becoming a managing director. Virginia just dreamt of being a salesperson.

Composing herself again, she pushed open the heavy doors, flashed her pass at the tired security guard and called the lift. Then she played the game she played daily: if the lift came in less than five seconds it would be a very good day; if it came in less than ten it would be an OK day; if it took longer it would be a horrible day. Thirty seconds later the lift arrived.

Virginia pushed the button for the fourth floor, the trading floor, her floor. She knew as she watched the other floors pass that this was definitely where she wanted to be, but in an entirely different job.

At twenty past six, she was at her desk. She was one of the first people on the floor and she liked this time. It gave her a chance to study the markets, watch the screens and feel that she was part of it – before Isabelle, her boss, came in and reminded her that she was nothing more than a secretary and destroyed a little bit more of Virginia's hope.

Clara Hart was running late. Again. She cursed loudly as she surveyed the mess surrounding her, the knickers, socks and laddered tights that littered the floor. She grabbed the last pair of tights in the drawer and prayed that they were whole. Her prayers were answered. She went to the wardrobe and pulled out her last clean suit, a navy blue pinstripe skirt and jacket. She made a mental note to find her dry-cleaning tickets as she hauled herself into it. She pulled a brush through her long, matted blonde hair as, on cue, the buzzer went. She grabbed her coat and bag and ran to pick up the intercom. 'Hello,' she said, knowing who it was.

'Taxi,' a gruff voice replied. Her chariot had arrived.

The driver looked familiar; he had probably taken her to work thousands of times, or taken her somewhere, she was never sure. As she settled into the back seat she pulled her trusty compact out of her Prada handbag and applied her makeup like an expert. Clara had never quite got the hang of public transport, as her taxi firm had observed. Once she had put on her face, she grabbed her purse from her bag, counted out the fare and, as the cab pulled up outside the office of Seymour Forbes Hunt, she was ready.

She winked at the cab driver as she walked away and he smiled. She knew she still had 'the charm'. Clara had discovered 'the charm' at an early age: not the brightest child in the world, she had used it to get her through prep school, her strict boarding-school, finishing-school and eventually to her job in sales at SFH. It always got her what she wanted, and allowed her to break every rule in the book to do so.

It wasn't that she wasn't gorgeous, everyone thought she was. She had long blonde hair, pretty blue eyes, sweet lips and a figure to die for. But Clara knew how to make the most of her looks. She dressed to kill — skirts were always short, tops showed just a hint of cleavage: makeup emphasised her good points and hid the bad. Clara was an expert in making the most of what she'd got, and although she had more than most, she made herself desired by practically every man she met.

As she waited for the lift, she thought of Tim. What time had he left her bed? She didn't remember him going, but she knew that at some point after she passed out, he would have slunk home to his wife. She also knew that he would already be in the office, at his desk, wearing his immaculate suit that would have been laid out for him by his immaculate wife.

Christ, if I was as organised as a wife, I'd make a much better mistress, Clara thought as she climbed into the lift, which would take her to begin her day.

Chapter Two

When Ella got to work, she could tell it was going to be a busy day. The salespeople were on the phone, collecting information; the traders were reading research. Ella picked up the report that the researchers prepared every morning and flicked through the market predictions. As soon as the markets opened, she checked her screens, watched the prices jumping and felt an adrenaline rush as she prepared to trade.

She checked her positions and was happy that her trading book was as it should be. Then she called her favourite broker, Danny, and proceeded to sell a number of stocks she had bought cheap on Friday, which had upped in value that morning. After working her positions for the first hour, Charles, one of the sales-guys called over to her: 'Ella, can you get me a price in Orchid Corp for a million shares?'

'Buyer or seller?' Ella shouted back, checking the screens.

'Dunno, he wouldn't open,' Charlie replied.

It was the response that Ella expected: clients never said if they were a buyer or seller, there was only so much information they felt a trader needed. Ella flipped a coin in her head and guessed that the client was probably a buyer. She shouted back her price.

'I'll buy at twenty-five or sell at fifty cents higher for up to five hundred thousand. I'm happy to start like that and work the balance if you still want a million.' She waited as she watched Charlie speak with his client.

'You've sold five hundred to SAM at twenty-five and a half. You've got a balance of half a mill to buy for them. Top limit is five-eighths. Try to improve. Oh, and, Ella, you've got one hour.'

Ella remained cool but she knew this was potentially a good trade. She also knew it was risky: she didn't own the stock she had just sold. She was short of half a million shares, and needed to buy them back at a lower price to make a profit. 'Sure thing, Charlie,' she shouted, as she sat down and picked up the phone.

Half an hour later, the order was filled, the price good, both Ella and the client were happy, and Charlie asked Ella to marry him.

Ella was a trader on the European Equities desk. She bought and sold shares in European companies both for clients and for SFH's own trading account. Her own trading account, 'her book', gave her more satisfaction than the client trades. It was her book that had made her a small fortune in commission over the last few years.

Ella had had a good day. She pulled out a calculator and worked out how much money she'd made for the firm. Not bad at all. Picking up her gym bag, she grabbed her coat, said goodbye to anyone still on the desk and left. It was a quarter past five.

When she reached the stop the bus was waiting, which was always a good sign. It was a fitting end to the day. Ella was buzzing all the way home. She loved nothing more than making money, and the thrill it gave her was better than sex. Well, better than the sex she remembered. She thought fleetingly back to Tony, her ex-fiancé, and tried to push him out of her mind. God, no matter what she did or where she went he was always there, haunting her, and she didn't even know if he was dead or alive.

Ella knew she was one of the best traders at SFH, and she had proved herself. She worried about the lies catching up with her, about Tony finding her, if he were alive, or the police finding her, if he were dead. She also worried about her brother Sam. Her only contact with him now was the monthly cheques she insisted on sending him. She still couldn't see him; she still couldn't give him her address. She couldn't even bring herself to call him. As far as Ella was concerned, she was a fugitive. Before she allowed herself to dwell on her past for too long, the bus pulled up and she got off.

She walked from the bus stop to her smart, riverside Docklands flat, laughing at herself through the sadness as Sam would have laughed if he could see her. With her smart flat and her TVR in the underground car park he would call her a yuppie, although they no longer existed. It was these imaginary conversations with her brother that kept her going. If only Sam could see her now, she knew that, along with the jokes, he'd be proud of what she had achieved.

She let herself in, kicked off her shoes and made herself a cup of tea. Then she put the stereo on and relaxed on the sofa, sipping tea and thinking about her work. She knew that she was in line for promotion to manager within the next year or so. Then who knew? She was looking forward to being the first black female managing director of SFH.

Her flat was incredibly tidy, because Ella could hardly bear for it to be lived in. She could remember when she had got the mortgage, signed the forms, been given the keys. It was hers, the first thing in her life that had belonged to her totally. She loved it: the polished wooden floorboards, the big red leather sofa, the huge television she hardly watched, the stereo, the abstract paintings she had chosen. The bookcase was jammed full of books: books that offered Ella the escapism she craved. She had a few knick-knacks from her old life: a china elephant Sam had given her, a photo of her family, and some wooden boxes she had once kept her treasures in, but that was all. The coffee table had only today's *Financial Times* on it and the book she was reading at the moment.

The kitchen was small but functional. It was fitted and a bit too chrome for Ella's liking, but she had never thought of changing it. The bathroom was lovely, white and clean, and the bath was large. Ella loved her bath. She had a separate shower room, which she barely used. Her bedroom was *huge* with big, fitted wardrobes, one filled with work suits, the other with casual clothes; it was empty by comparison with the first. She had a navy blue duvet cover and a plain wooden blind on the window. It was not an interior decorator's dream, but Ella thought it was nice; and she only wanted her life to be nice.

She picked up the *Financial Times* and read it for the second time that day. The one thing she loved about her working day was that although it demanded an early start, an early finish was the reward. She had a routine in the evenings that made her feel secure. She would read the paper, listening to music. Then she would cook herself some dinner, and after dinner, she would have a long soak in the bath with a book, which she would then take to bed with her. During the week Ella rarely went out. She was too concerned about staying focused. So after her tuna salad, she picked up her Jackie Collins novel, and took it with her to the bathroom.

Ella was normally in bed by 10 p.m. and asleep by half past. She sometimes wondered why she wasn't in the Army, her life was so regimented. But this routine was necessary for her to do her job well, and her job was about the only thing she had left.

Ella fell asleep dreaming about her work. She knew that there was more to life than work: her one friend, Jackie, whom she had met when she first moved to London, was constantly reminding her of that, but Jackie was the only person who could get away with it. Jackie, with her down-to-earth ways, and her down-to-earth restaurant was the only person Ella could afford to let into her life. Friends did not happen in Ella's life; she was afraid of anyone finding out too much about her. She shivered as she thought about what would happen if ever the truth came out. God, she loved her job and, as she often pointed out to Jackie, at the moment that was enough for her.

Because all these thoughts were running through her brain, it took Ella longer than usual to fall asleep that night.

'Virginia, can you get my line?'

'Virginia, can you fax this?'

'Virginia, can you print me out the figures again?'

'Virginia, can you photocopy this ten times?'

Virginia smiled weakly at the giver of each instruction. It was a typical Monday.

After fulfilling requests all morning, she left the office for ten minutes at lunch-time and tried to collect her thoughts. It was a bright winter's day; the dull haze of the morning was long gone. She was slightly cheered by the weak sunshine and that the temperature had risen above freezing for what felt like the first time in ages. She walked past the other City buildings and wondered what they were like inside. She wondered if they shared the same routine as SFH, and what it would be like to work in one of them. She wondered what the trading floors were like. Dragging herself past them, she felt like a child passing toyshops. What she wanted so badly might have been in each of these buildings, yet all Virginia could do was walk past them.

She went into the Italian sandwich shop where she always bought her lunch. She ordered a cheese-salad sandwich on brown bread and a bottle of mineral water. She returned to SFH, went to her desk and ate her lunch. At the same time she read and dealt with her e-mails (all from her boss), checked the diaries for the afternoon, and by the time that everyone had returned from lunch and the desk was full again, she was ready for the afternoon orders.

Virginia worked as a secretary to Isabelle Holland and ten

salespeople. She organised all their diaries, booked their client dinners, arranged their travel, photocopied, filed, typed, organised. She rarely had time to breathe. Isabelle was a demanding boss and most of Virginia's time was spent working for her. The ten salespeople were also demanding, and kept Virginia busy for the day and most of the evening. Although she was an efficient secretary, no one on the team took much notice of her or seemed to appreciate her. The truth was that they had seen how Isabelle treated her, and heard how Isabelle talked about her behind her back. They had even laughed at her cruel jibes. No one was quite sure why Isabelle hated Virginia so much, but they had no intention of jeopardising their own positions by being nice to her. Virginia did not question their coldness. This was how she was used to being treated.

She looked at her watch. It was a quarter past seven and she still had a pile of filing to do. She looked across the trading floor. It was thinning and the quiet buzz of the computers was the only sound once again. As she was close to being the first person in every morning, she was close to being the last there too. Thinking back over the day, her heart sank. Isabelle had been in a nasty mood. She had shouted at her for not doing things that she had never asked her to do. The people on the desk hadn't left her alone all day, then before they left they'd all handed her their expenses, which were such a mess. Virginia knew she might not be able to bear the job for much longer, but what else could she do?

She turned pink with embarrassment at the memory of last week when she had bravely walked into Isabelle's office, bravely given her rehearsed speech, bravely stood as Isabelle once again stamped on her dreams.

'Isabelle, have you got a minute?' Virginia had asked timidly.

Isabelle had looked at Virginia over her glasses; the lack of interest was evident. 'Sure.'

As Virginia had walked into the office, she noted again

what a mess it was. She often referred to her boss's office as Paper Mountain, due to Isabelle's inability to organise and tidy. When it got so bad that Isabelle couldn't see over the top, she would summon Virginia to clear it up.

Virginia sat down, facing Isabelle. She looked at her and wished she herself was more sophisticated. Although Virginia wasn't short, Isabelle still seemed twice as tall and made her feel so inadequate. Her hair was tied up in a bun, but a couple of strands hung over her face to make her look less severe. Her wire glasses sat on her nose and Virginia always had to resist the temptation to push them back. Her pink lipstick always looked immaculate, as did her long, painted nails. The designer suit she was wearing complemented her slim figure, and if Isabelle hadn't been such a bitch, Virginia would have said she was stunning.

'I've been working for you for three years, and I really enjoy it, but I've come to a stage in my life where I need a new challenge, fresh opportunities, and I wanted to speak to you about what I could do.' Virginia had said it without daring to take a breath.

'Go on,' Isabelle had said icily.

'Well, I really want to get into sales. I was wondering if I could do my exams for a start, then maybe you would let me apply for a junior sales position here, or maybe on another desk ...' The frost in Isabelle's eyes had made Virginia stop prematurely.

'But you're a secretary,' Isabelle had said.

'Yes, but I don't want to be a secretary for ever. I have a degree, you know, and I have learnt loads while I've been here – and it's something I've always wanted to do.'

Isabelle sat up straighter. 'Virginia, do you know how long I've worked here?' Virginia had shaken her head. 'Fourteen years. Fourteen long years. I have been at SFH as a salesperson for the whole of that time. So, please forgive me when I tell you that I know what makes a good salesperson. I know instinctively, it's in my gut. And as I have had an extremely successful fourteen years, you'll be able to trust me when I say that you would not make a good salesperson. You're all wrong. Virginia, I value you as my secretary, but believe me when I say that that is the only job you will ever have at SFH. Sorry to disappoint, but I feel situations like this need an honest approach.' With that Isabelle turned to face her computer and Virginia was dismissed.

She had not cried in the office, although she felt like it. She had waited until she got home and cried there, sobbed. Big fat tears. Virginia knew that Isabelle was wrong, but how was she ever going to get the chance to prove it?

She turned back to her pile of work, and realised that no one would know if she left the filing for another day, and who cared if her desk was a mess? Virginia no longer felt like playing Miss Efficiency and, with that rather decadent thought, she shut down her computer and left the office.

The drive home was quick and traffic-free. She stopped on the way to buy a bottle of red wine, something she rarely did but today had been such hell that she felt she deserved it. She unlocked the door to the studio, picked up a bill and a letter from her parents that lay on the mat. She put them aside and opened the wine.

Her studio had two rooms. One, her living area, housed a small double bed, an armchair and a counter that ran alongside and was her kitchen. She hated having her kitchen in the same room as her bed, but she kept it religiously clean and had learnt to bear it. It had a small stove on top of a small oven, a sink, a small fridge and a cupboard. Virginia cooked herself dinner every night; she kept the food simple. Her room was magnolia, dirty magnolia. The carpet was dark beige and had seen better days, as had the armchair, which had lost half of its stuffing. She had a small bookshelf, which mainly contained books about the City, a small colour television and video. She even had her own phone, but as it never rang she often forgot it was there. She had only one picture on her wall, a print of a country landscape her mother had given her when she moved to London. It was oddly depressing – you could see all of Virginia in that one room. The shower room was just a shower, a basin and a loo, small but clean, which Virginia felt applied to the rest of her life.

As she drank her first glass of wine, she tried hard to think about what she could do. She felt that she was at the end of the line. She had tried everything. After the initial rejection by all investment banks when she applied for the graduate programme, she had wanted single-mindedly only to work at SFH. At her first interview for her current job, she had talked about her ambition. In return, she had been told that SFH had a strong policy for internal promotion but she was also told not to expect it to happen overnight. It hadn't happened overnight; it hadn't happened at all. Now that Virginia had learnt that Isabelle had no intention of ever promoting her, she felt she had nothing left.

Virginia drained her glass and went to take the second shower of her day. She tried to scrub off the disappointment; she tried to wash away her despair. Once dry, she poured another glass of wine, put the news on and finally opened the letter from her parents. For as long as she could remember, Virginia had had a pitiful relationship with her parents. They had been fiercely ambitious for her and Virginia had never lived up to their expectations, even at seven when she didn't get the most Brownie badges in her pack. They wanted her to be the best, the brightest, the prettiest, and Virginia was none of those things. She was a failure. Her parents had pointed out their disappointment at every stage of her life. First she didn't win the sack race; then she didn't have the highest reading age in her class; she didn't get into the top sets at secondary school; she didn't get any As at GCSE; she didn't get any As at A level. Then she went to what they saw as an average university, and true to form she didn't get a first-class degree.

Never once had Virginia's parents congratulated her or told her they were proud of her. They had done the opposite and, consequently, she had never had any confidence. Now, of course, they reminded her, every time they wrote, that she was just a secretary, and wasn't it a shame that a girl with all her opportunities had never managed to make the most of any of them?

The letter started as usual. How are you, how's work, have you managed to get anywhere yet? Then it spoke of the wonderful achievement of her cousins: Mary-Ann was going to Oxford University; Sally was getting married to a computer programmer no less. What a shame, it said, that Virginia had neither their talent nor their luck with men. She screwed up the letter and threw it on the floor. It sat there, a solitary blimp on an otherwise spotless carpet. 'Damn, I can't even make a mess properly,' Virginia hissed, and went to pick it up.

She tried to remember where she had gone wrong. How had she, the girl from Coventry, managed to go through life with no friends, no one to love, and no happiness? She was twenty-four years old with a job she hated, not one friend – unless she counted Susie her penpal from Canada, a poky bedsit in London, and a reputation for being odd.

And she *was* odd. When she started working at SFH, the other secretaries had socialised together and invited Virginia to join them. However, she had always declined, preferring to stay at home reading books about the City. She had learnt about the markets, she'd read every bit of research she could get her hands on, she read the newspapers and watched the City news. Virginia figured that her education was more important than her social life. Inevitably, the girls stopped asking Virginia to go with them, Virginia ran out of books to read, and lost the conviction that her education was even remotely important.

Now, every evening stretched before her, empty and dull. She had tried to tag along with the secretaries a couple of times recently, but they ignored her: they felt that because she had snubbed them before, she thought herself better than them, and Virginia's defence against that charge was weak. She had put herself in Lonely Land and the only social life she had was her French classes — so she had something else to put on her CV — which were mainly full of people much older than her. Virginia had spent the last three years of her life trying desperately to better herself and her prospects, and she had failed.

The nights spent reading, weekends visiting galleries, exhibitions, watching movies had resulted in loneliness, immense loneliness.

With the third glass of wine came tears, with the fourth nausea, and with the last drip of the bottle, sleep.

As Clara made her way across the floor to her desk, she noticed the manic activity that was already under way. A number of salespeople were on their feet with phones glued to their ears, shouting across to the traders. 'Am I done?' seemed a popular chant. As she approached her desk she noticed that Sarah, the most senior member of their team, excluding Tim, was also on her feet. 'Is it filled?' she was shrieking at Liam, a trader.

Liam was barely visible: his head was low on his desk, a phone at his ear, and he screamed, red-faced, 'Hit the bid in fifty. *Now!* You fucking useless broker wanker.' His voice rose above the other noise in the office. Silence ensued.

Liam stood up with his telephone handset still attached to his ear. 'No! Fucking useless bastard missed it. We sold half a point lower.'

'Shit!' Sarah screamed at him, but he shrugged and moved on to his next call. Sarah took her client off hold and attempted to pacify him.

Although Clara loved scenes like this, she did not have the first idea what any of it meant. Therefore, when her first client of the day called she wrote everything down.

Clara smiled sweetly at her neighbour. 'Toby, I have this client who wants to buy some stuff and, well, I'm just not sure what to do.' When Clara wanted anything, she fixed her eyes so intently on the person who could give it to her that they buckled.

'Sure, give me the information, I'd be glad to do it.' Toby blushed.

'You're such a darling. I insist you let me take you out for a drink tonight to say thank you.' Toby thought he'd died and gone to heaven. He readily agreed, still blushing.

Clara's work theory. When she started as a secretary, she hadn't been expected to do much. Most of the men in the office were too in awe of her to ask her for anything, and her boss, Tim, flirted with her rather than showering her with work. In the rare instances that anyone wanted anything, Clara would asked one of the other secretaries to do it, and bought them handmade chocolates as a thank-you. Now that she had become a salesperson things were a little different. Although not exactly overworked, she now had a number of clients for whom she was responsible, and when they called to asked her to buy or sell stock for them, she didn't know what to do. She knew in principle that you got a trader, wrote a ticket, put something in the computer, but it didn't sound like fun, so she didn't bother learning how to do it. She loved talking to her clients and they loved her. She often went for lunch or dinner with them and they were all big fans. Although she did not have a clue how to do her job and everyone on the desk thought she was useless, her sales figures were good. This was because Toby or Francine made sure the orders went through after Clara had taken them, and Clara rewarded them with a smile, chocolates, or a much-coveted after-work drink.

She flicked through her e-mails, sent a couple of jokes to her brother then went to see Tim.

Clara took perverse pleasure in visiting Tim's office. She would knock on the door, enter, sit facing him and make him squirm. The office was glass-fronted and looked out on to the trading floor. He had to talk to her as if he was talking about business, but they weren't talking about business.

'Timmy, what time did you leave me last night?' Clara pouted.

'About one. You were fast asleep.'

'I know, and nothing can wake me when I pass out. So, when I am going to have the pleasure of your cock again?'

'Clara, please.'

'Please what, Timmy? Do you want to do it right now?'

Tim went red and turned his back to the trading floor. He knew that most of the men would be staring at Clara and he didn't want anyone to see his discomfort. He adored Clara; lately he had even been thinking about leaving his wife and family for her. Although it had started as a lust-filled fling, he thought of how great it would be for Clara and he to be together all the time. His wife was OK but dull, his children, well, they would be at boarding-school soon, and with Clara he would be able to indulge in his favourite pastimes, cocaine and sex. And not just sex with Clara either: sex with prostitutes, his 'special treat' girls he called them. His prudish missionary-position wife would probably die if she found out, but he told Clara all about them and he was sure she found the idea quite a turn-on. He was a lucky man. He was beginning to think he would like to be lucky all the time. The trouble was, they both sometimes forgot who was boss. He needed to bring her back in line.

'Stop it. Now, baby, I know you're gagging for me, but you have to be a patient girl. I won't be seeing you tonight because I'm visiting one of my hookers. Probably the tall one with long red hair and boobs bigger than both of yours put together. I shall be screwing the fuck out of her, and when I've finished, I'll go home and have sex with my wife. You see, you don't deserve me tonight, so you're not going to have me.' Tim smiled at Clara, his whole face lit by a confident grin. Oh, yes, he thought, she's putty in my hands.

Clara smiled back at him sweetly, wishing he wasn't such a prick. She didn't find the way he behaved remotely sexy, although he thought he was. She often felt sick about the prostitutes, and she hated him having to convince himself that he was in control. Clara knew he was thinking of leaving his wife, he'd told her. Of course, he had made it sound like a huge privilege, ('you lucky, lucky girl'), but the idea filled Clara with dread. An affair was one thing, but full-time Tim was another. That was not what she wanted.

All the signs pointed to it. First, he had been with her last night and it had been Sunday: rule one in affairs was that you never saw your mistress on a Sunday. Also, in a moment of extreme ecstasy (or weakness, as Clara saw it), he had told her he loved her. Rule two broken. All that left was never leave your wife, and never ask your mistress to wash your underwear. Clara prayed that he wouldn't break the last two rules. She would mind horribly if he left his wife, and she would mind if he wanted her to wash his underwear. Clara hated it, but she knew that Tim was all she deserved. She had been through an amazing number of men in her life, and she had only ever wanted one, but he had not wanted her. Tim was retribution, punishment, for the way she had discarded men carelessly.

Clara tried not to panic as she thought about what she had to do. She couldn't have him all the time; she didn't want to be with him at all for much longer. But, and it was a big but, she couldn't give him up yet. Tim had three roles in Clara's life. The first was as her boss, but that didn't worry her: he couldn't sack her for ending their affair – there were laws to prevent that. The second was as her lover, and not a particularly good one: as a lover, he was dispensable. The third was as her supplier of cocaine, good coke, and that was the one thing she couldn't give up.

Clara put on a false smile. 'Well, I hope you have a good time, bad boy, and I'll be at home alone for you whenever you want me. Oh, and by the way, as I'll be lonesome, have you got a little something to keep me company?' Clara licked her lips.

As she got up to leave the office, she brushed past him and took a little package from him. She lingered near his hip for longer than necessary, and smiled at him. 'See you later, baby,' she cooed, as she left his office.

It was half past five and Clara was bored. She had e-mailed, surfed the Net and talked to a couple of clients, but she was just waiting for the moment that she and her powder would be united again. At six, she took the lift to the floor below, which housed the accounts department. She went to the ladies' loo – she always felt too paranoid to use the one on her floor. As she chopped and lined up the white powder, Clara felt relief flood her body. After she had snorted her first two lines of the day, she felt as if she could conquer the world.

She left the loo, smiled at the accounting staff, who were staring at her, and returned to her floor. She practically flew through the doors and ran to her desk, where Toby sat looking anxious. 'Are you ready, Tobe? I'm absolutely dying for a drink.'

'I'm definitely ready.' The panic Toby had felt that she might have changed her mind left him.

They went to Bertie's, the wine bar to which everyone from work flocked. It was large, with a light wooden floor and furniture to match, elegant, cool, and reflected the personalities of its clientele perfectly. Or, at least, the way its clientele saw themselves. It was enormously successful due to after-work business; it did not open at weekends.

They sat at a wooden table, Clara with a glass of champagne and Toby with a bottle of beer. Clara was chatty, a symptom of the coke, and she talked while Toby drooled over her. She barely noticed him; she just talked at him, smiling, flirting and even touching his leg. It took all of Toby's strength to stop him fainting with lust. After a number of drinks, most of which Toby bought, and a few more lines of cocaine on Clara's part, she made a decision. The most astounded person in the world was Toby Bradley as Clara jumped on him and kissed him.

In the taxi that took them back to Clara's flat, Toby willed it to go faster. He could not believe his luck. Here he was with a goddess, a woman most of the men on the floor felt was out of their league. He was twenty-eight; he was an experienced salesperson, yet he doubted his sophistication. Especially when he was with Clara. He knew as he kissed her in the back of the taxi, that this was like a dream for him and that it wouldn't happen again. But as he fumbled with her left boob, he was determined to make the most of the best dream of his life.

Clara had stopped thinking at about half past nine. Now, as they approached her flat, she knew that she felt wonderful and she wanted to feel more wonderful. That meant she needed Toby. It was nothing personal, she just needed sex. When the need for sex took her over, Clara always submitted to it. It took her over a lot.

When the taxi drew up, she got out, walked to the door of her building and waited for Toby, who was paying the cab driver. She called the lift, and kissed him as they rode to her floor. When the door opened, Clara strode out with Toby panting behind her. She unlocked her front door and waited for Toby to enter. As soon as he was inside, she grabbed him and tore at his clothes. Off came the tie, the jacket and the shirt, then the shoes, the trousers and his boxer shorts. When he was naked, Clara ripped off her own clothes. Toby was rooted to the spot. She kissed, licked, teased until Toby could stand no more. Pushing her down on to the floor, just inside the front door, Toby finally found his balls and started making love to Clara.

Shortly afterwards they crawled into her bed, where Clara passed out. Amazed that he was actually in Clara Hart's bed, Toby fell asleep with a smile the size of London on his face.

Chapter Three

Ella walked into the office, looking forward to the day. She'd already forgotten the strange girl who had stared at her by the lifts. Flicking her screens, she saw that the markets were doing exactly what she had predicted. At close of morning business, it was looking like a promising day. The whole desk was in a good mood as they bantered, teased and chatted. Then Jeff, her boss and a managing director, rolled up. He was one of the most respected managing directors at SFH. He was young, dynamic and a hard worker. Ella had looked up to him from the moment she met him. 'Ella, can I have a word?' he asked.

'Sure,' Ella replied, and followed him into his office.

'What's up?' she asked.

'We have a junior, Johnny Rupfin, coming to join us next week. Now, I know you weren't involved in hiring him, which was an oversight on our part, but I would like you to mentor him.' Jeff smiled. Ella did not. The thought of a trainee being her responsibility didn't appeal to her. However, she knew that it was a forerunner to her management aspirations being met.

'Who is he? Some kid fresh from university?'

'He's just passed his MBA, from Harvard. Smart kid, lots of brains, not sure about his balls – which, Ella, is why you have been asked to do this. You are our best trader, you know that, and you've got a bright future ahead of you here. We need you to pass some of your brilliance on to our youngsters.' Jeff laughed; so did Ella.

'Right, fling him my way. I'll soon find out if he's got balls.' She laughed again as she left his office. Basking in the praise Jeff had given her, she forgot for a moment that she would have some youngster under her feet, and she forgot to be annoyed about it. After all, she had been a junior once.

Thinking back to how she had got here still made Ella feel as if it had all happened to someone else.

Four years ago her life could not have been more different. She lived in Manchester; she was engaged to Tony, the manager of the nightclub where she worked behind the bar. She had no qualifications, apart from a couple of GCSEs, and no real ambition. She was twenty-three. Her name was Elloise Butcher. She was happy.

As soon as Tony had put a ring on her finger, he started using his fists. Increasingly, Elloise was housebound, with bruises, black eyes and the occasional broken rib. He would take her to Casualty if the beating had been particularly bad and the doctor, although suspicious, never did anything. Elloise didn't do anything either. Tony was tall, broad, with dark blond hair and a lovely smile. He didn't look like a woman-beater; he didn't act like one at first, which is why Elloise had fallen in love with him.

When he became violent, she felt trapped. Even now she couldn't remember why she had stayed with him, and she couldn't remember wanting to be with him. She knew that he had made her so weak that she lost the strength to leave. Her brother Sam was her saviour. He got suspicious and went to visit her at their flat. As she was covered in bruises, Tony sent him away. Sam waited until Tony had gone to work then went back. When Elloise refused to let him in, he broke down the door and carried his sister home.

Sam was a year older than his sister, but she was the most important person to him in the world. This had almost destroyed him. As they held each other, back in their parents' home, Sam told Elloise what she would do. His plan was for her to leave Tony and Manchester, to escape and build a new life. Although this terrified her, she knew that her brother was right. As her parents fielded any attempts from Tony to get near her, Elloise and Sam plotted and planned. Sam, who had a couple of dubious connections, got her a driving licence, a birth certificate and a passport with the name Ella Franke on it. He arranged for some money so she would have enough to live on for a couple of months, and he bought her a one-way ticket to London. He also arranged for Tony to be taught a lesson. He paid some men to do to Tony what he had done to Elloise. They were supposed to make it look like a robbery at Tony's nightclub, and Sam had asked them to give him a beating he wouldn't forget. They did, but they went too far.

When the hospital called to tell Elloise that Tony was in a coma, Sam visited him with her, spoke to the police for her, and arranged for her to leave rather more quickly than she had intended. Although the police thought it was a robbery gone wrong, Elloise knew the truth. Elloise left Manchester and Ella arrived in London.

Once over the initial shock and panic when she arrived in London, she felt stronger and better. Her only regret was that she didn't know if Tony was dead or alive and that she couldn't see Sammy. She found a bedsit and a job as a waitress, and every night when she slept she had nightmares of Tony coming to get her.

At first she called Sammy every week just to tell him she was all right, but the phone calls became too painful, especially as there was no news of Tony. After a while she told Sammy she would stop phoning him and she would write to let him know she was all right. He agreed reluctantly, but argued that he should be able to contact her. Ella couldn't bring herself to give him her address or phone number. She failed to explain it to him, but to herself it was a punishment. By messing up her life as she had, and she still blamed herself, she now had to pay. And paying meant that she had to cut herself off from the person she loved most in the world: Sammy. Elloise Butcher had a family; Ella Franke had no one.

One day she picked up the London paper and saw an article about how too few black people worked in the City. Ella did not know what they meant by 'the City' but she read on and was hooked. The description of trading appealed to her; she fell in love. Although it was a crazy idea, she discussed it with her friend and boss, Jackie. Jackie saw this as an opportunity for Ella to put her past behind her and look to the future, so they began to plan. Jackie found someone who could get her a fake university degree certificate and then they set about reinventing her CV. She substituted PR for bar work, and management consultancy for waitressing. References were obtained, and as she hadn't given phone numbers, whoever she applied to had no way of checking other than by writing. Setting up the deception had been easy but costly. It had taken all the money Ella had. Ella sent this embellished CV to Serena Dalton at SFH, the woman who had commented in the article. She was sure that it had all been a load of bull but she attached a photograph of herself, and in a matter of days Serena had invited her to interview.

When Serena saw that Ella was not only black but also a black female, she had almost had an orgasm. The Equal Opportunities Board would love her. Serena had been given a hard time over the article in the paper, which had practically accused SFH of racism. Although the press office had sent out statements denying this and reiterating SFH's equal-opportunities policy, they had told Serena to go and get some ethnic minorities. Well, now she had Ella and maybe Ella could save her life. Ella's interview was short and not terribly difficult; within two weeks she had met a number of managing directors, all of whom wanted to prove the press wrong, and was offered a position as junior trader.

Ella had prepared for her interviews with meticulous

research, and knew a great deal about the field; any questions she was asked she answered confidently. Everyone was impressed. At the time of the interviews, Ella believed she was all the things she had said she was, educated, bright and ambitious. She wasn't Elloise the punchbag; she was Ella the girl with potential.

Human Resources was keen for Ella to start, especially as she had been so well liked; they skimmed over the usual checks that they did on all their employees. Luckily for Ella, they had collected the references, but they neglected to check with the university; they decided that the degree certificate was enough.

Although she knew that what she had done was wrong, Ella couldn't help but think she should be forgiven for it. Tony had abused her for years. She had had to leave her family and friends because of him. He was a woman-beater, the worst type of coward. The cowardly man who can only hit those too vulnerable to hit back. Ella knew that Sam had been right to teach him a lesson. He had deserved it; he deserved worse. However, the implications still scared her: the implication that she or Sam might get into trouble. She rationalised her deceit in getting her job by telling herself that she deserved a good life. She also knew that while getting the job had been easy, keeping it would not be. When she walked through the doors of SFH, she knew one thing: if she was no good, she would be fired within minutes.

Ella was ever conscious of her rocky foundation. And the fear of Tony that had once dominated her had now been replaced by a fear of her losing her wonderful new life.

Virginia was hung over. For the first time that she could remember, she felt like throwing her alarm clock across the room when it went off. She crawled out of bed, her head pounding. Instead of putting the kettle on, she pulled a bottle of water out of the fridge and, another first for her, drank straight from it. She then hauled herself into the shower.

As she dried herself, she dropped the towels on the floor. She pulled on a pair of grey woollen trousers and a jumper ignoring the suit and the crisp white blouse that lay waiting for her. She had another drink of water before she left the flat. She wasn't sure if she should drive – she wasn't likely to be over the limit, but it was still more of a risk than Virginia liked to take – but she jumped on the scooter and drove to work. The cold air helped to clear her head, but it did nothing to improve her mood.

She had to wait ages for the lift. She saw Ella, the black trader from her floor, standing next to her, tapping her foot impatiently. Virginia couldn't help but stare. She knew that Ella was one of the best traders at SFH, and longed to ask her how she did it. Ella sensed that she was being stared at and looked Virginia in the eye. Virginia nodded; Ella tipped her head slightly and looked away. Then the lift came.

Today, the quiet hum of the screens on the trading floor seemed too loud to Virginia. The flashing lights made her feel as if she was in a cheap disco. She grabbed a cup of water and a cup of coffee, and marched up to her desk. She decided that she might as well do her filing. She finished it just as the office was filling up. The people on her desk said good morning to her, but Virginia just nodded. She had had enough of being nice to these morons who gave her grief. She couldn't understand how, when all she wanted was peace and quiet, she was busier than ever.

She felt a chill run down her back and she turned to see Isabelle standing behind her. 'Hi,' Isabelle said, as if she couldn't quite remember who Virginia was. 'Have you got a second?' Virginia picked up her notepad and followed Isabelle into her office. 'Right, I've got a lot on at the moment, and I need you to get these things done quickly. I hope you understand.' Isabelle sounded even more bitchy than usual.

Virginia guessed it was another of her moods. Isabelle seemed to have bad moods most of the time. The only person she ever took them out on was Virginia. Virginia nodded; speaking would only give Isabelle more ammunition.

'First, I want a private room in a restaurant for Tuesday the seventeenth at lunchtime. Choose the restaurant, somewhere classy. I mean my version of classy, not yours. I do not want to entertain my clients in Pizza Hut. We are hosting a lunch for thirty people. The names are on this list. I also need the invitations printed and out by the end of this week. I can leave you with that. Standard invites. Put on them "SFH Emerging Markets Equities is delighted to invite whoever to lunch," you know the sort of thing. Then I am hosting a conference for women in the City – you know, to encourage more women to get ahead. I want all female professional employees invited, so you'll need to get a list from Personnel. By professional I mean all level four and above, but I'm sure you know that already. Then I need invitations to go out – here, I've written a blurb – and people for both events need to RSVP to you. You need to get lists drawn up, and give me final numbers by the end of next week. Oh, the conference will be on the twenty-fourth, and I need the big conference room booked. Right – oh, here are lists of meetings I want you to arrange, including rooms, then ensure my calendar is accurate. Also, I want some brochures on Barbados, only luxury resorts, of course. Here are my dry-cleaning tickets. I've paid for it, so I need you to collect it for me today.' Isabelle still didn't look at her.

'Right,' Virginia said uncertainly. Although she'd written everything down there was so much to do. Her head pounded even more.

'Oh, and don't fuck anything up. If you do I'll fry your sulky head.' Isabelle looked at her coldly and dismissed her. Not only was the workload unfair, especially the personal chores, but since they had had their 'chat', Isabelle had been even nastier to her. Virginia walked back to her desk scowling. She was close to tears.

Virginia's place at Canterbury University hadn't made her

parents happy. They would only have been happy with Oxford or Cambridge but Virginia, who was studying economics, had looked forward to going there. She packed her suitcase, bade farewell to her parents and Coventry, and went to Kent.

Her life as a student was a little subdued. She joined the Economics Society and made friends with people who seemed to share the same interests. They went out together and became a clique. To the trendy people and the sports stars, this little group was known as 'the spods', because they put study before sex, museums before beer. They were not proper students.

After three years together, Virginia's friends all took their first-class degrees to postgraduate courses around the country, even around the world. Virginia had decided to take her third-class degree in economics to the City. When she failed to secure a job she felt too embarrassed to keep in contact with her successful friends. While they took off to their new lives, Virginia returned to Coventry and her parents. Desolate, she found her parents devoid of sympathy. Instead they told her how disappointed they were, and Virginia began her phase of loneliness.

She had forgotten how bad living with her parents could be, so she told them she needed to live in London to find a job, took her savings and went. Every recruitment consultancy told her the same thing: the only way to get into the City was as a graduate trainee, or as an assistant/secretary. When Virginia was offered a job as secretary to Isabelle at SFH she took it, knowing that it was only temporary, that it wouldn't be for ever, that it wouldn't be for long. Now, she had stopped telling herself that.

As she worked like a horse for Isabelle, she prayed that soon she would find something, anything that would make her happy.

Clara's mouth felt dry and she couldn't feel her teeth. The second thing she noticed was how much her head hurt. She felt shit. She tried to turn over slowly, without moving her head too much, and when she did, the third thing she noticed was Toby. She closed her eyes and opened them again to make sure.

Forgetting her thumping head, she sat upright. It was 6 a.m. Slowly she got out of bed and walked to the kitchen. She tried to ignore the fact that she was naked and why she was naked. Gulping down a glass of water, she scrabbled in a drawer for some headache pills. Praying to the god of paracetamol, she heaved a sigh of relief when she found them. Swallowing four, she gulped down another glass of water and crawled back to bed.

As she walked back in Toby was awake and watched her. No matter how much she needed to crawl back under her duvet, she was unable to do so, just in case he got ideas. Of course, he had ideas: after all, she had screwed him. She grabbed a towel that lay on her bedroom floor and wrapped it around her. This was turning out to be a bad day already. Headache or not, Clara decided to sort things out. 'Good morning, Toby.'

'Hey.' Toby had that lovesick look in his eyes that Clara had seen a million times before.

'Toby, I want to thank you. Last night was wonderful.' She paused as she tried to remember if it had been wonderful and found she could remember little of it. 'But, well, you know it can't happen again.'

It was exactly what Toby had been expecting, but he still felt crushed.

'It's not that I don't like you — God, I think you're great and sexy and fun — but we work together and I wouldn't be able to handle it, you know.' Clara felt nauseous; the conversation wasn't helping.

Toby looked crestfallen. 'I understand. But I really enjoyed last night.'

Clara smiled. Thank God, he wasn't going to argue. She kissed his cheek. 'Toby, you're the best.' And with that, she ran into the shower. When she returned, Toby asked if he could have a shower and he asked if she would mind them going to work together. The only thing Clara minded was that she was early and she couldn't crawl back into bed for another hour. She ordered a cab, got dressed and tried to remember another time when she had gone to work so early.

She hoped that no one would notice that Toby was wearing exactly the same clothes as yesterday.

The day was harder than most. She refused to pick up the phone, refused to speak to anyone and when any of the senior guys asked her to do anything, she told him or her to 'Piss off,' 'Get screwed,' and 'Stick it up your arse.' The people on the desk knew to expect such outbursts from Clara. They were used to her mood swings. Even when Tim came to sit on the desk for a few hours, as he did most days, she scowled. At lunchtime, Clara announced that she felt ill and unless anyone wanted her to be sick all over the desk she had better go home. They all stared at her, amazed that someone so junior could behave like that and get away with it as she stalked out of the office.

Hailing a cab, Clara thought about getting home. She was feeling dreadful – tired, sick, and her head was exploding. As soon as she got home, she took a line of coke then went back to bed. As she fell into a weird, dream-filled sleep, she thought about nothing but the white powder flowing contentedly to her brain.

Tim was facing an onslaught in the office from Sarah Parks, one of his senior salespeople. She had worked at SFH for a long time and with many salespeople. 'Tim, Clara's as good as useless. I mean, she swans in late every day, doesn't have time to fill her clients in on the markets, even if she could. She gets Toby or Francine to do all her orders for her and she just chats, e-mails and looks decorative.' Sarah couldn't bear to see Clara in such a good position: she gave working women a bad name.

Tim was silent. He was in a difficult position. He knew Clara wasn't the greatest salesperson in the world and he seriously doubted that she knew what an equity was, but she was Clara and he wanted her, and therefore he couldn't do anything about it. 'Sarah, you're exaggerating. I've had loads of compliments about her from her clients. They really like her, and I think you'll agree that that is the important thing. How many clients do you have who would go elsewhere just because they didn't like you? It's not based on anything else.' This was true. Clara's clients loved her, and Tim knew that they would hate it if she was removed from their accounts.

'Fine, but she's not doing what she should be doing. Tim, I mean it, she's really bad for team morale. If people see her getting away with murder, they'll expect to do the same.'

Tim sighed. There was only so much logic he could argue with. 'I'll speak to her.' As Sarah left, Tim knew he had no intention of speaking to Clara. It was important to him that her job was reliant on him. If she had been competent, his power would have been greatly reduced. This way he held all the cards.

He sat at his desk and remembered when he had first employed Clara. The managing director of the Private Client Division had called him and asked him if he had any secretarial vacancies. It was good timing, because his current secretary was leaving to travel the world. He had just requested that Human Resources find him a new one. When Phillip Reid told him that a client's sister wanted a job and it would be a great favour to him if Tim would consider her, Tim agreed to an interview.

James Hart looked after the family business and the family wealth. At thirty-two, he was considered one of the most eligible bachelors in England and he was the heir apparent to his father's empire, of which he was now mostly in control so that his parents could spend time at their various overseas homes. James was proving a great success. When Clara told her parents of her intention to get a job, they scoffed. Her mother said she should be finding a suitable boyfriend, and her father said that she was a rich party girl, and why did she need a job? 'Clara, we didn't send you to finishing-school so you could come out with ideas about getting a job, we sent you there to learn to cook.'

Clara didn't know why she wanted a job. She knew that she had no qualifications, that she couldn't cook and that she was bored with her life. She liked the idea of putting on a suit and having somewhere to go during the day other than for lunch. She resented the way that her family treated her like an airhead. She hated her parents for having no expectations of her other than marriage; she hated herself for constantly proving them right. She always behaved like an airhead. She was crying when James found her. James and Clara had always been close, so it was natural for him to step in to protect his little sister. He told her he would use his contacts and help her to get a job in any way he could. Hence the interview with Tim Pemberton at SFH. Clara agreed to let James help her because she felt she had something to prove. She just had no idea how she was going to prove it on her own. Everyone saw Clara as a confident, beautiful bitch. If they had known the amount of times she cried herself to sleep, they would perhaps have thought more kindly of her.

When Clara walked into his office Tim nearly fell off his chair. She was so lovely, so gorgeous and so sexy. Her blonde hair curled over her face, her big blue eyes were hypnotising, her figure slim but curvaceous. Tim thought that if he were to describe his ideal woman, she would be Clara. She smiled, showing two rows of perfect white teeth; she shook hands, revealing lovely long nails; and she spoke to him in a cut-glass accent. She was heavenly.

After that the interview was a bit of a blur. Tim couldn't help staring at her, managing to ask questions somehow but not listening to answers. The minute she left his office, he called Human Resources and instructed them to offer her a job. How she had gone from being his secretary to his mistress was a bit of a blur too. All he knew was that from the moment she had started working for him he hadn't been able to get her out of his mind. He was aware that her work wasn't really up to scratch and that she was always late, but he was most aware of how much he wanted her. So much that, for a while, when he slept with anyone, from his wife to his prostitutes, he imagined Clara.

His amazement was great when he took the folder of mail she gave him and found a note from her asking him for a drink. Although he knew that he was attractive and successful and could have any woman he wanted, Clara had given him the impression that she wasn't interested in him. This had puzzled him: women normally fell at his feet. Tim had come a long way from his first job as a trainee stockbroker to managing director of SFH, and his rise was down purely to hard work and opportunism, but he had never lost his disappointment at being from the wrong background. As his income grew he married Constance; an upper-middle-class girl whom, he hoped, would help him attain the status he craved. He did not marry for love; he did not fall in love. Tim Permberton was only in love with himself and his aspirations. As soon as the ink had dried on the marriage certificate he was having affairs with other women. Girls, both paid for and free, became his passion, as did cocaine. Tim believed in his own publicity. He was a sexy, successful man. A man who snapped his fingers and girls flocked to him. He wanted Clara, but he didn't think she wanted him. When she made her approach, Tim's belief in his infallibility was restored. Tim always got what he wanted. He arranged to meet her in a bar in Kensington, and he knew it was his lucky day.

Clara was late getting to the bar and Tim was nervous, although he wouldn't have admitted it. When she walked in, wearing a short, tight black dress and black heels, he nearly fell off his chair. She moved towards him and he hardened immediately. He had to have this woman.

And he did. He bought champagne; she told him how she loved working for him. He bought oysters; she told him she wanted to be a salesperson. He bought more champagne; she told him she had wanted him from the first time they met. He took her back to her flat, where they made love several times before he went home to his wife.

The affair started quickly. Clara flattered him, serviced him and treated him like a king. In turn, he always bought her champagne, cocaine and, in the end, promoted her to salesperson because she begged. Then she said that if he didn't she'd have to end the affair. Clara's logic was that if she was his secretary, having an affair with him was tacky. As a salesperson, although he would still be her boss, it was more acceptable. That was the word she had used. Tim didn't want to give up Clara so he promoted her.

He had swayed it with the board by reminding them that the family was a big private client. It was better than telling them the truth. She was promoted, but although the clients indeed loved her — especially the male ones — Clara didn't have a clue what the job involved, as Sarah had pointed out.

Tim looked at his watch. If he was lucky he could get out of the office early, see Clara for a couple of hours and be home in time for a late dinner. He picked up the phone to call his wife.

Clara was not proud of the way she'd got her job but, then, she was never proud of herself. She didn't think she had any value, apart from her body, so she used it. She knew she was no better than a whore; she didn't know how to be better than a whore. Confidence was her defence mechanism; being rude and bitchy to others was the wall she hid behind. The humiliation she felt at the way she had come by her job was compounded by the degradation she felt with Tim.

Chapter Four

Ella went to the gym after work. Another good day, another profit; she felt that she had been born to trade. On the treadmill, minus Jim, she felt all the tensions of the day fall away. She ran for half an hour, showered and got changed. She said hello to Isabelle, the manager of the emerging markets sales desk, who had just finished changing into an immaculate white outfit and was brandishing a squash racket.

'Ella, how are you?' Isabelle smiled.

'Fine, Isabelle. You?' Ella bristled: Isabelle's smile was even colder than Ella's and this intimidated her. Isabelle was a successful manager at SFH, and Ella knew her by reputation as someone who would stamp on anyone who got in her way. She was thankful that she had never been involved professionally with Isabelle. Although they were both ambitious, Ella was not a corporate bitch. Isabelle's heart was made of stone.

'Oh, you know, the usual stress of being in our jobs. Anyway, I wanted to invite you to a conference about women in the City. I'm hosting it and, well, it looks like we're going to get a good turnout. We've got a number of female members of staff coming and I was wondering if you'd do a bit on trading.'

Ella smiled. This was the longest conversation she'd ever had with Isabelle. 'Sure, I'd love to.'

'Great, I'll get my useless secretary to send you a schedule. See you.'

''Bye,' Ella said, to Isabelle's departing back. As she left the gym, she hailed a cab and told the driver she was going to Camden Town.

Her friend Jackie had an amazing house there, bought when Camden was cheap and Jackie was in the first throes of success with her Soho restaurant. When Ella first went to the restaurant for a job as a waitress, she had seen the survivor instinct in Jackie and they had immediately become friends.

She had told Jackie a condensed version of her story, and had been surprised to get Jackie's in return. Jackie had been only fifteen when she left home and moved in with a thirty-year-old man. She had been in love, he had been old enough to know better and her parents had been heartbroken. They still hadn't forgiven her. The man had lost interest when she aged a couple of years, and left her. He had, however, left her with money. Her subsequent fight with her feelings had made her a successful businesswoman but, like Ella, her heart was hard.

Jackie met Ella with a hug and a kiss then ushered her into the house. They settled in the huge old purple sofa with a bottle of wine and began to catch up.

'How's the dream job?' Jackie asked.

'A dream.' Ella giggled. 'You know, I can't wait to get to work every day. I mean, I know you think I'm crazy, but here I am, trading millions of pounds, getting a huge buzz and a lot of respect, and I am totally in love with it.'

'I do think you're crazy. I, on the other hand, am fed up with slaving away in the sweatshop that is my restaurant. I've decided to hire a manager. I'm going to college.' Jackie beamed.

'Get away. Shit, Jac, you're amazing. What to study?'

'English, can you believe it? I think I'm recapturing my youth.'

'What, all twenty-eight years of you?'

'Yeah, I know, but don't forget, I've been twenty-eight since

I was fifteen.' Jackie's grey eyes clouded as they always did when she thought about her hard lesson in growing up.

'Please tell me this isn't a mad ploy to date the eighteen-year-olds you missed out on?' Ella teased.

'Shit, I didn't even think of that, I guess it must be.' Jackie laughed.

'To be honest, Jac, I don't think I'd care how old the bloke was, I just wish I had one.'

'What you? No man could compete against your love affair with your job.'

'I guess not. But it would be nice. Someone to hug, someone to ... well, you know, someone to talk to ...' Ella became dreamy.

'Ella, stop. You sound like a sap.'

'Thanks. Anyway, you're probably right. I love my job so much. Who would have thought I'd change from a pint-pulling punchbag into a City slicker?'

'Well, not me, that's for sure. Ella, do you still have nightmares?' Jackie did what she always did: now that the chitchat was over, she turned the conversation to more serious matters.

When Ella had walked into the restaurant, Jackie had been struck by how fragile she seemed. In front of her was a striking girl, who was tall and slim with long hair, yet who looked as if she would break if she was touched. She noticed the sadness in her.

When Ella told her story, Jackie felt nothing but sorrow. She remembered what it was like to be used by a man, and although Alan had never hit her, the mental scars with which he had left refused to heal. Ella's mental state was bordering on the imbalanced. She couldn't cope with being on the run although, rationalising it, Jackie decided that no one could point any blame at Ella. She encouraged her to start her new life, but knew that she was still exorcising the ghosts of the old one. Tony wouldn't leave her head, so the nightmares had started.

Jackie knew they had got worse when Ella went to work for SFH. It made her so angry to see Ella's guilt when she was the victim. Jackie had become a friend, but she had also become a counsellor. She got Ella to talk, and she had listened, rather than judged. She had pieced together parts of Elloise's story, and she had tried to rebuild the new Ella. That was why, when Ella had decided she had had enough of waitressing, Jackie had encouraged her in her pursuit of a job that neither of them thought she had a hope of getting.

Although Jackie knew that what she was doing was wrong, she had an even stronger feeling that she was saving Ella's life. She had been right. From the moment Ella had walked through the doors of SFH, she had been a different person. She didn't find it easy but, then, she hadn't worked in that industry before. She worked harder than she ever had in her life and proved herself. Jackie had nothing but admiration for Ella: she was one of life's remarkable women.

'Yes, but they're getting better. I still have the one where Tony is dead and chasing me through the streets, and the one where I go to work and find Tony in the office with my boss. Although that's something I think about when I'm awake too. I think it will take me a long time to get over it, don't you?'

'I'm afraid so, but, Ella, it's been more than three years. Don't you think it's time to put him behind you?'

'What if he's dead?'

'What if he's not? For all you know, he could be alive and well and beating the hell out of some other poor woman. Christ, Ella, it's time to move on. Call Sammy, find out the truth, and get yourself some friends, maybe another boyfriend. Listen, darling, I really think you need to start living.'

'Jac, I can't. I just can't.' And with that, she burst into tears.

Jackie held Ella, the frightened, fragile Ella, and she knew that one day Ella would have to make that confrontation. She just prayed that Ella would be strong enough to cope.

Virginia could hardly carry Isabelle's dry-cleaning. She was weighed down with it as she struggled back to the office. She had barely had a chance to breathe all day, and she had had to run to the shop to collect the clothes just minutes before it closed. She was tired and out of breath when she handed it over, but she didn't even have time to be annoyed when Isabelle failed to thank her. She was so busy arranging the conference and the lunch that all her other work was still waiting for her. Cursing again, Virginia prepared herself for a long night.

That evening, driving home at nine, all Virginia wanted was to shower and go to bed. Huddled like a child under her pale blue duvet, she wanted never to get up again. She felt so trapped and she didn't know how she would ever get out.

Tim didn't think to call Clara, he just turned up at her flat. Clara was awake, although she had a headache and had been about to take a couple of sleeping pills then go to bed. She thought about not answering the door, but decided she would in case it was someone important.

She regretted the decision as Tim landed a sloppy kiss on her lips. 'I thought you'd like to hear about how many prostitutes I screwed last night.' He leered and Clara cringed inside. This was the game he always played before sleeping with her: he believed it turned her on.

Clara walked to the sofa, sat down and smiled her best smile. Once she had asked herself why she made herself so sexy for Tim, but she knew the answer really: she did it for the cocaine.

'So, tell me,' she purred.

'Well, darling, I started with the redhead. I licked her boobs and she had an orgasm there and then. Then I fucked her. I moved on to the blonde girl. God, my stamina is unbelievable. Next week I'm going to sleep with both of them together and they'll do a show for me, if you know what I mean. You should consider joining us.'

Tim smiled. Clara felt sick again.

'Well, Timmy, you'd have to be a very good boy before I'd do that for you.'

Tim scowled. Just as he thought he was in control, making her jealous, turning her on, making her want him, she always tried to snatch it back. 'I think it's time you did as you were told. Get into the bedroom.' Tim used his sergeant-major voice, the one that Clara thought made him sound even more of an idiot than he was. However, she did as he said.

After an hour of sex, which involved foreplay, on Clara's part, then huffing and puffing, on Tim's part, he collapsed on top of her and kissed her lips. As he put his tongue into her mouth Clara realised that this affair could not last for ever. Lying in his arms, she concentrated hard on not feeling sick, but she was sweaty and feverish.

'You know I told you I'm thinking about leaving Constance,' Tim said. Clara was not in a fit state to deal with this.

'Um,' she replied.

'I'm not promising, but carry on looking after my needs the way you do and maybe, just maybe, I will.' He planted another kiss on her lips and went to the shower.

Clara got up, went to the kitchen and drank a glass of water. She tried to cool herself by dabbing her forehead with a damp cloth, but she was feeling dreadful. She went into her sitting room and picked up the wrap of cocaine that Tim had given her yesterday. She took a line, immediately felt better, and returned to bed.

Tim came out of the shower, put his clothes on.

'Sorry I can't stay but I have to go home and shag my wife,' he sneered as he kissed Clara goodbye.

As the cocaine settled into her body Clara felt much better, especially when she saw the two wraps that Tim had left on her bedside table. Thinking of his wife, who was about to be shagged – if he was to be believed – Clara couldn't help feeling sorry for the poor cow.

Chapter Five

Ella's week was getting better. She felt tired and a little headachy from last night – she and Jackie had talked well into the small hours – but still in control. The markets, once again, were doing exactly as she had predicted.

'Nice one, Ella.' John smiled at her. They had debated a position last night and, on Ella's judgement, had sold the stock before the price fell.

'Hey, it's nothing,' Ella joked.

'I may ask your advice more often.'

Ella felt her face go warm. She basked in the compliment; she didn't know how to react to it.

'John, boy, why don't you ever ask my advice?' Liam had joined the growing crowd around Ella.

'Because you don't know shit. I ask you which way a stock is going, you toss a coin.'

'Yeah, but then I have a fifty-fifty chance of getting it right.' Liam laughed loudly and returned to his desk. 'Hey, I know, let's go out tonight,' he suggested. Now he was juggling with two plastic rugby balls.

'OK. Where?' John asked.

'We'll go to the Met bar, I've got membership.' Liam threw one of the balls at John's head. John caught it and threw it straight back at him.

'How the fuck did you get membership there?' Trevor, one of the more senior members of the desk, asked.

'I'm a classy guy, of course I have membership. Anyway, you coming?'

'Count me in,' John said, returning to his seat.

'Me too,' Trevor agreed.

'I'll be there.' Jimmy indicated although he was still on the phone.

'And me.' Bob, who sat next to Ella, smiled.

'Come on, Ella, what about you?' Liam asked.

Ella looked at him. She only socialised with them at official desk dinners, and felt panicked about the idea of them and her outside the office.

'No, I don't think so. Five disgusting men and me? I'm not sure I could cope.' She giggled in an attempt to make her refusal sound inoffensive.

'Ella, you're one of us. Come on, we insist,' John said.

Ella realised that it would be rude to say no. She remembered what Jackie had said about moving on. Perhaps one night out wouldn't hurt.

'You're on,' she said, smiling widely.

'And I promise we won't go to any lap-dancing clubs,' Liam finished.

Ella flashed him a look of fake disgust, and they got back to work. Well, almost work.

Ella surveyed the schoolboy scene, always in evidence when the markets went quiet after a good morning. The traders would throw things, make paper aeroplanes, tell jokes, dance, sing, and generally act as if they were in the playground. When the day was bad, they sat at their desks sulking and cursing quietly. When nothing was happening, they played practical jokes on team members and caught up with Internet porn. Ella thought that there was nothing as bad as a bored trader.

She often thought that the trading desk resembled the most glamorous school in existence. The pupils wore Armani, Gucci,

Savile Row, the teachers the same. The behaviour, however, reflected the spoilt, rich kids that they were. But you couldn't help having fun in such an atmosphere.

When the bell rang to signify the end of trading, John and Liam were exchanging high fives, and Jeff was beaming like a proud father. 'Fabulous day. Great work. This is the way it should be,' he said.

Everyone voiced their agreement.

At five thirty Ella excused herself to go and put on her makeup in the ladies' room. She didn't wear much: clear mascara that lengthened her lashes, a subtle lip-gloss, a tiny amount of eye-shadow. Her look was understated but professional. It was an image Ella had taken pains to cultivate, and now it was like second nature to her.

When she walked back in, Liam wolf-whistled and she hit him. She went back to her desk to finish up, but the guys had already started telling jokes so she found it impossible. Looking at each of them, she felt that they had finally accepted her, they had included her, which they didn't often, they had complimented her, and they were treating her as one of the guys. It had only taken three years.

Ella remembered the terror she had felt when she first walked on to the trading floor. She had been training with Human Resources for two months, in which time she had taken her reglatory exams. That morning she was so full of nerves and excitement that she spent it being sick.

Everyone turned to look at her. She was not just the new girl, she was the new black girl, and in an office that was full of white faces, she felt conspicuous. Jeff, whom she had met at the interview stage, soon put her at ease, and when he introduced her to her fellow traders her knees had almost stopped knocking.

The rest of the desk all eyed her with mild interest. They were civil, they were polite and sometimes they were even kind. However, until she could prove that she was good, they did not accept her. As soon as she started making money, they thawed slightly, but still they whispered that this might be beginner's luck. Her 'beginner's luck' lasted three years, which culminated in her getting the biggest bonus and making more money than anyone else. Their attitude turned to respect and now they were even offering a kind of friendship.

She felt that although initially she had perhaps not deserved to get the job, she had justified herself.

They piled into a cab, and Ella knew that, whatever happened, tonight would be a long one. They had dinner at Indigo before moving on to the Met bar. Ella enjoyed the food, the wine, the champagne. They were all drinking as if Prohibition were to be introduced the following day. The guys were getting through twice as much as she was, but that was because they were animals. The jokes were blue, the language was unrepeatable, but they were courteous towards Ella.

She, however, was more than able to handle anything they threw at her. At the Met bar, she was fascinated by the handful of celebrities they encountered. Although most were wannabes, there were people that Ella recognised: a few music stars and a couple of sexy actors whose names she wasn't sure of. Liam was ordering champagne and smiling suggestively at anyone female. Trevor's tongue was hanging out – he was standing near some girls who looked like models. Bob was asleep on a table, and John and Jimmy were taking care of Ella.

She got home at some time in the small hours and fell into bed. When her alarm clock went off at 5 a.m., announcing that it was a gym day, she mumbled, 'Fuck the gym,' and reset the clock for an hour later.

On Wednesday Virginia kept her head down, and worked twice as hard as usual. She completed Isabelle's tasks efficiently, and was thankful that due to 'hangovers from hell' the desk were too ill to ask her to do anything apart from get them bacon sandwiches in the morning. She logged into her directory of investment banks, looking for any to which she could apply.

She made an alphabetical list, then looked at it despondently. 'Change career,' a voice in her head told her.

'No,' she replied. 'No, no, no.' If anyone else on the desk noticed her talking to herself, they didn't say anything.

Virginia went through the list again. She knew she didn't want to work for anyone as much as she wanted to work for SFH. But her loyalty to a bank that made her miserable and gave her no opportunity to advance was inexplicable. Except that it wasn't SFH, it was Isabelle. If it weren't for Isabelle she would get somewhere. For a moment Virginia felt faint: her grip was going, her reason and rationale.

How can you carry on when you have nothing? Virginia rubbed her temples, she felt like she was going mad, and there was no way she could go mad.

She left the desk, rushed to the ladies', and sat on the loo seat with her head in her hands. She had to think. She knew that today was Wednesday. Right. Her routine had been as usual: she had got up, she had had her tea, she had come to work, it was quiet, and she would go for lunch in twenty-seven minutes. That was OK. Everything was OK. She wasn't going mad.

She washed her face and went back to her desk. Everyone seemed to be leaving for lunch and they told Virginia not to expect them back for a while. Isabelle had already left for her afternoon meetings; Virginia could expect a quiet afternoon.

She left for lunch exactly twenty-five minutes later. She went to her usual sandwich bar; she walked past the banks she always walked past. She returned at the same time she always did, she sat at her desk, she ate her sandwich. She had her composure back.

In the afternoon, Virginia made lists. Her first list was her work list. Then she wrote a shopping list for the weekend, which was unnecessary as she bought the same things every week. She followed with a list of clothes that needed washing and a list of clothes that had to go to the dry-cleaner's. Then a list of shoes that needed polishing, a list of household items that would run out soon – washing powder: one more week; shoe polish: two months; shampoo: three weeks. Her final list was her dinner menu for the following week – Monday: pasta; Tuesday: tuna salad; Wednesday: soup; Thursday: chicken and vegetables; Friday: fish and chips (takeaway). She made a separate menu list for the weekend. Then she filed her lists in her Filofax and felt better. How could she be going mad when her life was so well organised?

Virginia's routine was military. She could not cope if she didn't know what she was doing and when. If she broke it, as she had a couple of times recently, it unnerved her – if she went to bed half an hour late, if she got up even minutes late, if she didn't watch the news. She wasn't a control freak, she knew she wasn't, but what she did know, her big secret, was that due to her many failures her grip on her life was so fragile that if her routine was disrupted she would lose that grip altogether. The only way she made it through the day was by behaving like a robot.

Virginia often told herself that she had failed at getting a personality as well as failing at everything else. She often wondered if her life had purpose, but the one thing she was certain of was that she would prove her parents wrong. One day they would no longer call her a failure.

She had been an unpopular child, a gawky teenager, and was now a boring adult. She had had one boyfriend in the whole of her life, Noël, a fellow economics student and member of the group she went round with. Noël was a committed Christian, and she was still a virgin. But she quite liked kissing him and having him hold her. With Noël, for the first time, Virginia had affection. He would hold her hand, hug and kiss her.

Noël was very bright, very bossy, and spent hours preaching either the Bible or economics at Virginia. She didn't mind; she would sat for hours listening to him, and she felt wanted. Noël got a place at Stamford to do a postgraduate course. He had flown to the States where celibacy before marriage was fashionable and Virginia had gone where the prospects of having either sex or marriage were slim.

Virginia left work at a reasonable time. That evening she had a French class. She brightened: for once she could escape spending the evening in her depressing room. Her French-class routine involved leaving the office at six, driving home, changing into her casual uniform of jeans and jumper, eating dinner, leaving at a quarter past seven and arriving, by scooter, at the local adult education centre at half past.

Virginia had thought long and hard about what evening class she would do. When she first moved to London she took classes to help her get a social life: she had tried pottery, art history and badminton. She had not made a single friend, or motivated herself in any way. The French class was as unsophisticated as the language was sophisticated. Its intellectual demands were few, and Virginia was nowhere near being fluent, but she believed that, one day, she would be if she kept going.

There were seven people in the group, which was taught by a frazzled middle-aged Frenchwoman. Virginia sat next to Pat, a housewife who had ideas of moving to France when her husband retired. She was plump and grey, and Virginia often wondered if she really had a husband. Two girls were taking extra lessons to help with their GCSE's. A man of about fifty, called Graham, wanted to learn French to go with his Spanish and German conversational skills. Completing the group were the Trout sisters, two women of about eighty as far as Virginia could tell, who giggled through the lesson and had so far never uttered a word of French.

Virginia applied herself to the class with the determination she applied to everything and she was good. Madame often said that she was the best in the class and she was a natural. Virginia basked in the pleasure of such a compliment and she tried harder and harder each week. The reality of the class made being the best quite easy, but at least she was the best somewhere.

After the class, Virginia hung back. The two girls rushed out of the classroom then Pat picked up her massive tote bag and trundled off, buckling under its weight. The Trout sisters collected their walking sticks and moved slowly out of the room, while Graham, the international conversationalist, stopped to ask the teacher something.

Tonight, Virginia waited to speak to madame. 'I just wanted to tell you I'm really enjoying the course,' she said shyly.

Her teacher smiled. 'You are the best pupil I've got.' They laughed, and as Virginia had now collected her weekly compliment, she left. She didn't think about how sad it was that the only person in the whole world who was nice to her was her French teacher; she thought that at least she had someone to be nice to her.

She drove home, had a shower and went to bed. The difference between the French night and any other night was that after the class she went to bed smiling.

Clara looked at the screen again. It was changing constantly, but she didn't know why. She hated numbers. Tim was away on business in Paris, but would be back tomorrow with perfume, chocolates and a story about French whores. She could hardly wait.

Sitting at her desk, she checked her calendar and realised that she had to go to dinner with her family tonight. She checked her bag and felt relieved to find a wrap of cocaine sitting at the bottom. At least she would be able to cope with her parents. She called James and checked that he would be joining them. Clara had had what she thought was a good day, but wished that Toby would stop looking at her in that lovesick way – she still felt guilty about him.

Clara knew that she had a problem. She knew she was an addict. She believed she was addicted to sex. Ever since she had experimented with her roommate at boarding-school, Clara had been insatiable. She had climbed out of her bedroom window on numerous occasions to meet boys from the nearest boys' school. In the holidays, she slept with her brother's friends, much to James's annoyance, and when she was sent to Switzerland, she developed a predictable liking for ski instructors. But it had always been controlled. Clara had always liked sex, but she had been discerning about whom she slept with: only the boys she liked at school, only the best-looking of her brother's friends, only the young ski instructors. Now she had slept with a number of men in London and was no longer in control of whom she took to bed. In fact, if you asked Clara how many men she had had, she would tell you that it was far too many to count. Clara knew it was in London that she had developed an addiction to sex.

Occasionally she wished she could control it, and in Toby's case, she did. He was nice and he was hurt. Most of the men she slept with didn't deserve her sympathy. There were rich businessmen who treated girls as trophies. There was Tim, who had so little respect for women she couldn't give a stuff about him. There were a couple of family friends who were out-and-out playboys, and although in the past they had asked Clara to marry them and promised to give up the wild lifestyle, she knew they didn't mean it. There were strangers. Now there was Toby. Toby was sweet, Toby was her friend, and now she was feeling guilty – Clara's one foray into unrequited love had taught her how it hurt. But although she often hated herself for hurting people, she knew she couldn't control her addiction.

There were only two ways she could resolve the problem with Toby. One, she could have a relationship with him, which didn't appeal to her, or two, she could find him a new girl to lust after. Her eyes lit up. She would find someone to make Toby happy again. Then she would be rid of the guilt.

Clara decided to talk to Alexandra Poole, a secretary she liked. She was blonde and pretty, and ideal for Toby. She walked over to Alex's desk and told her that she had heard Toby was

interested in her. Alex looked over at him and proclaimed him
'cute'. Clara persuaded her to e-mail him and ask him out.

The plan worked perfectly. Clara watched as, that afternoon,
Toby left his seat, went to Alex's and obviously arranged the
date. Clara hoped she would be invited to the wedding.

At six she left her desk and made her usual evening visit to
the ladies' loo on the accounts floor. She had her fix, went back
to grab her bag, said goodbye to everyone and skipped out of
the door.

As she arrived at Claridges to meet her parents, she was still
in good spirits. She walked into the bar and straight away saw
her immaculate mother. She was wearing a cream suit, probably
Chanel, her dark hair was streaked with light brown, a Chanel
handbag sat on the table, and Clara knew instinctively that she
was wearing matching shoes. The same pearl jewellery that Clara
received on birthdays and at Christmas decorated her throat,
wrist and ears. Clara thought her mother dressed predictably,
like all middle-aged rich women. Her father sat opposite her
mother, looking tall, grand and grey. They were both sipping
champagne.

Clara took a deep breath and approached them. 'Mummy,
Daddy. How are you?' She kissed them both and sat down.

'Fine, darling. You look tired – do you think she looks
tired, Paul?'

'You do look tired, Clara. It's all this work nonsense.' He
poured her a glass of champagne. Clara knew what was coming
next. 'I've decided to give you a bigger allowance.'

'But, Daddy, I don't need one. I've got my fund interest
and my wages.'

Her parents tutted. 'That's my point. If you have a bigger
allowance, you won't need wages.' Her father smiled, her mother
smiled, and Clara knew that she didn't need wages anyway.

And, darling, I know you think you look professional in
your suit, but you can wear suits to lunch too, you know,' her
mother pointed out.

Clara wondered how such a stupid woman could have conceived her and James. 'I like my job,' she protested, although she cringed when she thought about telling them how she had got it, or how she kept it.

'Don't be ridiculous. I didn't send you to finishing-school to become a career woman. Look at your mother. At your age, she was married with James. You should be thinking about doing the same,' her father growled.

Clara was always pleased to see her brother, but never more so than at that moment. James strode confidently to their table, shook his father's hand, kissed his mother then his sister, sat down and poured some champagne. Clara envied him. Envied and loved him. He was tall, good-looking, sweet, bright and hard-working. He was also male.

The conversation soon turned to business, as James and his father debated the future, the past and the present. Clara sipped her drink and watched her mother, who had cultivated the perfect-wife qualities. She was decorative, classy and, most of all, she had an intent look of interest on her face as the men talked business, even though it was not only boring but double-dutch to her. If her mother understood a word of what was being said, Clara would eat her fur coat.

Eventually she had had enough. 'Do you want to hear how my business is?' she asked, trying to get her father's attention and to sound important.

'Of course,' James replied.

'No,' her mother said.

'Clara, I wish you'd stop pretending and give up that silly job of yours,' her father said.

Clara beamed at them and excused herself to go to the ladies', where she put a much-needed line of cocaine up her nose.

As the powder hit, the sensation took away the desire to scream, and replaced it with calm. Nothing mattered. Everything was under control. She could handle it. She knew her parents only wanted her to turn into a carbon copy of her mother; she knew they would never appreciate that she needed something of her own. She herself could barely understand it. She was doted on, adored, lusted after and wanted. No one had ever expected anything from her so she didn't know what she should expect from herself. She knew she didn't want to end up as her parents wanted her to, but she was also dangerously close to it. Her parents thought she was too pretty, rich and stupid to work. She hated the thought that they were probably right: that being pretty and rich had got her the job, and although she denied that she was stupid, she didn't understand what she did.

At finishing-school her teachers, who had all loved Clara, were bitterly disappointed that, unlike her mother, she had been so uninterested in their classes. She had not learnt to play a musical instrument, or the art of dressing a dinner table and she certainly couldn't cook. They felt she was useless.

Clara's father had been upset. He had wanted the school to turn Clara into a good marriage prospect, and he belonged to a generation who believed that women should have talents. Brazenly Clara told him that she would hire a cook, a table-dresser and a musician. To which her father replied that women had to oversee their staff and if they could not do their jobs, they would not know how to supervise them. Clara replied that she would marry a man with no class who would never know, and her father said she was a waste of space. The row was never resolved. Clara's mother watched them, fiddling with her pearls and never quite catching Clara's eye. Eventually Clara stormed out, went to find James and cry in his arms.

That was how Clara had sunk into her confusion. She moved into a three-bedroom flat in South Kensington, which her father had bought her after a particularly nasty row. From the moment she started living there Clara loved London. She caught up with old friends and made new ones. She discovered the joy of parties, shopping, drugs and men. Clara's life involved being out all night, sleeping all day and occasionally going for lunch with friends. She had a different man every night, and every night she was at a party or a club, and she was as high as a kite. She did what her parents expected her to do.

Her parents thought this was a good development. She was mixing in the right circles and would find a suitable husband. They were pleased she was having fun; a girl in her position was expected to settle down in a couple of years. (Clara's father was of the mind that as he was so rich and successful, he should choose Clara's husband. It irritated him that arranged marriages were no longer acceptable.)

Clara soon tired of this lifestyle. She had been through most of the men in her circle, and the girls were getting on her nerves. All they talked about was hooking Britain's most eligible bachelors (and Clara had already slept with all of them), shopping and doing the season. Clara wanted more from her life and decided to get a job.

As Clara sat down again, her parents were making moves to go out to dinner. They left Claridges and went to the Ivy, her parents' favourite restaurant. Clara didn't touch her food, or speak much. Her father was questioning James on the business again as her mother twirled her pearls. Clara thought the whole thing was so painful and felt freshly determined that, whatever she did, she would not turn into her mother. Even if it meant that she would have to learn how to do her job. At that moment, Clara realised that having a job was not going to make her successful, but being good at it would.

When dinner was over, her parents went home in their chauffeur-driven Bentley, while Clara jumped into James's Ferrari, and revelled in the envious stares of a couple of passing females. Not only was the car hot, her brother was too.

'Clara, are you going to tell me what's wrong?' James asked.

Clara pouted. 'Nothing. I don't know what you mean.'

'Look at you. You're jittery, you hardly said two words this evening and you didn't even argue with Dad. That's not like you.'

'I couldn't be bothered and, anyway, we had our usual row before you arrived. Look, James, I'm tired, I'm working hard, and the parents think I should just get a twinset and find a suitable bridegroom. God, the thought of turning into Mother makes me feel sick. The woman is a walking tomb.'

'That's my mother you're talking about. And you'll never be like her, you're a career girl.' James smiled at her proudly. He was pleased with the way Clara had proved herself at SFH and been promoted. He would probably have crashed his Ferrari into the nearest wall if he knew how she had got the promotion.

'Jamie, she's a zombie and Daddy's a pig. They aren't the faintest bit interested in me. All they care about is how successful *you* are, and how *I* can't boil an egg. Christ, I really don't know why I don't just excommunicate them. They make me feel so unloved and so fucking inadequate.'

'Well, I know you're none of those things. Listen, when you're ready you can come and work with me. We'll be the best brother-and-sister team the business has ever seen.'

'Daddy will never allow it.'

'Daddy will have no choice,' James said, as he pulled up at Clara's house. He jumped out of the car, opened her door and kissed her on both cheeks.

'Love you, Jamie,' Clara said.

'Love you too,' he replied, got back in and drove off.

Clara let herself into her flat, dropped the keys on the floor, pulled off her coat and kicked her shoes at the wall. She felt desolation welling up. She felt the walls closing in on her – life closing in on her. She ran to the bedroom, fell on the bed and sobbed uncontrollably. She always ended up that way after a Hart family dinner.

Chapter Six

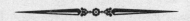

As she reached her desk Ella's head was hammering. From the sight that greeted her, she guessed that the others were suffering as much as she was. Liam wasn't there, Jimmy held his head in his hands, John was green, and Trevor was telling them that when he had got home, his wife had refused to let him into their bed. Bob was out on a bacon-sandwich run.

Ella tried to focus; she checked the market and was relieved that it was quiet. She went through her overnight positions: everything was fine. Bob returned with a sandwich for her and proceeded to hand out Nurofen. Liam arrived with a McDonald's Breakfast. No one could be bothered to speak.

They didn't notice Jeff approach with a short man in tow. He was not in the best of moods at seeing his vibrant trading desk all looking half dead. 'Morning, guys,' he said, unnecessarily loudly.

They all turned their heads. Trevor had ketchup dribbling down his chin, Ella had a mouthful of bacon, Liam was noisily drinking Coca-Cola, Bob had his head on his desk.

Only John and Jimmy responded. 'Hi, boss,' they said weakly.

Jeff sighed and glanced at his new companion, who was looking at the people in front of him with a mixture of disgust and despair. 'This is Johnny Rupfin. He's joining us on Monday as a trainee trader.'

Everyone but Ella looked at the new boy blankly. She sat up straight: this short, dark-haired man with a pinstripe suit, a red tie and what looked like acne was her new charge. Jeff introduced him to everyone and explained to him that there had been a big celebration last night, which was why everyone was looking 'under par'. That was a huge understatement. Johnny made a big show of shaking hands with everyone, but left Ella until last and barely looked at her.

At that instant Ella knew she hated him. He was the sort of kid who thought he was smart because he'd been to Oxford and Harvard, who was sexist and probably thought she was the team secretary. When Jeff explained that Ella was to be Johnny's mentor, she did not miss the momentary look of horror on his face. She knew that this man was going to be a problem.

After a few minutes, Jeff took him away and the group returned to their hangovers. It was going to be a long day – and time dragged. The amount of money traded on the desk that day was pitiful. They all left as soon as five o'clock hit, and walked out as slowly and painfully as they had arrived.

Ella hailed a cab, she couldn't face the bus. As soon as she got home, she took a long bath and went straight to bed. Thursday, as far as Ella was concerned, had not happened.

Virginia arrived at work as she always did. Her morning routine and her drive to work were exactly as usual. The lift came in five seconds; her desk was as she had left it.

During the night Virginia had had a dream. It had been so real that, for the first few moments after her alarm woke her, she had had to rack her brain to try to remember if it was a dream or not. She was 90 per cent sure that she had been asleep, but the other 10 per cent felt it had really happened.

In this dream, Virginia e-mailed Human Resources with her CV and a covering letter so strong that she could remember every word. She had not copied Isabelle on the e-mail, she had done it all on her own. To be sure, Virginia opened her mailbox and looked in her 'sent' folder. There was definitely no e-mail in it. She started typing and, with every word, she knew that this had not been a dream but a prompt. She knew it was the right thing to do. She selected Helena Fortane from the internal mail list and sent her an e-mail, explaining her situation and asking for advice. She attached her CV.

That morning she did her work as usual, nervously checking each e-mail she received as soon as it came in. Although her heart was beating fast, she kept a cool head and made sure she did everything in her usual organised way. At eleven thirty her computer flashed to inform her of new mail.

The sender was Helena Fortane, and she was inviting Virginia to make an appointment to see her. As she read it Virginia was trembling. Her hands shook and she felt the colour drain from her face. This was great: this was the response she had wanted. She called Helena's secretary and arranged an appointment over lunch-time that very day. Instantly Thursday became Virginia's favourite day.

The time crept slowly until half past one, when Virginia felt able to leave her desk. She announced to anyone who cared to listen that she was going to lunch, and took the lift to the fifth floor.

She found Petra, the secretary, easily and was ushered straight to Helena, who greeted her as if she were an old friend. She motioned for Virginia to sit in the chair opposite her own and looked directly at her as she spoke. 'You're looking to become a salesperson?' she asked.

'Ideally, yes. I've always wanted to do sales, but Isabelle doesn't have any opportunities for me. I don't want to go to another firm but, well, I expect you understand.'

Helena nodded. 'Yes, I do. This is a big firm. Let's look through your CV.'

An hour later, Virginia got up to go. Helena had listened and advised. The conclusion was that, although she could not make any promises, Helena would talk to a number of different managers about her and would get her interviews with any departments that had opportunities.

Virginia felt lightheaded as she took the lift back to her floor. She sat down at her desk, a pleased shade of pink.

If anyone were to ask Virginia what happened that afternoon, she would not have been able to say. She functioned somehow, but was on autopilot; her mind was still with Helena and the opportunities of the future.

As she left that night, she drove her scooter to the supermarket. It wasn't her shopping night, but she felt the need to celebrate and floated around with her basket. She selected Italian ham, expensive Brie, fresh soft bread and a bottle of sparkling wine.

'I'll live like this all the time when I'm a salesperson,' Virginia said to herself, happy to indulge in a little luxury.

When she got in, she laughed as she popped the cork and it flew into the air. She poured the wine into a glass, and made a mental note that maybe soon she could buy champagne flutes and drink real champagne. She cut the bread, and spread it liberally with Brie and ham. Sitting in her small chair with a documentary on the television, she drank the fizz, ate her supper and, for once in her life, felt like royalty.

She giggled to herself as she poured glass after glass. She danced around the room, she jumped up and down and, although anyone watching would have thought she was mad, it was clear to Virginia that she was merely celebrating the start of the end of her madness. She was finally becoming sane.

When Clara woke her head hurt. She recognised the headache as one she got from crying. She woke most days with a headache, and she had learnt to distinguish the causes. Normally it would be a hangover from either drink or cocaine. Today her eyes were puffy and sore, and her throat was dry. She pulled herself out of bed, noticing that it was already eight: she would be late again.

She felt like crawling back to bed, but she remembered her vow of last night to work harder, to prove herself worthy — and her parents wrong. She knew what she had to do: go to bed earlier, get up earlier, drink less and, as soon as she felt she had secured her position, dump Tim.

Dressed in her sharpest pinstripe suit, she jumped into the cab she had ordered and, with a new feeling of determination, started her journey to work.

That morning Clara looked at the SFH building through new eyes. The building impressed her, standing tall; its marble floors gleamed with pride. She smiled at the security guards as she showed them her access pass. She strode confidently to the lift. She got out at her floor and went to her desk. 'I'm so sorry I'm late.' She smiled briefly and sat at her desk. As she logged on to her computer the others watched her, astounded. They could count on one hand the days that Clara had arrived on time. She had never apologised before.

Clara read her e-mails, responded to the senders and then she turned to Sarah. 'Do you think we could have a word?'

Sarah nodded; she was still in shock. They both got up and went to a nearby meeting room.

'Look, this is a bit embarrassing, but I know you don't really like me,' Clara said.

'Right,' Sarah replied. She felt uncomfortable.

'And I don't blame you. I'm lazy and late and scatty and I don't work very hard,' Clara went on humbly. Sarah nearly fainted. 'But, well, I want to prove myself. I want to work harder, make more money for the company, and I want to be successful.'

The conviction in Clara's voice triggered sympathy in Sarah. 'What does this have to do with me? I'm pleased, but what can I do?' Sarah asked.

'I was hoping you could point me in the right direction.' Clara opened her notebook and took the lid off her Mont Blanc pen. 'Would you mind terribly helping me a little?' She smiled sweetly.

Sarah sat down. 'No, of course not, fire away.' For the first time since Clara had started working on the desk, maybe she was being serious, she thought.

'First, when you arrive in the morning, what exactly do you do?'

Sarah realised then that the bit of help Clara wanted was not going to take five minutes. 'Look, Clara, let's be honest. You don't know the first thing about being a salesperson. You call clients, you have lunch, but that's it. If they give you an order, Toby or Francine handles it for you. If they ask how the markets are you just say, "Fine", and change the subject. If you're serious about this, and you had better be serious, you'll have to learn an awful lot in a very short time.'

Clara took a deep breath. She *had* to learn – she had to prove herself – and she needed to be taken seriously.

'I *am* serious.' They stared at each other for a short while. Clara thought that Sarah was the ultimate professional. She was a lot older than Clara, about forty, she guessed. She had curly brown hair, which always looked neat. She always looked immaculate. She was married, and she kept photos of two children on her desk. Once Toby had told her that Sarah had been with the firm for ages, and although she hadn't reached management, she was respected as a salesperson. Clara could understand her initial hostility, but was grateful for her professionalism and kind heart.

'Fine. You sit with me today. I'll go through everything with you. After that you're on your own, but I'll be there to help.' Sarah smiled. All of a sudden she felt motherly: Clara was obviously lost, and although she didn't have any respect for the girl, she felt an overwhelming desire to help. She couldn't work out what had brought about this transformation in Clara. Perhaps Tim had threatened her with dismissal or demotion.

They left the meeting room like old friends. Sarah instructed Toby to take over any queries from Clara's clients, grabbed Clara's chair and pulled it up to her desk. A few raised eyebrows and questioning glances passed, but the rest of the desk was too busy to take much notice.

'Let's start with the mornings. Every morning you call your clients and tell them what the markets are doing. You prioritise your clients in order of importance and call the biggest first. OK?' Sarah was responding to e-mails, looking at screens and talking to Clara all at the same time.

Clara felt dizzy. 'Could we possibly just take a step back? How do I know what the markets are doing?'

Sarah felt like tearing her hair out. 'We have a meeting every day at seven, just a ten-minute rundown from the research people, which we take notes on. You didn't know about these meetings?'

'Not really, but I'm never here at that time. The one morning I did get in early this week, I didn't realise that when you all disappeared you'd gone to a meeting. I thought you'd just gone to breakfast or something.'

'How long have you worked here? Never mind. Anyway, you get in at seven, go to this meeting, take notes, then call your clients and give them a market run-down – it might prompt more orders. Clients like to know what's going on. Whenever anything of note is happening that affects our markets, it's our job to inform our clients. OK?'

'Yes, that makes sense. Should I prioritise my clients now?'

'Sure.'

As Clara worked on her client list, Sarah studied the markets. When Clara had finished, Sarah began to explain how she used the screens to look at prices, trends and markets. She taught Clara how to get the most up-to-date news, how to use the sales system and how to book client orders.

Clara listened intently, and realised that it wasn't as baffling as she had thought. She had spent her life suffering from number phobia – as soon as she saw a number her mind went blank. Now she realised that figures weren't the evil bastards she had thought they were and everything made sense to her.

They worked through lunch, getting the desk assistant to fetch them sandwiches. Sarah gave Clara research, reports and magazines to study. She put them in a pile to take home. Then they moved on to the client orders. Clara listened as Sarah spoke to clients, took orders, wrote tickets, shouted to traders, got confirmations, gave confirmations. Although this was stressful, and sometimes it seemed that the traders messed up, there was a methodical pattern, which Clara filed in her brain as well as taking notes.

Then Sarah gave her the opportunity to take an order herself. Clara spoke to the client, took the order, double-checked that the numbers were correct, shouted the order across, filled in a ticket, and ten minutes later called the client to tell him the order had been successfully filled. The buzz that Clara felt when she put the phone down was immense.

Sarah smiled at her. 'There's hope for you yet.'

Clara had been so caught up in her new-found enthusiasm that she hadn't noticed Tim return to the office. He watched her, puzzled that she and Sarah seemed so chummy, especially as the other day Sarah had made plain her feelings about Clara. He had brought Clara perfume and chocolates – he had even been to his favourite underwear shop and purchased some sexy lingerie. He was looking forward to the evening when he would see her in it. He had told his wife that he would not be back until late. She would probably be so busy with the children and homework that she wouldn't even notice what time he got home. Even if she did question him, Tim would tell her that he had been with clients. As Constance liked the money his position gave them, she would never push further. Tim smiled to himself as he realised how well he had organised his life.

Just before five that afternoon, Clara was calling all her clients to give them an end-of-day round-up. She smiled, she laughed, but she also gave them some interesting information. When she hung up at the end of each conversation, they were all a little confused: Clara never talked to them about anything other than lunch or dinner.

Tim came up behind her and felt desire flood him. Clara didn't turn round but she caught his reflection in her screen. He paced round the desk, asking each of his salespeople in turn how they were doing.

'Have you got a client dinner booked tonight?' he asked Clara.

Clara's hair stood on end: she understood the code. Although she wanted to read her research and have an early night, she also needed cocaine. It would be a while before she could ditch him.

'No, I'm going to stay in and study the markets.' She smiled at him innocently: she was the old Clara again.

She left at six that evening, after making her usual visit to the downstairs ladies'. On her way home she popped into Harrods, where she bought handmade chocolates for Sarah.

As soon as she got into her flat, she draped her coat over the armchair, poured a glass of red wine and started reading. She found it interesting, although she had to reread some sentences a number of times. She was still immersed in it an hour later when the doorbell rang. She opened it to find Tim standing there.

He kissed her sloppily on the lips and walked in, handed her a bottle of Krug, and an expensive-looking shopping-bag. Then he took back the champagne and marched into the kitchen. Clara followed him, wishing that he didn't behave as if it were his flat.

As he poured two glasses of champagne, she opened the bag. In it was Chanel perfume, the kind he always bought her. Clara was astounded at how much perfume he must think she wore because she had loads of unopened bottles. The reason they were unopened – apart from the fact that he gave her so many – was that Tim, an expert adulterer, gave her the same perfume his wife wore, which Clara didn't like as it made her smell 'wifely'. She always wore her own perfume and, not as clever as he thought, Tim had never noticed.

Next she found French chocolates, which she put in the fridge; she regretted her trip to Harrods – she could have given these to Sarah. Lastly, wrapped in tissue paper, she found the flimsiest, laciest underwear she had ever seen. 'Go and put it on. I'll line up,' Tim ordered.

Clara took it to the bedroom. She prised herself into the black bra, pants and suspender belt (she had to cut the top off a pair of tights because Tim hadn't bought her any stockings). When she finished, she reapplied her lipstick, doused herself liberally in her own perfume and slipped on her sexy stiletto shoes. When she glanced in the mirror she had to admit that she looked like a whore – but a damned sexy one.

When he saw her Tim's eyes nearly popped out of his head. He snorted his line, let her have hers, then ripped at her tiny pants and thrust himself straight into her.

After the 'passion' ended, Clara made herself another line and poured another glass of champagne. Tim did the same.

'Darling, you are so sexy.' He tweaked a nipple.

Clara giggled, feeling the effect of the cocaine. 'So are you, Timmy,' she replied, and kissed him.

Tim was still half dressed – he never took all his clothes off because he was always so desperate for Clara. 'I'm going away this weekend. Taking the girls to Scotland to see Constance's parents. I wish I could be with you, though.' His voice was soft, he was being nice, and Clara almost liked him when he was nice.

'I'll miss you,' Clara lied.

'Of course you will. Come on, give me a blowjob.' Clara stifled a sigh. Nice Tim had disappeared again, as he forcefully pushed her head down to his crotch.

He left at midnight, after more sex, cocaine and champagne. He had also left Clara with four grams, which would get her through the weekend. She went to bed smiling. She had cocaine, she had her new ambition, and she had a weekend without Tim. Life was looking up.

Chapter Seven

At half past five, Ella was in the gym. The horror of yesterday had passed and she felt human again. She had decided to write off yesterday. Today she was not only working out, she was mentally preparing herself to make money, and she intended to make a lot. As she walked into the shower room, Ella sang. She was in a very good mood.

By the time Ella got started the markets were flying. Once again, trading activity was the way she liked it: fast and aggressive. Two hours later, she had traded millions of pounds worth of stock and her account glowed with profit.

'Ella, I need to discuss Johnny with you.' She hadn't seen Jeff creep up behind her.

'In your office?' she said, cringing inside. She had been hoping for a nice salad and the *Financial Times*. Now she had to have a discussion with Jeff on the man she had mentally written off.

'No, I thought we'd discuss it over lunch. My secretary has booked a restaurant.' Jeff's tone suggested that this was not optional.

'What time?' Ella asked.

'One.' He strode back to his office.

'Oh, lunch with the boss! Who's special?' John teased.

'Maybe Jeff has a more than professional interest in you,' Liam teased.

'Or maybe he has a more than professional interest in the new cupcake guy. After all, I don't remember him being so anxious about any of us,' Trevor suggested.

'He's probably just worried that after one week with you, Johnny'll leave the firm and never want to come back. And who would blame him?' They all laughed and Ella glared at them, then giggled.

'Yes, Miss Boss Lover. We'd better watch what we say in front of you,' Jimmy shouted.

Ella had time to read the *Financial Times* quickly before Jeff came for her. She pulled on her jacket and followed him. She glanced back to see her desk all standing up making faces at her. She stuck two fingers up behind her back and quickened her pace to catch up with Jeff.

The restaurant was a fifteen-minute walk away and Jeff spent the time asking her how she felt things were going on the desk. Ella told him how happy she was; Jeff nodded and smiled.

They reached the restaurant, which was a typical City lunch spot: white tablecloths, wooden floors and anxious waiters. They sat down and Jeff ordered a bottle of red wine. Ella respected Jeff, but his management method included doing as he liked without asking anyone. With Johnny, Ella had been *told* she would be his mentor, not *asked*. The funny thing was that, where it mattered, Ella trusted Jeff's judgement, so she didn't mind. But she also felt she should give her opinion, even if it was ignored.

Ella took a sip of the wine and studied the menu – a salad to start, she thought, and chicken for her main course. She hoped that Jeff wouldn't want dessert – she wouldn't be able to work that afternoon if she ate too much.

'We've had a great week,' Jeff said.

'Certainly have, in fact one of my best.'

'Yes, actually, Ella, it is one of your best, and one of our best. Well done.'

Ella glowed. She was like a little girl when it came to praise; she basked in it. The waiter approached and they ordered the food.

'What did you think of Johnny?' Jeff asked, when the waiter had left.

Ella thought for a few seconds about how to respond. Then she said, 'I'm going to be honest with you. I was disappointed at the way he dismissed me. It was a typical sexist reaction. He looked at all the men before looking at me. He obviously thought I was a secretary. And when you told him I would be his mentor, he was horrified.'

'I agree. Listen, Ella, Johnny is a very clever boy. First from Oxford, MBA from Harvard – he's definitely SFH material. We want the best and Johnny fits the bill. Now, I know none of you interviewed him, but I did and there's no question he's bright. He knows about the markets, he understands how the City works. The only thing I don't know about him is whether he can trade. And if he can't we'll deal with it, but at the moment he's our junior trader and I want you to try your best. The sexism is something we can overcome easily.'

Ella smiled. 'Fine, but I don't think you're as taken with this guy as you make out.' She knew this was a bold statement, but she made it anyway.

'Maybe you're right, Ella. But I'm supporting him, and I suggest that, if you see yourself in my position one day, you do too.'

Ella smiled again. She understood everything now, and she liked the feeling it gave her. Jeff was still behind the scenes directing her career – he cared about her as a mentor should – and she resolved then and there to do her best with Johnny, to try to make it work. 'Jeff, if I can be half the mentor to Johnny that you've been to me, he's one hell of a lucky man.' She raised her glass in a toast and Jeff smiled at her affectionately.

'I may be a bully, but I do have your best interests at heart.'

'Isn't that the sort of statement Hitler made?' Ella teased, and they both laughed.

After lunch, they walked back to the office in companionable silence, and Ella enjoyed the sun on her back and the warmth of her boss.

As she left the office to spend Friday night alone in her flat, she knew that soon she would be ready to find herself a social life ... However, it would never be as important to her as her career.

Virginia was at work even earlier than normal. She was so excited about the prospects Helena had suggested might be there for her that she couldn't sleep. She had spent most of the night daydreaming about getting interviews and being promoted. She wondered where she might work, and who with, and she pictured Isabelle's face when she found out that her secretary was good enough to be a salesperson. She couldn't wait to prove her wrong. It was time for Virginia to start taking control of her life, which she had never done before. From now on she would be a success, and would do it for herself. Because of her nervous excitement, she ensured that she stuck to her routine. The timing was off, but she still had her shower while the kettle boiled; she made tea as soon as she was out of the shower. She watched the breakfast news as she drank it. She got dressed. She left the house. She drove to work.

The only change in routine was that she bought a copy of the *Financial Times* on the way into the office and read it. Normally Virginia waited until mid-morning when free copies were given out. She wanted to make sure that she knew what was going on. She also checked out the markets, which she usually did but today she felt she had a real reason for doing so. She smiled as the office filled, and was rewarded with a couple of impersonal grins.

As the morning progressed, she grew more nervous. She

knew that at any moment an e-mail might come through from Helena, but she didn't know when. She kept telling herself to be patient, Helena had said these things took time. Virginia had been waiting years; she felt that, with discipline, she could last a little longer. She had to slow her breathing consciously: she felt as if she might hyperventilate. She counted: one, two, three, four. By four she was calm. She hadn't had these feelings for such a long time, value, opportunity, optimism. It had been such a long time since she'd faced anything like this: she had no controls in place to deal with it.

If she got an e-mail today and it contained good news, she hoped she could contain her excitement – she didn't want anyone else to know, especially the dreaded Isabelle. As the panic rose, she began to think of ways to avert it.

She caught up on all her work, the filing and outstanding expenses, but her ten-minute checks on her e-mail led to nothing. At lunch-time she went on her usual walk, to the usual sandwich shop and bought her usual sandwich. When she returned to her desk, her e-mail box was as it had been when she left.

As her work was largely done, she decided to e-mail her penfriend, Susie. She started typing, asking questions about how she was, how her job was going – her friend was a research assistant for a pharmaceutical company – and how her family were. She had been writing to Susie since she was thirteen. Her English teacher had introduced the idea and had allocated each child in the class an address in a different country. Virginia was offered Canada, and for a while she was disappointed as she had hoped for America, Africa or even Australia.

After a while, she and Susie knew so much about each other that Virginia counted her her best friend. They were soulmates. They wrote to each other regularly, exchanging secrets, news, troubles, and hopes for the future. If Virginia were less neurotic she would have seen that Susie was like herself: she would have recognised that they shared many characteristics. She would have seen that there was a good reason why, at thirteen, she had been given Canada. She would know it was fate, but no one could have guessed that this linking would lead to a lifelong friendship. When they started working, they had swapped letters for e-mails, which meant that their correspondence became easier and more regular. They had never spoken or met, but that didn't matter. At least Virginia had someone to confide in.

Virginia told Susie of the latest development at work, then asked how the problem with Susie's boss had been sorted out. The message was long, and when she was satisfied that it contained no spelling errors she clicked on send. If she got a new job she would visit Susie in Toronto: she would love to go there, to see her only friend, and have a holiday. Yes, that was exactly what she would do. She would go on her first ever holiday. The excitement of planning for the future infected Virginia's whole being.

At half past three on that Friday afternoon, her diligence and patience were rewarded by an e-mail from Helena saying that she was setting up an interview next week for her with the head of the Private Client sales department. She read it and re-read it, felt herself go pink and took a deep breath. Here in front of her was a real opportunity. An opportunity that might take Virginia to her dream job.

Virginia went through the directory and found out who worked in the Private Client department. She needed to make sure she had a full knowledge before the interview. It was on a different floor in the building, which made things easier. Then she found the Private Client site on the Internet and read all about SFH's prestigious division. She was going to be prepared.

Just before half past five Helena e-mailed her more information about the position. There was an opening for a junior salesperson in the Private Client business. The division had its own floor, the second, due to the kudos attached to the SFH Private Client list. They were clients who carried a lot of money and influence. It was like a dream come true for Virginia. A real job, with real prospects. As she watched the others on her desk, she wished she could jump for joy.

She also wished she had someone with whom to share the news, but her parents would only ruin the moment, and she didn't want to send another e-mail to Susie until she had heard back from her. The only thought that consoled her was that when she got her new job she would make friends. She would stop being surly, serious and insecure. If she got this job, and something told her she would, she would be friendly and she would learn how to be fun. She looked forward to that. She would be friends with her colleagues because she would be *someone*. She would no longer be a failure: she would be a salesperson.

After work Virginia went home and had her dinner. Then she got on to her scooter and went to the cinema to see a Hollywood blockbuster rather than an art-house film, which she usually chose. She sat on her own, eating popcorn and laughing at Julia Roberts interacting with a gorgeous actor on the big screen. She told herself that this was the beginning: she would become normal, and she would stop trying so hard to be someone she wasn't. The only flaw in her plan was that she still wasn't sure what normal was. And she wasn't sure how to find out. The other problem was that she didn't have the first clue about who she really was.

When her alarm clock went off Clara woke up with a start. She looked at the time, which she couldn't quite comprehend. Six a.m. She almost went back to sleep before she remembered about her new start. She crawled out of bed, jumped into the shower and washed quickly. She pulled on the suit she had put out the night before, and when the taxi-driver rang the doorbell at half past six she was ready.

She applied her makeup in the cab and was amazed at how short the journey was at this time of the morning when the roads were empty. She had to ask the driver to slow down a number of times. If this was the way things were going to be every morning, she might give up wearing mascara, she thought. She had just applied her lipstick when the cab arrived at her office.

As she walked to her desk she ignored the stunned faces. She smiled at Sarah and handed her the chocolates. Sarah looked touched. Clara pulled out the research that was always left on her desk and read it through before they all walked to the conference room for the morning meeting. When he saw Clara Tim's eyes nearly popped out of his head. What was she doing there?

Clara barely looked at him. She was too busy feeling self-conscious. Here, in a room full of her peers, she felt unsure. They had got their jobs by the usual means while she had not. They saw her as a slacker and were probably wondering, as Tim was, why she was there.

She sat near Toby, grateful for a comrade. She took notes as the researcher gave a rundown of the market movement and any predictions for the day ahead. The meeting was short and soon they all filed out. Clara felt nervous as she picked up the phone and called her first client. If he was surprised to hear from her, he didn't show it. He was perhaps a little more shocked when she told him she was calling to fill him in on 'market developments'. She gave him a five-minute summary of the markets – Sarah had said the secret to a good morning call was to keep it short. He thanked her and she hung up. She repeated this with all her clients. The only person she spoke to for longer was Jenny Pickard, a client she liked and with whom she socialised. They had arranged to go out together that night, so they agreed a place to meet.

When Clara had finished she checked her screens, and then her phone started ringing. She took order after order, and executed them as though she had done it all her life. Toby watched in amazement as she shouted to traders for prices, wrote tickets, and although she was confused at times with the quantities, she got them all right. By lunch-time, she had taken more orders than in all the time she had been a salesperson.

✻   ✻   ✻

Tim felt edgy. He watched Clara working hard and wondered what the hell she was playing at. He knew she didn't need to work, and she knew that the only reason she was a salesperson was because he was sleeping with her. She didn't even know what a salesperson did. That was the way Tim wanted it. She had to owe her job to him totally; she had to be dependent on him. His claim on her would be considerably weakened if she began to do her job well.

The other problem was that Tim did not want Clara to work at SFH for ever. The plan was that when he left his wife for her and they were together full time, she would give up work because he would need her to look after him. If it didn't work out between them, which he doubted, he needed to be able to fire her from SFH for incompetence. Tim had set this whole thing up so that he held all the cards. Now, it looked as if Miss Hart was taking control. Tim knew that he had to put a stop to it. He had to get her back to being dependent on him.

There were two ways in which he could do this. First, he could tell her of his plans for them, of how she would be his full-time woman, how she should give up working sooner rather than later to prepare for the role. Somehow he thought she might insist on working for longer, at least until he left home. Tim sighed. He knew that was what she would do, and although he had decided to leave his wife, he wasn't sure when. Therefore, he had to make sure that Clara's good intentions didn't last. He wouldn't be able to do anything about the situation that weekend, but he knew someone who could. He picked up his mobile phone, called his dealer and arranged for six grams of cocaine to be discreetly delivered to the office that day.

If he gave Clara huge amounts of her favourite white powder, she would soon be unable to keep up with her job. All she would be good for would be to wait at home, legs wide open, for him. If Clara wanted to play hard to get, Tim Pemberton would always be one step ahead of her. That was why he was in the position he was in. No one could get the better of him.

Just after three, Clara received an e-mail from Tim, asking her to come into his office but to make sure she told everyone it was she who wanted to see him. Clara pressed the delete button. 'Thank fuck the slimy bastard's away this weekend,' she said to herself, as she got off her chair and shouted to the desk, 'I'm just going to chat to the chief,' as she walked away.

She knocked, waited for him to beckon her in then closed the door behind her and forced a smile. 'Timmy, how are you?'

'Fine, darling, but you have some explaining to do.' He was using his curt, pissed-off voice. Clara suppressed a giggle as he let his cut-glass demeanour fall and sounded like one of the cast of *EastEnders*. Clara was one of the few who knew that the public-school persona was all bullshit. Tim was such a snob and he couldn't bear to admit his past. Clara had only found out about it by accident. She respected him for his achievement, but despised the way he made out he was a direct descendant of the Queen of England.

'I don't know what you mean, hot cakes.' Clara feigned innocence.

'The morning meeting. What were you doing there?' All his elocution lessons forgotten, Tim sounded rougher than sandpaper.

'I thought I was supposed to be there, but I just hadn't made it before. Anyway, baby boy, I decided to make things easier for you by being good at my job.' She smiled enigmatically, the sort of smile that always made grown men swoon.

Tim looked uncertain.

'Um, well, yeah.' He stopped speaking and stared into Clara's sparkling blue eyes. The silence lasted a few seconds, in which time Tim seemed to remember who he was supposed to be. 'Very commendable, Clara. I was just surprised. I'm all for you making my life easier but, darling, just remember whose cock you suck, and discuss your ideas with me in future.' He ended with one of his sleaziest smiles, which he thought of as a turn-on but made Clara feel like investing in granny knickers and a floral nightdress. She made a mental note to think seriously about doing so.

Clara sighed. She'd known he'd hate the sudden turn-around in her – she knew it meant he had less control over her – but she decided to play up to him. After all, granny knickers or not, she still needed him for now.

'Darling, I'm only interested in keeping you happy. The job thing is just something I wanted to do to ensure no one finds out about us. Well, until you want them to, of course.' She gave him her best little-girl smile.

Tim was mollified. Actually, he had a huge hard-on. That smile always made him think of Clara in a gymslip. He made a mental note to buy her one. All thoughts of anything but what was happening in his trousers fled from his mind.

It was at times like this that Clara wondered what had happened to the intelligence that had got him to the top. She decided long ago that where she was concerned he must have buried it beneath his ego and his cock.

'Fine, good. Listen, baby, as I'm not going to be with you this weekend, I've got something to remind you of me.' He passed over five wraps, checking furtively that no one could see them, and watched as she tucked them expertly into her skirt. She blew him a kiss, and walked back to her desk, where she put them safely in her handbag.

Before he left the office, Tim thought, after that she won't even get out of bed on Monday, let alone make the morning meeting. As she saw Tim leaving, Clara thought, Thank God the talking testicle's gone. She turned her thoughts to the weekend ahead and thanked God, Buddha and the god of cocaine for the precious freedom that had been bestowed upon her.

At five, she took her usual visit to the ladies'. Although adrenaline had got her through the day, she felt wobbly and shaky and her head was pounding. After her line of coke, she felt better. She still couldn't believe the amount Tim had given her and couldn't work out what had brought on the stroke of generosity, but she was too in love with cocaine to imagine that his motives might be destructive. She ran back to her desk, grabbed her bag and announced she was off to meet a client.

She walked the short distance into the heart of the City to meet Jenny in a bar in Bishopsgate. Clara seldom walked anywhere, but today she took rare enjoyment in the early-evening bustle that greeted her. Traffic sat still in every road, people squealed about the night ahead; the grey sky, dotted with clouds, seemed to smile at her. Clara smiled back. People shot puzzled glances at each other as they passed a gorgeous girl who seemed to be smiling at them; some even debated following her. Unaware of the effect she was having on the inhabitants of the City of London, Clara reached the bar still smiling.

She and Jenny got on like a house on fire. Jenny was a tough London fund manager who liked to get drunk and pick up men. Her background and Clara's were a million miles apart. Jenny, the hard-nosed, loud-voiced Oxford girl with an amazing brain had no qualms about being working class and liked to tell Clara about 'all the toffs I've shagged'. The two girls had developed an unlikely but wild friendship, which meant that when they went out they didn't talk about business. They got plastered, high on cocaine and usually ended up with men.

Clara ordered a bottle of champagne, lit a cigarette, and found a table. She didn't have too long to wait and Jenny bounded in ten minutes later.

'Clara, how are you?' Jenny's voice was so loud that most of the bar turned to look at them. They were not so quick to look away. The two girls cheek-kissed and Jenny sat down. Jenny was a stunning brunette. Her big brown eyes had inflicted many a broken heart, and she was a good-time girl, a lot like Clara, although she had worked hard for everything she had. She didn't have Clara's privileges but she had ambition.

'Fuck, I've had such a shitty day. Give us some of that plonk.'

Clara poured her a glass of champagne; Jenny always said she had had a bad day and Clara suspected that she never did. 'So, what do you fancy doing tonight?' Clara asked, having forgotten to make any plans past the bar they sat in.

'Why don't we drink this, have another, then when we're too pissed to eat, we'll go to Soho, laugh at the nobs in Mezzo and go to China White. Is that all right with you?' Jenny suggested.

'Fine, darling. Now if we're drinking here, how about a little something to make you sparkle?' Clara raised a questioning eyebrow at Jenny.

'Clara, I'll keep giving you all my business. You're a star.' Clara handed the wrap under the table to Jenny, and Jenny literally went off to powder her nose.

An hour later they were flying. They had both had a few lines of coke, they had drunk a bottle and a half of champagne and the conversation had turned blue.

'Darling, take my advice, keep away from married men. My Mr Married is so foul, I don't know quite why I keep sleeping with him. He thinks he's sexy and kinky and, oh, such a turn-on, but I find the idea of shagging a turnip more appealing.' Clara looked momentarily sad.

'Dump him. When I slept with this married man last year — he was some sort of egomaniac — I dropped him like a shitbrick as soon as he said he was leaving his wife. I mean, what's that all about? Married men are supposed to have affairs and never leave their wives. It's such a crock of shit,' Jenny said.

'Exactly, absolutely. He wants to leave his wife and I don't want him to. I want him to stay with her. For ever and ever. And leave me.' Clara started to laugh. 'Perhaps I should anonymously send him a book on how to be a proper unfaithful bastard. There must be one that says never leave your wife for your sexy-bit-on-the-side hussy.'

'If there isn't we could write one. And in it we should also say that married men are only attractive to single girls *because* they're married. If they were remotely single, we wouldn't touch them.' Jenny was warming to the idea.

'Yes, and we should also say that married men should be better in bed because they're married, and if they're not what's the point? Oh, God, I think I'm getting confused.' Clara broke into drunken giggles.

'Anyway, I met this bloke on Tuesday and he's a bit of all right. He's single, tall, and rich. Oh, and he's hung like a donkey.' Jenny giggled.

'Christ, all that in one package! Tell me the delicious details.'

'He's a footballer.' Jenny and Clara burst out laughing.

'He's not David Beckham, is he?'

'No, he's bloody not. No, my man plays for West Ham, and he's rich but he's common as muck. Bit like me. Oh, yeah, and he's so good in bed, I was walking like Woody from *Toy Story* for the rest of the week.' Jenny shrieked.

'So, are you going to see him again? Aren't all footballers common? They tend to prefer rugby and cricket in public schools.'

'Clara, you fucking snob. You clueless snob.' She always got famous people mixed up. She had once been at a party with loads of celebrities and she managed to upset quite a few. The most memorable was when she met one of the Gallagher brothers and told him she thought it was very brave of him to leave Take That, especially as he was so good at break-dancing.

Jenny continued, 'Although you're probably right. But my footballer's quite bright – not enough kicks in the head or something. Anyway, I'm seeing him tomorrow night for a marathon sex session.'

'Lucky you. Christ, do you think we'll ever find men that are enough for us? I can't imagine settling for just one.' Clara looked frightened.

'I don't think there's a man on this planet who's enough for you. Sorry, darling.'

'Well, in that case, I'll stick to Charlie.' Clara laughed and went to powder her nose again.

When she got back they left and took a cab to Mezzo. At the bar, men surrounded them. After another few lines of cocaine, they started to behave like a double act. Clara would flirt and get drinks bought for them, then Jenny would pull each man to pieces until they could endure the misery no more. They were both having fun; the men they met were not.

By the time they got to China White, they were as high as helium balloons. They walked straight past the intimidating doorman, who smiled at them, and sat down at a table. Clara tossed the reserved sign over her head. Although the staff gave them odd looks, no one questioned them. When they were together, they could get away with whatever they wanted.

After their first drink, two men approached them. Unlike the rather sad types who had mobbed them in Mezzo, this pair wore trendy suits, had slick haircuts and model good looks. They said they worked in the music industry, then proceeded to prove the point by plying the girls with champagne, cocaine and talking about bands Clara and Jenny had never ever heard of. Mick and Jerry – which couldn't have been their real names, even Clara could see that – took it in turns to flirt with each girl, giving them no clues as to who fancied whom. And the flirting was full on. They were touching cheeks, hands, knees, as well as giving the girls the most amazing eye contact.

When Mick and Jerry made a trip to the loo, together, Jenny and Clara had an opportunity to gossip.

'I think we've met our matches. Perhaps we're too pissed but I can't figure out what the hell is going on,' Jenny said despondently. Whatever game they were playing was beyond her.

'Only because we're wasted. Listen, Jen, I think they want to sleep with both of us. You know the sort of thing – they'll entice us back to their flat, give us more champagne and cocaine and then they'll make a move. They'll probably suggest sleeping with both of us, some sort of orgy. I bet that's what they want.'

Jenny wasn't shocked. 'Are you sure? Cheeky bastards. Listen, Clara, I'm way past the stage of reason. I've got my date tomorrow night and I'm not really up for an orgy tonight. I just want to go home and pass out.'

Clara looked thoughtful. 'You're probably right. I'm not sure I want sex anyway.'

'So, you don't mind if we make a move?' Jenny asked.

'No, but I want another drink and I think we should say goodbye to them.'

'Do you mind if I split? I don't want them to try to talk me out of leaving.'

'Of course not, darling. I'll explain, have another drink, then go home too.' Clara was glad Jenny was leaving first, because she wanted sex and she needed it. If it had to be with two men, she was ready for it.

Mick and Jerry returned to find only Clara at the table. 'Where's your friend?' Mick asked.

'She had to leave – she had a headache. I hope you don't mind that I'm staying,' Clara said.

'No, not at all. But that leaves us with a problem,' Jerry said.

'Why?' Clara asked innocently.

'Because there's two of us.'

'Yes, and there's one of me. But I think I'm enough for both of you ...'

At half past two, they left to go back to Mick's flat in Primrose Hill. In the cab, they were both groping Clara, who made sure she gave both men an equal amount of attention. The cab pulled up outside a mansion block and they all got out.

The flat was big and untidy. Mick made a half-hearted attempt to put all the mess in one pile, and they sat on a battered leather sofa. The men were obviously excited, but seemed unsure of what move to make. Jerry lined up the cocaine; Mick produced a bottle of champagne. They took turns at kissing Clara as the other drank or snorted the coke. Clara decided to take control.

'Do you want me to undress?' she asked, pulling herself out of her suit.

Mick and Jerry's eyes were wide.

'Come on, boys,' Clara teased, and they tore off their clothes.

Clara had sex with both men several times. They proved insatiable and expert – she couldn't remember the last time she'd had such good sex. Her libido was working overtime when the realisation hit her that perhaps she would always need two men to satisfy her.

When Clara woke up it was seven in the morning. She got out of the bed and found a large, messy bathroom where she splashed herself with cold water and dressed. She knew she had behaved like a whore; she liked the feeling. When she kissed them goodbye they thanked her like gentlemen and Mick offered her his number, suggesting a repeat performance. As she went outside to get a cab, Clara decided she wouldn't want to see either of them again, ripped up the piece of paper Mick had given her and left it on the pavement. She got into the cab and laughed as she felt in her pocket the two grams of cocaine she had taken from the sitting-room table. It was her reward and she deserved it.

Clara directed the cab to Kensington. She felt ill from lack of sleep and over-indulgence as she pulled off her suit once more and fell into bed. As she slept, she dreamt of nothing.

Chapter Eight

Ella spent Friday night alone. She awoke early on Saturday and decided to blow away the cobwebs. She took the lift to the underground car park and stood admiring her pride and joy: her beautiful blue TVR. Although it was cold outside the sun was shining, so she put down the roof and drove off. She drove for the sake of driving. She loved driving fast more than anything in the world, and as soon as she found the road clear she put her foot down, broke the speed limit and risked the wrath of the law. It was at times like this that she forgot she had a fake driving licence and a fake identity.

She drove for about an hour before she decided to turn round and head home. She didn't know where she'd gone, had paid no attention to road signs or scenery: she had been lost in her thoughts.

She thought of Tony: dead perhaps, buried somewhere; alive perhaps, kicking the hell out of another poor woman. She thought of Sammy. She hoped he had moved out of home — after all she'd given him enough money to get a place of his own. She hoped he had a nice girlfriend, a job he liked. She hoped he was happy. Clenching her jaw to stop herself crying, she accelerated like a Formula One driver.

She stopped at the supermarket, bought some food for lunch and the newspapers. She walked round in a daze, not taking in anyone around her. If she had, she would have noticed people giving her odd looks. She was stalking round the supermarket, hair askew from driving, and wore a vacant zombie-like expression on her face.

At home, she parked her car, kissed it goodbye and went up into the flat. She chopped some salad, cut some bread, ham and cheese and took it into the lounge. She put some music on and ate her lunch.

As a compilation classical music CD flooded the room, Ella's mind cleared. She wasn't a huge fan of classical music and didn't really know her Chopin from her Mozart, but she liked the way it relaxed her. She lay down on the sofa and drifted into a trance.

It took ten rings before she heard the telephone and the answer-machine had clicked in before she could pick it up it. She heard Jackie's voice, saying that Ella should meet her at 8 p.m. tonight at her restaurant. It wasn't an invitation that required an RSVP. Ella went back to her trance.

At seven, she took a shower. It was only as she was washing her tangled hair that she realised she had spent all afternoon lying on the sofa. She felt a shiver down her spine: so much time spent without moving. It scared her that she could just lie still unaware of time passing. It was a habit she had developed since being in London. Something Elloise would never have done.

Elloise never sat still for more than five minutes at a time. Since childhood, she had been a bag of nervous energy, running around, barely able to stop, fidgeting in school, being shouted at frequently. And she was an incessant talker: she was christened 'Little Miss Chatterbox' by her primary-school teacher. Elloise and Ella were so different, no one would have believed they were the same person.

Elloise used to laugh a lot and play practical jokes. She was known as the class clown, the person who did the minimum work and had the maximum fun. She was popular and she always led a crowd. She was the first girl to start smoking – B&H behind the bike sheds — she was the first to turn up to school with a joint, courtesy of Sam, and at thirteen she was the first to lose her virginity, to Pete Smith, the most rebellious boy in her class.

When Elloise left school at sixteen with a couple of GCSEs, she went to work in a trendy clothes shop. It was there, when she was seventeen, that she met Tony. He was every young girl's dream. If sophisticated Ella saw him now she would cringe at his lack of style but Elloise thought he was the most stylish man in the world. He came to the shop three times before asking her out. His slow, lazy grin, his boasts of running the most popular nightclub in the area, his designer-labelled clothes and his overpowering aftershave meant to Elloise that this man, this god, was sex on legs. She agreed readily to a date.

He took her to dinner. Elloise had never been out to dinner before and, at seventeen, she felt incredibly grown up. When they left the local steakhouse, he took her to his club. He knew Elloise was under age but he plied her with cocktails, then took her back to his flat to smoke dope and shag her. When he drove her home the next morning in his second-hand BMW, he kissed her hard on the lips and told her he'd see her tonight in the club.

Elloise's parents didn't ask where she'd been and she didn't tell them. They had always given her all the freedom she wanted. Sam questioned her and was not happy with the answers but he was being an overprotective brother. She ignored him and rounded up a group of her friends to take to Dino's nightclub. She called Tony and cheekily told him to make sure they were all on the guest-list.

Ella shuddered at the memory of Dino's. She would never set foot in such a tacky place now, let alone ask to be on a guest-list, but to her and her friends then it had been incredibly cool. The bar was huge and busy; the music was whatever brand of dance happened to be in vogue that week. Ella would have spotted straight away that it was a haven for under-age girls and paedophiles, but to Elloise the scene was cool. The biggest prize a seventeen-year-old girl could have was an older man. Tony was twenty-five.

Not only did Elloise and her friends enter the club free, they were given free drinks all night. Tony lorded it around his club, shouting orders, greeting favoured customers, grabbing and kissing Elloise whenever he felt like it.

After that night, which ended with more dope back at Tony's flat, this time with a number of his friends, then more sex, then being driven home in the morning, Elloise was well and truly in love.

Their relationship developed quickly. Tony seemed to adore Elloise too, and she was head over heels, arse over tit in love with him. Everything he did impressed her: the red roses he bought on their one-month anniversary, the champagne in bed, the kinky underwear and the sex. Elloise had only ever had sex with school-boys before; now she was having sex with a man. She loved it.

Within a year Elloise was given a job at the nightclub; Tony said that they would be together so much more. Elloise was the luckiest girl in the world; Tony was a real gentleman, a real romantic, a dream come true. He was everything a seventeen-year-old could wish for.

The relationship carried on in the same vein for two years. As Elloise left her teens, they were a couple. She worked with Tony; she slept with Tony. Tony behaved like the king of the world. Elloise's parents were wildly impressed with him. He had a nice car and a good job, everything they wanted for their only daughter. Her brother Sam thought him an idiot. It was the only subject on which Elloise and Sam disagreed, and it got to the point where they avoided talking about it. But Tony didn't like Sam: he knew that Sam was a threat to his relationship.

On Elloise's twenty-first birthday Tony proposed. He believed he was in love with her. Normally after a few months he switched his girlfriends and a year was the longest anyone had lasted before Elloise. But Elloise made him laugh, had an amazing body and liked to please him. At twenty-one she wore clothes selected by him, styled her hair as he suggested and used the makeup he liked. Elloise was Tony's doll.

She moved into Tony's flat as soon as the engagement ring was on her finger, and her mother started planning the wedding. Two months later, Tony and Elloise had a fight over a man who had flirted with her at the club and she received her first black eye. Elloise was baffled. She said that in her job men flirted with her. Tony accused her of enjoying it. Of course, he apologised afterwards, and said it wouldn't happen again. Two months later, she got her first all-over beating: he kicked her in the legs, the stomach and the back. Her bruises resembled a cloudy sky, dotted all over her body. This time he cried when he apologised.

With each beating, Elloise lost a little more of her spirit. She stopped making jokes, stopped laughing, chewed her fingernails and constantly had panic attacks. When the beatings were so bad that she needed medical help, Tony would escort her to the doctor and say that she had been attacked in the nightclub, or that she'd been mugged, or fallen, or been pushed. Every casualty department in Manchester took turns to treat her: Tony was far too clever to arouse suspicion. He also fed her Valium and sleeping pills. She worked at the nightclub less and less, she saw her parents only on the occasions that she was bruise free and she hardly ever met up with Sam. The wedding plans ground to a halt.

Elloise didn't think any more, she didn't dare look and she hardly dared to speak. The man she loved was a monster, but she couldn't see that. All she could see was that she was a rag and she had no will to live. She didn't know how she felt about Tony because she'd stopped feeling about everything. She didn't know about love, she didn't know about hate. The only thing she knew now was physical pain or doped-up state. Those were her only realities.

A couple of years passed before she received the worst beating of her life. She had become a zombie, a shell, and the only person who saw this was Sam. He had spent the last year trying to get to her but Tony, with his slick excuses, had fended him off. When Tony had had a row with the owner of the nightclub about the lack of profits and was told his job was hanging by a thread, he went mad. He got home that evening to find Elloise had cooked him chicken stew. He threw it at her. He then proceeded to hit her, blackening both eyes, and knocking out a tooth. Elloise didn't make a sound. Increasingly frustrated, he threw her repeatedly against the fridge. Then he held her arms and slammed her back into it. Still she made no sound, so he threw her to the floor; the blood on her face was mixed with chicken stew. As he kicked her in the ribs, screaming, swearing at her, 'Bitch, slut, cunt, cunt, cunt!' still she made no sound.

He broke her arm then gave up and left her on the floor.

After an hour he went back to her. She lay still, contorted, and Tony began his clean-up. He apologised, put her in the bath, put her in the car, took her to yet another casualty department. Elloise still made no sound.

She spent the night in hospital. It was the first time Tony had allowed her to stay overnight but before he left he made up yet another elaborate story of how she had come by her injuries. When the hospital mentioned the police, Elloise shook her head. When Tony left he kissed her and whispered in her ear that she had better keep quiet.

When he brought her home the next morning, Tony put Elloise to bed, unplugged the phone, then went out. In the background, she heard the doorbell ring, but as Tony had given her two Valium she was unsure and anyway she could not move.

That night when Tony returned, she heard her brother's voice. This made her stir. She heard Tony telling Sam that Elloise wasn't well and couldn't be disturbed. She heard raised voices; then she heard Sam leave.

The next day, while Tony was at work, Sam broke down

the door, packed Elloise's things and carried her out to his car. He took her battered body to their parents' house.

Ella snapped out of her dream and realised she'd been in the shower so long that she'd turned into a prune. She dried herself and got dressed. She was verging on being late so she decided to get a cab. Standing on the street with her hair still wet she waited about ten minutes, cursing, before a black cab appeared.

She arrived at the restaurant, where the waiters greeted her as an old friend. It was a modestly trendy bistro, offering reasonably priced food, and Ella felt at home there.

'You're late,' Jackie said, as she kissed Ella.

As they had dinner Ella told Jackie about the afternoon's trance and her long shower. Jackie felt pleased that for the first time Ella had filled in the details of her relationship with Tony. They talked and ate, and before they knew it, the restaurant was emptying. It was midnight.

Ella helped Jackie close up. They had a last cup of coffee and left.

When Ella got home she jumped into bed and drifted into a dreamless sleep.

Saturday was Virginia's chore day, and although she had a glimmer of a brand-new life, she still needed her routine. After showering and dressing, she cleaned her room. She dusted, hoovered and washed, then did her laundry. She divided everything into dry-cleaning (her suits), hand-washing (her jumpers), and launderette-washing, (everything else). Virginia's weekly washing routine was so important to her that she often ended up washing things that didn't need to be washed.

She did her hand-washing, then left the flat. She dropped off the dry-cleaning, then sat reading the paper while her washing whirred around in the machine at the launderette.

On the way home she thought of the new flat she would

rent when she got her new job. It would have a washing-machine. Perhaps she could even have a flatmate. Virginia hugged herself as she let herself into the studio.

Once she had ironed, she put her clothes away then looked on her list for the next thing. She went to the supermarket to get her weekly shopping, then to Boots to buy her vitamins, and drove home.

She called her mother and kept the conversation deliberately short. She always phoned her parents once every two weeks to avoid being told that she was an ungrateful, neglectful daughter. She didn't tell her mother about the new job, and her mother talked on and on about how well all her friends' offspring were doing. The call left Virginia feeling depressed.

Afterwards she had lunch – a tuna sandwich – then checked the flat for any missed bits. Satisfied, she took out all her old economics books and spent the afternoon reading.

In the evening, she decided to get a video. Her smile widened with irony as she selected *Wall Street*, and she allowed herself a bag of popcorn.

Cooking dinner that night, she whistled to herself, and watched the movie pleased that she was watching a normal film. She went to bed that night to dream of Gordon Gekko.

On Sunday, she had a full English breakfast, and went out to buy the Sunday papers. She willed the time to pass into Monday as she half watched the *EastEnders* omnibus.

That night she hardly slept a wink as she thought about her brand-new life. Weekends when she would no longer be alone. A social life, maybe even a boyfriend. She blushed to herself as she thought about meeting men. The new Virginia would know how to talk to men. That was another thing she was determined about.

Clara woke up at six on Saturday evening. She pulled out

her emergency earplugs and saw her answerphone flashing so insistently that it made her headache worse.

She sloped into the kitchen and grabbed a bottle of water from the fridge. She felt famished but the fridge was empty except for the chocolates Tim had given her. She grabbed the box and went into the sitting room.

She pressed play on her answerphone then lay on the sofa eating chocolates as she listened to her callers: her mother, her brother, then Tim: he spoke in a whisper from some God-forsaken part of Scotland. She couldn't even hear what he said. Clarissa had called to remind her that she was expected at a party that night, and a man Clara didn't know had also rung.

She finished the chocolates and felt better. She phoned Clarissa. She had no memory of any party.

'Darling, where have you been? I've been calling all day,' Clarissa said.

'In bed. I got laid by two guys last night, had about a zillion lines of coke and the same amount of champagne and got home at seven this morning. What have you been doing?'

'Really, you are such a tease. You always make up such elaborate lies. Anyway, I'm having this party at my house, the one I invited you to months ago and I expect has a little star next to it in your diary.'

'Um.' Clara thought that this probably wasn't the time to break the news that she didn't keep a diary.

'So you're in. Oh, darling, I have the most divine men coming. You'll be spoilt for choice.'

At this Clara perked up. Until she remembered the kind of men Clarissa knew. 'What time am I expected?' she sighed.

'Oh, you really are hopeless. I'm serving cocktails in thirty minutes. I need you here then.' Desperation had edged into Clarissa's voice.

'I'll do my best,' Clara said. She thought about trying to get out of it, but Clarissa didn't take kindly to being stood up.

She had a line of cocaine, jumped into and almost straight

out of the shower, put on a nice little black dress, pulled on a coat and ran outside to hail a cab. It wasn't until she was in the taxi that she realised she had forgotten where Clarissa lived.

Clarissa was miffed when Clara called her from the cab.

'How many times have you *been* here? Clara, I live in the next street to you.' Clara laughed and directed the cab. She gave the cab driver a ten-pound tip because he looked pissed off.

Clarissa was one of Clara's oldest friends although they had little in common any more. She was busy trying to be a society wife, although she didn't even have a boyfriend; she would only drink in moderation and she thought cocaine was something gangsters took. Clara found it hard to understand how Clarissa had changed so much, especially as they'd been the first ones to give each other an orgasm at boarding school. Whenever Clarissa and Clara met, Clarissa always looked at her as if she was terrified of having that little secret let out. They had nothing in common.

'Darling, you look so gorgeous,' Clarissa said. Clarissa was stick thin, blonde and bony. The biggest thing about her was her nose. She looked awful.

As soon as Clarissa answered the door, Clara remembered why she hardly spent any time with her. Dressed in a style that would have pleased Clara's mother, Clarissa looked like a rich-wife-in-training: a simple designer suit, matching gold earrings and bracelet, sensible shoes with just a little bit of height, and a scarf tied neatly round her neck. Clarissa looked boring and middle-aged. Clara shuddered.

Clarissa had been Clara's first best friend, and until the age of eighteen they had been inseparable. Then Clara had skipped off to finishing-school and Clarissa had gone husband-hunting at Cambridge University. After university, Clarissa became straight, poised, and ready to marry well. Her friends were the same as her.

Clarissa looked nervous, which she usually did when she gave a party. She placed so much importance on these social gatherings that she sprouted another wrinkle with every one.

They air-kissed and Clara tried to sound pleased to see her. She immediately saw a number of people she knew. They were old schoolfriends, and suitable boys – so dull that she couldn't bear to spend the evening with them. They all pounced on her, asked her what she was doing, and proceeded to bore her to death. If that wasn't bad enough, the cocaine was wearing off.

Clara extricated herself from a lawyer called Jeremy, ran into the bathroom and closed the door. She took out her coke, cut up two lines and snorted them both. She sat on the side of the bath and felt her panic ease. Damn Clarissa and her friends. She had to think of a way to get out, but she knew she couldn't leave just yet.

A different Clara swept back into the sitting room. She was relaxed and charming. She asked after Ginty's horse, Laura's young son and Kate's divine husband, then asked Clarissa who she had her eye on. They giggled for a while, as they stood in the girls' corner, and the suitable men watched them. Although she was bored, Clara managed to look as if she was having fun. Just as one of the braver men looked about to approach her, the doorbell rang.

'I'll get it,' Clara said, and ran to the door. This was her escape plan. She would open the door, slip out then call someone to take her to a club.

On the doorstep was a man in his mid-thirties, with longish, greasy hair, wearing leather top to toe. Clara did a double-take. 'Crikey, I didn't think Rissa had friends like you.'

'And if I knew who Rissa was I'd probably agree.'

His accent was pure East London and Clara shivered with excitement. 'Clarissa lives here. She's having a party.' She gave him her best seductive smile.

'Really? Well, I guess I'm the gatecrasher. I'm Martin.' He smiled back sexily.

Clara grabbed his hand and dragged him inside. 'Martin's here,' she announced to the whole room, which fell silent. Clarissa was frozen in shock.

'Hi,' Martin said.

'Hello,' Clarissa squeaked, without moving. Everyone else mumbled.

'Let me get you a drink.' Clara grabbed a glass of champagne out of someone's hand and gave it to Martin. She was mesmerised.

Slowly the party resumed its subdued tone, but Clara and Martin were soon shrieking with laughter. Clarissa still hadn't moved.

'Would you like to have some fun?' Clara raised a questioning eyebrow at Martin.

'Sure,' he said.

She led him upstairs and into the bathroom.

'Nice bathroom,' he said, and seemed interested in examining it. Clara lined up some cocaine.

Martin stopped looking at the piping long enough to have a line. Clara chopped up two more — and her sex addiction kicked in.

'I'm not wearing any knickers,' she announced, and lifted her dress.

Martin looked as if he was going to pass out so Clara just jumped on him. It was quick. It wasn't entirely devoid of pleasure, and Clara had had her sex fix. She sat on the toilet seat as Martin put his trousers back on and lit a cigarette.

'So, tell me why you're here,' she said.

'I'm a plumber. I was doing a job across the road and I saw this bloke come in here and when I left I noticed his car still had its lights on. I came to tell him.' Martin looked faintly embarrassed.

'I guess he's got a flat battery by now,' Clara said.

'He's not the only one,' Martin replied.

Clara let the plumber out. She didn't know whether to laugh or cry. She decided on laughter. Just as she was contemplating leaving, Clarissa found her. 'Clara, are you going to explain just what that man was doing here and what you were doing with him?' Clarissa tried to keep her voice quiet, but the pitch was shrill.

Clara had worked out her story: 'Actually, darling, he told me he was a plumber and had come to mend the cistern, and I thought I'd save you embarrassment in front of your friends by making it look like he was part of the party then taking him to mend your loo. Anyway, he looked at it, said it was fine and I made him make sure. Then he realised he was in the wrong house – he'd actually been called next door. How funny.' Clara laughed.

'At this time on a Saturday night?' Clarissa's voice was practically breaking glass.

'Darling, it was an emergency call-out. Anyway, I thought it was all very amusing. I can't wait to go and tell everyone.'

Clarissa turned pink. 'Clara, I hardly think it's appropriate to discuss such matters with my guests.' Clara smiled at her; she still felt loyalty to Clarissa although she couldn't understand why.

'OK, darling, I understand. I have a headache anyway, so I really should be going.' Clara kissed Clarissa on both cheeks and saw relief spread across her tight face.

Clara walked home, let herself in, took a couple more lines of coke and drank half a bottle of vodka. She just lay on her sofa, smoking, drinking, listening to music and playing her life in her head. Everyone else tried to control her, her parents and Tim especially. And, to top it all, she was addicted to sex so to an extent other men controlled her too. She felt sad about that, sad about it all, and she was determined to pull back her control. As tears fell on to the empty vodka bottle, Clara vowed she would make a success of her job.

She woke at 5 p.m. on Sunday. She shuffled to the kitchen, drank half a litre of water and took some headache pills. Then she went back to bed and slept through to the morning.

PART TWO

Changing Trends

Chapter Nine

'Ella, I need a price in AMZ.'

'Ella, what's the bid for Coni?'

'Ella, I need an update on the Lin trade.'

Ella threw back the answers. The markets had taken a beating that morning and stress was evident in the office. People were either shouting, sulking or screaming at each other. Ella was doing her best to keep cool; it always looked worse than it was. Her positions had made losses, but not catastrophic ones, and she had managed to limit the damage. The main problem was other people losing their cool and bugging her.

The other problem was Johnny Rupfin, the new boy. He had flinched when Jeff told him that Ella was his boss. Ella hadn't had to manage anyone before. They had a couple of trading assistants on the desk, but they were so efficient that they worked on their own and didn't require much supervision. Johnny was part of the desk; at some stage Johnny would be trading. And when he flinched, and all his pimples moved, Ella guessed that he liked the idea of her being his boss as much as she did.

Ella had started out by being warm. She had welcomed him, introduced him to everyone again and apologised that she would be busy this morning due to the state of the markets. He had barely looked at her or spoken to her. He went on to annoy her all morning. Why had this market done this? Why was that stock like that? What does this mean? What does that mean? The questions were irritating enough, but the worst thing was the way he treated every answer she gave him with disdain. He questioned her, then seemed to dismiss her answers, and she didn't have the time or the patience for it. The others on the desk were already being rude to him, but although he deserved it, Ella tried to be nice to him for Jeff's sake. However, Johnny was turning out to be a major pain in the arse.

'Johnny, it's time for a very important job,' Liam said, not trying to disguise his hostility.

'What's that?' Johnny asked, pompously. If his short, greasy hair, his acne and his lack of height made him unattractive, his tone made him positively disgusting.

'Lunch run,' Liam replied.

The whole desk was quiet as they listened to the discussion.

'What?' Johnny asked.

'Lunch. I'm sure they had lunch at Harvard,' Liam said.

'Yes, but why do I have to do the lunch run?'

'Because, matey, you're the new boy and all new boys do the lunch run.' Trevor was kinder than Liam.

'I may be new to this desk, but I'm not straight out of university. I went to Harvard, I got an MBA. I think I'm probably the most qualified person here. I don't get lunch. Anyway, I thought that was what trading assistants were for.' Johnny was on his feet. Everyone looked at him, and the two trading assistants cocked their ears. They only got lunch for the desk when there was so much going on that no one could leave.

Liam laughed. 'Johnny, even if you think you're the most qualified member of this desk, it doesn't change the fact that you're a junior. And, as a junior, you do what every junior has to do. That includes lunch.'

'As I said, I don't get lunch. I'm not a slave and I don't think it's the most productive use of my time. I could probably teach you all a thing or two and I thought you'd be grateful for the help. If I answer to anyone I answer to Jeff. Even though you seem to think you're my boss, you're not.' Johnny's voice was raised as he looked at Ella.

Ella's blood boiled, and she lost her temper. 'You little cock-sucker. Just because you went to business school does not give you anything over us. You're a trainee, not a real trader, and from the way you've behaved this morning it's clear you're not going to be a real trader any time soon. So, if you think you have a future on this desk, then you better get your scrawny little arse down to the sandwich shop and get our fucking lunch.' Ella was looking Johnny straight in the eye as she said this. When she stopped, everyone else gave her a round of applause.

'Fine. I'll be speaking to Jeff about this.' Johnny picked up the sandwich list and the money and swept out.

As soon as his back was turned everyone burst out laughing. 'Way to go, Ella, I didn't know you had it in you.' Liam slapped her on the back.

She mock-bowed. 'I better go speak to Jeff before he does.'

Ella went to his office and stopped on the way to speak with his secretary. One thing she had learnt early on was to be nice to secretaries. She knew that Johnny Fuck-face wouldn't work that out. Unfortunately, they didn't teach social skills at business school.

'Jeff, we have a problem.' Ella refused his offer to sit down.

'I know. The markets are a mess. What are our losses?' Jeff was still staring at his screens.

'Not huge. The accounts at the end of today will show you — but it's not as bad as it looks. Anyway, that's not the problem.'

'OK. What is, then?'

Jeff was so approachable, so friendly and so smart. Ella prayed he was smart enough. 'I had a run-in with Johnny. Liam asked him to do the lunch run and he said that he didn't get an

MBA to get lunches and that he was more qualified than all of us. Then he said that you were his boss and he wouldn't answer to me. Due to everything that's going on we're all a little fraught, so I got angry – but he needs to get used to this atmosphere. You know as well as I do that it's not playschool, and he just isn't tough enough.'

'I was afraid he'd turn out to be a bit of a sissy. Listen, Ella, I'll back you on this one – even I had to get lunch for people when I started. But, well, there's something else.'

Ella's heart sank. 'What?'

'He's the nephew of one of our biggest clients. I didn't tell you before because I hate nepotism. The trouble is that he wants to trade, and he wants to trade on the best desk we've got. Which is ours. I had no choice in hiring him, really – his uncle put the squeeze on. So we're stuck with him.'

Ella was angry. Johnny had no skills and would make a crap trader; she'd put money on it. But he had a job for as long as he wanted because of who he was. Life was unfair. 'Does that mean we have to be nice to him?' she asked.

'No. Treat him as you treat everyone. Ella, I mean it. I said we'd hire him, but I also said there would be no special treatment. If he complains to his uncle, then I'll speak with him personally. Apparently, his uncle isn't even that fond of him anyway.' Jeff managed a weak laugh.

'Well, I guess he needed to get him a job. After all, no one else would hire him.' Ella swept out of the office.

Johnny took his time returning with the sandwiches. He had purposely forgotten Ella's. 'Sorry, I guess they don't do jellied-eel sandwiches,' he said. He had balls, Ella noted, but the wrong kind. He was rude to Ella and, as he had been told she was his boss, that wasn't the smartest move. He was so secure in his position yet this was only his first day. Ella remembered fleetingly how she felt on her first day. Nerves had been eating her. Johnny Harvard-Rich-Uncle had probably never felt nervous in his life.

'I'm from Manchester, not the East End of London, you little prick,' Ella said. She told herself to calm down and be nice to him, but she wasn't convinced she could be.

'Well, north or east, it's all common, isn't it?' Johnny sneered. Liam looked as if he was going to hit him; Trevor had come over and stood behind Ella; John was looking at Johnny as if he had crawled out of his backside. Everyone else was ready to fight.

Ella indicated to them to let her deal with it. 'Yes, it is. But, then, I'm a fucking good trader and you're a cock-sucking, pimple-faced little turd. Is that common enough for you? You, Johnny No-balls, will never be a good trader, in the same way that you'll never get laid. But don't worry, because Uncle Job-fairy got you this job, and I'm sure he'll get you another one if you fuck up. Because that's the only way you will ever stay in this industry. Now, I am your superior in every way, and if you don't listen to me, I'll kick your arse into Jeff's office and perhaps you'll listen to him.' When she had finished, Ella found that she had drawn quite a crowd. Johnny was red-faced, in anger and then embarrassment, as Ella received her second round of applause that day. He sat down. Ella reached across, picked up his sandwich and ate it.

Johnny seethed all afternoon. Some black woman with a northern accent was telling him what to do. Him, an MBA graduate from Harvard. His uncle was one of the biggest private clients this bank had; they should remember that and give him the respect he deserved. He was special; she was common, and she was a woman. She would regret treating him like this. All she was good for was sucking his dick, not calling him a cock-sucker. How dare she? She had no right. Johnny decided there was no way he would be spoken to like that by a woman. He would find a way to make her pay.

He was quiet for the rest of the afternoon, much to Ella's relief. She wasn't sure how much more she could cope with. When the day ended, she went home and drank two whiskies.

She didn't know why, but Johnny bothered her. His presence and his attitude unnerved her. Especially as everything else seemed to be going so well.

Monday seemed to set the atmosphere for the rest of Ella's week. Her relationship with Johnny deteriorated every day. He ignored her when she tried to explain things, he scowled at her when she asked him to do anything. The rest of the desk were close to hitting him, and Ella was tired. Jeff spoke to Johnny to reiterate Ella's position but that had no effect.

The markets were still volatile, which meant the traders had to concentrate hard and she found that increasingly difficult when she had a little wart like Johnny to deal with. She was finding it hard to keep her nerve; she was finding it even harder to keep control. They rowed daily. Ella swore at him and Johnny answered back. Although Ella always had the last word, she was fed up with fighting, fed up with Johnny, and for the first time since she had been at SFH, she was not enjoying herself.

The worst argument happened on Thursday. Ella could barely believe that Johnny had been there less than a week – he was acting as if he owned the place. She had told him that she would let him know when she felt he was ready to trade. He told her he was ready now. She told him he was not. He told her he was a better judge of his abilities than she. She told him he was an arrogant shit. Ella hated what she had become. She was swearing, shouting and behaving badly. Johnny brought out the worst in her. He didn't listen when she tried to be nice and calm, he didn't listen when she shouted. So she just shouted louder. Ella wanted to make management. She could easily manage anyone else on the desk. Her approach would be to listen, to care and to conciliate. She would be gentle and she would earn respect. With Johnny, her management approach was on a par with a bull in a china shop. She hated herself for it, but she hated him even more.

At lunch-time Liam dragged Ella out of the office before she killed Johnny. They went to Bertie's.

'Uggghhh,' Ella said, and drank a glass of wine quickly.

'Ella, keep calm. He's just a little wanker.'

'Then why is he making my life such a misery? Why is it getting to me? Why can't he just fuck off?'

'Look, I know it's tough now but he won't last. I've seen this before. Idiot clients think their idiot relatives deserve jobs, then idiot relatives can't do the job and we all get pissed off. They'll relocate him soon and we'll be free to do our jobs. Just wait. Let him make mistakes, then go to the boss with those mistakes. One thing no one in this company will tolerate is people who lose money. And Johnny has "shit gambler" written all over his forehead. Just be patient, and although I don't blame you one little bit for the way you speak to him, try to count to ten before every outburst. You may find it helps.'

'Liam, I almost love you. Well, I might love you. God, that little weasel is really getting to me. I hope you're right. If he does fuck up, I'll buy you dinner in the restaurant of your choice with champagne. Christ, I hope you're right. I'm not sure if I can cope with this much longer. And I will try not to shout, but you've seen the way he reacts when I'm nice. Shit, it doesn't make any difference.' Ella smiled.

'Well, I've opened a book on how long he lasts. We start at a hundred to one for three months, and evens for two weeks. I'll give you a range in between.'

'I'll bid seventeen days,' Ella said.

Liam typed it into his electronic organiser. 'OK, I'll give you two to one. I tell you, seventeen days, what a good guess. I'm going for two weeks because he's such a dickhead, I think I'll have to kill him before then anyway.'

'Christ, Liam, I didn't think he bothered everyone else as much as he bothers me. That makes me feel better.'

'He's pure evil. OK, let's go back and start making his life hell.' Liam paid the bill and dragged Ella back to the office.

Johnny was sitting at Ella's desk writing a ticket. Ella and Liam exchanged worried glances. 'Whose trade are you writing that for?' Ella said, anticipating the answer.

Johnny grinned smugly. 'Mine.'

Ella took a deep breath and counted to ten. Liam stayed close. 'Right, let me see it.' She grabbed the ticket. 'So, this is a client trade and you bought one million dollars' worth of Ironco. This trade has been executed. The price was seventy cents and the salesguy is aware that the trade is complete?' Ella asked calmly.

'Yes, to all the above. I told you I could trade.'

Ella ignored Johnny and shouted across to Harvey, the salesperson who had initiated the trade. 'Harvey, can I check this ticket with you?'

Harvey made his way to the desk. 'Sure, what's up.'

'I just want to check the details of this Ironco trade. Quite a big trade in this atmosphere.' Ella was surprised that a client was buying: even though the amount wasn't huge, no one had been buying much at all this week.

'My client needed to offload quickly. Didn't care about the price, just wanted to get rid of the stock,' Harvey explained.

Ella's heart flipped. 'This ticket says bought, not sold.'

'What the fuck? They wanted it sold. Shit, you said it was done, Christ.' Harvey was going mad.

'Harvey, calm down. I'll sort it.' Ella waved him away and sat at her desk to work out exactly what she should do. She turned to Johnny, who was defiant. 'Johnny. A word of advice. If you really think you can be a trader then you better fucking well learn the difference between buy and sell. Oh, and the losses we are inevitably going to incur from this fuck-up are going on your very own account. You wanted to be a trader, you told us you were capable, so you can take the losses. Which in this case will not be pocket money.' Ella smiled at him and turned to Liam.

'I think seventeen may have been a bit optimistic.' She

picked up the telephone as the rest of the desk started laughing.

'Fuck you, you stupid bitch,' Johnny hissed, before storming out of the office.

Johnny went for a walk and tried to calm down. How dare they laugh at him? With a first from Oxford, an MBA from Harvard, a member of one of the most successful families in this country, he was head and shoulders above the animals on that desk. Everyone made mistakes. He only made mistakes because Ella, the black bitch, didn't teach him properly. He deserved their respect, not their mockery. He wouldn't put up with it.

When he had told his uncle he wanted to work for SFH, it was because of the prestige of the bank. He had thought he would be with like-minded individuals with intelligence, breeding and brains, not with a bunch of farmyard animals, a black woman as a boss and common people. SFH was not supposed to be full of comprehensive-school idiots. But his desk was. He would make Ella pay. The bitch had nothing, no brains, no breeding, only a degree from Durham University. Nothing compared to his achievements. She was obviously from a council estate. He couldn't believe they let people like that into the City. Especially at such a respectable institution as SFH. There must have been some mistake with her application.

He decided to go home. He was not about to let that bunch of idiots get the better of him, Johnny Rupfin, son of one of the top lawyers in the country, nephew to one of the leading computer entrepreneurs, friend to the rich. SFH's whole trading desk possessed less class and breeding than he had in his little toe. And he would teach them that you should always respect class.

What Johnny hated most was the lack of respect Britain had for class. It seemed to him that, in this day and age, whatever their background, sex or colour, people were given opportunities to which they were not entitled. Johnny believed that everyone should know his or her place. He knew his: rich, well educated, with a successful future ahead of him. He wouldn't let Ella ruin that. Ella, who should be living in a council flat, cooking black food for her black husband and her black children. She should be claiming state benefits along with the other lower-class oiks who would never climb out of that class. It wasn't just colour: it was colour, sex and class. People needed to know their places, and families like Johnny's should ensure that they did.

He walked to his flat in Clerkenwell. It was a huge warehouse conversion, open-plan and interior-designed, a flat fitting his status. He would get Ella; he would make her sorry she had ever been rude to him. As he let himself in, he was formulating a plan. He couldn't be sure what it was, or even what he was looking for, but he knew that there would be something in the background of Ella Franke that would show her up as the common slut she was. Something that would bring her down.

He would probably find out that she had been a prostitute or into drugs. Something he could use to humiliate her in front of her cronies on the desk. He would embarrass her so much that she would have to leave. And even if she didn't leave she would be put firmly in her place. Then the rest of the desk would transfer to him the respect they showed her. He was sure he could find something. And if not, he would make it up. There was no way she was going to survive. Not now he was in her life.

Johnny knew he was clever. Now he would prove just how clever he was. He would soon be the most respected member of his desk, and then it would be only a matter of time before he was the boss of someone. He would ensure that they only employed people with class.

Johnny called his father's secretary, Claudia. Claudia loved Johnny and had worked for his father for years. She had a job fit for a woman, and she knew her place. She was always willing to help Johnny out: she had typed his homework, would do any research he needed and was generally a brick. He knew that with her expertise and her contacts she would be able to do the initial digging for him.

He called her and gave her all he knew about Ella, which wasn't much. He knew her name and her university. It wasn't much to go on, but Claudia was a professional. Claudia asked him to give her until the beginning of next week. Johnny said that would be perfect.

He knew that he would probably get a lecture from Jeff when he went back to the office, but he would talk his way out of it. Especially as his uncle was an important client and they couldn't upset him. His job was secured, he was about to bring down Miss High-and-Mighty Ella, and he was going to get what he wanted. He felt his excitement grow, and he lay on the bed masturbating to his impending victory.

Ella was amazed that he had had the nerve to leave the office like that. She felt like a schoolgirl as she walked into Jeff's office, crawling to the headmaster like the sneaks that everyone, including Ella, had hated. She wished she could deal with Johnny herself, but she couldn't. He had a strong position, and although she was respected, Ella had got her job under false pretences. She couldn't afford to rock the boat and she couldn't afford a feud with anyone, even if he was a pimple-faced little shit. She needed to deal with the problem before it spiralled out of control.

'Ella, I see more of you now than ever before.' Jeff looked sympathetic as she sat down.

'I know and I hate it too, but I just don't know what to do.'

'Johnny?'

'Johnny. I asked him not to trade until I felt he was ready, but while I was at lunch today, he took a client trade. Unfortunately, he bought rather than sold so we've got a load of stock we don't want, plus the same amount again that we had to buy from the client to keep them happy. The deficit is quite big, and although we're working on selling, it's too much in these market conditions and the price is dropping fast. We're going to make quite a sizeable loss.'

'Shit. Not now – this is such a bad time to have these losses. What did Johnny say?'

'As soon as I pointed out that he needed to know the difference between buy and sell, he stormed out of the office.'

'Great. What a mess. Ella, my hands are tied for now. I can't move him after less than a week. I spoke in length to Phillip who heads up Private Clients and his feeling is that we need to try for a bit longer before we do anything. He's sure that Johnny will work out if we persevere. There's nothing I can do.'

'Jeff, I hate to admit defeat, you know that, but Johnny shows me no respect and has no regard for my instructions. This climate means that I need to have one hundred per cent of my attention on the markets so mistakes aren't made. I came up with an idea that we get him to spend time with the others on the desk, starting with Trevor, who is the most experienced. For the next couple of weeks, we rotate him around the desk, and I'll keep an eye on him. Perhaps then he'll start to listen to us,' Ella said. She was trying to buy herself some breathing space until she figured out what to do. She knew that Johnny would probably react better with men, and especially with Trevor, who had a similar public-school background. All Ella knew was that she wanted to trade, and she didn't want to deal with Johnny.

'OK. Let's try it. I'm going to the monthly managing directors' meeting next Thursday and I will emphasise there that this type of policy is not working for us. I'm sorry you had to deal with him, but I know you're right. Everyone on the desk has complained about him and they've all said the same as you. Even when *I* speak to him, he's arrogant. I can't stand him either. It's just that until this meeting my hands are tied.' Jeff hated being told what to do, but he also felt there was no other way out of this one. The company was a partnership, so he would have to wait until the majority of the managing directors agreed before he could do anything.

'Thanks,' Ella said.

'He really is a little shit?'

'Of the highest degree.'

The rest of the desk took a brotherly view of the Johnny situation, and Trevor was more than happy to beat him into shape. They were all behind Ella and hostile to Johnny. She had everyone's support, even Jeff's. So why did she feel so wretched about it? Ella was scared and she knew it was because she loved her job and that somehow Johnny could ruin everything.

She left work that evening and went to the gym. Then she went home and read a Jilly Cooper novel until her eyes closed. Just before she fell into a deep sleep, Ella prayed to God that she would not have everything taken away from her. She wasn't sure she would survive the second time round.

On Friday, Ella had regained her composure. After all that had happened to her in her life, the one thing she had clung to was composure. If she lost that, she would fall and never get up again.

Johnny didn't speak to her. When he got to the desk she said hello to him and he just looked away, which suited her fine. She told him he would be spending a few days with Trevor; again, he didn't speak. Throughout the day he remained quiet. When Ella stole glances at Trevor, he seemed almost to lose his cool a couple of times, but for some reason Johnny was being almost amiable. It saddened Ella: it seemed to prove her right. Trevor could handle him and she couldn't. However, now she could do what she loved, and she traded well all day.

The markets looked as if they were recovering, which was a relief. Short-term dips weren't a problem and they added to the excitement. She made back her losses and more, and the week ended on a high, just as it had started.

That weekend she was seeing Jackie again and she knew that her friend would help her to rebalance. When she came to work on Monday she could put the new nightmare behind her. She hoped that the managing directors' meeting the following week would put an end to Johnny so she could get on with her life. She hoped and prayed for it.

Johnny ignored Ella. He was glad he was sitting now with Trevor, who seemed more like the type of person who should be working at SFH. He kept relatively quiet, apart from asking a few questions, because he had his secret now. His secret meant Ella would soon be destroyed. He was sure of it. He had a feeling in his stomach.

As soon as he left the office Johnny turned on his mobile. He had a message from Claudia asking him to call her. He decided to walk home and rang her on the way. 'Claudia, it's Johnny.'

'Hi, darling, how are you?'

'Fine. You're working late.'

'Well, you know what a slave driver your father is.' She laughed a high-pitched laugh.

Johnny felt impatient. 'Was there something specific, Claudia?' Johnny asked. He liked her, but hated the way women always wanted to make small-talk.

'Yes, darling. I'm a bit puzzled by the information you needed. I called Durham University. God, you'd think they were MI5 from the way they treated me. Anyway, I told them I was from a law firm and had an issue with one of their ex-students and they bought the story.'

Johnny was standing still, trying not to shout. He didn't have time for this waffle. 'And?'

'They told me they'd never had an Ella Franke at the university. I got them to check and recheck, but as far as they were concerned she doesn't exist.' Johnny went hot, then cold. Then he felt like jumping for joy. This was better than he had ever expected. 'Claudia, thanks, but don't worry. I

must have got the wrong university. I'll talk to you soon.
'Bye.'

'Let me know if you need anything else. 'Bye, darling.'

He almost ran home. He had never expected it to be so easy.
The whore hadn't gone to university. She had lied her way into
her job. He wasn't sure how she had done it; normally SFH and
places like it did rigorous background checks. They should have
made the phone call Claudia had made. He couldn't understand
it, but he felt better than ever about his life. Unless she had a good
explanation, which he was sure she hadn't, she'd be finished at SFH.
Not just humiliated as he had planned, but fired. He knew he hadn't
got the university wrong: he had checked that bit of information
– it was the only information he had. She had proved so easy to
destroy that he was almost sorry. He knew she would be finished,
and he knew he had made her pay. He would prove to everyone
that no one got the better of Johnny Rupfin.

That night, he went to his club, a private club for discerning members: his father had given him membership as
a gift for passing his MBA. It was full of young people,
professionals from the right families who enjoyed a drink
and a chat after work. He met up with a couple of his old
schoolfriends and enjoyed intellectual chat. The girls were
pretty and well groomed, and as he was feeling good about
himself, he bought champagne. Although none of the girls
showed an interest in him, seeming to prefer his friends, he
knew it would only be a matter of time. Once he was a big
swinger in the City and his dermatologist had cleared up his
skin they would flock round him. And he would date only the
prettiest, most aristocratic women. They wouldn't shun him
any more.

He left at eleven and took a taxi home from Mayfair. He
thought he should start going to some trendy places in London
as well. After all, he would soon be important, a big man in
London, and he needed to be seen in places that befitted his
image. He made a mental note to call Claudia and get her to find

out where these places were and how he could get membership. That would make him popular and he deserved to be popular. And once he had got rid of Ella, he would be the most popular person around.

Chapter Ten

On Monday, Virginia practically floated to work. She paid so little attention to her normal routine that she was unable to say whether she followed it or not. She reached her desk at her usual time and flicked on her computer. There appeared to be more people in the office than usual, but Virginia paid barely any attention to them. She took out her notebook, and checked that she had finished her to-do list. She had. Her Monday list was still blank. She had time to indulge in her favourite pursuit: studying the markets. She looked through them all and saw the rollercoaster pattern that seemed to be the reason for the full office. The breakfast news had said the markets were 'volatile', but in fact they were messy. She did not need to participate in the hysteria that gripped the trading floor so she had time to look through, study them closely and draw her own conclusions as to why they were as they were. When her interview came, she would be ready.

Isabelle marched up to the desk screaming about the markets. She demanded that everyone get on the telephone and speak to every client. The emerging markets had taken more of a beating than most others had, and Isabelle hated taking a beating. Once she had finished shouting at the salespeople, it was Virginia's turn. 'I need coffee – go and get me some. And hurry. My desk needs tidying, I need my filing done, and then

I have about a hundred letters for you to type. Go on, what are you waiting for?' she glared at Virginia. The stare that could turn you to stone. Virginia went. Her face was hot, her hands sweaty, her stomach tight. She was on the verge of tears. By the time she reached the coffee bar, she had decided that she would get the sales job whatever it took and then she would shove two fingers up at Isabelle.

When she had finished tidying and filing for Isabelle, she returned to her desk to type the letters. The atmosphere seemed to have relaxed a little and no one was doing much business. Virginia predicted that this was the cautionary period when everyone waited to see what was happening before taking any action. Virginia felt the markets would fall further then recover by the end of the week.

It was nearly 5 p.m. before she got a message from Helena saying she had an interview on Tuesday morning. Virginia sent Isabelle an e-mail saying she would be in late due to a dental appointment and glowed until she had finished her work and could leave.

She sat in her tiny room, studying, researching and glowing. She would no longer be Virginia the Failure. She would be Virginia the Salesperson.

Virginia's interview on Tuesday was with the manager of the Private Clients sales desk. She felt confident as she asked for Phillip Reid at the reception desk. The first thing she noticed was the difference between her floor and the floor she hoped to work on. It was smarter, neater, quieter, and more comfortable than the trading floor. Virginia felt at home.

The interview went well. Phillip was impressed with Virginia's knowledge, he was interested in her aspirations and he seemed to like her. He told her that he wanted her to meet other people and, if that went well, she would need to talk to Isabelle. He understood that Isabelle wouldn't want to lose her – it seemed that Helena had been very good in explaining things — but he said that as it was an internal move, if it went past the second interview stage Virginia would have to discuss it with her boss as a matter of courtesy. Virginia said she understood and that she was looking forward very much to the next stage.

Virginia didn't recognise the girl in the interview. She was confident, she didn't blush, she said what she wanted to say and she was personable. Not like the Virginia she normally was: the surly, uninteresting girl who no one liked. She was nice.

She went to her desk, where the atmosphere was despondent. She looked at the markets and saw why. They had all taken a battering but Emerging Markets had suffered more than most. She e-mailed Helena and told her how the interview had gone; Helena sent a return message saying how much Phillip had liked her. Virginia was floating. She was so busy in her dream world that she didn't hear Isabelle creep up behind her.

'Don't you have any work to do? Just because you go to the dentist doesn't mean that you don't have work to do when you come in.' Everyone on the desk looked up.

The confident Virginia disappeared. 'I — I only just arrived,' she mumbled feebly.

'Really? Next time go to the dentist in your own time and get on with some work.' She was shouting and Virginia flinched. Isabelle glared at everyone else on the desk and stalked off. For the first time, the others on the desk shot Virginia sympathetic glances. All she could think of was how much she wanted to be rid of Isabelle. She set to work.

Later, the interview times of her second-round interviews were confirmed for Thursday after work. She wished it was sooner, but she understood that it couldn't be. She would just have to be patient. After all, she had waited so long, what difference would a couple of days make?

She had almost forgotten that Isabelle's big client lunch was scheduled for that day. She was glad that Isabelle and her bad mood would not be there to upset her and neither would anyone else on the desk. Virginia would enjoy a heavenly afternoon alone. Isabelle told the others that at least the quiet markets meant it was a good day for them all to be off the desk. She said it as if she had arranged personally for the market to fall. Before Isabelle left she instructed Virginia to man the phones, to take messages and not to do anything else. She said that all the big clients would be at lunch anyway, and if any other clients called, she was to explain that there was a conference so no one was available. Isabelle seemed to think it was worth losing an afternoon's income to wine and dine clients who would give them more business in the long run, but Virginia felt she should leave at least one salesperson on the desk: even if the big clients were with her, some others might want something and it was never a good idea to lose business. Virginia did not mention this theory to Isabelle.

'I'm sure you can cope, although you'll probably prove me wrong again. Oh, and get the filing done while we're out — this desk looks like a paper mountain.' Isabelle was still in a bad mood about the markets and now she was in a flap about the impending lunch. She took out all her frustrations on Virginia.

There was no filing and no paper mountain, so as soon as they left Virginia prepared for her second interview on Thursday. The office was quiet and she was enjoying the time she had to herself. Isabelle was proved right about the phones. It seemed that only mothers, boyfriends, girlfriends and internal people called. She effectively had an afternoon off.

At half past three the phone rang on a client line. She snatched it up, panicking inside. It was a fund that didn't normally do a lot of business with them and had not been deemed important enough to be invited to the lunch.

'SFH,' Virginia said, worrying.

'Hi, I need a price in Griffin,' a gruff male voice barked. Virginia felt her heart stop. It was a sales call, a trade. This was what she would soon be doing.

She bumbled, 'I'm sorry, but there's no one ...'

'What? Look, don't mess around. I want to buy ten million dollars' worth of shares in Griffin and I need a price now. I can always use another bank.' The voice was insistent, and the order was huge. Virginia didn't know what to do but she didn't have time to think. Without even realising it, she shouted over to a trader.

If the trader was shocked to hear an order from her, he didn't show it. He shouted back a price, which Virginia, voice shaking, communicated to the caller.

'Fine, you got the order. Call me when it's complete. John Towers. Got that?'

'Yes,' Virginia squeaked, and John hung up. She shouted to Mark, the trader, who congratulated her.

'Nice work, darling,' he said.

Virginia felt sick. She shouldn't have done it. Although she had made a lot of money for the desk, she wasn't registered with the SFA; the official body you had to be regulated by before you could take client orders or trade. She had broken the law. And that wasn't all. What would Isabelle say?

Virginia panicked. She put her head in her hands and took deep breaths. She kept telling herself she had done the right thing; she hadn't passed on an opportunity that would make them money. But she shouldn't have done it. She wasn't allowed to. 'Oh, God,' she said to herself, as she rested her head on the desk.

'Trade complete,' a voice boomed at her.

Mark came over to the desk and gave her the prices. He looked at her strangely; she had turned green and was sweating. 'God, darling, you shouldn't get in such a state. It's a lot of money, but you need to keep cool, like me.' He grinned and walked off.

Virginia's hand was shaking as she called John and gave him confirmation. He even said thank you. Then she filled out a ticket. As she booked the order, she knew she would have to face Isabelle in the morning and she hoped she wouldn't be horrible about it. The implications of what had happened flooded Virginia's whole body. 'Oh, hell,' she said to herself, and rushed to the ladies' loo to throw up.

She went home and, unable to face her French class, she crawled under her duvet without eating. She didn't sleep that night, agonising about what she had done. She couldn't get it out of her head. She hoped that Isabelle would be pleased and would brush the incident under the carpet. She feared that she wouldn't.

Virginia was at work even earlier than usual. She had given up any hope of sleep in the middle of the night; coming to work was her only escape. She still felt sick. She watched the door for Isabelle's entrance. For the first time, she willed Isabelle to arrive. Then she did. Virginia marched as confidently as she could, with her legs buckling under her, into Isabelle's office.

'Hi, Isabelle,' she said quietly.

Isabelle looked up. She looked ghastly. Her hair was unusually messy, her eyes were swollen, and her skin grey. Virginia guessed that she was hung over. 'What?' she growled.

'Well, yesterday when you were out . . .' Virginia faltered.

'Get on with it, I'm not in the mood,' Isabelle said.

'Well, John Towers called, from Mitos. He wanted to buy ten million dollars' worth of Griffin shares. At first I said no one was around, but he said he wanted us to do it and if we didn't we'd lose all his business. So I got Mark to give me a price and, well, we did it. And it's a lot of money and I know I shouldn't have done it and I wouldn't have done, but it was such a good order and he was really insistent, saying he would never use us again if I didn't give him a price. So I did.' Virginia's legs were shaking so much she could almost hear them.

Isabelle looked up slowly. 'You took an order?'

'Yes.'

'You took an order and it was big?'

'Yes.'

'Give me the trade code,' Isabelle instructed.

Virginia told her and Isabelle typed it into her computer. Virginia saw a flicker of interest in her eyes as she looked at the figures. She knew that, whatever happened, Isabelle would take credit for this. She wanted her to.

'OK. Well, no harm done, I don't think. But, Virginia, I will have to think about this. What you did could have got the firm into a lot of trouble, and although I don't think it will, it was still a risk. Don't worry, I'll try to keep it quiet and if we don't tell anyone I can't see you getting into trouble. I'll just say you called me on my mobile with the order and I filled it. Which is what you should have done. You should consider yourself lucky. That's it.' Isabelle smiled coldly at her and turned back to the screen.

Virginia didn't know whether to be relieved or angry. Isabelle said she'd take care of it, so it looked as if she was out of trouble. However, Isabelle had told her yesterday that she wasn't to be disturbed for anything. She had told her not to call her mobile under any circumstances. At least Virginia still had a job and at least she still had an interview tomorrow. Once Isabelle claimed the trade for herself, there was no way she could backtrack and blame it on Virginia. Isabelle would enjoy taking the glory for this, so she would keep Virginia out of it. Virginia could put it out of her mind.

For the rest of the day Isabelle kept herself locked in the office. Everyone else on the desk looked as grey as she did. Apparently the lunch had turned into a huge drinking fest, culminating at a nightclub. Virginia gathered this from snatches of conversation, none of which was directed at her. As she didn't see Isabelle, she managed to put herself at ease about the illegal order. It wasn't such a big criminal act after all, and it had worked out. Instead, Virginia decided to take this as a positive sign that proved she could be a salesperson.

❊   ❊   ❊

Thursday was hell. She waited all day for six o'clock to arrive so that she could go to her interview. She was unable to concentrate on anything else and she was jittery. If anyone noticed they didn't say anything, and for the second day running, Isabelle stayed in her office most of the day, probably working out her commissions. All Virginia had to do was the usual day-to-day work, and although she was busy, she was on autopilot.

At six she rushed to the Private Clients' floor and asked for Phillip. She tried her best to remain calm: she was determined not to ruin the opportunity. Phillip met her, took her to a conference room and then, her interviews began. She met four people – a manager, a senior salesperson, another salesperson, and the newest member of the desk. Although she wasn't exactly dazzling, she was articulate, intelligent, asked the right questions, and by the time the last person had left, she felt confident that she had interviewed well.

Phillip returned and apologised for keeping her so long. He said that they would be in touch via Helena tomorrow, but he also said that it was time for her to tell her own boss she was interviewing. This was a good sign: he wouldn't have told her to do that if he wasn't keen, but she dreaded speaking to Isabelle when she hadn't been offered the job. She agreed with Phillip, although she didn't really, and she knew that she would have to speak to Isabelle the following day. Another sleepless night stretched ahead of her.

Friday was a repeat of Wednesday. As soon as Isabelle arrived at the office, Virginia pounced. This time her legs were shaking so much that her knees were knocking together. 'Isabelle, I need to speak to you.'

Isabelle looked amused. 'Again? What is this? Did you take another order?' She was cold even when she smiled.

Virginia shivered. Although she had gone through her speech in her head a thousand times, she still faltered. 'No, nothing like that. Well it's just that I've been for an interview in the Private Client division and, well, they thought I should tell you before we take things further.' The way Virginia said it, rushing to get to the end, meant she didn't explain things the way she had so carefully planned.

'I see. You've been interviewing elsewhere.' Her face grew colder.

'Yes.' Virginia almost fell over.

'I see. For a sales job?'

'Yes, as a junior salesperson. Well, you said you couldn't find me a job, so I called HR.'

'How very innovative of you. I was sure you didn't have it in you. And if you don't get this job?'

'Well, I think I will.' Virginia tried to sound assured.

'That's confidence for you. OK. Let me know what happens.'

'Is that it? I mean, well, I'm not sure, but ...' Virginia was lost.

'That's it. Let me know if you get the job. In the meantime, just remember you're still my secretary and I need you to do a load of typing.'

Virginia was astounded. Her face was red and hot, but at least Isabelle hadn't shouted at her. She hadn't even seemed to mind. She turned to her typing and tried hard not to think about the moment when she heard if she had the job.

Isabelle counted to ten before she looked up. The little mouse had turned into a rat. How dare she go behind her back? How dare she not listen to Isabelle when she told her she would never make a salesperson? How dare she almost go and get a job?

Isabelle called Helena from Human Resources and asked her if what Virginia had told her was true. Helena said it was and they were very impressed with her in Private Clients. Isabelle came off the phone and wanted to spit. She despised Virginia, with her timid way, her cheap suits and her permanent scowl. She despised her for crossing her. Isabelle didn't like being proved wrong. She was riding high at SFH, she was respected, and she had a great future ahead of her. She would not accept someone like Virginia trying to prove her wrong.

She thought for a while, then picked up the telephone again and called David Marker, co-head of Sales at SFH. His office was on the same floor, but David was her boss and she never went to see him unannounced. His secretary answered the phone and said that he would be free in half an hour. Isabelle asked to be put in his diary.

She thought it all through. She would ensure that Virginia didn't get her nice new job; she would ensure that she didn't work at SFH; she would ensure that she never crossed Isabelle Holland again.

When Isabelle walked into David's office, she noted as she always did that it was twice the size of her own. She had often dreamt of having an office this size and one day knew she would make managing director. She would be as powerful as David and no little girl would dare cross her.

'Isabelle, how are you? Sit down.' David was very professional.

'Thank you, David, I'm fine.' Isabelle was sugary sweet.

'What can I do for you? I hope we're not still worried about the dip at the beginning of the week. I know your desk took a battering, but things are looking up.'

'Yes, they are. No, unfortunately I have another problem and I really need the benefit of your experience to sort it out.'

'Go on.'

'You see, David, my secretary made a mistake. On Tuesday while we were having our big client lunch, which by the way was a great success and I think will generate a lot of business for the firm, Virginia Bateman, that's my secretary, was given instruction to man the phones. I told her if any client wanted to do business she was to call me on my mobile and I would let one of the traders know and get them to execute it. She isn't terribly bright and she's certainly not SFA registered. I told her that the lunch was important, but I also knew that I couldn't leave the desk with just a secretary on it. She had my number and all she had to do was call. The markets were quiet so I didn't expect anyone to phone, especially as most of our clients were with us.'

David looked impatient. 'Yes?'

'Virginia took an order from a client we don't do a great deal of business with. It was a big order, which made us a good commission. But the point was she dealt with the order herself. She didn't call me and if anything had gone wrong we might have been sued.' Isabelle looked serious.

'Good God. What was she thinking of? Anyway, no harm done and we made money. Or is there more?'

'Yes, I'm afraid there is. She marched into my office the following day and was actually bragging about the order. I pointed out that what she had done was wrong and I asked her why she hadn't called me. She was very flippant. I told her we couldn't afford for anyone to find out because if they did they might report us. I told her that this must never happen again, and I emphasised that although we made money, it was still a bad thing she had done. She laughed and said that I was always so over-cautious and then she informed me she was successfully interviewing in Private Clients and she would soon be a salesperson anyway. She basically told me to stick my opinion. I should have come to you sooner, but I tried to work out what to do myself. I tried talking to her again, but was met by the same attitude. She just didn't care that she had broken every rule in the book. I know what she did was a sackable offence, but I wanted to talk to you and get your opinion.'

'Really? God, she sounds a loose cannon.'

'My sentiments exactly. She had obviously managed to

charm Phillip Reid, who is very keen, and if it hadn't been for her indiscretion, I would be supporting her the whole way. But we can't afford to have people with so little regard for the rules in this department, but even more so in Private Clients. She hasn't been offered the job yet and I don't know whether I should tell Phillip or not. Even more, should we sack her? I hate to sack people, you know that, but as you say she is a loose cannon.' Isabelle smiled demurely.

'I see. Well, she sounds dangerous. What we'll do is this. We have our monthly managing directors' meeting next week. I will speak to HR and then see where we stand on firing her. If there is no reason why we can't, we can make the decision at the meeting. I'll get HR to keep it quiet, although I'll have to speak to Phillip. He can always stall his decision. Then at the meeting we'll decide if she has a future here and in what capacity.'

This was better than Isabelle had imagined. 'I knew you'd have the answer.'

'Yes, but I don't want her getting wind of it. This meeting is where we discuss all matters of staffing and any problems. Just think of the scandal if we were caught using a secretary to fill orders. Clients would leave us in seconds. She needs to think that everything is normal until HR can sort out the details. We don't want her flinging any accusations at us, so we need to make sure our case for firing her is watertight.'

'Right. But I think she's expecting to hear about the job before next week.' Isabelle was worried that the woolly Human Resources woman would find a rule that meant Virginia would get off with a caution. Firing people was so hard these days.

'Don't worry. The decision to move someone internally has to be approved at the meeting. It's just a formality but it gives us time to look into things. Phillip will tell her she has to wait.'

'Doesn't it all seem a bit cloak and dagger?' Isabelle didn't want to let on quite how excited she was.

'Isabelle, she put our whole reputation at risk. This is a

very delicate situation. We need time to figure out how to handle it. OK?'

'Thanks, David. I knew you'd know what to do.'

Isabelle left David's office, smiling. She was looking forward to drowning the rat.

Virginia received a call from Phillip, saying that he would have to discuss the hiring of her at the monthly managing directors' meeting the following Thursday. Virginia timidly asked him if this was a good sign. Phillip assured her it was. Virginia didn't know how she would be able to bear it for the next week, but she still felt she had it in her grasp.

Phillip put down the phone feeling fed up. He had liked her; the rest of the team had liked her. The call from David had just said that they had an issue with her that he hoped to clear up before the meeting next Thursday. Phillip hoped it would be cleared up, because he didn't want to have to start interviewing from scratch again. However, he knew he would have to sit tight and await David's decision.

Chapter Eleven

Clara woke on Monday and felt utterly miserable. This was not unusual: she often felt like this when she woke. There was a deep gloom inside her, which she couldn't explain and she couldn't fight. She wanted to pull the duvet over her head and sink back into sleep, but something stopped her. The old Clara would have done that but she was the new Clara. The new Clara would go to work.

She wore her sharpest trouser suit, a beige Armani, which made her look professional and not too sexy. She took pills to banish her headache and she put on her makeup in the flat for once, trying to cover up her grey skin.

She strode into the office to be met with a flurry of excitement and panic. At the meeting she discovered that the markets had dropped considerably and no one really knew why. Problems in Wall Street had occurred on Friday night and seemed to have had a domino effect on the other markets around the world. They were told of causes, effects, and what the predictions were. For a couple of weeks the markets would be in a state of flux, then recovery would come. It was a short-term drop; everyone should keep calm and pass on the calm to their clients.

Clara understood what was being said and relayed it perfectly to her clients. Although there was panic in the office, Clara kept cool and felt professional. Until Tim e-mailed her demanding her presence in his office.

It seemed like ages since she had seen him. She had felt a lot happier without him and she didn't want him near her any more. She wanted to tell him, but she didn't know where she would get her cocaine. She felt like crying as she walked into his office. No matter how professional she looked, Tim always made her feel cheap.

Tim was annoyed. He had been sure that Clara would be at home, recovering from the excesses of the weekend, not looking great, strutting about the office as if she knew what she was doing. Clara was his bit on the side, not a legitimate member of his staff. If she was getting ideas about being career-focused, then Tim knew he was going to have to give up the idea of leaving his wife. His life seemed to be in as big a mess as the markets were. He was in love with Clara and he wanted her in his bed, not in his workplace.

'Hi.' Clara sat down in the chair facing Tim's desk.

'Hi.' They stared at each other for a few seconds. Clara noticed that Tim looked old: she had never considered his age before. He was forty-five, but had managed to remain youthful. His short brown hair showed no signs of greying (he dyed it) and he dressed in a smart but fashionable manner. Clara saw the lines on his face, which made him seem old, and he looked tired. For the first time, Clara thought he was too old for her.

'I'll be at your flat at seven tonight,' Tim said.

Clara's heart sank. 'Fine,' she replied.

'That's all then.' Tim dismissed her. As Clara walked out, she knew that she needed to be nice to him. He was feeling threatened by her behaviour and she understood why. But she needed to follow through with her new determination, and she decided she would look into alternative cocaine suppliers.

The rest of the day passed in a blur. She worked hard, and she chatted and swapped opinions with the rest of the desk.

By the time she left, she had banished the black cloud that represented Tim's impending visit.

At home, Clara opened a bottle of champagne and had a line of cocaine. She spoke to James and reassured him that their mother was being hysterical when she had told him she thought Clara might be dead. She promised to call him more often but explained that she was very busy at work. It was almost the truth. They arranged to have dinner the following weekend, and ended their conversation just as the doorbell rang.

Clara opened the door to Tim. Despite the cocaine and the drink, she felt nervous and clammy.

'Hi, beautiful.' He sounded almost tender. They kissed.

'How was the weekend?' Clara was devoid of conversation.

'Boring and cold. What about you? I called you several times.'

'I was with my parents this weekend.' Clara took Tim's hand and led him to the sofa. He lined up the cocaine and she poured him a glass of champagne.

'Clara, you know I don't want you sleeping with other men,' Tim said, as he finished his first line.

Clara almost choked on her champagne. Then she lied, 'Of course. I only want you.'

'That's what I thought you'd say. And as a reward I brought you a present.' Tim handed her a bag containing more cocaine than she'd ever seen in her life. She almost fainted, but instead she kissed him, unzipped his trousers and started to thank him properly.

Clara passed out before Tim left, and her dreams were filled with white fluffy clouds.

Tim watched Clara as she slept. She was so beautiful; he couldn't let her go. She was so eager to please him, would do anything he wanted; she was dynamite in bed. Tim wanted to be in her bed more often. He was tired of his wife's lack of imagination, her insistence on making sex a duty, not fun. Sometimes this excited him, having her lying there like a plank, but other times it bored him. At the moment, it bored him. He knew that Clara would never be boring. Now he felt the time drawing near when Clara would be his full-time bed partner. If only she hadn't got some notion in her head that she enjoyed her job.

As Tim got dressed he couldn't help but feel puzzled about the change in Clara's attitude. Admittedly, it had been only a few days, but it was enough to be a worry: Clara getting to work early, Clara in the morning meeting, Clara becoming popular with her colleagues, Clara increasing sales. And she was showing no signs of wanting to leave. Tim sighed. There was nothing for it. He needed her to need him. He needed her to be there for him whenever he wanted her. He would not tolerate her not needing him. He couldn't even contemplate that she might not need or want him any more.

If Tim was in love with Clara, it was a perverse love. Although he told himself he was good for Clara and she was lucky to have him, he wanted to control her. He was going to do this by plying her with so much cocaine that she wouldn't know what day of the week it was, what her name was, or even how to get to work. Oh, Tim loved Clara. He just needed to ensure that she felt the same.

Clara woke to an empty bed; she had slept through her alarm clock. Although she still had time to get to work, she had to forfeit her shower and pull on her clothes in double-quick time. She was angry about sleeping in, she was angry about feeling terrible. She blamed it all on Tim.

She managed to get through the day, but without the enthusiasm of last week, or even yesterday. She was worried about Tim; she didn't know what to do about him. She kept thinking she would mess things up, and she couldn't bear to do that. She was full of contradictions.

Tim joined the desk in the afternoon. He glanced at Clara. 'You don't look well. Are you coming down with something?' he said, for the whole desk to hear.

Everyone looked at Clara.

'I'll be all right, just a bit under par,' she replied, seething.

'Yes, well, you should go home. I insist. I don't want any illness in the office.' Tim smiled.

Clara's anger grew. 'Fine,' she replied curtly, grabbed her coat and her bag and walked out. She didn't see Sarah shaking her head and no one saw the tears in Clara's eyes.

At home, she went straight to her Louis Vuitton vanity case, which held her huge supply of cocaine. She had a line, still upset. She knew Tim was undermining her hard work. He was trying to control her in the office. She knew it was all her fault, as everything else was. She had slept her way into her job and had abused it until now. Her punishment was to be obstructed by Tim at every step of the way. But she wanted her job. She wanted to be a career girl. She didn't want to be like her mother and Clarissa and all those other girls who filled their heads with dreams of husbands. However, Tim did not share her views. She guessed that if he was serious about leaving his wife for her, he wanted her in bed, legs akimbo, waiting for him to come home. The thought made her feel sick.

She went to bed and ignored the phone as she cried herself dry.

The next day Clara went to work, feeling ill due to her bout of tears but determined not to let that ruin her job. She would fight with everything she could muster. It was nearly lunch-time when Tim called her into his office. 'You still look ill. Are you sure you should be here?' he said.

'Thanks for your concern, but I'm fine,' Clara replied.

'I'll be over tonight at about nine. I'm going to a strip-joint first, and when I'm incredibly turned on I'll be over to turn you on.'

'Tim, I'm busy tonight. Can we give it a miss?' Clara asked.

'No, we can't. I have to make arrangements to see you, and I expect you to make yourself available. Is that a problem?' He was cold.

'No,' she said quietly, and left his office. She looked back at him sitting calmly at his desk and wondered why he had to do this to her. She had invited his attention and now she wanted out. Getting rid of Tim was going to be a huge fight.

When Clara returned Sarah was waiting at her desk. 'Do you want to go to lunch?' she asked.

'Yes, I bloody do,' Clara replied, and grabbed her coat. They went to Bertie's and ordered pizza and mineral water.

'Are you OK?' Sarah asked. She was genuinely concerned.

'Yes. No. I don't know.' Clara shrugged. The tears she had thought she used up last night were threatening to come back.

'Is it Tim? I can't help noticing how much attention he pays you.' Sarah was fishing for information. She had her suspicions about Clara, fuelled by the way that Tim continually singled her out.

'I'm sleeping with him.' As soon as the words escaped her, she knew she should not have said them. Sarah was speechless. Clara wished she could take them back. She thought fast. 'I mean, well, I did, once, and now he's a bit, you know, well, I think he wants us to have an affair and I don't, and he's making things hard for me at work and I don't know what to do.' Clara lied so convincingly she almost believed it was true.

'Christ. You know that's harassment and you can do something about it?' Sarah said helpfully, while trying to absorb the information.

'Yes, but I did sleep with him and now I'm scared that I'll

lose my job if I try to do anything and, well, he's very powerful.' Clara was already regretting having lunch with Sarah.

Sarah's mind was working overtime; she had just won the lottery. What a piece of information. Despite Sarah's motherly feelings, she couldn't help but think she should have guessed. All the time Clara had behaved like an idle brat, she had known that if Tim did anything about it she could tell everyone about sleeping with him. But although Sarah had had serious doubts about Clara's ability, recently Clara had proved her wrong. Clara was quite competent and she was working hard. She wondered if she had slept with Tim before or after her promotion; she assumed it was before. Tim fancied her, slept with her and promoted her. How wonderfully unprofessional, Sarah thought. Although she was not sure that she could use the information, it certainly felt good to have it. 'I know. But, well, don't let him destroy things. Put it down to a silly mistake and keep away from him. I won't breathe a word, I promise.' Sarah meant it for now.

'Thanks, Sarah. I feel much better just getting it off my chest.' In fact Clara felt ill with the thought that another person knew. Not just any other person either but someone who worked for Tim. She burned inside with fear at the thought that it might come out into the open. Then she would lose her job and Tim would probably lose his. Moreover, her family would hear and she wouldn't be able to live with the scandal. She tried to calm down by telling herself that Sarah had said she wouldn't mention it. However, she couldn't quite bring herself to believe her.

For the rest of lunch they resumed normal conversation, although they continued to think about the same thing.

On Thursday morning Tim was sitting in his office watching Clara work. He had been with her for an hour last night, and it had been hell to go home. He would leave his wife sooner rather than later. He would get Clara to resign from SFH and then they would be together properly. That was his new plan.

He thought back to the previous evening when, after an erotic strip-show, he had gone to Clara's and made her perform a striptease for him. Then he'd had mind-blowing sex before he left her to go home. He didn't want to leave her: he wanted to wake up with her, get her to do things to him in the morning, not just in the evening. He knew he was addicted to her. His wife had become an obstacle in his desire for Clara and he hated obstacles.

He wondered if he could see her that evening. He had a dinner arranged with his top client, Stephen Lock, and he knew he couldn't sneak off. Stephen liked to party and would probably insist they go on to a club. After that, it would be too late to go to Clara's. He would be stuck with his wife.

He was still reliving the details of the previous night, when the telephone rang. It was his wife and she was hysterical: Jemima, their youngest daughter, had appendicitis and had been rushed into hospital. His presence was required. This meant he wouldn't be able to see his client that evening, and he didn't know when he could see Clara again. He cursed Jemima. He picked up the telephone.

Before he finished dialling Stephen's number, he changed his mind. He called Clara and told her to come straight to his office. He was too far away to notice the sympathetic glance Sarah gave her as she left the desk.

'Hi,' Clara said, wondering what he needed now. She was increasingly on edge after the conversation with Sarah, and being at his beck and call was not going to get her any sympathy from the rest of the desk.

'Jemima has appendicitis. She's in hospital.'

Clara thanked the god of appendicitis. 'Oh, I'm so sorry,' she said sweetly.

'Yes, well, I have to go, but I'm supposed to have dinner with Stephen Lock from MMN. I want you to go instead.' Tim had decided that if Clara was with Stephen he could kill two birds with one stone. The client would have his dinner; Tim would know where Clara was. Stephen was over fifty, married and unattractive. He was not a threat.

'Me? But I've never even met him.'

'Clara, this is an order. Here's his number. Call him and let him know what's happening. I've booked Nobu and you just need to be your normal charming self. Hopefully I'll see you tomorrow.'

Clara took the details and left. She called Stephen, who sounded old, and she arranged to meet him at Nobu. She spent the rest of the day working as hard as she could, knowing that Tim wasn't there to distract her. He would not be able to call her into his office; he wouldn't be able to call round to see her. She was free of him. Even if it was only for a day and a night, it was a wonderful feeling.

Before leaving for the restaurant she had a line of cocaine. When she arrived, Stephen was already there. She sat down and ordered a bottle of champagne. At first glance, it was worse than she thought. Stephen was so pleased to see her, which he would be considering that he was over fifty, with little hair and a huge belly. At best he was distinguished; at worst he was over the hill. He was not a date, he was a client. Clara told herself this as the cocaine swam around in her brain. She found it hard to distinguish between the two.

As they ordered, Clara enjoyed the conversation. Stephen could tell a good story and he kept her laughing for most of the meal. She had to sneak to the loo for another couple of lines, after which she couldn't remember what she ate, if she ate. She knew she was charming. She was always charming. Stephen became charming too. After brandy, Stephen suggested going to a club, and Clara readily agreed. She was high as a kite and having fun. He was drunk and could barely draw his red eyes from Clara's cleavage as he explained that he had membership at Annabel's. Clara loved Annabel's. As he called to reserve a table, she paid the bill.

At Annabel's the fun continued. Stephen might not have had the looks, but he knew how to make Clara laugh, how to compliment her. He didn't know she was wasted. They had a bottle of champagne and Clara had more cocaine. They danced – Stephen was as amusing on the dance floor as he was off it – they laughed, and suddenly Stephen became very, very attractive.

Clara could barely remember who she was, let alone why she was there. And she had that feeling of need, which she couldn't fight when her addiction kicked in. 'Let's go,' she breathed, knowing what she wanted.

'But I thought we were having fun.' Stephen looked confused.

'Oh, what I've got in mind is far more fun,' Clara replied. She asked the door attendant for a taxi, which he flagged down quickly. As they drove to Clara's flat, Stephen tried to speak, but Clara hushed him with kisses. As soon as they got inside the flat, she pulled off her suit and stood naked; Stephen looked on in awe. She peeled off his clothes slowly and tried not to look as he stood before her in all his glory. He was far too fat to contemplate.

She seduced him in a way he didn't know existed. They had sex on the sitting-room floor and when it was over, Clara glanced at the sweating whale in front of her. He was leaning back against the sofa, his tiny penis flapping against his thigh. Clara looked away and offered to call him a cab. He nodded – too amazed at his good fortune to speak.

He thanked her as a gentleman would, and Clara smiled, as a good salesperson would do. The only thought in her head was that she wasn't an SFH salesperson, she was a sex salesperson. She took another line of cocaine and then another. Then she saw the truth. She had had sex with a client. One of Tim's biggest clients. She was enveloped in a cloud of disgust. She couldn't believe she'd done it. She calmed herself down by reminding herself that she was a sex addict: she couldn't help herself. She had an illness. She hadn't been rational. She was in deep shit.

Wrapping herself in her crisp linen duvet, she took a couple of sleeping pills and forgot to set her alarm.

She woke at midday. The answerphone was beeping. She hadn't heard any telephone calls, but she never did when she took sleeping pills. The only voice on the answerphone was Tim's. He was barking that she had better call him straight away at the office. She burst into tears as she heard the anger in his voice.

Tim was fuming. 'How dare she do that to me?' he said to himself. He had gone to work after spending a stressful night at the hospital. Jemima had had her appendix removed then demanded that he stay with her. His wife was hysterical and his elder daughter was sulking because she wasn't the centre of attention. No one would listen to him and he began to hate women. In the morning he excused himself, saying he had important meetings at work. In reality, he needed to get away from his family.

At the office he found some peace until his client, Stephen Lock, the fat, respectable married man, had called him to thank him for the 'great piece of arse' he had sent. Then he had been unable to stop himself telling Tim how much of the arse he had seen. And the breasts, and the other bits. Clara had betrayed him. She had slept with another man. Tim wanted to kill her.

As soon as he had an explanation, he would decide what to do. He told himself that Clara might not have slept with Stephen. Stephen might have lied. He had probably tried it on and she rejected him. Tim hoped that this was so. Unable to bear it any longer, he told his secretary he had a last-minute appointment and took a cab over to Clara's flat.

Clara opened the door wearing her towelling dressing-gown. Tim barely looked at her.

'Hi,' she said.

'Clara, did you sleep with Stephen?' His fists were clenched.

'Yes,' she said.

'No. The answer was supposed to be no. Clara, you are a fucking little whore. You slept with one of our most important clients. You said you only slept with me.'

'Yes.'

'Fuck, Clara, how could you do that to me?' Tim had never before felt this angry.

'I didn't mean to. It just happened.'

'Nothing just happens. You make it happen. You bitch, I should beat the shit out of you.' Tim's face was contorted with rage.

Clara hoped he wasn't going to hit her. He looked as if he might.

After a few minutes' silence, he grabbed her roughly by her bathrobe and pulled her to him. She screamed and he put one hand over her mouth. He undid his trousers with the other, trapping Clara with his legs. She tried to push him away but she had no strength. He took his hand away from her mouth, undid her bathrobe, pushed her to the floor and climbed on top of her.

'Don't you ever have sex with anyone but me!' he spat, as he entered her.

Clara cried out in pain. 'Shut the fuck up. You behave like a whore, I'll treat you like one,' he said, and thrust into her even harder.

Clara's head was spinning. She had lost control of her body. She could feel Tim prodding at her, and it hurt, but she couldn't say anything. She couldn't lift her arms to push him off. She saw that he had pinned them down, but she couldn't feel it. By the time he'd finished she couldn't feel anything.

Tim's face was red and contorted as he climbed off her. Clara stayed still. She tried to work out what she could do or say, what she should do or say. He'd raped her, but maybe he'd had a right to. She was a whore. A worthless whore who gave her body to anyone who wanted it. This was her fault; this was what she deserved.

'I'm sorry,' Clara said, still lying on the floor.

'You'd better be,' Tim said, as he stood over her.

'I'll come to work,' Clara started crying.

'Don't fucking cry. I don't want you at work. Don't even think about work. You stay there with your legs open waiting for your next fuck. You're not fit to work.' Clara knew this was true. She was in no state to move, let alone work.

'I'll be there on Monday. It's my job, Tim. I need to come in on Monday.' Clara was pleading.

'Fine. Do that. In the meantime, I want you to know I'm very angry, disappointed and upset. I don't know what I'm going to do, but I'm going to do something.' Tim stormed out, leaving her lying on the floor in a puddle of tears.

His first thought after he had calmed down was how he could turn this to his advantage. He could offer to forgive her if she agreed to his terms. His terms would be that she would resign from her job, he would leave his wife and move in with her. The sex he had just had with her had proved that she would let him do what he wanted. She would let him have her whenever he chose. He wanted that; he wanted her all the time. Although he was eaten up with jealousy at her sleeping with Stephen, he could use it to own her. He wanted to own her. Tim believed that this was love.

Clara spent the rest of the day crying. She needed to talk to someone but she didn't have anyone. Her brother would be disappointed in her, and he was the one person in her life who had any faith in her. She couldn't risk losing it. Her parents would probably drag her home, lock her up and make her marry the first man they could persuade to take her off their hands. She had no friends. Clarissa would probably have a heart-attack if she knew what Clara had done. No one would understand, no one would forgive her. How could they when she couldn't forgive herself? Tim's violation was something she pushed to the back of her mind as she got up and went to get her cocaine.

Clara felt disgusted with herself. But it wasn't her fault that she was addicted to sex. How could a person say no when they were addicted? She tried to figure out when she had first needed sex this much, but she couldn't remember. If she was being honest with herself she would have realised that it was probably at the same time she had started taking cocaine, but to Clara, cocaine was her one and only friend. She couldn't betray it.

How did I end up like this? Clara thought, as she lay on her cream sofa and stared at her cream walls. Her immaculate flat represented her life. It felt empty right now.

That afternoon Tim made a decision. His wife called him constantly with updates from the hospital. Jemima cried, Jemima wanted ice-cream, Jemima wanted comics. It went on endlessly. Tim pointed out that it was a simple operation that many people had, but to his family it was a Greek tragedy. And Tim felt tragic. He sat in his office not really working, thinking about the Clara problem.

Clara was young, sexy, keen and open-minded. She doted on him. He knew that although she had slept with Stephen he would forgive her. He had to forgive her. The alternative to forgiving her would be to lose her. He couldn't lose her.

By the end of the day, Tim picked up his briefcase and knew exactly what he was going to do. He would tell his wife that on Saturday he was going to play golf with an important client. Instead he would go to see Clara. He would tell her that she had to resign and he would leave his wife and move in.

They would buy a new house – he didn't like her flat – after the divorce had been finalised. He would marry her as soon as he was divorced and they would live happily ever after. Tim would have what he wanted: Clara in his bed.

Clara had to pull herself together. She had slept so much lately, cried so much and been totally unlike herself. She needed to get a grip on her life. She was seeing James on Sunday for lunch and by then she would be so together that everything would be fine. She would start next week with a new outlook and a new life. She would finish the affair with Tim and throw herself into work. The new Clara. This Clara would not be called a whore; she wouldn't let Tim force himself on her ever again. No man would be allowed near her unless she wanted it. She needed to take control.

She started planning how to get rid of Tim, but before she had made any decisions, he called her and told her that he was on his way. She got dressed in jeans and a sweatshirt. She pulled her hair back. She looked positively ordinary.

When Tim arrived, she was prepared. He entered the house, moved straight into the lounge and sat down. She stayed silent.

'I need to talk to you,' Tim said. He wasn't shouting as he had been the day before.

'Fine.' Clara felt her resolve falter, but she knew that after he said what he had come to say she would tell him it was over. She hoped he wouldn't do to her what he had done yesterday. For the first time, Clara felt afraid of Tim.

'I'm leaving my wife for you. I realise that you only slept with Stephen so you could get my full attention and now I'm going to give it to you. But first you have to resign from SFH.'

Clara nearly threw up. Her heart started beating faster and faster and she felt as if her insides would explode. This was not what she had wanted or expected. 'Tim, I can't resign. I love my job.' Her job was the only thing she could cling to. It was all she had.

'Clara, we all know why you got that job. It was because you gave great head. I gave it to you in exchange for what you gave me. Now I'm offering you the position of being with me full time. A highly coveted position. You can leave your job for me, the way you got it because of me.'

Clara felt her heart slow down. She was angry. He had never said that before. He had never said why he had promoted her. She could not leave her job and she didn't want him.

'Tim, I think it's time to call it a day. You have a wife and kids and they need you. I'm young and I have a career. I don't want us to break up, but I don't want this. This is too much. I don't want to become your next wife.'

Tim stood up and started pacing the room. 'You don't mean that. You need me.'

'No. I need my job. I don't want this any more.' Clara felt very tired.

'So, what are you saying? You don't want me to leave my wife. You won't give up the job?' Tim looked almost panicked.

'That's what I'm saying. Please understand.'

'No, I fucking won't understand. I'm not letting you do this. You will resign and you will become my full-time girl.'

'I won't.' Clara couldn't take this any more. She needed out.

'Right. I'm not sure I understand. You love me.' Tim sounded almost like a small boy.

'I don't love you. We have fun. That's what affairs are for, not for leaving your wife for or making me leave my job. Tim, I really love my job and I want to be successful. Please, you can't take that away from me.'

'Actually I can. Remember that. What I gave I can take away. I will see you in the office on Monday. You can give me your decision then, but I expect you to come round to my way of thinking. Remember what I've said.' Without glancing at her again, Tim walked out.

Clara looked at her wooden clock. She stared at it and watched the hands move. She moved with them, but she stayed still. It wasn't long before she was crying again.

She knew that Tim couldn't sack her without good reason. He couldn't take her job away from her.

She couldn't remember the rest of Saturday. She needed coke to calm herself down. She went to the shop and bought vodka and cigarettes and she ordered a pizza. She couldn't remember in which order they came; she just remembered the objects. She ate somehow, she drank and she had more cocaine. She awoke on Sunday morning on the sofa. The panic was still there as she put on her brightest smile and prepared to meet her brother.

PART THREE

Black Thursday

Chapter Twelve

After another encounter with Jim, her personal trainer, Ella went to work on Monday. It was as painful as all the others had been, except it was her last. She had spoken to Jackie at length about Johnny, her job and her life, and Jackie had advised her to loosen up a little. If she wanted to make management, she would have to deal with people like him, and she would have to make him show her some respect. She also realised that she could get rid of Jim without feeling it meant that she didn't fit in. The façade had been in place for too long; it was time to start letting go. That morning she told him she would no longer be training and she was amazed at how good that felt.

Now she had the support of her team she felt she could relent a little; she deserved that. She even smiled at Johnny when he arrived at the desk and almost fainted when he smiled back.

Johnny smiled at Ella, safe in the knowledge that she was about to fall from a great height. He had made an appointment with Jeff and he had his story worked out.

'Johnny. What can I do for you?' Jeff wasn't welcoming: he was expecting a new list of complaints. Every time Johnny had ventured into his office, it was to complain about something.

Jeff was tired of him. He was also loyal to his team and, so far, he had no time for the new boy. He had already decided that he would make a point at the meeting on Thursday, and he hoped he would be able to persuade the others to back him in his quest to move Johnny to another department.

'Well, it's a bit awkward, really.' Johnny was playing coy.

'Fine, well, why don't you just tell me what's on your mind?'

'Well, it's Ella.' Jeff had been expecting another complaint about Ella.

'What about her? She's a highly respected member of our team. One of the best traders we've ever had.' Jeff was firm.

'That's why this is awkward. You see, my father is a friend of one of the deans at Durham University and he was visiting this weekend. I happened to mention that Ella was my mentor and I asked him if he knew her. As she's obviously a smart girl, I thought he would remember her.'

'Where's this going, Johnny? I'm quite busy today.' Jeff looked at the man standing in front of him and felt nothing but contempt.

'He'd never heard of her, and, well, he knows all the students. It's part of his job.' Jeff looked at Johnny uninterestedly.

'No one knows every student at a university. I don't see what this has to do with anything.'

'No, what I meant to say — gosh, this is embarrassing — is that he heads up the humanities department and Ella mentioned she did history at Durham and, well, she definitely didn't. My father's friend would have known her if she had.' Johnny was red-faced. This wasn't going as smoothly as he'd hoped.

'Johnny, you know what you're saying, don't you? And I cannot take your word for this just because someone doesn't remember her. I'll get it checked out and I'm sure there's no cause for concern. I would also rather you didn't mention this to anyone else. I'll speak to you later when I've investigated.'

Johnny felt relieved. He had wanted this to happen. Now

Jeff would have to get someone to make the same call Claudia had. Then they would discover that Ella was a fraud. In addition, Jeff would never find out that Johnny had gained the information on purpose. He would think it was just a coincidence. Johnny was angry with himself for not sounding more convincing, but as he left the office, he knew he'd won.

Jeff thought about ignoring the whole thing. He was not a fool and he knew that Johnny's accusations had to be a misunderstanding. Of course Ella went to Durham – she had a degree certificate from there. But he had to get everything checked out. If he didn't, Johnny would make waves in the office. He couldn't afford for this to get out – he couldn't believe it was true. Ella was his best trader, the best the desk had. She was a natural, always making money, showing wonderful judgement. Jeff didn't want to lose her. He knew, too, that Johnny had not been lying. He had probably asked some eighty-year-old professor about Ella and he hadn't remembered her. University people were renowned for being old and out of touch with reality. Jeff asked himself why he was making excuses; all he had to do was get it checked out. He would take delight in proving Johnny wrong. Although he still didn't believe that the accusation was true, he called Helena in Human Resources and asked her to look into it.

Virginia found work even harder than usual. She was counting the minutes until Thursday, and she was sinking under the amount of work she had. Isabelle was being nicer to her than usual, but that was the only good thing. She could hardly bear to breathe: she was so excited that her dreams might come true at last. On a number of occasions she found her concentration wavering, but that was only to be expected. She had a big decision to await. She had to try to remain calm.

*   *   *

Isabelle had decided to be nice to the rat. Make her think she could get away with going behind her back and trying to get another job. Well, soon she would find out that you don't cross Isabelle Holland. Especially if you were a stupid secretary. Especially if you were *her* stupid secretary. On Thursday David would make the rest of the board see that Virginia was a threat to the company and they would welcome her dismissal. They wouldn't, however, welcome it quite as much as Isabelle Holland would.

As soon as she got into the office Clara went to see Tim.

'You've made your decision I take it?' Tim asked coldly.

'Yes, I have. Tim, the answer is no. I will not resign and I don't want us to be together. I'm sorry, I'm really fond of you, but I need to succeed at this job. Please understand.'

'You know how you got this job, don't you?'

'Of course, but I'm good at it. And, anyway, you would implicate yourself as much as me if you tried to sack me because of it. And don't forget my family is a big client with this bank, which is really why I got a job here in the first place.' Clara had played her best hand. She hoped it would be a winning one.

'So, your family will protect you, will they? I suppose they don't know about our affair, or about how you sleep with clients, or your little cocaine habit?' Tim was angry.

'Of course not, and you wouldn't tell them. You have as much – no, more to lose than I ever do.' Clara was angry.

'Fine, if that's your final word you'd better get back to work.' Tim turned his back on her.

'Is that it?' she asked, surprised.

'Yes, it is. From now on you're just another employee. 'Bye.' Clara left the office. She could hardly believe her luck.

*　　*　　*

As soon as she had gone Tim picked up the telephone. He spoke to Helena in Human Resources and told her that one of his salespeople had slept with one of their best clients, which was against SFH policy and potentially damaging to the company. Helena asked him what he wanted to do and Tim explained that her family was a client. He told her who she was. He said that, despite this, there was no way they could risk her continuing to work for them, and that he was confident Clara would keep her dismissal from her family: she would never be able to tell them she had slept with a client. He said she had to go, and he'd square it at the managing directors' meeting. Helena said she'd look into the implications of sacking Clara, although as she had broken the rules it was an open and shut case. The only problem would be in convincing Private Clients that this had no implications for them.

He smiled as he put down the receiver. He knew that Clara wouldn't blow the whistle on their affair – she couldn't bear her family to find out. However, she would be sacked and she deserved to be. If she didn't want to be with him she wouldn't be allowed to work with him. No one rejected him without paying the price.

He felt justified because he was broken-hearted. He called up Heather, a prostitute he sometimes visited, and arranged to see her that evening. He explained he needed some tender loving care, and as he was paying handsomely, he knew that that would be exactly what he got.

Helena was having the day from hell. She had three cases in front of her, all from the fourth floor, all of which could lead to dismissal. She had been in conference with the head of Human Resources over this and the whole department was working on it.

By the end of Tuesday, the results were clear. Ella Franke had never gone to Durham University and her degree certificate was a fake. She would have to be dismissed, and to avoid any scandal they would have to ensure it was kept quiet. Helena called Ella's boss to tell him. He sounded close to tears.

Virginia Bateman had taken an order illegally. This was now a major issue and might have resulted in the firm being sued. Her bosses wanted her fired. She had no legal come-back.

Clara Hart had taken a client out to dinner and slept with him. Again, there were implications for a scandal. In a salesperson's contract it said that relations with clients were forbidden. Especially married clients.

Files on all three cases had been prepared. The managing directors would meet on Thursday to discuss them and discuss damage limitation. That day, Helena developed another seventeen grey hairs.

Chapter Thirteen

The monthly managing directors' meeting was held over lunch on the top floor of SFH's building. They had a three-course meal and discussed any matters of urgency, company policy and any new issues that arose. They also reviewed each department and often ended up patting each other on the back.

The meeting this Thursday was to be different. Helena from Human Resources was joining them to discuss three urgent staff issues, which were also matters of potential scandal for the firm.

Helena was frazzled. She hated attending these meetings. The managing directors intimidated her, but then, they intimidated all of HR. She tried to ask her boss if perhaps someone more senior should attend, but her boss, who equally hated such meetings, told her that she was responsible for the departments in question, therefore she had to go. She had prepared the files meticulously and she knew that the probability would be that these three people would have to be fired. Helena had her own views, although she knew she would never have the confidence to voice them.

Virginia Bateman had broken the rules, but nothing had gone wrong and Helena felt she was not the risk to the company that she was being made out to be. She had met her when she had first started looking for a new job, she had heard how hard

Isabelle Holland was to work for, and from what she knew of Isabelle she tended to believe Virginia. She felt that Virginia had made one mistake and as the repercussions hadn't been high, they should give her a warning and let her take her new job if it was offered. She had proved herself a capable salesperson.

Ella Franke was a huge problem. Everyone in Human Resources had been upset. They all saw Ella's appointment as a triumph. Unfortunately, they had hired her without being thorough and they were paying the price. She had proved to be good at her job, but she didn't have a degree. She had lied and somehow faked a degree certificate. She could represent a huge scandal for the company. Helena felt sorry for Ella, although she wasn't sure why, but she knew that they couldn't keep her in their employ.

Clara Hart was also a problem. She had slept with one of her desk's major clients, showing unprofessional behaviour and bad judgement. However, her family was a client of the bank and upsetting them was a consideration. Helena thought it was time she went to work in a less stressful environment.

Helena walked in as everyone was sitting around the table, drinking aperitifs and studying the menus. She sat down and waited until they had ordered their lunch. She wasn't given a menu. She didn't mind: she couldn't have eaten anyway. The twenty-one men sitting before her in their immaculate suits with their immaculate haircuts intimidated her so much that food would have choked her. They all looked at her expectantly. Her heart was pounding and she felt sick. She could not understand why she was in such a state.

She outlined each case without stumbling, then sat back while the discussion ensued.

'Well, let me start with my opinion of Virginia's situation as she is directly under my wing, although also yours, Tim, as you are co-head of Sales. I thought the same as Helena, that it was a mistake, and then I found out she might soon be working as a salesperson with Phillip, which would mean she would get the exams she needed and be able to take orders. But after speaking to Isabelle Holland who manages Emerging Markets, I discovered that Virginia was unrepentant about what she'd done, felt that she had done nothing wrong and was a bit of a loose cannon. If anything had gone wrong with the order we could have been sued, ridiculed for letting a secretary deal with clients and perhaps even ruined. I know it seems far-fetched, but one person can bring down a bank. Look at Nick Leeson,' David Marker said.

Helena almost fell off her chair at the comparison between timid Virginia and Nick Leeson. However, she lacked the nerve to say anything.

Tim spoke next. 'I quite agree, David. We cannot put our clients at risk, and I'd be surprised if Phillip wanted to hire her after hearing that anyway. We need professionals in this business and you're right, one mistake with a client could cause us irreparable damage. Which brings me to Clara. She compromised our reputation by sleeping with a client. Phillip, I know the Hart account is important to us, but I don't think that she'd run to Daddy with the reason she was sacked, and even if she did, then he wouldn't be in any position to cause trouble, would he?'

Phillip took over. 'No, not at all. We cannot afford people who do not embrace the company culture and the company rules. I wouldn't employ Virginia now. She's trouble and I'm glad I found out before we hired her. As for Miss Hart, well, you can't sleep with clients in this business. I can't bear the disregard for company policy. It should not be tolerated. I propose we offer her confidentiality from revealing the reason for her sacking to her family in return for her not rocking the boat with us. I think you're right, Tim, she wouldn't want them to know. Gosh, who would? As for the last girl, well, there's no doubt, is there, Jeff?'

Jeff felt ill. His ulcer had been playing up over Ella. He liked her and he respected her. She had lied to him, but he didn't want to lose her. He had always felt fatherly towards Ella from the moment she had joined the desk. Her ability to do the job was rare, and Jeff had recognised it almost immediately. However, he knew that he didn't have any choice.

'Yes, Ella, well, as you say, there's no defence. She lied to us to get a job, and although she was incredibly good at that job, she didn't have the qualification she claimed. We don't even know if she is who she claims she is. There is no alternative but to let her go.'

Simon Havant, a senior managing director spoke. 'We are on the edge of crisis. If the world finds out we hired someone with a forged degree certificate and kept her for years before we realised, we'd be a laughing stock. If the client the girl slept with decides to spread it around, we'd be seen as a knocking shop. And if the young lady who took an order when she was a secretary tells the press we're in big trouble. As well as having to sack each one, which saddens me, I think we need to ensure that none of this ever gets to be common knowledge.' He smiled at everyone. Helena smiled back, but inside she was pissed off. Chauvinistic pigs like him made her job so hard.

Peter Seymour, the chairman, and one of the few members of the board from the founding family, spoke. He was very old and his only involvement in the company was the monthly meetings and collecting his huge salary. 'I agree. It all started when we let women into the business. Men never behave this way. You know where you are with men.' Helena was appalled; everyone else coughed with embarrassment.

Giles Thornton was one of the most experienced and well-respected members of the board. 'We have to dismiss all three women. We also need to look at damage limitation, as Simon said. Now, all three signed confidentiality agreements I take it?' He looked at Helena, who nodded her newly grey head. 'Good. In that agreement, as I'm sure all you know, it says that no one can talk to the press about SFH while working here or after they leave. If they signed that we can sue anyone who talks. Moreover, I think we emphasise that when we dismiss them. Not that I think they will talk. After all, they were all in the wrong, they can't claim unfair dismissal – they can't claim anything. We have acted in the best interests of our shareholders and clients, and if there's any trouble, we will issue statements to that effect. Now, are we all in agreement that this is the right path to follow?' Twenty men nodded. 'Does anyone feel we need to take a vote?' Twenty men shook their heads.

'Great, fine. Well, Helena, you'd better go and dismiss them. I expect them out of the building before the end of the afternoon. Don't forget to remind them of the confidentiality clauses. And can you ask the waiter to come in with the main course on your way out? Thank you, Helena.'

Helena left and felt that the next stage would probably cause her hair to fall out.

Chapter Fourteen

As she walked back to her office, she clutched the files to her chest and knew that the afternoon would be awful. She got her secretary to call each woman into her office and prepared to deliver the news. Ella said she was too busy but in the end she agreed to come. Clara sounded pissed off and reluctant. Virginia sounded excited and evidently thought she was going to be offered a job. Helena's boss was sympathetic, but unwilling to get involved in the dirty deed. Helena sighed. As she prepared to see Ella first, Clara next and finally Virginia, for whom she felt incredibly sorry, she hoped that the following week would be better.

All three women reacted differently. Ella sat impassively in front of Helena. She looked as if she might faint when Helena explained that she had deceived them and her deception had been discovered. When she asked Ella for any defence, Ella shook her head. Then Helena explained that they had no alternative but to dismiss her. Ella dropped her head into her hands and nodded. Helena went on to explain about confidentiality. Ella sat silently for ages after Helena finished. When Helena asked her if she was all right, Ella looked at her as if she was an alien. 'Sorry' was the only word she uttered as she left the office.

Clara shouted, screamed and swore. Helena explained that she had broken her contract, and Clara said that it was all Tim's fault, but when Helena asked her to quantify that statement, she shook her head. She said this was a travesty and a total miscarriage of justice. Helena explained that if she hadn't slept with the client then she would be in the clear. Clara replied that of course she had slept with the 'fucking' client, but it wasn't her fault. She wouldn't quantify that either. She was told her career at SFH was over and reminded of the confidentiality clause. Clara screamed some more, called Helena a 'corporate bitch' and stormed out of the office.

Virginia shook with fear. She said that Isabelle had said it was going to be fine; she asked about Phillip. Helena said she was sorry, but the rules had been broken and the decision taken at the managing directors' meeting. Virginia said she didn't understand. She cried. Helena tried to comfort her, but she had nothing good to say. She had to remind Virginia not to talk to the press, at which Virginia looked confused. She told her that unfortunately she would have a few problems getting a reference after this incident and Virginia looked even more confused and hurt. Helena figured that Isabelle Holland would probably ensure that Virginia never worked in the City again. Virginia showed little sign of leaving the office and Helena's heart went out to her. She was a frightened child, not a devious monster plotting to bring about the fall of SFH, which was how she had been painted at the meeting. Eventually Virginia whispered that she was going to clear her desk.

Liam asked Ella what she was doing as she walked into the office, grabbed her bag and her coat and left. Ella ignored him. Everyone watched as she left and only Johnny had the faintest idea what was happening. Liam tried to go after her, but Trevor pulled him back. He thought she might have had bad news and probably needed to be alone. Johnny smirked inside. They didn't know how bad.

*   *   *

Clara marched up to her desk still fuming. She sent an e-mail to Tim, copying her whole desk on it. It read:

> *Tim, you are low-life scum. As soon as everyone else in this pissy firm realises what a small-minded, small-penised man you are you'll be finished. You were even fucking useless in bed. In fact, you just are useless and ugly and a complete slimeball. Have fun with your boring wife and boring family. Oh, yeah, and the hookers you're so keen on. Everyone else will now know what I know. You have the charisma of a turd.*

She smiled at everyone on her desk, picked up her bag and coat and pressed send. She was at the lift when everyone read her message.

Virginia walked to her desk; her legs were shaky. She felt sick. She ignored everyone as she picked up her diary, her pen, her notebook, and thrust them into her bag. She found her coat and tried to get her legs to take her out. Isabelle blocked her path. 'That will teach you to try to cross me,' she whispered. Virginia hardly registered her presence as she concentrated on getting herself out of the office. 'You will never, ever get a job in the City again,' Isabelle hissed, and laughed quietly as she saw the tears streaming down the little rat's face.

Ella was seething. She had never felt so angry, not when Tony hit her, not when she left Manchester. She was angry with herself and with the firm. They hadn't given her a chance. Not a chance. OK, so she had done wrong, she had lied and cheated, but she'd been good at her job and she had proved herself. The lie about having a university degree didn't seem so big in the scheme of things. For the first time in her life, she felt that what had happened to her wasn't her fault. She wasn't sure whose fault it was, but it wasn't hers. If they had just let her get on and do her job, she would have been fine. She had known this might happen – she almost felt that she had been waiting for it since she had first walked through the doors at SFH.

When she first decided to try for this job, had faked her CV and purchased a dodgy university certificate, she had not thought anyone would take her seriously – they would realise straight away. That was what she had told herself. When they didn't, she had done everything in her power to ensure she made up for the lie and she became an asset to the company. She felt as if she had been born for her job. She believed that, out of her nightmare, her true destiny had emerged. It gave some reason for the pain she had suffered at the hands of Tony. She often told herself that although she would never wish on anyone what she had gone through, there had been a reason for it. The reason was that she had got a position she would never have dreamt of. She made more money than her parents had from working all their lives. She lived a lifestyle she could barely comprehend. She loved her job.

She couldn't figure out how they had found out now, nearly four years later, and she hadn't been able to ask the Human Resources woman. When she thought about being fired, she could barely remember what had happened in that office. She was suspended in space and someone was controlling her. She didn't know who. But that someone had stopped her talking, thinking or understanding. She couldn't function. She couldn't believe it had come to this. Now she had nothing. Her façade had been destroyed and she was destroyed too. She let herself have one last glance at the building she loved before she turned and walked away.

Clara didn't know what to do. She wanted to kill someone, but that wasn't really the done thing, was it? She went down to the accounts floor to use the ladies' and took a line of cocaine.

Fuck, she thought. What the fuck do I do now? She stormed out of the building swearing to herself, leaving a line of glaring visitors watching her. She didn't care what they thought. She giggled as she remembered the message she had sent everyone, but then felt sad knowing that Tim would tell everyone *his* version of the truth.

'Clara slept with one of our top clients,' he would say, 'so we had no alternative but to let her go. She sent this malicious note to get back at me. Please ignore it and carry on as usual.' She took comfort in the fact that Sarah would believe her, but she knew that Sarah valued her job too much to do anything about it.

'You fucked up again,' Clara said aloud.

She stood on the front steps of the building and looked at it. She wanted to feel bitter, but she knew deep down that this was what she deserved. She hadn't got the job on her own merit and she had only just begun to do it properly. If she had taken it seriously from the beginning this mess would never have happened. She felt a sour anger towards Tim. Anger so physical, she felt it all over her body. He had got rid of her just like that because she wouldn't do what he wanted. The only good thing was that he was now out of her life. Unfortunately so was her job. She felt sick at the memory of her lunch with her brother, only last Sunday. He had told her he was proud of her, and she so wanted someone to be proud of her. He wouldn't be now. She was a worthless whore. She took one last look at the Seymour Forbes Hunt sign, which seemed to gloat at her. She walked away.

Virginia was puffy from tears. She had only just made it out of the building, but seeing the gleaming sign, the sign she spoke to every day, the sign that represented her hope, she broke down.

She kept thinking about the new failure she could add to her long list.

Isabelle had done this to her. She could have kept the trade quiet as she had said she would. She knew there would have been no repercussions. Then Virginia would have been offered the job in the Private Client division. She knew she would. Instead, her dream had been cruelly snatched from her by a woman she hated. And, evidently, one who hated her. Although Virginia had known that what she did was wrong, it wasn't something she was likely to do again. Isabelle knew that Virginia was dependable, so why had she lost her job? She couldn't understand why someone would do that to her. She started to walk away from the building leaving a trail of teardrops, the only evidence that she had ever been there.

Chapter Fifteen

Keith was washing glasses. He had taken the job as barman at the Bull and Barrel as a desperate measure – he needed the money. Although he had done plenty of barwork, he had never worked in a pub like this. The clientele were mainly market employees, which meant that the first rush came at seven or eight in the morning when the stock had been delivered and the night workers were going off duty. He had never before seen men drink so much so early. The other rush was at lunch-time, which he was still clearing up from, and the last was the after-work rush, which almost made him feel normal again.

There was a great atmosphere in the rush times, even the morning one. He really enjoyed those times. Unfortunately, in between it was boring. He had polished glasses, cleaned tables, emptied ashtrays and now he was polishing the glasses again. There was nothing else to do. The landlord insisted that the pub stayed open, although they rarely got any customers. He was thinking about asking for a television or even a radio to keep him company. He thought the punters might like it too – when football was on a television might attract evening trade.

A television would be great, Keith thought, as he moved around the bar to decide on the best place to put it. Then he stopped in his tracks.

A tall black girl walked in and marched up to the bar. This

was unusual for many reasons: she was wearing a suit and suits never found their way in here; she was a girl, they didn't get many girls either, and she looked like she was crying. Her red eyes almost glowed against her gorgeous dark skin. Keith composed himself and flew back behind the bar.

'Drink, love?' he asked, in his friendliest barman's voice. The girl just stared at him. Keith stared back.

'Whisky,' she said.

'Shall I make that a double, love?' he asked. She scowled then nodded.

He poured the drink, and she paid him then went to sit in the corner. Keith was a surveyor of people. He often watched the men in the pub and thought about their lives. He could tell if they were married, single or gay, and he would while away the hours by thinking about their lives. He could see that this girl was upset. He suspected she'd been dumped. From her clothes she was probably a secretary, and he could tell by her demeanour that she was feeling hostile. Keith prided himself on his perceptiveness. He was just thinking about where she lived when he got another shock.

In walked a gorgeous blonde in a short skirt and jacket. She walked to the bar and smiled. She had nice teeth.

'What can I get you, darling?' Keith put on his best seductive barman's voice.

'Vodka-tonic, ice, make it a double.' She had stopped smiling.

'Coming right up.' Keith winked at her but she was staring intently at the girl in the corner. As Keith handed her her drink and she paid him, she looked as if she was going to ask him something, but she obviously changed her mind. She hovered by the bar for a couple of moments, giving Keith the chance to check out her breasts. They were very nice indeed. He thought she must be another secretary, probably working with the first girl, and he hoped she was single.

She lit a cigarette and Keith felt weak at the knees. He studied her legs as she decided to go and join her friend.

'What are you doing here?' Clara asked, blowing smoke into Ella's face.

'Piss off,' Ella replied.

Clara ignored her and sat down. 'Don't tell me you've been sacked as well?'

'What do you mean "as well"?'

'Well, I've been sacked and I guess you have too. Otherwise what would bring you to this God-forsaken place?'

'I have,' was the curt reply.

'Wankers,' Clara said, draining most of her drink.

Ella nodded. Now her world really was turning upside-down. Not only had she lost her dream job but she was also sitting in an awful pub with Miss Public School of the Year, who was claiming to be in the same boat.

'Can I get you another drink?' Clara asked. Ella nodded again. 'Christ I would have to get the sack on the same day as someone who has no conversation,' Clara mumbled as she walked to the drooling barman.

Keith took delight in serving the blonde again, but she didn't seem to share his enthusiasm. Keith guessed she was upset that her friend was upset. He wished he could hear what they had said to each other, but they were too far away. He wished he had waited before cleaning all the tables. As the blonde returned to her friend with two drinks and another wink from Keith, the door opened again.

What *is* this? A bloody secretary's convention? he wondered as yet another girl in a suit walked into the bar. He thought for a moment that she might be a dyke — her hair was short and she had on a trouser suit. Not bad legs, though. He nearly fell over as he came eye to eye with her and saw she had been crying too. Dumped by her lesbian lover. Or maybe the black girl was her lesbian lover. Keith wouldn't have minded seeing a bit of that. He composed himself as he waited for the latest girl at the bar to say something.

'Drink?' he asked, when she stayed silent.

'What?' the new girl asked.

'Drink?' Keith repeated. Maybe he was dreaming.

'Yes,' the girl replied.

'OK, what?' he asked, wondering if she was a bit simple.

'What?' she asked back.

He was now officially having a nightmare. 'What would you like to drink?'

The girl looked confused. Keith smiled encouragingly: he wanted to put her at her ease. 'Um, brandy,' she stuttered.

'Large?' Keith asked, but seeing the blank stare, he just poured it anyway. 'Are those your friends?' he asked, gesturing to the other two. The new girl looked over; she was in a daze. She stared at them for what seemed ages, but she made no attempt to move.

I think I'll quit while I'm ahead, Keith thought, and went back to polishing his glasses.

'My God, isn't that thingie's secretary?' Clara nudged Ella.

'Who?' Ella asked, looking at the girl who had just walked in. She seemed vaguely familiar.

'You know, Isabelle, head of Emerging Markets sales?'

'Fuck,' Ella said. She didn't know what was going on.

'It bloody is. Christ, what *is* going on?' Clara echoed Ella's thoughts, ran to the bar, grabbed the dazed girl and brought her back to the table. 'What are you doing here?' she asked.

'I don't know,' Virginia replied, before crying again. Ella said nothing, but she searched in her bag and handed a tissue.

'Christ, I thought I was in hell when I got sacked, but now I really am. My name's Clara, that's Ella and you are?' Clara looked at Virginia, who was still crying.

Ella looked surprised. 'You know me?' she asked.

'Yes, you've done some of my trades. We haven't really spoken, but I know who you are.'

'Oh,' Ella said, giving no sign of recognition.

'I'm Virginia.'

They sipped their drinks in silence. When Ella went to get another round, Virginia stopped crying and Clara nipped to the loo for a line of cocaine.

When she got back, she said, 'So, is anyone going to tell what happened? I was sacked for sleeping with a client. But the real reason they sacked me was because I was sleeping with Tim Pemberton, my boss, and he found out I slept with his client, and he got pissed off and asked me to move in with him, or him with me, and he was going to leave his wife and he asked me to resign and I refused, so he reported me for sleeping with this client and I got sacked anyway.' Virginia and Ella stared at her.

'Really?' Virginia asked.

'Yes, really. What about you?'

'Can't you report Tim for sleeping with you? I mean, that's against the rules just as much as sleeping with clients, isn't it?' Ella asked.

'I suppose, but I don't want my family to find out, and if I tell everyone I slept with Tim as well, they will. Anyway, I don't think they'd jump to give me my job back.' Clara's eyes darkened.

'Yes, but Tim might lose his and there'll be some justice,' Ella pointed out.

Clara felt she had made a breakthrough. 'I know, but my family – I couldn't bear to disappoint them. I always disappoint them.'

Virginia perked up. 'Do you? I do too. I don't know what they're going to say when they hear about this.'

'So what did you do?' Clara asked.

'I was alone on the desk. I am – I mean, I was Isabelle

Holland's secretary. They were all on a lunch and a client called and I took his order because he was really scary, and it was good and we made a ton of commission. I told Isabelle and she said it didn't matter. Then I was interviewing for a sales position in Private Clients and they told me I had to tell Isabelle and it was all looking really promising. Then Isabelle said that was fine, but she reported my illegal trade to one of the managing directors and they sacked me. I still don't understand.' She burst into tears again.

'I always thought Isabelle was a bitch,' Ella said.

'Christ, that place is run by egos,' Clara said. 'What about you, Ella?'

'It's a long story. But, well, in a nutshell I got the job by saying I graduated from Durham University and I didn't.'

'Where did you graduate from?' Virginia asked.

'Nowhere. But I was good at my job. Fucking good. I can't understand how they found out now.'

'Gosh, Ella, I didn't realise you were so interesting. It takes balls to lie about your qualifications. But how did they find out?' Clara was interested.

'I don't know how or why or anything. I was so upset. I couldn't ask those kind of questions and I doubt they'd have told me. They had to sack me but, shit, I loved my job.' Ella had drunk more than she was used to and she felt a little unsteady.

Virginia went to get more drinks, and they all sat, deep in thought.

'I say we get drunk,' Clara said.

'Clara, this isn't a jolly girls' outing.' Ella was sharp.

'Calm down. We're all in the same boat here. We've all lost our jobs and the only way I think I can get through the next twenty-four hours is to get rat-arsed,' Clara finished.

'What *am* I going to do?' Virginia started crying again.

They drank more and didn't notice the evening rush begin. They sat in silence for part of the time; they all asked what they were going to do. None of them could comprehend what had happened, what was happening. For three people who couldn't be more different, they all had something in common that day.

'I know. I'm going to fucking get my own back on that toad Tim,' Clara announced, through the cigarette haze that surrounded her.

'Give me a cigarette,' Ella said, reaching over and taking one.

'How are you going to get him?' Virginia asked, leaning back. The smell of the smoke coupled with all the drink made her feel queasy.

'I don't fucking know, but I am and you two should do the same.'

'What? Get back at Isabelle?' Virginia's eyes were wide open.

'Yes! Get the bitch! Make her sorry she ever messed with you.' Clara was angry.

'But how?' Virginia asked again.

'I don't fucking know, but somehow we'll all do it. Together. Yes, that's what we'll do. We'll take our revenge on those who ruined our lives.' Clara's eyes shone with determination.

'Clara, I think you're drunk. I don't even know who I'm getting back at. And, anyway, it's a stupid idea,' Ella said.

'Oh, really, Miss High and Mighty Fake Degree Certificate? Someone shopped you, or whatever they call it. Someone was behind your fall, mark my words, and it won't be hard to find out who.'

'Really? Fine! You find out, then. Be my guest. I just want to put the whole mess behind me. And I'm not the high-and-mighty one, Miss I Slept With Just About Everyone In My Job.'

'Well, at least I'm not too into myself to have sex. Ella, you remember this. We will never put this behind us until we've got our just deserts. I don't particularly like you and you obviously don't like me and, well, I don't know about her but I expect she doesn't like either of us. But we have to unite and do this. We owe it to ourselves.'

'Please,' Virginia squeaked. She was close to tears again.

'Fine, Clara. If you think that's what we should do then OK, but I warn you, it'll all end in tears. This isn't some adventure, you know.'

'No, Ella, it isn't. It's our lives, and if you don't give a shit about yours then crawl back into your hole, but I am not going to take this lying down.'

'Which, of course, you usually do,' Ella hissed.

Virginia put her head in her hands; she thought there might be a fight. 'Clara's right. We're not going to get up tomorrow and go to work. We won't ever work in the City again – they'll make sure of that. I don't know what I'm going to do and I don't even know how to begin to find out. We have to do something.'

The other two stared at her. That was the most she'd said all evening.

'Right. We're going to do it. Ella, I don't care if you like me or not. Or you.' Clara waggled a finger at Virginia. 'But we'll get the people who got us, then they'll be sorry they ever messed with us.'

Ella rolled her eyes. 'OK. But I told you I don't even know who ruined my life.'

'I'll find out. Don't worry. Say you're in,' Clara pleaded.

Something told Ella she was going to regret this, but the others were right. She had no idea what she was going to do now that the rug had again been pulled from under her feet. 'OK,' she said reluctantly.

'All right. We'll be like the Three Musketeers or Robin Hood or something.' Clara stopped. The others were looking at her as if she was mad. 'Anyway, we'll meet tomorrow. My flat will be our headquarters and we'll all write down our addresses and telephone numbers.' They did as she said. 'Tomorrow at four at my place. Anyone who isn't there better have a good reason.'

'Fine,' Ella said. She felt deflated.

'Fine,' Virginia said, before she started crying again.

Clara looked at the two girls in front of her. She was filled with an overwhelming anger. Anger at the injustice, anger at those who cared so much for themselves they destroyed other people's lives in the blink of an eye, anger that she was here, and anger that Virginia and Ella looked like the worst kind of fighting partners anyone could have. She stood up. 'I'd like to propose a toast. To revenge. To avenging. To giving these people what they bloody well deserve.' They all clinked glasses and Clara hoped that Ella and Virginia would find some enthusiasm before the next meeting.

Ella took a bath and tried to wash the day off her before going to bed. Due to the drink, she passed out almost immediately.

Virginia walked into her studio and felt depressed. She tore off her clothes and left them where they were. She climbed into bed and cried herself to sleep.

Clara paced the sitting room for a while before she could settle. Her head was filled with thoughts of revenge, and she felt almost positive about the process. She knew that whatever happened she would not just go away. She knew that she would ensure that her family didn't find out. She knew that they would all be proud of her one day.

When sleep finally greeted her, she dreamt of Tim Pemberton's head on a shiny silver platter.

PART FOUR

The Drawing Board

Chapter Sixteen

When Ella woke her head hurt and her mouth felt as if it had been stuffed with leaves. Her throat hurt, and the memory of the cigarettes flooded back. Then the memory of why she had been smoking hit her. She looked at the clock; it was 6 a.m. She picked up the telephone.

'Hello,' a sleepy voice said.

'Jackie, It's me.' Ella said, rubbing her temples.

'Ella? Are you OK?'

'No, not really. I got sacked.'

'You *what*?'

'I got sacked.'

'Shit, you're joking. Christ, Ella, I'm coming over.'

'Thank you,' Ella said, and dissolved into tears.

Ella hadn't been able to muster the energy to move from the bed. She waited for the door, clutching tissues and rubbing her throbbing head. She didn't know how much time had passed when the buzzer sounded.

Still in her bathrobe she opened the door; Jackie stood on the other side.

'Oh, babe, tell me what happened.' Jackie took Ella into her arms and she fell apart again.

Ella explained everything. The call from Human Resources, the accusation, the fact that she didn't know what had triggered it. The fact that she had no defence. She told her about the afternoon in the pub, the other girls, and even the plan for revenge. Jackie didn't interrupt; she just listened as she always did.

'Hon, I don't know what to say, I really don't. I thought that was it. Once we'd got away with it initially, I thought there was no way it could come out. I think that girl, Clara, was right. Someone must have been behind this. But who and why?'

'I don't know. Everything was going so well and the only thing upsetting me was Johnny. Do you think it could have been him?'

'How would he know? I mean, he would have had to go and find that information. It's not like it's common knowledge. Only you and I know. Maybe the company was updating files and they had to do checks on everyone or something. Maybe it was bad luck, after all.'

'I didn't have the nerve to ask. It was humiliating enough. I guess I'm just being paranoid about Johnny — I mean we had a few run-ins, but I only knew him for a week and there's no way he would do that. I guess my main fear was that it had something to do with Tony.'

'Ella, this has nothing to do with Tony. That's one thing I know for sure. How could he have found you? He can't. He might be dead. Christ, he's haunting you so much I'd like to kill him myself.'

'I know it's irrational. It could have been a routine check, as you said, but I can't help feeling that now I've lost my job the rest of it is going to come out. What if Tony did die? I let Sammy get his friends to beat the hell out of him. I wouldn't let him take the blame.'

'Ella, Sammy is not in trouble. He cashes the cheques you send him, doesn't he? He wouldn't if he was in prison. We'd know, you'd know, you'd feel it. Anyway, we're letting all this run away with us. Darling, if Clara does find out that someone did this to you, then you go along with her plan. And please, for me, think about calling Sammy and putting Tony behind you once and for all. Promise?'

'It's all too much, isn't it? Jackie, how can I cope? I feel like I've made such a mess of my life and I don't know if I'll ever put it back together.'

'You *will* put it back together. But we start here. Go and see Clara and Virginia when you're supposed to. It doesn't matter that you don't like them. This could be good for you, therapeutic, and God knows, you need it.'

They talked for hours until Ella started to calm down. Jackie made her some food, got her into the shower and got her dressed. As she prepared to drive to Kensington Ella realised that she was so lucky to have such a good friend.

Virginia woke up and found herself lying on the floor with her duvet wrapped around her. She felt awful; her head was thumping and her eyes were so sore she could hardly open them. She looked at the chair and saw her coat and bag. She remembered she had left her scooter in the City. Then she remembered why she had left it in the City.

The engulfing panic that followed left her short of breath and unable to move. She was physically wrecked. She knew she should be going to work now. She should be preparing to start her new job, not lying on the floor having a panic attack about the future. She dragged herself up and went to make tea.

Then she switched on the television and crawled back into bed with her cup. She thought about the girls she had met the previous night: Clara, who was confident and blonde and bossy, and Ella who was cold. She knew she didn't really want to spend time with them. She also knew it was her only hope. She had nothing but the thought that maybe they would put Clara's drunken ramblings about revenge into practice. That was the only thing she had left.

She wished she could speak to someone, but her parents wouldn't understand. And Susie was miles away. All she had was the mad girl who had slept with her boss and her client, and the cold girl who had lied her way into the job. She felt she was the most innocent of them all, but she also felt that they were victims too. Of what she wasn't sure. She thought that, whatever happened, they would be some sort of support for her. And she needed support. The only hope she had was of making Isabelle pay. Although she believed in her heart that she would fail at that too.

Eventually she managed to shower and dress. She put on jeans and a jumper and took the tube to pick up her scooter. Seeing her parking space and knowing she would never come here brought back all the pain. She checked the route to South Kensington in her *A–Z*, and drove off to meet the others with a heart that felt like a ton of bricks.

Clara woke and felt sick. Then she *was* sick. She crawled into the kitchen and drank water from the fridge. She didn't know what day it was until she remembered the black Thursday she had just been through. She checked her answerphone. There were no messages. She didn't know what she was expecting, but she was expecting something. She tried to banish the thought that what she had expected was a call from Tim saying, sorry, it had been a huge mistake, and offering her her job back. She decided to pull herself together.

She showered and dressed quickly. She was on a mission. First she called one of her old boyfriends and asked him if he could get her some cocaine. He told her he'd deliver some in person that evening. She still had quite a lot left from Tim, but she wanted to ensure that she never ran out. She knew she needed it more than ever now as she celebrated the result of her first mission with her first line of the day. Then she tidied the flat – her cleaner wasn't due in until the following week. She had strewn knickers all over the sitting room and there were remnants of cocaine on the coffee table, but the kitchen was clean – she never used it. She just shut the door of her bedroom.

Her next mission was to call her brother. Before she did that, she walked around her flat. It was in a lovely old building that had been a school or a hospital or something. It contained about fifty flats, but she didn't know any of her neighbours. She had three bedrooms, two that she never used and hers. The sitting room was large with a dining-table, which again she never used. There was a long white hallway and two bathrooms, one *en suite*, the other off the hall. She decided that although she hadn't paid much attention to the flat in all the time she lived here, she liked it.

She couldn't put off calling James. He handled the family's account at SFH, and she had to give him some reason for no longer being there. She hoped that no one at SFH felt they had to give him their side of the story. She decided that before she called James she would call the Human Resources bitch who fired her. This was damage limitation.

'Helen, it's Clara Hart. Sorry I was so rude yesterday.'

Helena sprouted another grey hair. She didn't have the energy to correct her name. 'What can I do for you?'

'You know my family has an account with SFH? Well, it seems I shall have to go and work for them now I no longer have a job. Therefore, I want to make it clear that I will not rock the boat for SFH with them if you make sure that SFH doesn't tell my family why I was sacked. In fact, I don't want them to know I was sacked at all.' Clara sounded confident.

'I don't see that as a problem.' Helena decided not to tell Clara that they had already decided to keep the reason for her dismissal quiet.

'Thanks.' Clara hung up.

Second mission accomplished. She felt a great sense of failure at having been sacked, but she believed she could cope with that as long as no one else knew about it. She dialled her brother's number.

'James Hart, please.'

'May I say who's calling?'

Clara hated his prissy secretary. 'You may. It's his sister.' She waited for a few seconds.

'Clara, hi.' James was always so nice it broke her heart.

'Jamie, listen, I've got something to tell you.'

'What? Are you all right?'

'Sure, I'm fine, but I quit my job.'

'You did what?'

Clara laughed falsely. 'Jamie, I left work. I was having a hard time there – you know, everyone thinking I was a result of nepotism. I decided that instead of fighting it I'd take some time out to figure out what I really wanted to do with my life. I know I'll never be the girl Daddy wants me to be, but I don't think I'm cut out for the City either.' She hoped she wouldn't be struck down for lying.

'Clara, are you sure?'

'Absolutely.'

'Well, then, congratulations. You're the proper grown-up, aren't you? Making all these decisions. Dad will be pleased. He'll probably think that now you aren't working he can marry you off.'

'Yes, but you won't let that happen, will you?'

'Not unless you want to be married off. Why don't you come to my place for lunch tomorrow? We'll celebrate.'

'I'll be there at one.' Clara hung up and almost believed that everything had been her idea. Shit, if he ever finds out, I'll be brotherless and friendless, she thought, as she picked up the telephone and moved on to mission three.

She was going to make Tim sorry. She might help Virginia make Isabelle pay. She wanted to know who had done the deed to Ella. She was only interested in the two girls because they were in the same position as she was, and she felt sorry for them as she felt sorry for herself. She needed to do something, but she didn't know what she could do next. Her plan would give her some breathing space.

There was only one person she could call on at SFH. Toby. She thought about calling Sarah, but Sarah would ask too many questions and she wouldn't be as easy to manipulate as Toby. Clara needed information about Ella, and Toby would get it for her.

Toby answered the telephone. 'SFH.'

Clara recognised his voice. 'Toby, it's Clara, but don't let the others know.'

There was a pause.

'Cl-Clive, are you OK?'

'Clive? Couldn't you come up with something better? Only joking. How are you?'

'I'm fine. What happened?'

'Oh, nothing much, I was busted, that's all, and I deserve everything. Just watch Tim. He's not a nice man.'

'He's not? What about the e-mail you sent?'

'Sour grapes. Anyway, that's not why I called. Can you do me a favour?' She put on her most appealing voice.

'Sure, what?'

'Well, I need to know what happened to Ella Franke.'

'The trader?'

No, Ella Franke the trapeze artist, Clara thought, but she didn't say it. 'Yes, Toby, Ella the trader. You see, she was fired and it transpired that she didn't have a degree and she lied. I want to know who found out about it.'

'Yeah, it's all over the office. No one knows why you went, although Tim has called a meeting of all of us this afternoon, but everyone's gossiping about Ella.'

'Well, listen, go to her desk and find out who dropped her in it. Then call me back, my number is—'

'I have your home number,' Toby interrupted, and Clara wondered how he had it.

'Great. Can you do it quickly?'

'Sure, can I ask why?'

'No, you can't.' Clara laughed again. 'All will be revealed later. Toby, don't tell anyone I called. Oh, and if you fancy a chat call me after Tim's meeting. How's Alex?' Clara thought it might be useful for her, Ella and Virginia to have an unsuspecting mole in the office.

'OK, I won't. And Alex is fine. We're getting along really well.'

'Good. Thanks, Toby, you're a real mate.' She put down the telephone and felt glad that Toby was with Alex. That meant she wouldn't have to sleep with him.

Sex. That's what it was. Clara had sex, Clara got into trouble. She had to try to cut down on the number of men she slept with. She had told herself this for a while, but now she really would try to do something about her sex addiction. Although now that she no longer had a job, she wasn't sure that she needed to.

She went to the kitchen and grabbed three pieces of kitchen roll – her cleaner bought all sorts of things for her. She took them to the dining-table, grabbed an SFH biro and started writing. On one piece, she wrote 'Tim Pemberton', on the second, 'Isabelle Holland', and the third she kept blank. She knew that when the girls came she would be ready for them. She would do this to prove that she had more about her than her parents would ever dream. At first she had thought the idea of revenge was just her being drunk and over-enthusiastic, but the more she thought about it, the more it made sense. People shouldn't be allowed to stamp on other people. It just wasn't fair.

The telephone rang when Clara was still daydreaming about revenge.

'Clive, it's Toby.'

'God, Toby, are you going to call me Clive every time you speak to me?'

'Probably. Anyway, I have the information you wanted.'

'I feel like I'm in a spy movie.' Clara giggled.

'Me too. I went to Ella's desk and I asked Liam Rice what he knew. He was really angry and told me to mind my own fucking business. I told him I was concerned and I said I was sort of a friend of Ella's. So he said he was sorry, but apparently everyone's very upset about it. Anyway, he said that some new guy called Johnny had boasted the next day that he had discovered Ella's secret and he was pleased with himself. Liam said they all hated Johnny, I don't know his last name, and now they hated him even more. Liam seemed really worried about Ella. He said that if I spoke to her I should get her to call him. As if I'm ever going to speak to her! I barely knew who she was. Anyway, does that help?'

'Toby, you're a miracle worker. Thanks. By the way, I know Ella and I'll pass on Liam's message, but remember, don't mention it to anyone.'

'I won't. I'll call you after the meeting with Tim, OK?'

' 'Bye, Toby.'

Clara returned to the table and wrote 'Johnny' on the last piece of kitchen towel. She settled down to wait for the others to arrive.

Virginia arrived early at Clara's flat. As she parked her scooter outside the magnificent building, she felt even more unsure of herself than she usually did. She looked up at it and was hit by the thought that this was the type of building she could have lived in one day if only she had the new job.

It was more intimidating inside. The doorman looked at her suspiciously, far more interested in keeping people out than the security guards had been at SFH. She hit herself on the head as she realised that every thought she had brought her back to SFH. She took the lift to Clara's floor, found her flat and rang the bell. She waited nervously for a few seconds until Clara opened the door. 'I'm a bit early,' Virginia said, turning pink.

'I see you dressed up for the occasion,' Clara said, looking at her. Although Clara was wearing jeans and a shirt, she looked nice; Virginia looked like a teenager in her old-fashioned jeans and big, baggy jumper. She felt embarrassed as she followed Clara in. The sitting room was bigger than Virginia's entire flat.

'Drink?' Clara asked.

'Water, please,' Virginia said, her mouth dry.

Clara disappeared and returned with a glass. 'Do you wear specs?' she asked.

'No. Why?'

'You just look as if you should.'

Clara sat at the dining-table and, not knowing what to say, Virginia sat on the sofa. Virginia wasn't a great conversationalist at the best of times, but here, in this lovely flat with a girl who reminded her of the mean but popular girl at school, she felt out of her depth.

'Do you think Ella will turn up?' Clara asked, after a while.

'Why wouldn't she?' Virginia had been so caught up wondering why *she* was here that the thought of Ella failing to materialise hadn't occurred to her.

'Because she seemed so cold and empty. I just felt last night that she might not.'

A few minutes later, the doorbell rang again and Ella appeared. She looked composed. She was wearing baggy grey trousers and a black cardigan.

'Hi,' Clara said, as she let her in.

Confronted by Ella's height and her style, Virginia felt even more inadequate.

'Drink?' Clara asked. Ella shook her head.

'Fine. Down to business. I have news for you, Ella. I know who stitched you up.'

'Who?' Ella asked quietly.

'Who do you think it was?' Clara replied, enjoying the drama.

'Clara, I don't fucking know. That's why I'm here. I didn't think anyone did.'

'Well, you're wrong. Someone did and it was Johnny, your new boy.' Ella sank down on to the armchair.

'Johnny,' Ella whispered.

'I called someone from my old desk who went to talk to Liam. Apparently Johnny was bragging about how somehow, I don't know how, he found out you were never at Durham. He told your boss, they checked it out, and that's why you're here.'

'Shit. I don't believe it.'

'It's true.'

'Thanks, Clara, I know it's true. But I only knew Johnny for a week – less. Why was he poking around?'

'Maybe he found out by accident,' Virginia offered timidly.

They shot her a look.

'Of course – he was just walking down the street and accidentally found out that Ella was a liar and a forger. How did you get that done by the way?' Clara said.

'It doesn't matter. We had a couple of run-ins, mainly because I was supposed to be mentoring him and he disliked me. He was scum, really egotistical, and I knew he didn't like me ... but to do that – to try to discredit me.' Ella rubbed her head; her hangover was returning.

'Ella, people are like that. Look at us. Tim did it to me, Isabelle to Virginia. He probably wanted to get rid of you. All he knew about you was where you went to university, and he started there. He didn't need to take it further – he must have thought it was Christmas.'

Ella took her head out of her hands. It all made sense. 'You're right. He probably didn't dream he'd find that but he was looking for a way to get at me, or to humiliate me. God,

I remember one argument we had when he was saying how he went to Oxford and Harvard and how he'd got an MBA as well as an economics degree, and I told him that just because I had a history degree from Durham, it didn't make him any better than me. Shit, I hate him.'

'Good. So we all hate someone. Now, can we move on?'

Virginia felt as if she was in a nightmare. Ella looked as if she was in a nightmare.

'Clara, wait. What else did Liam say?'

'Well, he was concerned for you and he asked if you could call him. They don't like Johnny either, but I'm sure he can't take down the whole desk.'

Ella knew she had been hard on Johnny, but he had deserved it. She could just imagine what happened. After the trade fiasco, he had stormed off wanting revenge. She still didn't know how he had found out, or what had possessed him to try. He was such a weasel. He had ruined her life.

Clara called them over to the table and they all sat down. She produced her pieces of kitchen paper.

'What's that?' Virginia asked.

'Kitchen towels,' Clara answered.

'Yes, but why?' Ella said.

'Oh, I didn't have any paper. Anyway, this is Virginia's, this is mine and this is Ella's.' She gave them each a bit. 'I thought we'd start by writing what we know about each person on them and go from there.' She handed them each a pen.

They started writing. Virginia finished quickly, Ella ran out of steam soon after and Clara seemed to take hours. When they finished, Clara read out what they had.

'Virginia, yours is first because I feel you had the biggest injustice done to you.' Virginia felt flattered. 'Isabelle Holland, manager of Emerging Markets at SFH. Tall, good-looking, a bitch. Is that it?' Clara looked at Virginia.

'I don't know much about her.' Virginia blushed.

'Ella, do you know anything more about Isabelle?' Clara asked.

'She plays squash at my health club,' Ella offered.

Clara wrote it down. 'Excellent, that's the sort of thing we need. Now, I know that she's heterosexual, single, thinks of herself as a cultural person and is as dull as dishwater.'

'How do you know all that?' Ella asked.

'I listen to things, I find out things, and if I didn't you two would be in deep water. Luckily for you, I've been to a couple of parties she was at. She was like a bitch on heat. Anyway, now Johnny. Johnny Rupfin. Ex-Oxford, Harvard MBA, has pimples and is an arrogant little cock-sucker. Do you mean that literally?'

'What literally?' Ella asked.

'Does he suck cocks?' Clara asked.

Virginia flinched.

'I don't know.' Ella was exasperated. She was beginning to regret coming.

'Oh, I suppose we couldn't be that lucky. I take it he's one of the computer Rupfins?'

'I don't know, but his uncle got him the SFH job. He's one of their private clients,' Ella offered. Virginia nearly burst into tears at this latest reminder of her lost opportunity.

'Then he is. My father knows his uncle, which might come in handy, although I'm not sure my father would approve of what we're doing. Oh, well, every little helps.' Clara wrote it down. 'Right, Tim Pemberton. Womaniser, takes cocaine, likes prostitutes and kinky sex. Never takes his socks off, likes champagne. Goes to the Tribor club on Thursdays, which is very exclusive, then goes to a seedy strip-joint or to see a hooker. Used to be having an affair with me. But isn't now, thank God. Wife, two children, both girls, a dog and a huge house in Hampstead. Used to be poor and common, is now common and rich. That's the type of information we need.'

'What? That he keeps his socks on in bed?' Ella giggled.

'What I mean is that all this information will help us to take our revenge,' Clara said reprovingly.

'Before we continue, I need to clarify something. I'm not prepared to break the law to do this,' Ella said.

'Me neither,' Virginia agreed, eyes wide. That idea hadn't occurred to her.

'Oh, God, don't be so silly. Of course we're not going to break the law. We're going to do this in a way that keeps us well and truly out of it. I have my family reputation to think about,' Clara said.

'I just don't want to go to jail,' Ella said.

'So, what are we going to do?' Virginia said.

'I don't know. God, you can't expect me to do everything. What I'm doing now is collecting information. What we need to do is to plan a revenge for each one that relies on their weaknesses. Tim's weaknesses are cocaine and sex. See? What about Isabelle?'

'Well, I guess she's motivated by money and power.' Virginia offered weakly.

'Good. Johnny?'

'He's egotistical, arrogant and a cock-sucker, although not literally.' Ella was surly.

'Fine. He probably thinks he's special when really he's an irritating, unattractive little wart. We use his ego to bring him down.' Clara was enjoying herself.

'So what are we going to do?' Virginia asked again.

'I don't know why you think I should have all the answers,' Clara replied.

'Well, this was your idea,' Ella said.

'I know, and I've done all the work so far. Oh, God, I'm not going to argue. What we do next is to think about what we've gone through this afternoon, then we meet tomorrow and every day until this is over. Same time, same place. It won't happen overnight. We need to put a lot of thought into it. I want to make sure that each of these worms gets what they deserve. And that is, no job and no reputation. We'll tear them to shreds. As I said, I think it's better if we deal with one at a time and we start with Isabelle. When we meet tomorrow we go over ideas of how we can get her. Are we all agreed on this?'

'Yes,' Virginia said. She was feeing stronger.

'Fine.' Ella was really pissed off. Clara's bossiness annoyed her, as did Virginia's timidity. However, she knew that they had to do this.

'Let's have a drink to celebrate.' Clara clapped her hands together.

'I'm driving,' Ella and Virginia said in unison.

'Well, one won't hurt,' Clara said, and went to get the wine.

While she was gone, Ella and Virginia exchanged glances. They didn't speak. Clara returned with three glasses and a bottle of chilled white wine. She filled each glass.

'Here's to revenge.' She held up her glass. The others clinked glasses unenthusiastically.

'Christ, you really are being very boring about this. Can't you see that we are going to do to them what they did to us? Can't you see how important this is?' Clara was stroppy.

'Clara, this isn't one of your public-school japes. This is real life,' Ella said.

'Yes, well, real life isn't great for any of us at the moment. Before tomorrow try to raise a little enthusiasm. Virginia, perhaps you could borrow a voice before you come back.' Virginia turned red.

'Leave her alone, Clara, we're still upset about our jobs,' Ella said.

'Yes, and so am I. I know you think I'm some silly rich bitch who slept her way into a job, but once I got there I loved it — well, recently I did — and I worked hard. Ella, we're not so different, you know. You lied your way in too.'

'I know. But I didn't whore myself.' Ella was losing her cool.

'Christ, you're so above that, aren't you? It didn't involve sex because you probably couldn't be appealing enough for long enough for anyone to want to sleep with someone as cold as you.'

'You fucking bitch.'

'Takes one to know one,' Clara said.

'Will you two stop arguing? We're all supposed to be on the same side.' Virginia was almost shouting. Ella and Clara looked at each other. Then they laughed.

'She's found her voice,' Clara said, and Virginia laughed too, because it was better than arguing.

By the time Ella and Virginia left, they had reverted to the cool, civil tones with which they had started. Clara knew she would have to lead them: they were both so docile.

Ella knew she would never like Clara or Virginia for opposite reasons: Clara too pushy, Virginia too quiet.

Virginia didn't know who scared her most: pushy Clara or cold Ella. She shivered and hoped that everything would be all right.

Ella drove to the restaurant. Although Jackie was working, the Friday-night rush hadn't started and they sat down together to have coffee. Ella filled her in on the meeting, Clara's irritating manner, the news about Johnny – she even told her about Liam wanting to talk to her.

'Bloody hell! What a couple of days. So, are you going to go through with it?'

'I don't know. Clara bosses us around and always sounds condescending. I know I shouldn't judge anyone after the way I got my job, but she slept with the boss. Things are always easy for people like her. She's great-looking, she's got a lovely flat, which I expect was bought for her. She doesn't look like she ever suffered in her life. And she treats this whole thing like an adventure from Enid Blyton. The Terrible Three Go to Get

Revenge. Although I'm angry about what happened to me and I'd like to kill Johnny, I know this isn't a game. And Virginia, well, she's just such a loser. Won't say a word, although she got angry with us in the end. I feel sorry for her, but she's so painful to be around. She goes pink every time you talk to her. I guess she's insecure. God, I should be nice to her to make her feel better, but she has this sulky expression on her face the whole time. It makes you want to slap her.'

'Ella, you've got to go through with it,' Jackie said suddenly.

'Why?' Ella asked.

'You'll find out. First, these people you told me about deserve to get done and if you don't do it they'll probably go on ruining people's lives, and second, those girls sound like they're really messed up. If you don't help them they'll probably screw it up. You're calm, you're intelligent, and you're probably the one with the most brains.'

'I'm doing this for the good of the public and so the other two don't fuck up?'

'Basically yes.' Jackie laughed.

'I've got to go back tomorrow. God knows how we're going to do this. Oh, and can you believe these plans are being masterminded on pieces of kitchen roll?' They both laughed.

'Ella, do you want to stay with me for a few days?'

'Yes, please.' Ella knew she didn't want to be alone. She went home to pack up a few things then drove to Jackie's house. She let herself in and started to think of ways to get Isabelle Holland for Virginia.

Virginia drove home. She should have known they wouldn't like her and the only comfort she took from this was that they didn't seem to like each other either. And, of course, she didn't like them.

She got home, lay on her bed and thought things through.

She was fed up with people treating her like that. She knew one thing: she would see this thing through. She would get her own back on Isabelle. She had to. She would do it for all the times when her parents had tutted their disappointment at her, for all the times Isabelle had shouted at her, for all the friends who had left her, and for all those who didn't even want to know her. She would do something that would make her proud of herself. She would stand up for herself.

She sat down and thought about all the things she could do to get back at Isabelle. She thought long and hard. As she went to sleep, she was dreaming of revenge.

Clara had another couple of glasses of wine when the others left. She really didn't know what she had done to deserve being mixed up with those two, but she guessed this was all part of her punishment. Ella the cold bitch; Virginia the nobody. She would follow it through, though, because she had nothing else to do.

She had a line of coke to calm herself and looked over the notes. She had no idea how they were going to do this, and she hoped that one of the two deadheads came up with something. They had to. They just *had* to.

She decided to change before Matt, her coke-bearing friend, arrived. She had dated him before she went to work at SFH, when she was seeing several men at the same time. He was cute, charming and had a huge crush on her. He wasn't exactly a cocaine fiend, but he used it and he had agreed to supply it to her. He was Clara's age, which she considered too young for her. Matt was one of the many men Clara called when she wanted a night out. It had never been a proper relationship.

He was tall and clean-cut with dark hair, the type of boy her parents would love for her. He came from the right family, he had good manners, he was rich, and he had his own career in advertising. He wasn't a playboy. He was an ordinary boy. Far too ordinary for Clara.

He turned up smelling of aftershave. A nice smell. He gave Clara the cocaine and told her she didn't have to pay. It was a gift.

'Can you get me this regularly, darling?' she asked.

'Sure, but I don't use much. I hope you don't either.'

Clara sighed. She hoped he wasn't going to be a bore. 'No, of course not. I have a couple of friends who I get it for too, but my supplier fucked up and I don't want to deal with him any more. You must have loads of suppliers – you do work in advertising, after all.'

'Yes, I do, but not everyone's a coke user. Anyway, it's just a recreational drug. I normally only take it at weekends.' Matt smiled, and Clara knew he *was* going to be a bore.

'So how have you been?' she asked.

'Fine. It's good to see you, though.'

'Come on, let's have a couple of lines and then I'll take you out,' Clara said, unwrapping the paper and lining up the cocaine.

'It's a deal.'

The next morning Matt kissed Clara tenderly. 'I'll call you. We'll go out next week.'

'I'll look forward to it. I don't suppose you can bring me more cocaine then?' Clara kissed him hard.

'Are you sure you don't have a habit?' he asked suspiciously.

'No, I told you, I need to give some away. I just use a bit. I think you saw that for yourself last night.'

'True, honey, you're like me. We just need a little bit for relaxation.' He said goodbye and left.

'Some people need to relax more than others,' Clara said to herself, as she went back to sleep, mentally striking Matt off her Christmas-card list.

Chapter Seventeen

By four that afternoon, Clara had washed, dressed, been to lunch with her brother and had two lines of cocaine. Then she panicked about Matt. Trust her ex-boyfriend to have turned into a square. She knew she didn't want a relationship with him, she'd always known that. What she needed was her own dealer, and Matt was not going to give her the number of his. She was back to square one and she was angry that she had no supplier and that Matt had suggested she was an addict. Clara was not an addict: she was just going through a very trying period in her life. Matt did not understand.

She picked up her address book and looked through it. In frustration, she ripped out most of its pages. Then she spotted Josh Lambert's address and phone numbers. Her heart flipped. Josh was an old family friend with whom she had practically grown up. She had loved him since she was a little girl. He had succumbed to 'the charm' when she was older, but their relationship had not lasted. 'Needs must,' she said to herself, and dialled his work number.

Her heart flipped again when Josh answered. He sounded so pleased to hear from her. She said she needed a favour and they arranged to meet the following Monday. Josh was the only man who had rejected Clara, although he had just stopped telephoning rather than dumping her directly. She didn't know if Josh still took cocaine, although he had when they were together, and she knew he had a friend who was a dealer. He was her best chance. When she hung up she was calmer.

The bell rang. Clara opened the door to Virginia.

'You are punctual,' she said.

'Yes.' Virginia blushed. Clara ushered her in. She had put a bottle of water and three glasses on the dining-table. Virginia handed her a package.

'What's this?' Clara asked.

'A notebook,' Virginia answered.

Clara laughed. 'Are you always this organised?'

'Yes,' Virginia admitted.

'Right. So, will the delightful Ella be honouring us with her presence today?'

'I think so,' Virginia answered.

Clara took out the new notebook and copied her kitchen-towel notes into it. 'I'll call it our mission book,' she announced. Virginia nodded, and felt like a fool.

Shortly afterwards Ella turned up.

'Sorry I'm late. I took the tube but I didn't know how slow the fucking thing was.' She walked past Clara, sat down and poured a glass of water, ignoring Virginia.

'Virginia, can we call you Ginnie?' Clara asked.

'Why?' Virginia hated the name Ginnie.

'So you can sound like one of her jolly-hockey-sticks friends,' Ella said sourly.

'No, it's just that I have a problem with the name Virginia. It sounds like Vagina.' There was silence.

Virginia blushed yet again and Ella tried not to laugh. 'It's my name, and I hate Ginnie,' she said.

'Fine. I'm really glad we had that discussion, can we get on with it.' Ella cut in.

'Who has any ideas, then? Vir-gin-ia?' Clara asked. Virginia shook her head. 'Neither have I. Ella?'

'Shit, this is ridiculous. I mean, what are we really doing here? So, we put itching powder down Isabelle's back, we write a letter to Tim's wife telling her what a cheating scumbag he is and we get Liam to put Superglue on Johnny's chair. What the hell are we going to achieve?' Ella had spent all night thinking and she'd got nowhere.

'No, Ella, that is not what we're going to do. Shit, this is far more serious than itching powder,' Clara said.

'Right. But that's the only idea I came up with. I knew this revenge stuff was stupid when we started.'

'Christ, Ella, I thought you were with us. Look, I don't know what *you* really think but this is what I think. It took three people to destroy our careers. Those three people have to pay, and we are going to make them pay by destroying *their* careers. There are three of us, Ella, we've joined forces and we can do this, we really can. But you have to start taking it more seriously and you need to stop being such a fucking pain in the arse.'

'Fine,' Ella said.

'What?'

'You're right. I'm just frustrated. I have no idea how we even start.'

'Neither have I, but that doesn't mean we give up. Not yet.'

'No. OK, Clara, count me in.'

'At long last.'

'I might have an idea.' Virginia's voice was barely audible.

'Well, then, speak up, for God's sake,' Clara snapped.

'It's really about money, I think. The thing that motivates her most of all. I don't know how, but I think perhaps we could set her up to lose money.' She was as red as Clara's lipstick, but at least she had said it.

'Like insider trading,' Ella said suddenly. Virginia nodded.

'What's insider trading?' Clara asked.

'It's where you get information about a company, a takeover or something like that, and you buy into a company on the basis of that information. Of course, the information isn't public so you get it before everyone else. It goes on a lot.'

'Is it legal?' Clara asked.

'No, of course it's not fucking legal. Christ, Clara, are you sure you worked in the City?'

'Yes, but I was still learning. OK, so we set her up with an insider-trading deal. But I don't understand how we can do that without breaking the law.'

'Neither do I,' Virginia admitted.

'Well, it's a start. What we have is the outline. We set Isabelle up so she buys shares in a company because she thinks it will go up. But, really, it's going to go down. Right?'

'Right.' Virginia felt quite excited.

'Perhaps she could have sex with a guy who owns a company and he tells her – you know pillow-talk that something's going to happen.' Clara offered.

'Clara, why does it always have to come down to sex with you?' Ella asked.

'This is the first time I've mentioned sex,' Clara defended herself.

'You got sacked because of sex, remember?'

'OK, but I like sex. I'm quite good at it. Do you like sex, Vir-gin-ia?'

Virginia was beacon red.

'I bet you've never had sex, have you?' Clara taunted.

'Clara, leave it. It's none of your fucking business,' Ella cut in.

'Do you like sex, Ella?' Clara asked.

'As I said, it's none of your fucking business. Are we going to do this or not?' Ella was increasingly losing her patience and Virginia was crying.

'What is it?' Ella asked her, not quite able to get concern into her voice.

'She's so horrible and I don't think I can do it.' Virginia jumped up, grabbed her coat and fled the flat.

Clara and Ella looked at each other.

'Look what you did!' Ella shouted.

'Oh, God. She needs to loosen up,' Clara moaned.

'But why did you have to upset her like that? Christ, Clara, just because she's not a loudmouth like you or confident enough to hold her own like me doesn't mean you have the right to treat her like shit.'

'But you don't like her any more than I do.'

'I don't like either of you. But if we're going to go through with this – and don't forget you're the one who is insistent that we do – then we have to try to get along. That means you don't tease her in that condescending way of yours and you behave like an adult.'

'Oh, I'll behave like you, shall I? I'll just be cold and calm and I won't try to have any sort of conversation with either of you.'

'Clara, you can have a conversation when you learn how to have one. You're just a spoilt brat.'

'I'm not. You don't know anything about me.' Clara was shouting now.

'No, and I don't want to either. So leave her alone, leave me alone, and we'll get on fine. Otherwise, we leave it here. Is that what you want? You want Tim to get away with it? Because when I arrived today I was ready to walk, and although I think we should take our revenge I still can.'

'She brought a notebook,' Clara said.

'Have you got her address handy?' Ella asked.

'Yes, it's here. Somewhere in Maida Vale.'

'You better call a cab. We're going to apologise.' Ella was firm.

Clara looked stricken. 'Fine, if I have to. But tell me, do you think she's a virgin?'

'Of course she's a fucking virgin, but that's just another reason for you to leave her alone.' Ella wished she had never walked into that damn pub.

Virginia drove herself home. When she got there, she cried some more. Why was Clara so mean? Why did she have to do this? Why was she in this position? She lay on the bed and cried hard. Her life was a mess.

In the cab Ella ignored all Clara's attempts at conversation, so Clara gave up. The cab took for ever to get through the traffic to Maida Vale. When they reached their destination, Clara spoke. 'OK. Here goes. I'll say sorry, then we can get back to the plan.'

They rang the door buzzer and Virginia's snivelling voice came over the intercom. 'Hello?'

'Hello, Virginia, it's us,' Ella said.

'Come in.'

When they stood in the hall, neither of them knew what to do: there were several doors, the wallpaper was peeling, the carpet worn. Clara had never seen a place like this; Ella hadn't been to one in a long while.

'What number?' Ella asked.

'Six.'

Ella started to climb the stairs with Clara hot on her heels. They reached the door and knocked. Within seconds, Virginia answered. When Ella saw her, with bright red eyes and in her old-fashioned jeans, her first thought was to leave. Clara would have been right behind her.

'Come in,' Virginia muttered. Before they could change their minds they were propelled into the bedsit. Clara tried to hide her horror. The room was a rat-hole, small, poky and badly decorated. It was nothing like she was used to. She didn't think anyone apart from refugees had to live like this.

They stood awkwardly as Virginia cowered on the bed. 'What do you want?' she asked, between sobs.

Ella nudged Clara. 'I'm sorry,' Clara said lamely.

'For what?' Virginia said.

'I didn't mean to be nasty. I just didn't think.' Clara looked at Ella; Ella rolled her eyes.

'You were mean.' Virginia sniffed.

'I know. I just apologised, didn't I? I had no reason to be nasty to you.' Clara could not help but feel pissed off. She didn't intend to be such a bitch, she just hadn't thought before she spoke. But Virginia was so wet she wanted to shake her into action. She was being cruel to be kind.

'OK,' Virginia said, and blew her nose.

'So, I'm forgiven?' Clara wanted to get the hell out of there. This room made her feel claustrophobic. She wished she had taken another line of coke before she left.

'Yes,' Virginia said.

'So can we go?' Clara asked.

'Go where?' Virginia asked.

'Back to mine, headquarters. We were getting somewhere before I started ... well, you know ... and I think we should get back to that lovely notebook you brought round.' Clara smiled.

'Are you taking the mickey again?' Virginia asked.

Clara threw her hands in the air. 'I just can't win, can I?'

Virginia wanted to drive round but they persuaded her to get a taxi with them. Clara said that as she was the one who had caused the argument she would pay. Ella promised she would drop Virginia home when she got a taxi back to Camden. Since they were being almost nice to her, Virginia didn't like to argue. She began to feel silly as they drove back to Clara's. She shouldn't have stormed out, but Clara had been so horrible and she had felt so out of her depth, so unsophisticated, so alone. She wondered for the millionth time why she was doing this, but something was telling her she had to see it through to the end.

They arrived at Clara's after a silent journey, and resumed their positions round the table.

'I guess we should go back to talking about Isabelle,' Ella said.

'Yes, absolutely. Now, where were we?' Clara tried to sound enthusiastic.

'Well, we were talking about her love of money and how we could get her on some sort of insider-trading thing,' Virginia said.

'Mm. But how?' The trio lapsed back into silence.

Clara lit a cigarette and Ella did too. Virginia looked uncomfortable.

'You don't mind if we smoke?' Clara asked.

'No,' Virginia said, although she hated the smell.

'Good,' Clara said, a little harshly. 'I don't suppose you'd like one?'

'No, thanks.' Virginia could see that Clara wasn't going to give up baiting her altogether. She decided she would have to grow a thicker skin.

'Clara, stop. Now, back to Isabelle. Christ, I didn't realise this was going to be so hard.'

'I need the bathroom.' Clara made for her bathroom and her cocaine.

Ella looked at Virginia. 'Don't mind her. She's just a bit . . . well, you know.'

'Yes, she's horrible. But she's right. I don't say much.'

'No, but if we all went on as much as Clara, we'd be in trouble.'

'I suppose.' Virginia wished she could talk the way Clara did. She didn't spend hours worrying that whatever came out of her mouth would sound stupid, or that she would be laughed at, or not even heard. Neither did Ella. Virginia wanted some of their confidence.

Clara took two lines of cocaine to fortify her. She was losing enthusiasm. She had thought it would be fun to plan and plot, but she hadn't thought out the details. She would have to spend more time with the two girls than she wanted, and she didn't want to spend *any* time with them.

She went to the kitchen and grabbed a bottle of wine out of the fridge. If she was going to get through this, she needed alcohol as well as coke. She also hoped that the others might become more interesting if they were drunk.

'Drinks time,' Clara announced, and poured out the wine.

'Isn't it a bit early?' Virginia said, and immediately wished she hadn't.

'No, it's six o'clock, which is a respectable time for drinking. Anyway, I think we need the inspiration.'

Ella leant over and took another cigarette as she sipped the wine. 'Sorry, Clara, I haven't smoked in years. I just fancy it. I'll buy you some.'

'Don't be silly. Help yourself – I've got loads.'

'Thanks.'

'Cheers, girls. Let's hope the wine gives us some idea of what we can do about Isabelle.' Clara prayed to the god of alcohol.

Again, silence ensued.

Ella knew what she thought they should do; she just didn't know how to figure out the logistics. They needed to give Isabelle some information saying that a company about to go bankrupt was to be taken over. Then she would buy stock, recommend it to clients and think herself very clever. The stock would go up briefly, then down before the company announced bankruptcy. It was simple, but it was also complicated. First, the information had to be rock solid: Isabelle wasn't stupid and it had to come from a source she would trust. And the company had to be going bankrupt: it was unfair to cause an innocent company to go out of business. That sort of information wasn't easy to get hold of. It was impossible to mastermind.

Virginia was thinking the same as Ella. If they could find a dead company with worthless stock and start the rumour, Isabelle would fall for it. She was so greedy and hungry for power that she would not only recommend it to her clients but she would personally buy it. And she would talk to the bosses about it. However, it seemed that putting this plan into action would be difficult, if not impossible.

Clara was wondering how they could use sex in the plan. She thought Isabelle looked as if she didn't get it very often. What man would be brave enough to try to seduce her? She was one scary woman. The others might have been thinking about insider dealing, but Clara thought sex was the answer.

The bottle was almost empty before anyone spoke again.

'Are you sure this insider-trading thing is the way forward?' Clara asked.

'I don't know,' Ella said.

Virginia felt things slipping away. 'It is. I know it. But we need to figure out how.' Virginia sounded surer of herself than ever before.

'OK. Let's review what we have so far.'

Ella looked at Clara, who took a gulp of wine, lit a cigarette and glanced at the notebook. 'She plays squash in Ella's club, so we have a venue for getting to her. Mind you, I can't play squash, can you? No, I don't suppose you can. She likes money, craves power and probably doesn't have much of a sex life. We want to set her up to lose a lot of money, but we don't know how. Shit! This is shit!' Clara jumped up and fetched another bottle of wine.

'There has to be a way.' Ella felt a challenge coming on and she loved a challenge. She was beginning to embrace the idea of revenge. She knew there would be a way, but after a couple of glasses of wine she didn't think she would be coming up with it.

'I agree. We'll think of something.' Virginia looked pleadingly at Ella.

'OK. Perhaps if we talk about something else, we'll be able to come up with an idea,' Clara suggested, as she poured more wine. The others looked at her warily. 'It's OK. I don't expect you to talk, I mean, you two have nothing of interest to say. Or, if you do, you keep it quiet. I'll tell you about Tim Pemberton, managing director of SFH.' The others exchanged glances.

'Tim fancied me the minute he saw me. But, then, most men do. Women too, sometimes. Anyway, I got the job as his secretary and as his mistress. He was such a sleaze and dreadful in bed. Actually, he wasn't that bad, but he was very demanding and kinky – God, I could tell you things that would make your hair curl, but I don't think Virginia's old enough. Anyway, he slept with me as often as he could and he always brought champagne round. Then I told him I wanted to be a salesperson and he promoted me. I made a rotten salesperson, but I realised I wanted to be a success so I started working hard. And I was getting there. But then Tim sent me out with the client and you know the rest. He fired me because I didn't want him to leave his wife and move in with me. Really, that was it. And, well, I slept with the client, who was old and fat, because ... well, I'm addicted to sex.' Clara stopped talking and looked at the others. They were open-mouthed.

Ella thought Clara was a drama queen. She had told the story with glee. She had enjoyed telling it. And the sex addiction? Ella didn't believe it for a minute.

Virginia had never met a sex addict before. 'You're really addicted to sex?' she asked Clara.

'Yes. If I meet a man, I sleep with him. I can't control it. Something comes over me and I'm powerless. That's my problem.'

'Why don't you go into therapy to cure it?' Ella asked.

'I don't really mind being addicted to sex,' Clara admitted.

'Even if you sleep with fat old men?' Virginia asked.

'Well, I don't care who I sleep with as long as I get it.

And some girls only get to sleep with fat old men.' Clara shot Virginia a look, which she missed.

'Clara, are you sure about this?' Ella asked.

'Yes, of course. I think I'd know if I was addicted to sex, wouldn't I?' Clara drained the rest of her glass and went to the bathroom again.

'I don't know what to think,' Virginia said to Ella.

'She's mad, that's all. Shit, I'm hungry. Are you?'

'Yes, I am.' Virginia was a little tipsy, and she felt braver. 'Shall we get a takeaway?'

'I was thinking more about going home,' Ella said, but instead she lit another cigarette. God, she loved how it felt. The first puff, the taste in her mouth ... she loved everything about smoking. 'OK, why not? I guess if we're going to spend time together, and it looks as if this could take a while, we should eat together.'

Clara returned and sat down. She lit a cigarette.

'We thought we might get a takeaway,' Virginia said.

'Oh, what fun. I guess this is probably the social highlight of your year. I'll get the menus.' Clara stalked off again. Virginia went red.

'Ignore her,' Ella said. Virginia shrugged.

'The sad thing is she's right,' she said, in a small voice.

Ella wasn't sure she was ready to handle these two, Clara with her fictional sex addiction, Virginia with no life. What had she done to deserve this? But she knew the answer to that.

They decided on Chinese and Clara rang through the order. When it arrived, they all dug in and ate it, although Clara had ordered the oddest things. Four portions of rice, sweet and sour pork and prawn crackers. Virginia ate a lot, Ella ate as much as she could stomach, and Clara ate hardly anything.

'So, do any of you two have any stories to tell?' Clara asked, bored again.

'Not really,' Ella said.

'I guess not. You're not terribly interesting are you?' Clara said.

'No.' Ella said.

'Well, I wish I could have got stuck with two more interesting people.'

'I wish you could too,' Ella retorted.

Virginia was drunk. She decided she wanted to be interesting. 'I'm a virgin,' she said.

'We'd worked that out,' Clara said, but she smiled almost kindly.

'I had a boyfriend. He was a Christian. He left to study in America. I never heard from him again.'

'Sounds like the best place for him,' Clara said.

'Yes, but I wish I'd, you know, done it before he left me.' The others giggled.

'He wouldn't have been any good. Christians never are,' Clara said.

'You've slept with one?' Virginia asked.

'I have no idea, I don't expect so. If they don't believe in sex before marriage, they're hardly going to sleep with a sex addict,' Clara pointed out.

'I just wish I wasn't such a freak.' Virginia looked sad.

'You're not. Sex isn't everything,' Ella said, not knowing whether to laugh or cry.

'It is to me,' Clara said, before breaking into hysterical laughter.

They left at nine, because Virginia was drunk and Ella needed to get out. Ella gave them Jackie's address and telephone number, telling them they could contact her there. They had arranged to take Sunday off and meet again on Monday.

Chapter Eighteen

The telephone woke Clara. She crawled out of bed to answer it, fighting the panic that engulfed her every morning.

'Hello.' She hoped she didn't sound as bad as she felt. She had stayed up late, taking cocaine and drinking until she passed out. Her flat was a mess and she had a monster headache.

'Clive, it's Toby.'

Clara sighed. 'Hi,' she said.

'Listen, sorry I didn't call you on Friday, but I think we should meet. Can we have a drink?'

'Sure, but why?'

'I'll tell you later. I thought you should know what a certain person said at that meeting we had.'

'OK. Why don't you meet me in Oriel's, next to Sloane Square tube?'

'Fine, I know it. About seven tonight?'

'I'll see you there.' Clara hung up. Then she telephoned Ella and Virginia and told them she had to go out that evening so they should come round at two.

Virginia had spent Sunday hung over. She was getting used to hangovers. They were the only thing in her life that made her normal. She spent the day in bed. Monday morning she went to the library and borrowed a novel about insider trading. She took it home and lay in bed, reading.

By the afternoon, she had an idea of how they could make the plan work. Virginia almost felt proud of herself.

Ella had breakfast with Jackie, who was delighted with the progress they were making.

'What a riot. These girls sound priceless.'

'Bloody hard work, more like. Jackie, what have I let myself in for?'

'Have you got any ideas for the first revenge?'

'Actually I have a great idea. I'm just clueless as to how to make it work.' Ella sipped her tea.

'OK. Here's what you should do. You outline your idea, let the others do the same, if they have any, then watch as it all comes together.' Jackie smiled.

'You really think it will?'

'Of course. Ella, there's a bigger reason why you and those two met. I don't know what it is, but I do know that until you get the plans actioned you won't know either.'

'Is this more hippie shit, Jac?'

'Of course it is. But it is bloody good hippie shit. So do as I say.'

'Where would I be without you?'

'Your life would be so much worse,' Jackie replied.

'Christ, you really think it could get any worse than this?'

Virginia arrived early again. Instead of facing time alone with Clara, she walked around the lush grounds of the flats. It would indeed be a wonderful place to live. When she saw Ella drive up she went to meet her. 'Hi,' she said.

'Hello. I guess we'd better go in.'

Clara opened the door wearing a skimpy top and incredibly tight trousers.

'Nice of you to dress up for us,' Ella said, as she walked in.

'Good God, it's not for you two. I told you, I'm going out later.' Clara smiled, 'How are you Virginia?'

'Fine,' Virginia said, red-faced. Clara shrugged and sat down. She was jittery because she had taken more cocaine than she had intended today. She was worried about her rapidly depleting stock and about seeing Josh.

'You remember telling us on Saturday you were a virgin?' Clara teased.

'Yes,' Virginia replied, blushing.

'Oh, well to be honest, it didn't come as a surprise.' Clara was bitchy again. Ella decided to change the subject and get on with the business they were there for.

'I've had an idea,' Ella said.

'Really?' Virginia felt excited. 'So have I.'

'Well, I haven't so why don't you tell us yours?' Clara said, fiddling with her pen.

'The problem was how we could set up a fake deal and get Isabelle to fall for it, right?' Ella began. The others nodded. She continued, 'Well, I was thinking about a function I attended last month, a women-in-the-City thing, and Isabelle was there. Anyway, I met this woman who was a lawyer, involved in company takeovers and she said to me that the information they were privy to would make your hair curl. So there we have it. First we find a company, then we find a lawyer to plant the idea in Isabelle's mind. It doesn't even have to be a real lawyer, just a convincing actor. We could pay someone.'

'Not bad. In fact I like it', Clara mused. 'So we set her up to meet this lawyer, who lets some information slip and she falls for it.'

'But lawyers aren't allowed to talk and Isabelle isn't stupid, so I was thinking we could produce a document that said X company was being taken over by Y company and arrange somehow for Isabelle to see it. The lawyer would fit in. But we need to get a document. The thing is, money. I don't have much.' Virginia was tomato red.

'Virginia, I think you have something there. Christ, yes! Instead of someone giving her the tip, we make it more official and get a document. But the problem is still the lawyer. We need to make sure she really believes it. Don't worry about the money, we'll keep it minimal.' Ella was getting excited.

'God, *don't* worry about money,' Clara put in. 'I've got plenty. Good idea, Virginia. And I have a contribution to make but I can't tell you until I've checked it out. It'll have to wait for tomorrow. I suggest that you two work out how we're going to get a company and how to get the document to look official. I will figure out how we're going to get the information to Isabelle.' Clara stood up. She wanted to get the others out of her flat so that she could have a large vodka and another line of cocaine without having to sneak into the bathroom.

'But how do we find a company?' Virginia asked.

'There are *loads* of companies,' Clara said.

'But Virginia's right. We need to find a company that's going to go bankrupt. We need a company that's traded on the stock exchange, which means that no one will know if it's going to go bankrupt or not. Christ, every time we get somewhere there's another hurdle.'

'Maybe we should rethink the whole thing,' Virginia said unwillingly.

Clara felt angry. A couple of good ideas were all they had between them. She might have to fill in all the blanks herself, with Josh's help, though he would probably think she was mad.

'Listen, girls, I'll sort out the lawyer and the company. OK?'

'How?' Virginia asked.

'Does it matter? Give me a day or two and I'll fill in the details. I'll call you tomorrow if I have any news so wait in, OK? I guess you know how to get a document forged, Ella.'

'Yes, I do,' Ella said. Clara really was a first-class bitch.

'Then leave it with me. I'll call you tomorrow.'

'OK.' Ella didn't feel confident. They had come up with such a rough framework and Clara was going to fill in the details. Left to her, it might turn out to be a huge mess. She got into her car, waved goodbye to Virginia, and, for the first time since she had been sacked, she made her way to her own flat.

Virginia was equally doubtful. The plan had seemed so easy in her head, but now it seemed impossible. She went home to her lonely bedsit and found a letter waiting on her doorstep. It was from her French teacher, reminding her she had missed the last couple of lessons. Virginia threw it into the bin. She couldn't think about the future right now and she didn't need to speak French. She decided that she would never go again.

Clara had a line of cocaine and a vodka. She knew the others would be pleased with her when she outlined her plan. Josh Lambert, the man who would ensure that she never had a problem getting cocaine, was also a corporate lawyer. As the plan formed in her head, she knew she had been right. Sex was always necessary as part of any plan.

Ella walked into her flat and felt as if she didn't belong there. In fact she had never felt at home there. Her life felt empty; she was empty. She called Jackie. 'Jac, could you use an extra pair of hands tonight?'

'You want to work in the restaurant again?'

'Just tonight. I fancy being busy.'

'Sure, come over. A couple of really cute waiters are starting tonight.'

'I'm there.'

Ella put on a skirt and a pretty top. She looked OK, not great but OK. She brushed her hair, applied makeup and left the house. She took a bus to the restaurant, not wanting to drive. She hadn't told Jackie that she hated her own company.

She waited tables all night, the job she had done when she first moved to London. The restaurant was busy and she was glad of the distraction. After she had cleared the last table, she flopped down opposite Jackie.

'Christ, I'd forgotten how tiring this is.'

'Good, so you won't be asking for a job,' Jackie said.

'Why? Aren't I the best waitress you've ever had?'

'Of course, but it's not for you. Come over if you're lonely, but don't work here, just eat.'

'Deal. Hey, how's the arrangements for college going?'

'Well, the course doesn't start for months so I'm going to start looking for someone to manage this place full-time for me.'

'I could do it,' Ella teased.

'Or you could start college with me.' Jackie got up and went to get a bottle of brandy.

That evening Virginia's mother called her.

'Virginia?'

'Yes, Mother?'

'Where have you been? You haven't phoned us for ages and we were worried.'

'I have some new friends. I've been out a lot.'

'Oh, really? I suppose they're unsuitable types.'

'No.'

'Well, you were never a good judge of character. Anyway, I don't suppose you've got any news so I won't keep you. We do appreciate a call every now and then, you know.'

'Yes, mother. 'Bye.'

Virginia felt angry as she hung up. Everyone treated her like dirt and she let them. Maybe she was as worthless as they all thought. She turned the lights off and sat in the dark, thinking about nothing and panicking about everything.

Clara was twenty minutes late to meet Toby. She had drunk too much, taken more cocaine and couldn't find her keys. She was trying so hard to hold it together but she was nervous about seeing Josh. Especially now that she needed so much from him. Toby was sitting at a table, looking from the door to his watch and nursing a bottle of beer.

'Toby, I'm so sorry I'm late.' Clara kissed him on both cheeks before Toby had a chance to stand up. 'Do you want a drink? Oh, I'll get you one anyway.' Before Toby had a chance to say a word, she had gone to the bar. Returning with a bottle of beer and a vodka and tonic, she sat down opposite him. 'What's up?' she asked.

'Well, it's a bit embarrassing, but Tim claims you slept with Stephen Lock and that's why you were sacked.' He looked hurt and confused. Clara's anger with Tim grew: why did he have to tell the rest of her desk that? Now they all thought she was a slut. Two could play at his game.

'Toby, if I tell you something, will you promise not to tell anyone else?'

'Of course.'

'Well, I didn't sleep with Stephen Lock. I went to dinner with him when Tim couldn't make it. A normal client dinner. But, well, the problem is Tim. When I started working for him he flirted with me. At first it was just fun, nothing serious, but then he became suggestive, kept touching me. He said if I didn't sleep with him my job would be in jeopardy. And, well, it was, wasn't it? He made the whole Stephen thing up but, you see, it was his word against mine. And he threatened to tell my family and, God, they would believe him and there would be a huge scandal, and I just couldn't cope with it. So I left quietly.' A tear ran down her cheek.

Toby had clenched his fists. 'There must be something we can do. He can't get away with that.'

'Tobe, there isn't and I don't want you to jeopardise your job for this. I'm OK. I mean, I miss the job, but I won't be destitute or anything. I want to forget about Tim and the whole mess. I just don't want you to think I'm some sort of tart.'

'I'd never think that. But if there's anything I can do, let me know.'

'I will, Toby, you're a good friend.' Clara wondered if she could use him in any of their plans, and filed him in her head.

They finished their drinks, chatted, and Clara went off to meet Josh.

He was already waiting for her at the Collection, and Clara kissed him warmly. Josh was another man her parents would've been happy for her to marry. In this case, she would have agreed with them. He was divine to look at, tall, well-muscled, dark hair and eyes. Delicious eyes. He was also well spoken, well mannered, successful, friendly, warm and funny. What they didn't know was that he was a serial womaniser but, then, they didn't know about Clara either.

The families had been friends for ages and, for a long time, Josh had seen Clara as an irritating younger sister. When they met again after she left finishing-school, his view of her changed and he pursued her vigorously. They ended up in bed, and embarked on a fling. Clara was ensconced in the life of a party girl and tried not to mind that he worked long hours, hardly had time to see her and still went out with other girls. She did mind terribly, but she always brushed it off by going to another party. It lasted only a month, then Josh stopped calling her and Clara didn't chase him. She didn't feel sad for long: she had a number of other men in tow, including Matt, and she had discovered the joys of cocaine – to which Josh had introduced her.

When Clara saw him, her heart flipped. She would never admit it to herself, but Josh was the love of her life.

'Clara, you look fantastic. How are you, darling?' Josh asked.

Clara sat down. 'Fine. You look fantastic yourself.' Clara decided she needed to flirt as she had never flirted before. It was the only way she could keep the butterflies at bay.

'How's James? I haven't seen him in ages, but he works so hard. God, he never has any time to play. Tell him to call me,' Josh said.

'He's fine, but you're right, he does work hard and he wouldn't be pleased if he knew I was with you. He thinks you broke my heart.' Clara giggled.

'And did I?' Josh's eyes twinkled.

'No one breaks *my* heart.' They both laughed. Josh summoned the waiter and asked for a bottle of champagne. When it arrived, they toasted 'old friends'.

'God, Clara, you are so gorgeous. I should never have let you go.'

'No, you shouldn't.' Clara had seen Josh at a couple of parties recently with a tall, skinny, blonde woman. She wondered if he had anyone special.

'I know. My mother always asks after you. Anyway, I was a bit too much of a playboy for you. You deserved better. Is there anyone in your life?' His voice was calm but his eyes betrayed his interest.

'No one special, although I'm not short of admirers. Anyway, I did deserve someone better, although no one came along.' Clara smiled. She felt thirteen again – and told herself to pull herself together: she needed Josh for her other tasks. He had hurt her once, he wouldn't hurt her again.

'I bet. Anyway, what was the emergency situation you needed me for?' Josh looked and acted like a lawyer now.

'It's a bit delicate. I need a dealer.' Clara spoke quietly, and she put her head close to him so she almost passed out.

'For cocaine?' Josh murmured. Clara nodded. He pulled out a pen and a piece of paper and started writing. 'Here's the number. He's the son of a peer. Nice chap and he gets great stuff, is reliable and lives in Camden. I'll tell him you'll be calling and he'll be fine.' He handed Clara the scrap of paper.

Clara read the number and her eyes lit up. 'Josh, you're a star, thank you.' She kissed his cheek.

'No problem. If you ever have any trouble with him, call me, OK?'

'OK. It's reassuring to know I can still call you. I've had a bit of a hard time lately. Mind you I'm putting that behind me. How much do you use?'

'Too much, but only to take away the boredom at parties,

never during the day and never when I have sex. Well, not too much anyway – it can stop me performing.'

'I didn't think anything could stop you performing.' Clara shivered as she remembered his amazing sexual technique.

'So, what's up? What problems have you had?'

'It's just, well, James doesn't know about any of this and I'm determined not to let him find out. You won't say anything, will you?'

'Of course not. Clara, tell me.'

She thought for a minute, weighed up the gamble she was taking and made a decision. 'I will, but first I need to go to the loo.' She stood up.

'You may want to take this with you,' Josh replied, handing her a wrap of cocaine before she went.

When she returned her mind was made up. Josh was the only hope she had for the Isabelle plan to work. He was also pulling on her heartstrings and she didn't know why. She felt vulnerable, and she couldn't cope with it. She had to get him to do this for her as well as for the others.

'You know I was working at SFH?' she said. Josh nodded. 'Well, I was doing OK there, but, you see, I was ... well, I was sleeping with my boss.'

'Christ, Clara, that's a bit clichéd for you, isn't it?' Josh wasn't laughing.

'I know. It didn't happen for long. He chased me, and he made me feel good for a while. I didn't feel very wanted after you stopped calling. Anyway, this isn't your fault. But then he got jealous and he told me he was going to leave his wife and move in with me but I had to resign from SFH. I refused. He got me sacked. End of story.'

'That's outrageous! You could do him for wrongful dismissal, sexual harassment, everything.'

'Yes, I know, but then James and my parents would find out. God, I couldn't cope with that. It's total tabloid sleaze and I can't put my family through it.'

'No, no, of course you can't.'

'Anyway, that's only my story. After I was sacked, I walked into the nearest pub. And in there were two girls I recognised from SFH, one was a secretary, the other a trader, and they'd both been sacked too.'

'What for?' Josh was interested.

'Various things, but although their dismissal was kind of fair, it was unfair, if you can understand that. Other people were instrumental in getting them sacked, like with me.' Clara lit a cigarette and drank some champagne.

'It all sounds a bit weird.'

'I know, it's bizarre — I mean, who would believe it? Three girls all sacked for things that meant they couldn't appeal — well, apart from me. But three different people led to this and those people should pay.'

'What are you getting at, Clara?'

'We're going to make them sorry. We're going to make them wish they had never messed with us in the first place. Of course, what we'll do is going to be legal, but they'll be destroyed, just as they destroyed us.' Clara was animated.

Josh reached over and took her hand. 'Baby, I had no idea. And you're right, they should pay. But are you sure you know what you're getting into? Shit, Clara, what a mess.' Clara nodded. Inside she knew what she wanted him to do, but he had enough information for now. The rest she'd save for pillow talk.

'Are you hungry? I'm famished,' Clara said.

'Great. We'll eat here, shall we?' Josh motioned for a menu. Clara felt like she had done a great job, and for the first time, she hadn't just done it for herself.

She wanted Josh. She knew it, but wouldn't admit it. She needed him, not his dealer, but she couldn't let herself feel like that. He might hurt her. He might be the only man who could hurt her. She didn't know what she could do about that, but she had to get him to help with Isabelle. She would sort her feelings out later. At that moment the plan was the most important thing.

After dinner, she went back to Josh's flat in the Chelsea Harbour complex, which reminded Clara of a hotel. When they'd been together previously he had never invited her there; they had always gone back to Clara's. She felt uneasy: the flat was functional, with a great view of the river, and it was definitely the place for a rich playboy. The décor was minimal, and there were no clues to his life in the sitting room, the kitchen or the bathroom.

When they kissed, though, she forgot everything. They took one more line of cocaine and she didn't notice how little she'd had that evening. They talked some more and kissed again. Sex hung in the air, but for once she was in no hurry. By the time they went to bed, Clara was fighting hard to keep her mind on her objective.

Afterwards she lay in his arms feeling safe and wonderful. She had to remind herself that she'd felt like that before and she hadn't been safe.

'Can we try again?' Josh asked. 'I mean really try this time. The two of us in a relationship. No one else, just me and you.' His voice was tender.

'Why, Josh? I mean, you say you want that, but last time you didn't. What's changed?'

'I have. I've grown up. I'm tired of airhead girls and you aren't an airhead. I'm sure you're quite mad, but you're lovely and clever and you have your own mind. I've missed you. I didn't know it until now, but I have.' Clara snuggled into his arms. She wanted to believe him, she really did, but she couldn't let herself. Her heart had been broken before. The parties, the cocaine, the job, Tim – although she couldn't hold Josh responsible for all of it, he had triggered it, and she knew that if she let him hurt her again, she might never recover.

'Josh, I really want to believe you, but because I've been messed around – or I've messed around – my life is a huge pile of shit. I need to do this revenge thing. I need to know that I wasn't fired in vain and I'm not sure I'm ready to take the risk of falling for you when I'm in the midst of all this.'

'So you haven't fallen for me already?' He looked hurt.

'I don't know, Josh. You're such a divine creature, and I've had an imaginary love affair with you since I was a kid. I'm not ready to try the real thing yet, not after last time.'

'OK. I'll prove I'm serious. What would it take to convince you?' Clara smiled at him; he sounded so sincere. However, he was probably just like Tim and all the others. He wanted her in bed, but he didn't want *her*. No one wanted her. She had an idea, and if it worked, she would at least be able to get Isabelle. If it didn't then she had only lost him again. She couldn't feel any lonelier than she already did.

'I want you to sleep with someone else.' Clara spoke so calmly it took a couple of seconds for the words to sink in. When they did, Josh sat upright.

'What? Are you fucking insane?'

'Probably, yes. But this is the most important thing right now. If I can help them get Isabelle, then they'll help me get Tim. Don't you see?'

'No, I don't, but I expect you're going to tell me anyway.'

'Isabelle is a manager. She's attractive, rich, successful and hungry for power. Virginia is this poor, boring creature, never had sex, probably never will. I mean, she's so boring who would want her? Anyway, although I don't like her I feel sorry for her, and I don't feel sorry for Isabelle, who's just the female equivalent of Tim.'

'Clara, you're babbling. I haven't a clue what you're talking about.'

'Josh, please, listen. Isabelle is a bitch. She chewed up this girl and spat her out. She deserves the same.' Clara outlined their plan. When she'd finished she looked at Josh pleadingly.

He sat in silence, making Clara feel nervous. Eventually he spoke: 'Very clever. The theory is sound – the share value will be low, it'll go up dramatically when people start buying, she'll think she's a hero, until the truth emerges and the company goes bust. Right?'

'Yes, that's right.' Clara said.

'Do you really think it'll work?'

'Well, I wasn't sure at first, but I know that it has to. Ella has some contacts who can forge anything, so getting a document to look authentic should be easy. But I don't know how we're going to find a company, which is one problem, and getting the information to Isabelle is another. But otherwise how can it fail?'

Josh couldn't help smiling. 'I can't believe you're doing this. I don't know if you're mad or brave or what. But where do I come in and why do you want me to sleep with someone else?'

'First, I thought you might be able to help us find a company. I know you lawyers take oaths and things, but if there's a company that's going down the tubes anyway you could let me find the information. If it works, there's no way they'll trace it back to us. If Isabelle screws up she'll never have the nerve to point the finger, especially if we make it that she steals the information. That's why you have to sleep with her. We need to ensure that Isabelle thinks the information is reliable. If she sleeps with someone who is a corporate lawyer and finds the information in his flat, she's sure to take the bait.' They sat in silence for a few moments.

'So I have to sleep with the bad guy?' Josh asked. Clara nodded. 'Fuck, Clara, I've just told you I want *you*, and you tell me to sleep with some horrible woman who upset your friend.'

'She's not my friend. Anyway, if you're serious about me you'll do it.' Clara pouted.

'No, I won't. If I want to be with you, I'll tell you to get some other guy to sleep with her because I only want to sleep with you. You are fucking mad. What if I agree to find you a company? That information is quite easy to come by and you can get someone else to sleep with her.'

'Josh, I can't trust anyone else to do this. It's just sex, you know. I was thinking you should take her out once, and whet her appetite by telling her how much insider information you get about takeovers. How much money you could get and so on. Then take her out again, take her back to your place, and leave a document on the coffee table. You only have to give her a bit of sex. Just once. And you never have to see her again.'

'Why do I have to have sex with her at all?'

'Because then she'll think she's been lucky finding the information. Otherwise it may look like a plant.'

'It *is* a plant. Clara, you don't want me to do this. You don't want me to sleep with anyone else.'

He was right, she didn't. But she knew he had to. Josh was their only hope. Without him, the plan would fail and then Tim and Johnny would get away scot-free. She had entered into this with a determination to see it through, and if Josh wanted her, he had to do this for her.

'I do. If you're serious about showing some kind of commitment to me then you'll do it.' She knew her logic was flawed, but she didn't care.

'I need some sleep, Clara. We'll talk about this later.' He kissed her tenderly then turned over, and Clara knew she'd won. If she lost Josh in the process, it was only part of a pattern. He would probably dump her again anyway. If he did this for her then maybe, just maybe, there would be a future for them.

She awoke the next day to find the bed empty. A note lay on the pillow. It read: 'You win. I'll prove that I'd do anything for you. I'll do this. Speak later. Love, Josh.' There was even a row of kisses. Clara punched the air with her fist. She could almost feel the impending victory.

Chapter Nineteen

By the time she got back to her flat, the answerphone light was flashing. She played the messages: one from her brother, wanting to take her to dinner, and one from Josh, asking her to call him.

'Josh, it's Clara.'

'Hi, darling, how are you?'

'Fine, you?'

'I'm OK, although I'm still shell-shocked. What you said last night, did you mean it?'

'Did you mean what *you* said?'

'About us? Yes, I did. I haven't stopped thinking about you.'

'Then so did I.'

'OK, here goes. If I'm sacked because of you, you have to agree to marry me.'

Clara blushed. 'Fine.'

'JF Technologies is the company you want. Stock has fallen dramatically. Bad management is destroying it. A friend of mine was called in to try to save it, but it's beyond saving. It has a lifespan of about a month, maybe less, so you need to act quickly.'

'You are fantastic.'

'What about the next bit?'

'I'll let you know. Josh, would you like to see me tomorrow night?'

'You know I would.'

'Then come round here and I'll cook you dinner.'

'See you at eight, then. 'Bye, darling.' Clara felt like crying every time he called her 'darling'. She had forgotten that she couldn't cook.

She called the others and summoned them. Then she made fresh coffee and ran to the shop to buy some pastries.

When the others arrived, Virginia first, Ella second, they were surprised to see food and fresh coffee.

'Have I come to the right flat?' Ella asked, and Virginia giggled despite the gloom that seemed to be eating her alive.

'We're celebrating.'

'What?' Virginia asked, sitting down. Ella helped herself to a pastry.

'Our first successful plan,' Clara said triumphantly.

'Go on,' Ella urged.

'Well, my friend is a corporate lawyer. His name is Josh and he's very successful and gorgeous. He has given us the perfect company to use. JF Technologies. Apparently it's about to go bust. And he's going to seduce Isabelle and ensure she sees the document.' Virginia and Ella were both dumbstruck.

'Really he is. You two should draft a document and get your forgers to make it up. Maybe we could say that Microsoft is interested in buying it or something.'

'Clara, you're a star,' Ella conceded.

'I know. And we need to move quickly. Josh needs to get into your fitness club. Can you get him a guest pass? Also, do you know when Isabelle plays squash?'

'Wednesday and Friday evenings at seven. That's when she always plays,' Virginia put in, excited now.

After the initial elation, caution returned. 'Why is he doing this?' Ella asked.

'Because he believes in what we're doing. I told him

everything – well, almost everything – and he cares about me and he wants to help.'

'Really?' Ella wasn't convinced.

'Yes, really,' Clara said.

'So you didn't sleep with him?' Ella said.

Clara resented this. 'My relationship with Josh has nothing to do with you.'

'So you did, then.' Ella laughed. 'Christ, at least you're putting your sex addiction to good use.'

'It's not like that,' Clara said.

'Oh? How is it, then?' Ella asked.

'I really like him.' They were all silent.

Eventually Ella said, 'Sorry, I don't understand. You really like this guy, yet you're getting him to seduce someone else. Are you mad?'

'That's what he said. I can't expect you two to understand.' For the first time Clara seemed unsure of herself.

'Try us.' Ella was bemused by the situation.

'Because he hurt me before. I've known him for ever and I had a crush on him when I was at school. Then when I was twenty we dated for a while. But he saw other girls too and he stopped calling me.'

'I guess not many men do that to you, do they?' Ella said.

'No, they don't. And it hurt. I threw myself into my party life and I met other men and I started taking cocaine and now I don't know if I can believe him when he says he wants me.'

'Clara, tell me you're not testing him with this,' Ella said

'I am.'

'Christ, you're mad. He likes you. You can't put him or you through this. You might lose him.'

'I'll lose him anyway,' Clara answered.

'Why?' Ella looked at Clara, and saw vulnerability for the first time.

'Because everyone I love becomes disappointed in me eventually. He won't want me for ever and he'll probably hurt me even more. If he does this, at least we get one of our plans under way before that happens.'

'Christ, Clara, you're fucked up.'

'So are you.' Suddenly Clara remembered who she was talking to.

'Maybe, but at least I'm not trying to destroy a relationship with someone I like.'

'That's because you're too cold to like anyone.'

'That's not true.'

'It is.'

'No, it fucking isn't.'

'Whatever. I knew you wouldn't understand.'

'You know something? I do understand. I just think it's wrong.'

'Do you want to get Isabelle or not?'

'Yes, of course.'

'Well, shut the fuck up.' Clara poured more coffee and lit another cigarette.

'What about the cocaine?' Virginia spoke for the first time.

'What about it?' Clara was not pacified.

'Do you still take it?'

'Yes, Miss Tight-knickers, I do. For relaxation, that's all. Christ, can you two just give me a break? I thought you'd be pleased.'

'But . . .'

Ella put a restraining hand on Virginia's arm. She promptly shut up. 'We are pleased. Well done, Clara. But before we put this document together, what can you tell me about JF Technologies?'

'It's a technology company, and the share price is rock bottom,' Clara said.

'OK. But is that all? What do they do?'

'Technology things,' Clara said, irritated.

Ella rolled her eyes. 'I'm going to call them and find out.

We can't write a realistic document if we don't know anything about the company.' Ella walked off to use the telephone.

When Ella had collected more information, she and Virginia worked on the report for several hours. By the time they had finished it sounded realistic enough for them almost to believe it themselves.

'This is great. Fantastic. I just know it's going to work.' Virginia had perked up.

'Clara, let's get a bottle of champagne – you know, to celebrate,' Ella suggested.

Virginia and Clara nearly fell off their chairs at Ella's unexpected burst of enthusiasm.

'I've got one in the fridge.' Clara smiled. She went for the bottle via the bathroom.

'How do we get this to your guys?' Virginia asked.

'I'll fax it tomorrow and they'll get it back to me in a couple of days.' Ella had already made the arrangements for the forgery.

'How much will it cost?' Virginia asked.

'Don't worry, it's on me.' Ella said.

'Thanks.'

'No problem.' Ella couldn't figure out why she was being so nice, but she felt nice.

Clara returned with the champagne and white powder stuck to the end of her nose. The other two tried to ignore it. 'What about timing?' she asked.

'OK. We get the document back in a couple of days. Can we arrange for Josh to meet Isabelle at the club on Friday?' Ella said.

'Don't see why not. You'll have to go to ensure that they meet,' Clara said.

'Why me?'

'Because I don't want to see the man I like seducing someone else. You won't have that problem and you know Virginia can't go. You need to make sure that Isabelle doesn't see you and Josh together. If she does she might get suspicious.'

'OK. Fair point. I haven't been to the place since you-know-when and I'll try to make sure she doesn't see me. I'll point her out to Josh and he can speak to her. Maybe he should ask her for a game of squash. If he asks her out straight away, it'll sound obvious.'

'Yeah, that should work.'

'Can Josh play squash?' Virginia asked.

'I haven't a clue. I'll call him.'

Ella lit a cigarette. She had never thought that so much detail would be involved in the plans.

Clara came back and announced he was a good squash player. Again, they relaxed.

'Clara, if this messes up your relationship, then I'm sorry,' Virginia said.

Clara looked at her. 'It won't. I would have messed it up anyway.'

'Clara, I think you and Josh will work out,' Ella said.

'What makes you say that?' Clara asked.

'Just a feeling.' Ella was beginning to sound like Jackie.

'Shit!' Clara screamed.

'What?' Virginia asked.

'I invited him round to dinner tomorrow night.'

'So?' Ella asked.

'I can't fucking cook,' Clara said. The others burst out laughing.

'It's not funny! I said I'd make him dinner – I can't give him a takeaway.' Clara was stricken.

'It's OK. I'll cook for you,' Virginia offered.

'Really? *Can* you cook?' Clara asked.

'I'm not bad. Have you got any recipe books?' Clara shook her head.

'Look, as a thank-you for what you've arranged for Isabelle, how about I come round tomorrow morning and we'll go shopping? Then I'll help you to make it perfect.' Virginia was red but she was holding herself together.

'Virginia, you're a star. You can cook something fantastic and we can put the finishing touches to the plan together. In a couple of weeks, phase one might be complete.'

Chapter Twenty

As Clara and Virginia pushed a trolley around the supermarket, they looked an odd couple. Virginia was wearing her usual uniform of jeans and a patterned jumper. Her short hair sat on her head like a hat and her awkward movements made her look as if she was still at school. Clara was wearing tight black trousers and a cropped pale blue cashmere jumper. A pair of designer sunglasses sat on her head and she clipped around the supermarket in high-heeled suede boots.

'Where do you buy your clothes?' Clara asked, as Virginia piled fresh vegetables and herbs into the trolley.

'What?' Virginia blushed.

'You should think about updating your wardrobe. I'll help,' Clara offered.

'Thanks, but I don't have money for clothes.'

'Well, what *do* you spend it on? You don't do anything.'

'I just lost my job, in case you'd forgotten.' Virginia moved on to the meat counter.

'I hadn't. I just wondered why you only seem to have one pair of out-of-date jeans and a number of horrific sweaters.' Clara now knew why she never went to supermarkets: she was bored out of her mind.

'Does he eat lamb?'

'I don't know. I guess so.'

Virginia picked out a joint.

'What are you going to cook? By the looks of my trolley not pasta and sauce.'

'Lamb with rosemary and a mint sauce, baby new potatoes and baby vegetables. That'll be the main course. For starters, you're having fresh watercress soup. For dessert, cheese. OK?'

'Well, it all sounds a bit ordinary, doesn't it?'

'Yes, but he's a man and men like roasts. And you can't cook so if I produce something complicated you'll be stuck for ever. Roasts are simple, but done well they're delicious. And don't forget, I'll cook the meal but I can't stay to dish it up. I'll leave you the instructions.'

'Good point. God, Virginia, where did you learn about men?'

'From Noël. He loved my roasts. And this isn't the sort of Sunday-dinner roast. This is a nice roast. The meat will be sliced thinly and decorated with herbs. And I'll make the soup.'

'OK. Sounds good, not that I eat much anyway. So Noël, he was the ex, was he?'

'Yes.'

'The Bible-bashing virgin who liked roasts.'

'Yes.' Virginia did her best not to get upset by Clara.

'Was he good-looking?'

'He was all right. He was tall and slim with dark hair, but he had glasses on which were always too big for his face.' Virginia had often wanted to tell Noël he should get new glasses but had never found the words.

'Sounds divine. It's probably a good job you didn't sleep with him. Did you do other things?'

'Like what?'

'You know handjobs, blowjobs and pussy-licking. That sort of thing.'

'None of your business.' Virginia blushed and Clara laughed.

'OK, let's go get some booze.'

When the trolley was stacked high with wine and champagne, they finally made their way to the checkout.

'Do you have a loyalty card?' The girl at the checkout asked Clara as she handed over her credit card.

'I don't do supermarkets,' Clara replied. The girl looked at Virginia who shrugged.

Back at the flat, Virginia started to make the soup and Clara sat on the sofa reading a magazine. That was how Ella found them.

'I see you've got her slaving in the kitchen,' Ella said.

'She offered,' Clara replied.

'I know, but you could help.'

'I went to the bloody supermarket, didn't I?'

Ella sat down. 'I faxed the document and it'll be ready in a day or two. We probably won't have it for Josh's first meeting with Isabelle, but that's just the introduction, isn't it?'

'Yes, that's fine. I'll make sure Josh knows what he has to do over dinner tonight. You'll meet him on Friday.'

Virginia appeared. 'Everything's under control,' she announced.

'She's so fucking organised,' Clara groaned.

'You OK?' Ella asked. Virginia nodded. 'So, what now?'

'Well, my cleaner must be sick because she hasn't been this week. I don't suppose you two could help me get this place clean, could you?' Clara suggested.

Ella looked sharply at Clara. She was the type of person who always got everyone else to do things for her. However, she had come through with the details for the plan that had eluded Ella. She felt she owed her.

'Sure,' they both said.

Ella was helping Clara clean the bedroom when she came across a vanity case filled with wraps of white powder.

'Your coke stash, I take it,' Ella said.

Clara snatched it off her.

'How much have you got in there?'

'Look, I don't take that much. Tim gave me most of this.'

'So he gave you cocaine as well as everything else.'

'I think he thought that if he kept me high I wouldn't be able to work.'

'Really?'

'When I started working hard, he gave me more and more coke.'

'How much do you use?'

'Not much.'

'Really?' Ella raised an eyebrow.

'Yes, really. Now, how do you put a duvet cover on?'

The flat was cleaned, the dinner was cooking and Virginia wrote out instructions for Clara before they left. 'Have fun,' she said, and Clara watched them go.

'I suppose one of us has to,' Ella said, feeling lonely.

'Ella,' Virginia said.

'Yes?'

'What are you doing now?'

'Going home, I guess.'

'I don't suppose you want some company. It's just that, well, being alone is hard at the moment.' Virginia was nervous about saying what she felt, but she finished the sentence.

'I tell you what, come to mine and we'll have pasta for dinner. Not quite the feast you whipped up for the queen in there, but it's better than nothing.' Ella was torn between wanting to reach out to Virginia and wanting to push her away. She felt sorry for her, but she didn't particularly like her. However, she didn't particularly like herself.

'Thanks,' Virginia said.

They sat in Ella's living room drinking red wine.

'This is a great flat,' Virginia said.

'I know, but it's so big,' Ella said apologetically.

'Compared to my shoebox.'

'Compared to most flats in London. Great views, though.

Look.' Ella led Virginia over to the window from where she could see the river all lit up.

'It's lovely,' Virginia said.

'I know, but it's so City. Shall I tell you something?' Virginia nodded. 'When I got this job, I tried so hard to become a stereotype – I guess I thought it would stop people finding out. I bought this with my second bonus. I'd already bought the fast car and a wardrobe of pinstripe suits. I worked out in the gym with a trainer recommended to me by the HR woman. I mean, how sad is that?'

'You wanted to fit in,' Virginia said.

'I certainly did. But you know what everyone thinks about the City? They think it's full of pinstripes and Porsches. But it's more than that. I loved the atmosphere, the buzz, the sheer excitement of making money, the frustration of losing it. It was more than fitting in. I took that to extremes, but I loved my job.'

'I know,' Virginia said.

'How?' Ella asked.

'I can hear it in your voice. I hated my job, and you know why. But I was about to get a job as a salesperson, my lifelong ambition. I wanted it for the same reasons you did, but I didn't get it. Well, I nearly did, but I guess that doesn't count, does it?'

'It does. I don't know how we can have something in common, but I guess we just found it.'

'I know you think I'm boring. I think so too,' Virginia said.

'I don't,' Ella said, but not convincingly.

'Never be a lawyer, Ella, you're no good at lying.'

'Virginia, was that almost a joke you cracked there?' They both laughed and went to make food.

By the time Virginia went home, she felt a lot better. And, for reasons she would never be able to explain, so did Ella.

* * *

Clara decided she loved Virginia. The food smelt divine and her step-by-step guide put Delia Smith to shame. When Josh turned up, Clara had changed into a sexy dress, she had put on her best underwear and had had a couple of lines of cocaine with a large vodka. She felt like a Girl Guide: she was prepared.

When Josh arrived, she almost fell apart just looking at him. She pulled herself together. 'I hope you're hungry,' she said, as he kissed her.

'Starving,' he replied, and pinched her bottom.

'Sit,' she commanded, and went to get the champagne. 'How did you find that company so quickly?' she asked, as she poured it into two glasses.

'Luck. My friend was talking about it in the office that morning. He'll go mad if he knows I've told you, but I thought it through and I don't see how anyone can ever find out.'

'Of course they won't. And if they do I'll tell them I seduced it out of you.'

'The judge would probably believe that. I should have held out for more seducing.'

'I'm cooking you dinner, aren't I?'

'Yes, I was rather surprised. What are we having?'

'Wait and see.' Clara couldn't resist kissing his champagne lips before they sat at the dining-table.

Ella had set the table saying that she had been a waitress in a past life. She had made it look lovely with candles and flowers.

'I'm impressed. You make better girlfriend material every second,' Josh said, tasting the soup. 'God, this is divine. How did you make it?'

'Secret recipe.' Clara blushed. Josh was about the only person who could make her blush.

'I'll drink to that.' They had white wine with the soup, red wine with the main course, and although Clara didn't eat much, Josh devoured it all. After cheese then more champagne, they settled together on the sofa.

'I need to talk more about the plan,' Clara said.

'You haven't decided to abandon phase two?'

'No, you said you'd do this, Josh, you have to.'

'OK. You win, I'll do it.' Josh was still smiling, but he was confused. He hadn't expected to fall for Clara so heavily, but he had the minute he saw her again. He had been a bit tired of her before: she loved partying and she was so silly and immature. At the same time, he was going through women like they were about to go out of fashion. No one had held his interest for long, but now Clara seemed more grown-up and even more beautiful.

'You're going to Ella's fitness club on Friday with Ella. She'll point Isabelle out. You need to talk to her at some point, so look sexy. She'll be playing squash and you should ask her if she'd like a game with you some time. Then you arrange it. That's all you need to do at this stage.'

'Right, even I can manage that. What if she tells me to piss off?'

'Josh, has a woman ever told you to piss off?'

'No.'

'Well, then. After you play squash you ask her to dinner and then you get her back to your flat. Don't forget to talk about your work all night, tell her how much information you're privy to. But we can discuss that nearer the time. I can't decide whether you should have two dates with her or just one. Um, what do you think?'

'Whatever. Clara, can we talk about us now?'

'No, but you can kiss me.' Clara never felt this good with any other man.

Josh wanted her to stop playing games and admit that she felt the way he did. He knew she would and he would wait. She was worth it.

Chapter Twenty-one

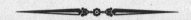

Virginia woke the next morning and did what she had been putting off. She wrote a letter to her parents and another to Susie, her penfriend, explaining what had happened. In Susie's letter she kept the details brief. She told her that the e-mails would have to stop for now, but she promised to be in touch when she sorted herself out. She didn't want Susie to respond, partly because she knew that for the first time in their relationship Susie wouldn't understand, and also because Susie's life was normal and hers was anything but. Her parents' letter was more difficult. For once, she wrote everything, Isabelle, the fateful order, the new job, and she tried to convey the unfairness of the situation. She knew what their response would be, but she hoped deep down that they might be just a tiny bit sympathetic. She vowed that if she were ever a parent, she would always be proud of her children.

She hadn't arranged to meet the others that day – they were all having a day off – and she was unsure of how to fill the hours. She felt the emptiness of losing her job even more. Although she felt closer to Ella, she was almost glad of a break from Clara. Her sniping hurt, and she knew she should fight back like Ella did, but she didn't know how. Virginia just took everything thrown at her.

*   *   *

Ella woke up and went for a run. She found that now she didn't go to the gym she missed the exercise. She ran along the river and back, picking up a copy of the *Financial Times*. As she read, she felt pangs of regret and sadness. After her shower, she settled down with a cup of tea and her latest romantic novel.

Clara woke at midday to find another note from Josh on the pillow next to hers. She smiled at the memory of last night then tried to put it out of her mind. She took a shower, dressed and made some coffee. She sat thinking about Josh for most of the afternoon. At four the telephone rang and interrupted her daydreams.

'Hello.'

'Clara, it's me.'

Clara's heart fell a million miles. 'Tim?' she whispered.

'Yes, of course. Clara, I need to talk to you.'

'So talk.'

'I need to see you,' Tim said.

Clara took a deep breath. 'Need all you want. Either talk to me over the phone or fuck off.'

'OK, I didn't expect you to welcome me with open arms but, Clara, remember what we had together. I miss you.'

'Really? What a shame.'

'I need to see you. Look, we can start over. If you don't want me to leave my wife I won't, but I want to be with you. Remember how good it was.'

Clara was fuming. She did not remember how good it was at all, she remembered how awful, degrading and humiliating it had been. As she clutched the telephone to her ear, she thought back to the last time they'd had sex, how Tim had had sex, and she felt sick at the memory. 'It can't start up again, Tim. I don't want you. You got me sacked, you ruined my life, you can't walk back in and expect me to forgive you.' She tried to sound calm but she wasn't.

'Can't I? No, of course I can't. But can we meet? Just to talk?' Clara wanted to tell him to go fuck himself, but she thought about the plan and she didn't know what she should do. She needed help. The only people she could ask were Virginia and Ella.

'Tim, I need time to think. I'll call you.' She hung up before he could say any more.

Clara was furious. 'How dare the little fucker call me?' she asked herself repeatedly. She had no answers. She picked up the telephone.

'Ella? It's Clara. I need you to come over, please. I don't know what to do.' She burst into tears.

'Clara, what's happened?' She was answered in sobs. 'Is it Josh?'

'No.' Clara gulped. 'It's Tim.'

'*Tim?*' Ella almost shouted.

'He called me. Please come. Bring Virginia.' She put the telephone down, still sobbing.

Ella called Virginia and went over to pick her up. Then she drove as fast as the London traffic would allow to Clara's flat. Clara opened the door with red eyes and tissue stuck to her face.

'Shit, Clara, sit down. Tell me what happened,' Ella commanded. Virginia hesitated by the door of the sitting room.

'He called. He told me he missed me and he said we could start again.'

'What a wanker. What did you say?'

'That he ruined my life and we couldn't start again. Then he asked if we could meet and I said I'd think about it.'

Virginia sat down. 'Why didn't you tell him to piss off?' she asked.

'Because although I wanted to, I thought the plan for him might be easier if we were in contact. Although I never,

ever want to see him again. I don't have to, do I?' She looked at Ella.

'No, you don't. Christ what a prick. Clara, don't let him upset you.'

'He didn't,' Clara said.

'You seem upset to me.'

'I am, but it just hit me. Talking to him hit me. I lost my job, I screwed around and I screwed up. I miss it – I miss the City, I really do.' She started crying again.

'So do we, Clara. Virginia and I were saying last night how much we missed it.'

'It was amazing. Walking across the trading floor, hearing the buzz, almost feeling the money being made. I loved it,' Clara said.

'So did we,' Virginia said, and she started crying too. For a while they all sat there in silence, apart from the odd sob from Virginia and Clara.

After a while, Ella spoke. 'Well, I guess now we *all* have something in common.'

They sat together for ages until Ella could stand it no more. 'Look, as we have no more planning to do today, why don't we get drunk?'

'I'll drink to that.' Clara giggled.

'Oh, God, I feel another hangover coming on,' Virginia said, and they all started laughing.

'I've got just the thing,' Clara said, getting up and walking to what looked like a cupboard but was really her drinks stash. She came back with a bottle of tequila and three shot glasses.

'I have never known anyone to keep so much alcohol in their flat,' Ella said.

'I'm not sure I can drink tequila,' Virginia said.

'You'll be fine. If you pass out you can use one of my spare rooms.' Clara poured the first shot. 'I should really get lemon and salt, but I can't be bothered.' They all downed it.

Virginia nearly choked. 'That's strong,' she said.

'It gets easier, just like sex.' Clara refilled their glasses. 'I know. We'll ask each other questions and we have to give honest answers. Like truth or dare, without the option of dares.'

'I'm not sure.' Ella felt hesitant.

'Ella, I know you have secrets and I intend to find them out.' Clara waggled her finger at Ella. 'First, I need the bathroom.' She made one of her routine trips. When she returned, she said, 'OK, boyfriends. Each of us has to talk about our most serious boyfriend.'

'You start, Clara, it's your game,' Ella said, downing the second drink. The others followed suit.

'I don't think I've ever had one. When I was at school I was with a number of boys, but always more than one at a time. Then I went to finishing-school and graduated to ski instructors. When I came back I was with Josh, and then I went back to seeing a number of men, none of whom can count as boyfriends. Then Tim.'

'So you've never had a boyfriend,' Ella said.

'Wow, I guess I haven't. Even now Josh isn't really my boyfriend because I've only seen him twice and I'm making him sleep with Isabelle. That doesn't really count as a boyfriend, does it?'

'No,' Ella said. 'Virginia, you next.'

'You know about mine. Noël the Bible basher, as Clara calls him. He was my first boyfriend and my last. We were together for one year and I worshipped the ground he walked on.'

'Did you?' Clara asked. 'Why?'

'I don't know. Because he kissed me, I suppose. No one had wanted to kiss me before – or since.' Virginia looked sad.

'They will,' Ella said.

'Sure they will. You're not bad-looking even if you should be arrested by the fashion police.'

'Clara . . .' Ella said, sternly.

'No, really. She's pretty. You have great eyes, you're tall

248

and slim. With a bit of makeup, your hair restyled and a new wardrobe you could look stunning.'

'Do you really think so?' Virginia asked.

'Yes, I do. Now, Ella, what about you?'

'I was engaged.'

'Wow,' Virginia said.

'Yeah, I was. In Manchester where I grew up. I dated this man when I was seventeen, we were engaged when I was twenty and I left when I was twenty-two. That's when I moved to London.'

'When did you start working at SFH?' Virginia asked.

'When I was twenty-three. I'd been there for years.'

'But what about the guy? Why did you leave him?' Clara asked.

'That's not the question. Another drink?' Ella poured the third drink and refused to say any more.

'OK, another question. Virginia, ask a question.' Clara said.

Virginia's mind went blank. She wished she could think of a great question, but she couldn't. 'Um. I don't know. Did you go out with anyone at SFH?' It was the best she could do.

'Well, you know I went out with Tim, but I also slept with this guy called Toby on my desk. It was my sex addiction, you know.'

'Well, I didn't,' Ella said.

'Me neither,' Virginia blushed.

'Oh, great question, Virginia. Ella, your turn.' Clara poured more drinks.

'Let me think. Has anyone here slept with a woman?' Ella giggled.

'I have,' Clara said.

'Who?' Virginia's eyes were wide.

'At boarding-school. Everyone was experimenting. Have you, Virginia?' Clara smiled at her, knowing the answer.

'No.'

'I did, someone in London, but that's all you're getting out of me,' Ella said.

'Fuck, Ella, you are full of surprises. Engaged, then a lesbian tryst. Wow.' Clara went to the bathroom again. Ella didn't know why she had told them that. She had slept with another waitress from Jackie's restaurant, only once and that was out of loneliness. She had found out that she definitely preferred men.

When Clara returned she brought a wrap with her. 'Now, you know I take cocaine, so I don't need to keep going to the bathroom. Would anyone else care for some?' Ella shook her head, much to Virginia's relief.

'This drink is really strong,' Virginia said, after their next shot.

'You already said that,' Clara pointed out.

'Sorry. I don't drink much usually.'

'Virginia, do you have any friends in London?' Clara asked.

'No.'

'Me neither. I mean, I have James, my brother, who is the person I love most in the world, and I have a number of men I can call on to take me out, but I don't really have any friends. Not one good girlfriend anyway.'

'I've got a friend called Jackie who's brilliant,' Ella said.

'Is she the one you slept with?' Clara asked.

'No, she's someone I talk to, laugh with, shop with, you know.'

'No,' Clara said, and they laughed.

'You all have more people than me. I have no one,' Virginia said.

'Oh, Virginia, there must be someone,' Clara said, and Ella added that if she had a friend, then Virginia was bound to have someone.

'I have a penfriend.'

Clara spluttered. 'A *penfriend*? Isn't that what you have when you're a kid?'

'Yes, but we're still in touch. She lives in Canada. I'd love to go and see her some day.'

'You are a sad fuck,' Clara said.

'Clara ...' Ella said.

'Sorry, but you are. You sound like a teenager, you drink like a teenager and you even dress like a teenager. Virginia, you need to get a life.'

Virginia burst into tears. She always seemed to be crying these days, she thought through her misery. 'I know all this, but I don't know how I can. It's all right for you, you're pretty, rich and surrounded by men, but I have no one. Not one person.'

'OK, Virginia, calm down,' Ella said, and glared at Clara.

'Virginia, I'm sorry. I shouldn't have said that. But you know, you could be someone and you're not,' Clara said.

'I couldn't. I never will be.'

'You will,' Ella said. 'Now have another drink.'

'Virginia, I'm really sorry.' Clara actually looked guilty as she lined up two rows of cocaine.

'It's OK,' Virginia said. But she knew she was sounding more of a wimp than ever. She wanted to take Clara on, to show her she was made of stronger stuff. She just didn't know that she was. They drank some more, the game abandoned. They made small-talk and Virginia felt safer. Clara took more cocaine.

'Are you sure you don't have a habit with that stuff?' Ella asked. Virginia was thinking the same but she couldn't bring herself to say it.

'God, Ella, are you turning into Miss Tight-knickers over there?' Clara waved a hand at Virginia.

Virginia felt anger well up inside her. 'I may have tight knickers but at least I'm not a drug addict. Perhaps you should try rehab.' Ella was astounded by Virginia's outburst, which didn't seem to rile Clara.

'What a jolly good idea.' Clara snorted a line of coke, drank another shot of tequila and lit a cigarette. 'Do you think that if

I tell them I'm addicted to cocaine and sex they'll give me a discount at the Priory?'

'Don't forget alcohol, I'm sure you're addicted to that too,' Ella said.

'Maybe I'll give them a call.'

'I don't think it's funny.' Virginia was bold suddenly.

'Have a line, Virginia. Maybe we can get you a vice or two.' Clara offered Virginia a rolled-up note.

'I don't need it,' Virginia said.

'*Au contraire*, you do need it. If you don't do something exciting soon your personality is going to die of boredom. Not to mention us.' Clara chortled at her own joke.

'Clara . . .' Ella gave her another warning look.

'I hate you. I can't wait until this sodding thing is over and I never have to see you again, Clara.' Virginia cursed herself. Until then she had been standing up to Clara, but now she sounded like a child again.

'Ella, I do believe that Miss Tight-knickers nearly swore.'

'Stop it! Stop being such a bitch,' Ella shouted.

'OK. Sorry, Virginia. I wonder if the Priory is open now.'

'If it is then add being a bitch to your huge list of problems,' Virginia suggested, and as they realised it was the first funny thing she had said, they all burst out laughing.

'Virginia, I knew you could do it,' Clara said, and squeezed her shoulder.

'Oh, my God, I feel sick.' Virginia stood up. The others jumped up and rushed her to the bathroom.

'It's a good job she has short hair,' Clara said, to the sound of retching.

'Why?' Ella asked.

'At least we don't have to hold her hair for her. When I was at boarding-school and someone was being sick, we drew straws to see who had to be the hair-holder.'

'God, your parents really got their money's worth at your school, didn't they?' Despite herself Ella giggled.

'Um, well, I guess they did. Virginia, have you finished?' Clara moved closer.

'Yes,' Virginia said.

'Come with me.' Clara led her to the kitchen. 'You know, this is good for you. It's all part of being a teenager.' She and Ella gave Virginia some water then put her to bed in one of Clara's spare rooms.

Ella called a cab and had another drink and a cigarette while she waited. 'You should lay off her, you know,' she said.

'I know, but I can't help it. She's almost showing a personality. If I rile her some more, who knows? She may be a likeable person.'

'What about you?' Ella asked.

'One day you may find out that I can be quite likeable too I'm not always a bitch.' They smiled at each other as the doorbell rang and Ella got up.

'Ella, before you go, what should I do about Tim?' Clara asked.

Ella looked thoughtful as she put on her coat. 'Keep him hanging for now. Don't see him – I don't want you putting yourself through that – but keep him guessing. Maybe we can use this when we get him.'

'OK. But I really can't cope with seeing him.'

'You won't have to,' Ella replied as she left to get her cab.

When Virginia woke the next day she thought she was in hospital. Then, as she stared worriedly at the white walls, the white duvet and the white curtains, memory flooded back. The tequila, being sick, the arguments. She remembered everything. And she had the worst headache of her life. She did something she'd never done before; she went back to sleep.

*   *   *

Clara woke and remembered that Virginia was in her flat. She groaned at the thought but she got out of bed, showered and put on some clothes. She had to pull herself together and get Virginia out. She had to call Josh, and she had a million other things to do. Tomorrow their plan would be put into action. If it worked, and she had no doubt that it would, Tim would be in the firing line soon. She wanted to be the one who pulled the trigger.

Ella woke up and felt old. She felt she was now mothering two messed-up, individuals, and she was as messed up as they were. She went out to get the papers and looked at the stock price for JF Technologies. It was very low for a firm that had floated only six months before, typical of the IT start-up companies that had flooded the world. Companies that were barely scraping by floated for huge amounts of money when they weren't even showing a profit. In fact, many showed huge losses. The public had been gulled into believing that these companies would make them rich. The shares were released at a high price, and then they plummeted. Some companies made it, many did not. This one showed all the signs of one that wouldn't. If Ella were still trading she would keep well clear of. It would be perfect for setting up Isabelle. Then it would only be a matter of time before Johnny got what he deserved.

PART FIVE

Just Desserts

Chapter Twenty-two

On Friday, Ella met Josh at Clara's flat. Virginia was already there, as was he.

'Ella, you're late,' Clara said accusingly.

'I'm not. You said five,' Ella replied.

'Oh, did I? Well, then, you two were early.' She glared at Josh and Virginia.

'I'm always early.' Virginia shrugged. After the other night, she had discovered something about herself: she was stronger than she had thought and Clara couldn't hurt her any more.

'Clara, I know you're a bit nervous, but I think you should calm down,' Josh said. 'Hello, Ella, I'm sorry Clara failed to introduce us, but I'm Josh.' He shook her hand.

Ella thought he was absolutely gorgeous. He also seemed charming and genuine. She thought Clara must be mad to send him to anyone else. Ella would have kept him for herself.

'Hello, Josh. Nice to meet you. Thanks for doing this by the way.' She smiled.

'I didn't have a choice. Shall we go?'

'Now, Josh, don't forget what I told you,' Clara said.

'I never forget anything you tell me.' Josh kissed her and he and Ella left the flat.

'And call us as soon as it's done,' Clara shouted after them.

'We will. Relax,' Josh said.

They stood in the lift in silence.

'Ella, I've got my car here. I'll drive, shall I?' They got into Josh's Porsche and set off. 'Are you all right?' he asked.

'Yes, but nervous too. I can't figure out if we're mad to do this or if we're doing the right thing.'

'Neither can I. Did Clara tell you about us?'

'A bit.'

'What did she say?'

'Josh, I can't figure Clara out at the best of times. If you want to find out what's going on in her mind, it's best to ask her.'

'Point taken. How long have you been friends?'

'We're not exactly friends. We all got sacked on the same day, but that's about it.'

'So why are you going through this together?'

'Search me.' She smiled weakly.

'I get the impression you confuse people as much as Clara does. Which way now?' Ella directed Josh through the streets until they found a car park near to the gym. They got out and walked. Ella's legs felt like rubber. Her stomach was churning, and her hands were shaking. Josh kept throwing her encouraging smiles and Ella thought again how charming he was. Isabelle didn't stand a chance. They got to the gym and went to sit in the bar.

'Ella, I'm getting you a brandy. I know this is a gym, but I think that under the circumstances a brandy is excusable. Anyway, I need some Dutch courage.' He ordered the drinks and Ella sat down so she could see the lobby.

'Are there any viewing galleries for the squash courts?' Josh asked.

'Upstairs. Why?'

'Because if I watch her play squash, I can tell her afterwards that I'd seen she was a good player then ask her for a game.'

'What if she's crap?' Ella asked.

'Then she'll be flattered. Trust me.' Ella did trust him.

They sat in the bar until they saw Isabelle walk in.

'That's her,' Ella said, hiding behind a plant. 'Over there.' She stuck out a finger.

'I see her. Tall, nice legs, glasses.'

'Yes,' Ella hissed.

'All right, you stay behind the plant, I'm going to the viewing gallery.' Josh got up.

It seemed like for ever before Isabelle and an overweight woman came on to court one. Josh stood and watched. He had decided to try to find this whole thing amusing, but it was anyway. Isabelle played to win; she had a killer instinct. Her opponent had obviously lost the will to live.

'Harriet, do try to concentrate. That's the fifth point in a row I've taken off you,' Isabelle shouted at the other woman, who was panting and cowering in the corner. As she lumbered about the court in stark contrast to Isabelle, who seemed to glide, she missed ball after ball. And when she did hit it, she seemed to hit it straight to Isabelle. Josh couldn't understand why they played together.

Half an hour later the plump woman could hardly breathe.

'I think we'll call it a day, shall we? You should practise more, you know,' Isabelle said, before stalking off the court leaving her opponent behind. Josh ran back downstairs. He knew now that Isabelle was a complete bitch. He gave Ella a thumbs-up but as she had moved her chair behind the plant now, he didn't know if she had seen him.

He waited in the lobby for what seemed like ages until Isabelle walked out. She was wearing a tracksuit and her hair was damp. He knew he had to approach her now.

'Hi,' he said, standing in front of her.

'Hello.' Isabelle tilted her head to one side questioningly.

'I know you don't know me, but I was watching your game,' Josh said, in his smoothest voice.

'Really?'

'You're remarkably good, aren't you?' Josh smiled his best smile.

'I wouldn't say that. I like to play twice a week, but there's room for improvement.' Isabelle was twisting a strand of her wet hair.

'Can I buy you a drink? It's just that I really need a squash partner. The person I used to play against has emigrated to New Zealand.'

'Oh dear.'

'Actually, he didn't play as well as you do. Perhaps we could discuss the idea of a game.'

'Sure, that'd be lovely.' Isabelle was practically swooning.

'What would you like?' Josh asked, going to the bar and trying not to laugh at Ella, who was invisible behind the plant.

'White wine, please,' Isabelle said, and sat down with her back to the plant. Josh ordered a white wine and a beer and sat opposite her.

'My name's Josh Lambert, I'm a corporate lawyer and I work for Garrett. Have you heard of them? I'm telling you this so you don't think I stalk squash clubs looking for pretty women.' He laughed, as did Isabelle, who was blushing.

'Isabelle Holland. I'm a sales manager at SFH. I've heard of Garrett, it's one of the most respected law firms in the City. I don't think you're a stalker.' She sounded less sure of herself than she had when she was shouting at her opponent.

'Wow, good job. You must be very clever to hold such a key position with a great firm,' Josh said. He knew he sounded like a creep, but he guessed that with Isabelle flattery would get him everywhere.

'Thank you, Josh, but it's hard work.'

'God, I know. I work such long hours myself. I understand. It's nice to meet other ambitious, successful people.'

'Yes, it is.' Isabelle thought it must be her lucky day. This man was a total babe.

'You have a wonderful forearm,' Josh said.

'Sorry?' Isabelle asked. Josh leant over, took her hand and pulled her left arm towards him.

'Such a well-formed arm,' Josh repeated, trying not to laugh.

'Thank you.' Isabelle was totally off-balance.

'So, what about it?' Josh said.

'Sorry?' Isabelle said.

'Squash next week?'

'Yes, that would be lovely. When?' Isabelle was hooked.

Josh decided to make her sweat a bit. 'I need to check my diary. But definitely next week. May I call you?' Josh saw disappointment flash for a second in Isabelle's eyes.

'Of course, here's my card.' She fished in her handbag and pulled one out.

'Fantastic. I'll call you on Monday. Is there any day you'd prefer?' Now that he was sure of her interest he could afford to be a little generous.

'Well, Wednesday's good for me.'

'Excellent. I'll make myself available on Wednesday. But I'll call on Monday to firm up arrangements.' He let his eyes fall to her tiny chest.

'Lovely, I'll look forward to it. So, I'll hear from you on Monday?'

'Yes,' Josh said, still trying not to laugh.

'Super. Well, I must go now. 'Bye, Josh, lovely to meet you. See you next week. Speak to you Monday.' Isabelle's calm demeanour had disappeared.

''Bye, Isabelle, the pleasure was all mine.' He kissed her cheek and could hear her heart pounding. He smiled again and she left.

As soon as he was sure she was gone, he bellowed with laughter. So did the plant.

'For God's sake, Ella, come out of there.'

Ella emerged. 'I can't believe how smooth you were. She was in pieces. God, no one but Isabelle would fall for the "wonderful forearm" thing.' Ella was hysterical.

'I hope you're not mocking my chat-up technique.' Josh feigned hurt.

'Christ, if you used that one on Clara, no wonder she's making you do this.' They looked at each other, and it was five minutes before either could speak.

'I've got to call them. They'll be having kittens by now,' Ella said, as she reached for her mobile phone.

Virginia and Clara had been watching television because they didn't know what else to do.

'Why haven't they called yet?'

'You've asked that a million times and it won't make the phone ring.' Virginia's nerves were in shreds.

'All right, just because you've got a personality now, or a bit of one, there's no reason to snipe at me.'

'I'm not sniping.'

'You are too. God, I created a monster.'

'Shut up, Clara.'

'I wish they'd phone.' Clara jumped up for the thousandth time and started pacing again.

'If you're going to be like this when it's only the beginning what are you going to be like by the last one?' Virginia said.

'In pieces. If we live that long.' Clara shot Virginia a warning glance, and Virginia shut up. She wasn't ready to be more like Ella and Clara just yet. The telephone rang. Clara grabbed it. Virginia only got Clara's side of the conversation, which consisted of 'yes'. She hung up.

'Well?' Virginia asked.

'He did it. They're meeting next week.'

'Thank God,' Virginia said, and felt better.

'Ella hid behind a plant,' Clara explained.

'Right.'

'I'm getting a drink. Want one?' Clara asked.

They sat sipping wine until the doorbell rang and Josh and Ella walked in.

'Mission accomplished,' Josh said, and sat down on the couch.

'You should have heard him, he was so slick.' Ella chuckled.

'Tell me all,' Clara commanded, and went to grab the wine bottle.

Josh told them what had happened, and Ella gave her 'behind the plant' version of how she had had to put her fist in her mouth to stifle her laughter.

'OK, I'm leaving now. Virginia, you want a lift?' Ella asked.

'I've got the scooter,' Virginia replied.

'You've been drinking,' Clara said.

'Only one glass, Clara, you had the rest.'

'Oh, yes. So I did.' Clara giggled.

After the pair had gone, Clara fell uncertainly into Josh's arms.

Chapter Twenty-three

The three kept apart until Monday, when Ella rang them both to tell them the document had arrived. She had paid handsomely for it and was pleased to see that they had done a great job. It looked like a genuine company report.

They met up at Clara's flat and pored over it. They were less nervous now. They knew that the stakes were high, and that if the plan for Isabelle didn't work they would have to abort the project, but now that they were getting close, they wanted revenge even more.

Clara told them that she'd spent the whole weekend with Josh. He hadn't left her side. 'Aren't you worried about him and Isabelle?' Ella asked.

'No,' Clara replied, indicating that the subject was closed.

Virginia shrugged. If she had someone like Josh interested in her, which would never happen, there was no way she would make him sleep with anyone else. They discussed the next phase of the plan.

'I know we want this over and done with quickly, but perhaps we should make sure they have two dates before he lures her back to his flat,' Clara said.

'I think you're right, although it seems a little unfair on Josh. She's not great company, is she?'

'Yes, but we need to be sure that she falls for it. If it

happens too quickly maybe she won't,' Virginia said.

'I agree. Two dates it is, then.'

Josh called Isabelle on Monday afternoon. Her secretary answered.

'Isabelle Holland please.' Josh put his business voice on.

'May I say who's calling?' the girl asked, in a singsong voice.

'Josh Lambert.' He could tell the girl was new because she forgot to put him on hold and he heard her shouting over to Isabelle that a Josh was on the line and he heard Isabelle say, 'Bloody well put him through, you idiot.' When Isabelle's voice finally came on the line, he had managed to stop laughing.

'Isabelle Holland.'

'Hi, it's Josh.'

'Josh, how are you?' Her voice was more sickly sweet than before.

'Fine. Are you on for Wednesday?'

'Of course, I've booked a court.' She was very keen.

'What time?' Josh asked. He wasn't sure how he would be able to sleep with her.

'Seven. Shall we meet at the club?'

'Yes, sure. I'll meet you in the lobby at five to, then.' Josh saw he had another call coming through.

'Lovely, I'll see you, then.' Isabelle was playing with her hair again.

'I must dash, I'll be looking forward to it. 'Bye.' Josh hung up, picked up his other line and wondered how he had got mixed up in all this.

Clara saw Josh on Tuesday night and gave him the report. He took her to bed, and after he fell asleep Clara cried. She got up and did another couple of lines of cocaine. Eventually she passed out.

* * *

Virginia sat at home and waited for the post. The response from her parents hadn't arrived yet and they hadn't called either. It was a worrying, if unsurprising, development.

Ella spent a lot of time with Jackie and tried to keep her mind off the other two. She found them occupying her thoughts more than she wanted. And she didn't understand why.

Chapter Twenty-four

On Wednesday as he got to work Josh was fuming. Clara had insisted he had two dates with Isabelle. He felt as though he had been hired to do this, and he felt cheap. He had tried to talk her out of it, but Clara wouldn't budge. If he wanted her, he had to do this, and he wanted her so much. He put Isabelle out of his mind at work, although he couldn't do the same with Clara. He would have loved to know what was going on in her head. But he had no idea. Resignedly, he got his secretary to order him a cab for half past six and went to the gym.

He was there before Isabelle, and as he stood in the lobby in his crisp white shorts, he realised he was nervous. He couldn't figure out whether going through with this would ensure that Clara and he could be together or whether it would do the opposite. He didn't have much time to dwell on it, though, because Isabelle arrived. 'Josh, hello,' she said, touching his arm.

'Hey, there. Ready to play?' he said, in his most seductive voice. He guessed that if he ever left the legal profession he could get a job as a male prostitute. He had wanted so much to say no to Clara, and all his common sense told him that he should have done so. But he knew this was his only option, so he threw himself into the role. They walked on to the court and the game began.

After the first few minutes, he had sussed her game. She wasn't very good and Josh had to play below his usual standard to ensure she got any points at all. By the end, although he won, he hadn't wiped the floor with her.

'Great game,' he said, as they stood on the court.

'Thanks, you play well,' Isabelle panted.

'Can I tempt you to have dinner with me as a thank you?' Josh asked.

'That would be lovely.' Isabelle's eyes lit up.

They changed and met in the lobby. Josh had been waiting for quite a while when Isabelle came out. She had doused herself in perfume, which made Josh feel nauseous, and she was wearing too much makeup. She looked unattractive.

'Ready?' Josh asked.

'Yes. Where are we going?' Isabelle asked. Josh had planned to take her to a restaurant near his flat, but that would have to wait for the second date.

'The Oxo tower,' Josh said. They walked outside and hailed a cab. Josh held open the door and ushered Isabelle in, lightly touching her bottom. He saw by the redness of her face that she had noticed.

'So, tell me about your job,' Josh said, and switched off as she talked about her own importance for the entire journey. She was the most egotistical and boring woman he'd ever met.

They arrived at the restaurant and she was still talking. She had told him about all the people she was in charge of, the money she made, the stupid secretaries she had to put up with. She talked and talked. Josh thought of Clara.

When they sat down, Isabelle finally ran out of steam and Josh took control. He ordered the wine and suggested the food.

'Tell me about your job, Josh,' Isabelle said finally.

'Well, as a City lawyer I get so much information about companies that I could make a fortune. Of course, I can't do anything about it, more's the pity. I'd be the richest guy in Britain – or nearly anyway.' Josh guffawed.

'Really? How come?' Isabelle asked, as the starter arrived.

'I specialise in takeovers. That's where the money is. Often the stock price is really low but about to go through the roof. Because I work on the takeovers I know what's happening well before the information is public. Of course if I acted on it I'd be fired, and as I quite like my job and have a decent amount of money anyway, it's not necessary. It's also illegal, as you know, but it would be nice sometimes.'

'So you get all the insider information. There are leaks, though – I've seen them myself.'

'Sure, but that's still illegal. Of course, if you got some information and used it no one could prove you'd been tipped off or worked on that tip. You could just have made a good judgement. But if I was involved, they'd probably hang me out to dry.'

'Josh, that's amazing. Imagine having that information and not being able to use it. It must be terribly frustrating.' Isabelle's eyes were shining.

'Yup, but that's life. It's frustrating.'

'I guess so.'

'There's one I'm working on at the moment that's a killer. It's going to be so big, but again there's nothing I can do about it.'

'Perhaps you could let it slip to me.'

'You know what? You've got a great sense of humour. And lovely eyes.' Josh looked into them. They weren't lovely at all; they were on the small side, like her chest.

'Thank you.' Isabelle flushed.

Josh kept the wine flowing. After dinner, they had coffee and brandy, and Isabelle was drunk. Josh drank quite a lot himself. As he wasn't going to sleep with her that night, the drink helped alleviate the boredom. He was not looking forward to seeing her again, but he had told himself he would, for Clara. As they finished the brandy, Josh leant his head close to Isabelle's. 'Isabelle, I've got a really early start. Regrettably, I must call it a night.'

Isabelle looked disappointed. 'Oh, well, of course, if you must. Where do you live?'

'Chelsea,' Josh said. 'You?'

'Hampstead. I guess we're on opposite sides of London.' She laughed weakly, but Josh could feel her disappointment.

'Yes. Isabelle, can I see you again?'

'When?' Isabelle asked eagerly.

'Friday?' Josh suggested. It was only two days away and then this would be over. He didn't want to waste any more time.

'OK. Are you sure I can't tempt you back for coffee?' Isabelle asked, licking her lips.

'Sorry, darling, but I really do have to work early tomorrow. How about dinner on Friday?'

'That would be lovely.'

'Good. I'll call tomorrow to fix it up.' Josh motioned to the waiter for the bill. When he had paid it, he stood up. 'Come on, I'll put you in a cab.'

The next day, Josh called Clara and told her that the evening had gone according to plan and he was seeing Isabelle again on Friday.

'Do you want to come over to mine tonight?' Clara asked, pleased with him.

'No, darling, I have to work late. I'll call you after Friday.' Josh tried to sound pleasant, but he was angry with Clara. He kept thinking she would realise the madness of the plan, or of his part in it. She would be so consumed by jealousy that she would tell him to stop, to pull back and not to sleep with Isabelle. But she didn't.

'OK, Josh, call me, and good luck.'

I need it, Josh thought as he hung up. Then he called Isabelle to make the arrangements.

*　　*　　*

Clara rang Ella and Virginia, and they decided to meet on Saturday after Josh had successfully taken Isabelle to bed. Until then there was no more for them to do. When Clara hung up, she felt restless. She was not sure why, but she felt dissatisfied with everything. She entered a cocaine haze that lasted for the next couple of days.

Chapter Twenty-five

Josh arranged to meet Isabelle at the restaurant he had booked in Chelsea, La Ciboulette. It was on the King's Road and therefore nearer to his flat than hers. Isabelle had offered another game of squash, but Josh had declined, saying he would not get out of work on time. He ensured that he was early and sat down, ordered a drink and waited.

Isabelle was on time. He saw her walk in and arrogantly ask the *maître d'* to show her to Josh's table. As she came over confidently, Josh took in her outfit. She was wearing a sharp navy suit with a white top underneath. Her skirt was short and showed off her legs, but the rest of her figure was boyish. She had no curves, unlike Clara, and her face was cold and unappealing. Josh grimaced at the thought of 'later', as she approached him.

'Josh,' she said enthusiastically.

He stood up and kissed her cheeks. 'Isabelle, you look lovely,' he lied. 'I hope you like French food.'

'*Je l'adore.*' Isabelle laughed. Her laugh was false, like everything else about her, and Josh felt depression engulf him. He told her what was good and ordered red wine. Isabelle chose her own food this time, but she asked Josh if she'd made a good choice. Josh guessed that she didn't date much — her sophisticated manner dropped every time she spoke to him.

Over the meal Josh flirted and flattered her. Isabelle ate barely anything, but he noticed that she drank quite a lot. She was interested in everything he said and hung on his every word. He also noticed that she took more than a polite interest in his work.

'I think your job must be so exciting. Tell me what you're working on,' Isabelle said, after numerous glasses of wine.

'Oh, it's not that exciting. I have to provide a lot of documentation for companies. I can't tell you what I'm working on right now, but it's taking up an awful lot of time. I have to take my work home with me. Actually, I have a lot to do this weekend. But that's life. I guess you get the same.'

'We never stop, do we?' Isabelle reached over to stroke his arm.

'No, but that's what makes us interesting.' Josh laughed.

After dinner, he decided to make his move. 'Would you like to come back to my place for coffee?' he asked, brushing his lips against her ear.

'Yes, please,' Isabelle said, and Josh paid the bill.

As they left the restaurant, Josh put his arm around her and Isabelle leant into him. He hoped he would be able to get an erection.

They walked into his flat where Josh pulled her to him and kissed her. She responded eagerly, too eagerly.

'I'll make coffee, you make yourself comfortable,' he said, steering her to the sofa. He walked out. The document was within her view on his coffee-table.

Isabelle was disappointed about the coffee. She didn't want coffee, she wanted Josh. As she waited, her eyes were drawn to a document that sat on the coffee-table. It was marked 'Private and Confidential'.

'Careless, Josh,' Isabelle mumbled, and tried to look at it without touching it. Then, checking that Josh was still in the kitchen, she picked it up and quickly put it down again. She tried to think what to do. She knew this must be the big deal Josh had spoken of earlier. She took deep breaths and looked again. Without disturbing it, she could only read the top cover. It seemed to consist of a load of legal jargon that Isabelle didn't understand, but then she saw the magic words 'takeover' and 'Microsoft'. Isabelle thought she had died and gone to heaven.

Josh watched her from behind the door, and knew they had succeeded. As he took the coffee in, he made a noise opening the door so he wouldn't catch Isabelle doing something she shouldn't be doing.

Isabelle turned to him. 'Josh, I don't want coffee. I want you,' she said. She took the cups from him, put them on the table and jumped on top of him. She ripped at his clothes passionately. Josh began to enjoy himself – he was a man, after all. She pulled herself out of her clothes, and although she was flat-chested, she had an athletic body. He pulled her to her feet and took her to bed. The sex was energetic, and Josh had no problems climaxing. Isabelle was wild. She jumped on top of him and screwed him as if she hadn't been screwed for ages. Josh supposed she hadn't. Afterwards he removed the condom, kissed her forehead and pretended to go to sleep.

Isabelle lay still for half an hour before she was convinced that Josh was asleep. When she was satisfied that he was, she crept out of bed and went to the sitting room. She lay naked on the couch and went through the report page by page. Although most of it consisted of legal terms, she understood that Microsoft were about to take over JF Technologies. And JF Technologies had very cheap stock. It was manna from heaven. She read it again committing the details she understood to her memory.

Although using the information would mean giving up Josh,

which was a huge sacrifice, Isabelle knew she could make money for herself, her clients, the company, and be a heroine. Her dilemma was between having Josh or being the first female managing director of SFH. The choice was simple. Isabelle had one golden rule. Work before sex. Josh would have to go.

She slipped quietly back into bed and fell asleep thanking her lucky stars.

Josh woke to find Isabelle's legs wrapped around his. He roused her gently, and before she could say anything he jumped out of bed and made for the shower.

Isabelle lay there for a few minutes. She couldn't stop thinking about Josh's report. Now she had read it she had a chance to make some serious money. She could advise her clients and her boss without them suspecting that it was a tip-off – she often worked on hunches. She resolved to work on a proposal that weekend so she could come up with feasible reasons why they should buy into it. She would use the information she had read in the report to do so. She licked her lips and felt horny at the thought of the money and success she was about to encounter. Fleetingly she was sorry that this would mean the end of her and Josh. But Isabelle knew you couldn't have everything. And Josh would get over her eventually. She needed to get home.

By the way that Isabelle rushed off, Josh knew she had fallen for the report. He saw a flicker of guilt in her eyes as he said he would call her. He knew she wouldn't answer his calls. Although it was only half past seven in the morning, he rang Clara.

'Hello,' a sleepy voice said.

'Clara, it's me.'

'Josh, it's the middle of the night.'

'No, it's morning. Anyway, I thought you might like to know how I got on last night.'

'Shit, yes. Sorry, I forgot.'

'Great, Clara, you make me do this by saying it's the most important thing in your life, then you forget.'

'Josh, just tell me what happened.'

'She fell for it.'

'You're sure?'

'Positive. I know she's going to do just what we want her to do.'

'Fantastic. Josh?'

'Yes, darling?'

'Did you sleep with her?'

'Clara, that was the idea. Your idea.'

'I know. Just checking. Josh?'

'Yes?'

'Was she any good?'

'No. It was like being in bed with a washboard.'

'Really?'

'Yes. I'll be over this evening. 'Bye, darling.'

''Bye.'

Clara leant back into her pillow. They had done it. They really had. It would only be a matter of time before Isabelle hanged herself with the rope they had given her. The drunken pub plan had worked. She called Virginia.

'Hello.'

'Virginia, it's Clara.'

'Clara, what time is it?'

'Late. You should be up anyway. Listen, Isabelle fell for it. Josh is sure. He didn't go into details, but he's sure she's taken the bait.'

'My God. Really?'

'Yes, I told you it would work, didn't I?'

'I can't believe it.'

'Well, you should. Be at my place for lunch. We'll celebrate. One o'clock?'

'I'll be there.'

Virginia didn't know what to do with herself. Although it was early, she couldn't contemplate going back to sleep. She couldn't believe it had actually worked. She made herself a cup of tea to celebrate.

Ella picked up the telephone, knowing it was Clara.

'Clara?'

'Ella, how did you know it was me?'

'I couldn't sleep last night for worrying about things.'

'Well, you didn't need to worry. It all worked perfectly.'

'Really?'

'Yes. Josh said it all went to plan.'

'So now we just have to wait.'

'I know. It's going to be hard. Lunch at my place, one o'clock.'

'Sure.'

Ella smiled, hoped that everything was going to work and fell asleep.

Clara had a line of cocaine to celebrate. She knew it was a bit early even for her, but this was a special occasion.

Chapter Twenty-six

Virginia was early again, Ella was running late and Clara was wasted. When Virginia first saw her she was shocked by her appearance. Clara was as beautiful as ever but her eyes were frighteningly wild.

'So, Virginia, aren't you going to thank me?' Clara was being bitchy already. Virginia didn't know what was wrong with her this time, but Clara scared her.

'Thank you.' Virginia sat on the sofa and crossed her arms. She wished Ella would turn up so she didn't have to be alone with the maniac.

'You don't sound like you mean it. Anyway, who cares? At least I know I was the one who masterminded the whole thing. I was the only person with enough balls to put the plan into action. You and Ella are useless. You're very lucky to have me.' Clara was waving her arms about; she seemed to have lost control. Virginia kept quiet, sat tight and willed Ella to hurry up.

When Ella arrived she looked at the scene in front of her and wished she had stayed asleep. Virginia was sulking on the sofa and Clara was doing some sort of rain-dance and mumbling to herself.

'What's going on?' Ella asked.

'Nothing,' Clara said.

'Clara, why are you dancing like that?'

'I'm keeping myself amused. Being with her is like being with a corpse.' She gestured at Virginia.

'I thought we were having lunch,' Ella said.

'Oh, yes. Well, we'll have to go out. I don't have any food. Come on.' Clara picked up her handbag and walked out. Ella and Virginia exchanged a glance and followed her. They walked down the street in silence, Clara stalking ahead. She chose the first restaurant they came to, a pizza place. She ignored the door attendant and went and sat at a window table. There was a reserved sign on it, which she flicked on to the floor. She lit a cigarette and shouted, 'Get over here,' at a waiter. Ella and Virginia were still silent.

'I want a bottle of Chianti,' Clara said.

'I'm not drinking,' Virginia said, and immediately regretted it.

'Of course not. You're far too boring to have a drink.'

'Clara, what's with you today?' Ella rubbed her temples, she had a headache.

'Nothing. It's you two. You'd think that you'd show me some gratitude, wouldn't you? If it weren't for me, you wouldn't have got Isabelle. But, no, you just act as if I didn't do anything. Well, I fucking well did. I risked my relationship for you and you can't even show me any gratitude.' The waiter nearly jumped out of his skin as he caught the tail end of Clara's tirade. She grabbed the bottle of wine out of his hands, poured herself a glass and noticed he was still standing behind her.

'Piss off,' Clara said. He did.

'Of course we're grateful, Clara, but can I just point something out? First, we thanked you before. Second, it isn't over yet. We have to wait for Isabelle to lose money and lose her job. Third, we both warned you about using Josh, and fourth, I hardly think what you have with him is a relationship,' Ella said calmly.

'You fucking bitch. How dare you come over all high and mighty with me? Maybe it isn't over yet, but look how far we've come. And it will work, thanks to me. And how dare you say that Josh and I don't have a relationship? What do you know about relationships? Nothing. Just because you once had one does not make you the world's biggest authority. So fuck off.' Clara was standing up and everyone in the restaurant was looking at her. The staff were trying to decide what to do, but no one was brave enough to evict her.

Ella took control. 'Virginia, go and pay for the wine.' She handed her twenty pounds. 'Clara, you have to stop this. I don't know why you're being like this, but you need to stop now.' She put her hand on her shoulder.

'Get off me.' Clara pushed Ella's hand away and collapsed in a heap of sobs.

They had to carry her home, where Virginia made coffee and Ella put her to bed, gave her Valium, which she hoped wasn't a mistake, and sat with her while she cried for an hour before suddenly falling asleep.

Virginia and Ella sat in the sitting room, exhausted.

'What is it?' Virginia asked.

'I don't know, but I think she has a problem with drugs.'

'Alcohol or cocaine?'

'Cocaine. Shit, Virginia what should we do? She really lost it today.'

'I don't know if it was because we've actually achieved something or whether it's Josh. I think he's really got to her. She needs help.'

'Well, I'm not going to be the one to tell her that. Look, we should stay until she wakes up, then leave and have a good think about calling it a day. If it's going to have this effect on Clara, I'm not sure it's a good idea,' Ella said.

'I agree. But if the Isabelle scheme works, we *have* to get the others.'

'And I don't know that I could leave it now anyway. When Clara called me today about Isabelle I felt so good. We have to do something about her, though.'

'But what?' Virginia asked.

'How about telling her brother? If she really is an addict we can't help her and she needs professional help. I can't tell her that, neither can you, but perhaps she'll listen to him,' Ella suggested.

'Ella, Clara adores James. She'd die rather than have him know about any of this. I think telling him might finish her off. It would certainly be the end for us.'

'You're right. Shit, we can't just leave her like this.'

'Maybe it's because so much is going on. When it's all over she might stop,' Virginia suggested, but she didn't believe it.

'Or it might be too late.'

'Well, I suppose the only thing we can do is keep an eye on her and try to keep her away from the drugs. God, I feel so helpless.'

'Me too,' Ella agreed.

They spent the afternoon watching TV and trying to think of things to say to each other. At five o'clock, Clara appeared. 'Hi,' she said, and sat down in an armchair. 'I'm so sorry about earlier. I don't know what came over me.'

'Clara, can I ask you something? Do you take cocaine during the day?' Ella was worried about the reaction she'd get but she had to ask.

'Of course not. Gosh, Ella, is that what you think? No, it's just that my period's due and I get the most awful mood swings at this time of the month. Virginia, I'm sorry I was so foul. God, I'll never be allowed back in that restaurant, will I?' Clara giggled.

'So you're OK?' Virginia asked suspiciously.

'Yes, thank you. Listen, girls, Josh is coming over later, so I need to get ready. As I messed up today, I'll take you to dinner tomorrow night. I'll book somewhere nice. I'll call you. Thanks.' Clara the demon had disappeared.

'That'll be fun,' Virginia said, thinking the opposite. She and Ella left and went their separate ways. Clara took more cocaine.

*　　*　　*

Josh turned up at seven. He hugged Clara, who pushed him away. The demon had returned.

'What is it?' Josh asked.

'I don't want to see you any more,' Clara said. She had decided this afternoon that she couldn't cope with her feelings for him. And Ella had been right: she couldn't cope with the idea of him and Isabelle.

'Clara, what are you talking about? We're just getting to know each other again.'

'Well, I don't like what I know about you. You're an egotistical fucker and you still shag any woman you come across.'

'I don't. And if you're referring to Isabelle, you asked me to sleep with her. No, you *told* me to sleep with her. You said if I didn't then you wouldn't see me any more.'

'Well, now I won't see you any more anyway, so there.'

'Clara, I think we need to talk.'

'No. You need to fuck off out of my life.'

'What is this?'

'Which word don't you understand? I know it's not fuck.'

'Clara, you're being a class A bitch.'

'And you're a prick. I don't want you. Do you find that so hard to understand? I guess no one has turned the wonderful Josh down before. Well, here you go. See how you like it.'

'Is that what this is? You're getting your own back on me for what happened between us before. Christ, Clara, that was ages ago, and I've changed.'

'Don't flatter yourself. I'm saying this because I feel like it. I want you out of my life.'

'How could you do this? You get me involved in your harebrained scheme by telling me that it's the only way we can be together, and now you tell me you don't want me. I really don't understand you, Clara. I'm going now, but I don't believe you. I know you still want to be with me. Clara, call me when you get your brain back.' Josh looked angry, then sad. He kissed her gently on the lips then left.

Clara sat on the floor with her back to the door. She started crying again. Now she'd lost Josh. She knew she would eventually so she couldn't risk leaving it until he got fed up with her. She knew he *would* get fed up with her. He was too nice for her, she didn't deserve him.

She pulled herself together and went to get some coke. This was all she needed. Josh could go to hell; he could never compare with cocaine.

Chapter Twenty-seven

The following day, Clara decided to pull herself together and start having fun. She booked dinner at San Lorenzo and hoped that they might just manage to have an enjoyable evening. She called Virginia and Ella to arrange to meet them in Knightsbridge. She also discussed with them how they would monitor the success of their plan.

Then she phoned Toby and told him she missed work. She suggested that he might call her every so often to update her on what was happening. Toby agreed that he would. Ella and Virginia were going to study the *Financial Times* and the financial pages of all the newspapers to see if there was any mention of buying in JF Technologies. They were also going to study the stock prices. If the price rose they would know Isabelle was buying. When the company went bankrupt, it would probably be in the press, but Clara felt there was no harm in keeping Toby as an extra information line.

Virginia stood outside the restaurant and glanced at her watch. She felt nervous that the plan was out of their hands. All they could do now was wait. She was worried that someone might find out what they had done, and although she didn't know how anyone could, it made her nervous. She still hadn't heard from her parents, which meant they had probably disowned her. She didn't know why this bothered her so much, but it did. She was as alone as she ever had been. Unless you counted Ella and Clara, which Virginia would rather not.

Ella arrived, looking fed up, tense and strained. They nodded to each other, but neither spoke. Virginia didn't really understand what was going on: sometimes she thought they were becoming friends, at other times she disliked Ella and Clara as much as they disliked her. She knew they were only spending time together to wreak revenge, but she wondered how much longer they could stand it. She even thought selfishly that she was glad Isabelle's revenge had been first.

Clara turned up fifteen minutes late, smiling broadly.

'Hello, girls,' she said, and led them into the restaurant. Clara was all charm as she flirted with the waiters and ordered champagne. Virginia flinched when she looked at the prices on the menu even though she knew this was Clara's treat.

'Let's drink a toast to our first success, which I know won't be long in coming,' Clara said.

'I wonder how long it will take,' Virginia said.

'I should think two or three weeks. If, as we predict, Isabelle buys shares for herself and her clients, the price will rise due to the buying activity. When the company is declared bankrupt the shares will be as good as worthless. It may even take less time than that.'

'Oh dear. Does that mean we'll have contributed to the company's downfall?' Virginia looked worried.

'No. Josh said it was beyond saving, but a few shareholders will get some money back, courtesy of Isabelle, so we're doing someone a favour.'

'That's one way of looking at it,' Ella said.

'The Clara way,' Virginia pointed out.

'Anyway, don't you want to know about Josh?' Clara asked.

'What?' Ella asked.

'I finished it,' Clara said.

'What?' Ella repeated.

'Yes. I realised we weren't suitable for each other so I thought it was easier to finish now.'

'I don't believe you,' Ella gasped.

'Well, it's true.'

'Are you ready to order?' The waiter interrupted them. They ordered main courses. Clara had decided they didn't need starters and the others didn't argue.

'Go on, Clara. Tell me why you felt you should end it with Josh,' Ella probed.

'Because he wasn't right. Or something. I don't know, it just wouldn't have worked out.' Clara couldn't quite remember why she'd done it.

'If I had a guy like Josh I wouldn't let him go,' Virginia said bravely.

'That's hardly likely, is it?' Clara looked at Virginia.

'Clara! Anyway, she's right. He was lovely and he seemed to adore you, although I can't think why,' Ella riposted.

'Oh, shut up. Can't we change the subject?'

'Do you think we should start talking about our next plan?' Virginia asked.

'No. Not until we know the first one has worked. It may be jinxed if we move on now.' Ella felt unusually superstitious.

'She's right. So until JF goes bust we don't need to see each other. If there's any information, we can call. Otherwise we'll have a couple of weeks off.' Clara smiled. Ella smiled. Virginia didn't. How was she going to get through a fortnight on her own?

Clara ate nothing, drank more than half of the champagne and the best part of a bottle of red wine. She also made two trips to the ladies'. Ella and Virginia were sober and worried about Clara. At one point when they were alone, Virginia turned to Ella. 'I think she's got a real problem.'

'So do I, but what can we do?'

'I don't know, but we should do something.'

'If we suggest anything to her now she'll just go mad. At least we can keep an eye on her.'

'What about Josh? I'd feel happier if he was around.'

'So would I,' Ella agreed.

Clara summoned the bill; she was swaying.

'Do you want to come back to mine for a nightcap?' she offered. The others agreed – they didn't think she would make it on her own.

They got a cab, which Ella paid for. When they got out, Virginia kept hold of Clara, who was on the verge of passing out, but Clara broke away from her and tried to walk to the front door, clutching the wall for support. Virginia and Ella watched as she searched her bag for her keys. Eventually she tipped it upside-down on the step outside the front door and giggled. Virginia bent to pick up lipsticks, a mobile, a purse, a compact and the rest of its contents. Clara stepped over her, grabbed her keys and opened the door. When they reached Clara's flat door, she couldn't get the key to work.

'Give it here,' Ella said and opened the door.

Inside the flat, Ella said, 'I'll get her some water,' and went to the kitchen.

'I don't want water, I want booze,' Clara shouted, and passed out on the sofa.

'Shit. Look at her.' Ella tried to wake her up, but failed, so they carried her to her bedroom. They gave up attempts to undress her and leaving her fully clothed they pulled the duvet over her.

'I hope she's going to be OK.' Virginia was upset.

'Who knows?' Ella replied, and went to call a cab.

After dropping Virginia off Ella went home, glad of her empty flat. She had a long bath and thought about what was happening. Events were taking over. What had started as their plan was now just something going on in the background of real life, and even that didn't feel very real at the moment.

After her bath, Ella went to the living room and pulled out a pen and paper. It was time for Sam's letter. She was going to keep sending him a cheque every month; she had enough money. Although she didn't know if he needed it, it made her feel better for him to have it. In the letter she told him how much she missed him, how much she longed to speak to him. She assured him she was still fine, but she didn't mention losing her job.

As she addressed the envelope her hand shook, and a tear rolled down her cheek. She wasn't so different from Clara. She loved her brother more than anything in the world, but she still wouldn't allow herself to talk to him or see him. She still needed to be punished for Tony. She was the same as Clara in many ways. Completely and utterly mad.

Chapter Twenty-eight

Isabelle almost floated to work on Monday. She had spent all weekend working out her plan, and she was ready to put it into action. She could hardly contain her excitement. She smiled as she thought of how stupid Josh was but, then, he was only a man. She couldn't believe he preached confidentiality then left out such a valuable document for anyone to see. Perhaps he hadn't expected her to go back with him, but he should have moved it the minute they walked in. He had made it so easy for her. He must be spending too much time thinking about her and not enough about his job. Isabelle would never make such a mistake.

Isabelle had spent Sunday in the office looking up all the information she could find on JF Technologies. At first glance it looked like bad stock but everything she had read in the document was verified. She could put forward a forceful argument in favour of buying the stock. She would make so much money; she would be a star. SFH would have to offer her a managing directorship. She would be powerful. She would get a bigger office and more money. She could hardly contain herself as she thought about how much money she would make. The managing directors were all multi-millionaires.

She would ensure that she took all the credit herself. She researched; she kept her ear to the ground. She was going to be known as the best. She *was* the best. Dear, sweet, stupid Josh. He was such a wonderful fool. And when they made the money, he wouldn't be able to say anything because his negligence safeguarded her position.

She spent the journey to the office thinking about what she would do with the stock. She would buy it personally, of course, but that was the easy bit. Making money for herself would ensure a nice little sideline and that was perfectly acceptable. She would also tell David Marker, her boss, and ask him what he thought. That way SFH could buy stock for its own book. If he didn't believe her he would soon see how much money they would have made if he had. She would use that against him. Then she would select her three best clients and get them to buy stock. She would use the same process with them as she did with David. Isabelle knew that as soon as the takeover was announced, the stock value would increase sharply. According to the document she had read, the announcement would be made within two weeks. Two weeks until Isabelle would recoup all she deserved. She was so excited, it was hard to think straight.

When she got to her office, she drafted an e-mail to send to David. She told him that the latest Microsoft press releases had said they were looking for small technology companies with good products to take over. She said that she had done copious research into the technology industry and JF Technologies fitted the bill. She pointed out the share price was so low that it was a prime Microsoft target. She also said that a Microsoft contact of hers had as near as admitted it. That wasn't insider trading. That was rumour. She sent the e-mail and waited. It wasn't long before David called her into his office.

'David,' she said, sitting down.

'Isabelle. This e-mail you sent me. How strong is the information?'

'I'd say it's rock solid. I'm willing to go out on a limb for this, David, and to make you feel better I should tell you I'm investing my own money in it. I was speaking to a contact of mine at Microsoft and I know that this is what they're looking for. All the signs are there. JF has a ground-breaking product but the management is falling apart. The share price is low and it's on its last legs. I could produce a full report if you feel it's necessary, but if you look at the company, you'll know I'm right.'

'I don't think that's necessary. I'll get our technology trader to buy into it on behalf of SFH. What about clients?'

'I'll tell my top three. No more. What we need to be prepared for is that the price is going to increase due to us buying. I don't want to panic anyone. So I thought that if we all buy simultaneously, it will be easier. The stock will rally and I guess there'll be copycat buying, but by then we should be in the clear. By the way, we need to sit on the stock for about two weeks, if not less, and certainly not much longer.'

'How sure are you?'

'One hundred per cent.'

'That's good enough for me. I trust your judgement. Let's go shopping.' With that Isabelle left him.

In her office, she called her personal broker and put him on standby to invest £50,000 in JF stock. Then she met with the SFH trader who was also on standby. She called her top three clients, who gave her orders to buy. She got someone else from her desk to fill the orders. That afternoon, wasting no time, Isabelle put her own money, SFH's, and three of her clients' money into JF Technologies. They managed to get the stock at its lowest price, then Isabelle watched as it rose after the buying spree. She went home a happy woman.

The following day the stock had risen again, and David sent an e-mail of congratulations to Isabelle. Ella saw the price in the paper and knew that they had won.

JF shareholders were puzzled by the rise. The managing director called their accountant, who said that it didn't make any difference: the share price might be high, but it was not high enough to save the company. Their lawyers were preparing bankruptcy statements to be released the following week. He advised the board to sell their stock now to recoup some money.

The City rumour mill was in overdrive, and the buying of JF Technologies stock became a big story in the financial press. Everyone said a takeover must be imminent, although the company denied it fiercely. Speculators in the City were buying stock on the grounds of SFH's trading activity.

JF Technologies had not seen such trading activity since it first floated on the market. Its staff was baffled and those who knew about the company's impending doom began to believe that it was going to be taken over and their jobs would be saved.

The following Wednesday the board members of JF were called into a meeting with the lawyers and accountants. They were all confused by the sharp rise in buying activity and the newly high share price. However, it was still not enough to save a company that hadn't shown a profit from the day it started trading, especially as their product had been slated by those who had used it. They said that there was no option but to announce that the company was bankrupt. They had been forced to make this announcement sooner than planned. The new shareholders would lose all their money and perhaps think again before listening to groundless rumours. There was no option.

On Thursday it was announced that JF Technologies was going into liquidation. Shareholders would have to apply to the bailiffs to recoup any money lost. Due to the renewed interest in the company, the story made the front page of the *Financial Times*.

Isabelle went to work oblivious of the massacre that awaited her. She sat down at her desk and picked up her copy of the *Financial Times*. 'Buying Rally Fails to Save Technology Company', screamed the headline that stared up at her. Her hands shook as she read that JF Technologies had gone into liquidation despite a huge rise in its share price. It went on to report how no one could understand the sudden buying interest as there was no way that the company could have been saved. It said that speculation about a takeover had caused the rise in stock price, but the rumour had been groundless. It also mentioned SFH as one of the biggest buyers of stock. When she reached the line that read, 'Was SFH acting on bad instinct or were they fooled into believing an untrue rumour?' Isabelle put down the paper, dropped her head into her hands and thought about running away. Her telephone rang. It was David.

'Isabelle, what the hell is going on?'

'I've just read the article.'

'Do you know how much money you've cost the firm? And we've ended up looking like fools. The PR on this is very bad. We've even had to call an emergency meeting. I'm going to have to explain this and all I can think is that either you gave us crap information or you believed some fool.'

'I'm sorry, I don't understand it myself.' Isabelle's head was spinning. How could she get out of this? Who could she blame? She couldn't tell them about Josh. That would implicate her as much as it would implicate him. She had to face the fact that she had no one to blame.

'I accept your resignation. Put it in writing and give it to my secretary. You can leave now, I'll inform HR.' David hung up.

Isabelle sat at her desk. She didn't understand. The document had been real, the deal agreed. She had seen it herself. Microsoft must have pulled out. The only explanation she could think of was that they had decided against it. But why? They wouldn't have issued a report unless the deal was concrete. The dull thud of reality hit her. Instead of having made her career, this disaster had ruined it. Isabelle wiped tears from her eyes as she typed a resignation letter. Not only had she lost her job, £50,000 of her own money and any respect her clients had had for her, she would never work in the City again. She didn't know how she was going to get through the next few minutes, let alone the rest of her life. She kept coming back to Josh. It was his fault, but how could she tell anyone that? If she did, she might be arrested for insider dealing. Perhaps he had set her up – she brushed that thought away with her tears. There was no way he could have done that.

She tried to feel brave as she called her secretary into her office. 'I'm leaving. I need you to, empty my drawers pack up my things and mail everything to my home address. Do it immediately.' She looked at her pitiful new secretary and scowled.

'OK.'

'And deliver this letter to Samantha, David Marker's secretary.'

'OK.'

Isabelle stood up, put on her coat, grabbed her briefcase and left the building for ever.

The emergency meeting contained most of SFH's managing directors. Those who couldn't attend in person were included via conference calls. David felt uncomfortable as he came under the angry scrutiny of his peers. He placed the blame firmly on Isabelle's shoulders. He said she had given him assurances that she knew what she was doing and, as a senior manager, she had the authority to do what she had done. He told them she had resigned, which meant she accepted full responsibility. They decided that they would issue a statement that day, naming Isabelle Holland as the person who had shown such bad judgement and distancing the firm from any blame or repercussions. The amount of money lost was not huge, and although David was told to keep a tighter control over his staff in future, his position was secure.

*   *   *

Ella ran down to the paper shop. She had been jogging every day, and on her way back she always stopped to pick up the paper. Lately, due to the reports that the stock was rising, her route had been getting shorter. She was impatient for the news. She paid for the paper and looked at the front-page headline. She blinked because she thought she must be dreaming, but then she looked again. Not only was the company bankrupt, but because so many shares had changed hands it was a top story. Her hands were shaking as she read that SFH was one of the major speculators who had lost money.

She ran home as fast as she could and picked up the telephone. 'Virginia.'

'Yes.'

'It's Ella. It made front page of the *FT*.'

'What?'

'JF has been announced bankrupt and it made the front page. Oh, and the best thing is that SFH has been given a mention for buying so many of the shares. It says here that they were either speculating or stupid. Well, something like that.'

'Ella, do you mean we did it?'

'Yes, girl, we did.'

'Does Clara know?'

'No, I'm calling her. We'll meet at her place in an hour. We can do this, Virginia. We got Isabelle, and we will get the others. My God, I can't believe how great this feels.'

'Me either. But is it real?'

'You bet your arse it's real.'

Virginia got dressed in a daze. She, Virginia, a little nobody, had helped to get Isabelle and the whole of SFH into trouble. God, if only her parents could see what she'd done. They would know she was no longer the fool they thought she was.

*   *   *

Clara heard the telephone and thought of ignoring it. Then, remembering the mission, she reached over and got out of bed, removing her emergency eyemask as she did so.

'Clara?'

'Yes.'

'It's Ella.'

'I know who it fucking is. What time is it?'

'Eight.'

'Great. Why does everyone seem to want me in the middle of the night?'

'We did it.'

Clara sat upright. 'We did?'

'Yes. Virginia and I will be over in an hour, or less if we can. I'll bring the papers. We fucking did it, Clara.'

'Ella, I'm so proud. I can't believe it.'

'With a little help from a friend.'

Virginia and Ella turned up at the same time, Ella carrying a bunch of newspapers. They rang Clara's bell and went in. She was making coffee.

'Hi, girls. We're celebrating.' Clara was smiling. Although she was tired and drawn, she still looked better than when they had last seen her.

'Here. Take a paper each and look through it.' They started reading. Although the *FT* had headlined it, the other broadsheets had picked up the story. They all mentioned SFH.

'Shit! I can't believe we did this,' Clara said.

'Neither can I.' Virginia giggled.

'There'll be more tomorrow. I bet everyone will want to know why SFH were buying such a stupid stock.' Ella chortled.

'I'm going to call Toby and see what he knows.' Clara ran

to grab the telephone. She returned, grinning, a few minutes later. 'Isabelle's gone.'

'My goodness,' Virginia said.

'Toby said that everyone's talking about it. The managing directors have gone into an emergency meeting and the press is camping outside the building. They smell a rat or a story or something.'

'If only they knew!' Ella laughed.

'They can't find out, can they?' Virginia asked.

'No,' Ella and Clara said.

Just then the telephone rang and Clara answered it. She walked out of the room with it and returned a few minutes later. 'That was Josh.'

'What did he say?'

'Congratulations. And then he asked if he could see me but I said no.'

'Why, Clara?' Ella asked.

'I just can't. End of subject.' They read on in silence, but they kept smiling to themselves. They were savouring their first victory.

'Who's next?' Clara asked.

'What for?'

'Well, now we've proved that revenge works, we should move on to our next victim,' Clara said.

'I think it should be Tim,' Virginia suggested. 'Well, it was you who got this done – you know Josh and everything. I think Tim should be next.'

'I agree,' Ella said.

'Thanks, girls, I appreciate it. Let's get Tim Pemberton.'

'I'll drink to that,' Ella said, and they clinked their coffee cups.

Chapter Twenty-nine

The media hounded SFH for a week. The company issued a statement saying that the bad judgement of one of their senior salespeople had resulted in the buying of the stock and that that salesperson was no longer with the company. They denied any foul play, or that they had listened to rumour; they pointed out that buying was often done on judgement and that was the whole story. They also said that they would be reimbursing their clients with any money lost as a show of goodwill. Their main priority was regaining client confidence. SFH had suffered as a result of JF Technologies, but they would recover. Someone was brought in from an outside company to take over Isabelle's job.

For the first time since they'd lost their jobs Virginia, Ella and Clara were happy. They had found something to fill the void in their lives. Virginia didn't feel any guilt towards Isabelle: the woman had treated her appallingly and now she was finished. It was a blow on behalf of everyone who had been treated unjustly, and Virginia felt empowered. Isabelle had been given a taste of her own medicine.

She still couldn't believe how easy it had been. The plan had been so simple, and it had all happened so quickly. She thought back to the times when she had let people hurt her.

Her parents, Noël, numerous friends and her boss. She had let them: she hadn't ever argued or stood up for herself. Well, now she was standing up for herself and everyone else who had been treated badly. It was a new feeling; a good feeling.

Ella was still unsure of how the plan had worked. She discussed it with Jackie, who was delighted by everything. She said they were lucky to have had Josh because it couldn't have worked without him, but Ella knew that Isabelle's ego and her greed had really caused her downfall. Ella knew that when she herself was trading she treated all information with suspicion. She would not have been quite so eager to take the information and use it — although she couldn't say that she wouldn't have fallen for it. It had been professionally executed after all.

It was the personal aspect of what they were doing that interested Jackie, and Ella told her she should be studying psychology not English. When she spoke of Clara's unpredictable behaviour and Virginia trying to find her voice, Jackie was fascinated. But Ella was frustrated by it: a friendship was not developing and they still knew little about each other, although they seemed bound together. Ella hoped this was only temporary.

Clara felt invincible. She only wished she could tell James what was happening. Whenever she saw him, she told him she was still trying to find her vocation. She didn't tell him that revenge was proving more rewarding than anything she'd done before. And then there was Josh: he kept calling her, asking to meet her. She refused him all the time, and she was sure that that was the only reason for his continued interest. It was obvious that he didn't really want her or care for her. He just saw a pretty girl who had rejected him and it grated on him. A man like Josh couldn't accept this. She just wished it didn't hurt so much.

Now she would look forward. She would look forward to

the day when Tim got his comeuppance. She would relish that. Until that, and until they had got Johnny as well, nothing else mattered. Clara had a mission and she loved it.

On Sunday, they met to discuss Tim, their success driving them on to the next goal. This one belonged to Ella. As they sat around Clara's dining-table, she outlined her plan.

'Here, look at this.' She reached into her bag and took out the *Sunday News*.

'Oh, lovely, Ella buys tabloids,' Clara said, barely glancing at it.

'Yes, I do, and I read them along with a huge number of the population of this country. The circulation is huge.'

'*I* don't read them,' Virginia announced.

'Well, there's a surprise,' Clara said.

'Shut up a minute. Look at the headlines. It's all about sleaze, sex, drugs and celebrities.'

'Really? Gosh!' Clara picked it up.

'OK. Imagine this. "Top Managing Director of One of Britain's Most Respected Investment Banks in Prostitute and Cocaine Scandal.' Ella sat back in her chair.

'Fuck, you're a genius,' Clara conceded, when what Ella was suggesting had sunk in.

'Thanks,' Ella replied.

'But how?' Virginia asked worriedly; this type of newspaper scared her.

'Well, let's just think. Tim uses prostitutes, we know that, and he uses cocaine. Reporters love to discredit people and he could be a prime candidate.'

'Yes. We could set him up so that he talks to them about his prostitutes and we could even get him to offer them cocaine. It's brilliant!' Clara was relishing the time when she would see the headline.

'But how?' Virginia repeated.

'Well, I haven't worked out the details, but the way I see it is that Tim is an egotistical man. We engineer a meeting with a reporter under some sort of pretence and he talks. Then they expose him. How smart is he, Clara?'

'Not very. At work he plays the clean-living married man, but I know he'll talk, given the right situation. After all, I know all about his sick life. If he told me then he'll tell anyone.'

'Yes, but you were sleeping with him.' Virginia pointed out.

'I know, but what I'm saying is that if someone comes along and he wants to impress them, it won't take much to get him to talk. He told me practically as soon as we started having sex, which was a gamble. I know we can't get anyone to sleep with him – well, unless *you* want to, Virginia,' Virginia turned crimson, and Clara continued, 'but we can easily get someone to make him talk.'

'So there we go. The thing is, what sort of people does he need to meet to spill the beans?' Ella asked.

'Surely we can't just get a meeting with a reporter and expect him to do that.' Virginia still couldn't understand how this would work.

'He'd need to be probed a bit. These reporters pose as other people, they don't just say, "Hi, I'm a reporter, can you get me some cocaine?" What are his weaknesses, Clara?'

Clara looked thoughtful. 'Class.'

'Class?' Ella prompted.

'He's working class, although he'd never admit it. He's from somewhere in London, he grew up in a council house, a real poor guy who made a fortune by working himself up.'

'So he's clever,' Virginia protested.

'No, he *was* clever but now he has everything he ever wanted he's more relaxed. How do you think we ended up together? I seduced him and he fell for me.'

'But you said he's revolting.' Virginia said.

'Yes, but I wanted promotion, you know that. He allowed

himself to be seduced and then he turned nasty. Anyway, I don't see what this has to do with anything.'

'In what way was he nasty?' Virginia asked.

'Well, he used me for his fantasies. He gave me cocaine to make me do what he wanted. He once, well he once, I think he raped me. Anyway, that's irrelevant. He's a major sleaze.'

'He *raped* you?' Virginia gasped.

'My God,' Ella said.

'Look, I wasn't going to tell you. I mean, he might not have done.'

'Clara, he either raped you or he didn't,' Ella said gently.

'I can't be sure.' Clara looked upset.

'Honey, did he have sex with you against your will?' Ella's voice was soft.

'Is there such a thing for a sex addict?' Clara asked.

'Yes, there is. Tell us,' Ella commanded.

'When he found out about me sleeping with the client, I didn't go to work because I overslept. Tim came over. He asked me if I slept with Stephen and I said I did. Then he shouted at me and then he, well, he pushed me to the floor, and he pinned my hands down and he opened my bathrobe and undid his trousers and put himself inside me.' Tears were streaming down Clara's face.

'Clara, that is rape. You should have called the police.' Virginia reached over and hugged her.

'I couldn't call the police – how could I? Who would they have believed? Him or me? And I really think he didn't see it as rape. Afterwards he acted like nothing had happened, and as we were having an affair, I guess I didn't think it could be rape. Oh, God. What a mess.'

'Clara, listen to me. He had no right to do what he did to you. I know that, you know that. Listen, darling, you don't want to go to the police but we'll ruin the bastard for you. I promise you we'll do this.' Ella's eyes were shining with tears. She felt so sad for the lost girl who sat before them. The girl who thought so little of herself that she could believe a man was allowed to rape her. Every bad thing she had thought about Clara in the past evaporated. Clara needed help. They sat together while Clara cried, then got angry and shouted, then screamed abuse about the man who had done this to her. They held her when she fell into their arms, they moved away when she wanted to vent her rage.

Eventually she calmed down. 'I've been such a fool. OK, we'll get him. Back to the plan. Remember what I said, his background is his weakness.' Clara looked at Virginia and Ella with determination. They saw this as a sign not to discuss the rape further.

'How about we get a journalist to pose as someone with a title – a lord or something? We can tell him to ask Tim where he can get cocaine and prostitutes. He'll fall for that, won't he?' Ella suggested. Clara smiled

'I'm sure he will. He would never be able to resist a title. My background impressed him – he was always asking about my family and school and everything. Wow, Ella, that's a fantastic idea.'

'How do we get this set up?' Virginia hated being the one who asked the stupid questions, but this sounded even more bizarre than the last project.

'Well, he wants to see me again,' Clara said.

'So you arrange to meet him, don't turn up and we get a reporter to start talking to him while he's waiting for you. He'll call you, you say you can't make it. He'll be pissed off and then he'll stay drinking with this guy who's posing as a toff.' Ella clapped her hands.

'Do you really think it will work?' Virginia almost whispered.

Clara and Ella looked at her sharply. 'Don't you?' Ella asked.

For some reason Virginia wanted to cry. The Isabelle plan had been something she could understand: it had involved brains and strategy. This was different. 'I suppose I'm just a bit worried about it being public. And, well, I know Tim deserves everything he gets, but what about his family?' That was her worry; going to the press might present all sorts of problems. If it came out who had started this set-up, their lives might be ruined. Although Virginia felt hers was ruined already.

'We'll be doing his family a favour. They deserve to know what he's like. You can't back out now.' Clara looked stern.

'But Virginia's right. There's a bigger risk to us here, because we're going to have to speak to a reporter to get the ball rolling.' Dread ran through Ella. If the press found out who she was, her life might be turned upside down. She might even be convicted of Tony's murder – or Sam might be implicated. They were bound to do some research on the person who was giving them the information – they wouldn't just take their word for it. She couldn't be the one to do this. She hadn't thought about it properly.

Clara went to get something to drink. Her head was filled with the same thoughts as Ella's. If she went to a reporter and they found out she was a member of the prestigious Hart family they'd have a field day. They would probably think it was more of a story than Tim's sleaziness. Especially if they did their research and found out she had been sacked from SFH. 'Shit, shit, shit,' Clara said aloud, as she slammed the fridge door. Then, as she grabbed three wineglasses, she had an idea. She knew it might turn out to be the worst idea she had ever had, but it was all she had.

'Here, have a drink.' She poured the white wine and lit a cigarette. 'One of us has to go to the journalist. It can't be me because I had an affair with Tim and these guys are smart. I doubt it would take any time at all for them to find out all the gory details. Then I would be headline news too. My father owns the Hart Corporation, which is a huge company, and my brother works there and it would be used to make the story even better. My parents are a bit society, often in gossip columns. My father even got a knighthood a couple of years back. I can't risk my family being dragged into this. They'd never speak to me again.'

'I understand,' Ella said. Virginia wished she had a family like Clara's, or any family other than her own.

'So, Ella, you'll have to do it.'

Ella turned a funny colour. 'No,' she said.

'What?' Clara asked.

'I said no.' Ella lit a cigarette. Virginia noticed that her hand was shaking.

'Ella, you have to. It was your idea and we can't contemplate letting Virginia loose with a hard-nosed reporter.'

'Then we won't do it.'

'But we have to! Shit, Ella, what is this? You can handle the situation. You just tell them you are an ex-SFH employee, you knew Tim well, and you saw what he got up to. They may look into your background, but the only thing they'll find is that you were fired and you'll tell them that anyway. We know why you were fired, but they won't find that out because SFH wants to keep it quiet. You say you're not doing this for revenge but you think it's a great story and you want some money. If they think you're doing it for the money, they'll accept it.'

'No. Just drop it,' Ella hissed.

'I fucking well won't. You just heard what I've been through. You have to do this for me. If you don't have a good reason like me, you have to do it.' Clara and Ella were on their feet, and Virginia wanted to run away.

After a while, Ella sat down and poured more wine.

'You don't understand. I can't do it,' Ella said quietly.

'Then tell us,' Clara demanded.

Ella winced. 'This is a day for revelations. OK. First, you know I was sacked because I faked a degree certificate. I know SFH have hushed it up and given another reason for my dismissal, but I can't risk the papers getting hold of it.'

'But I already said they won't find out. How can they? You just tell them you are Ella Franke, formerly from Manchester, worked at SFH, and they'll get the story that you were sacked for losing money or whatever it is SFH are saying. Traders lose money all the time, so you're not even remotely an interesting story.' At first Clara thought sending Ella to try to charm a journalist was going to be difficult because Ella was horribly un-charming. Now she knew it was their only hope.

'Because, Clara, if they try to do any research into my background they'll find out something I don't want them to.' Ella lit another cigarette.

Virginia reached for the wine, not taking her eyes off Ella. 'What?' Clara said.

'That I'm not Ella Franke.' Ella bolted into the bathroom where she locked the door and tried to think.

Her heart was thudding. No one but Jackie knew this and now she'd blurted it out to them! Ella couldn't believe what she'd done. Clara had riled her, but she could have said anything. Anything but the truth she had hidden for the last four years.

Clara looked at Virginia. 'Shit,' she said.

'We need to talk to her, find out what's wrong.' Virginia tried to remain calm.

'I know what's wrong. We're with someone and we don't even know her fucking name. What is she playing at?' Clara asked.

'Let's try to get her out of the bathroom,' Virginia sug-gested.

'You go. I need some coke.'

Virginia felt sick as she knocked on the bathroom door. There was no reply.

'Ella, are you all right?' she asked quietly.

'Yes,' Ella replied.

'Will you come out?'

'Of course I'll fucking come out. Did you think I was going to move in here?'

'No, Ella ... but, well, just come out.' Virginia was red-faced.

Ella opened the door, walked back to the table and sat down.

'Are you going to tell us who you are?' Virginia asked.

'To you I'm Ella, and that's all you need to know,' Ella replied.

'Actually, that's where you're wrong. We've sailed close to the wind with you — the whole Isabelle thing, now Tim, next Johnny. And if you think for one minute I'm going to continue working with someone whose real name I don't know, let alone what other things you're hiding from us, then think again.' Clara sat down, wiping white powder from the side of her nose.

'None of us knows who we are, so that's a pretty stupid thing to say,' Ella replied.

'I know who I am and I know who Virginia is, but you could be a major criminal for all we know.' Clara was shouting again.

Ella burst into tears.

In that moment, something happened to the three girls that they would never be able to explain. They had not seen Ella cry before. She had looked close to tears when Clara talked about the rape, but she had held them back. Clara had cried, Virginia had cried, but not Ella. Virginia moved her chair closer to Ella's and took her in her arms. As she held her, Ella cried and cried until Clara got up and put her arms around both of them. They waited until Ella's tears stopped before they let go. Virginia reached into her bag and gave Ella a tissue. Clara went to make coffee.

'Thanks,' Ella said.

Suddenly Virginia felt that after all she had heard today, she was the only one of them who had any normality left. 'Ella, whatever it is, whatever you're going through, you can tell us. God, we know more about each other than most people do. We know what really happened to Clara, we know I have no personality and I've never had sex, we know you lied to get your job. We ruined Isabelle's career together. I know we're not exactly friends but what we have is important to all of us. That's our bond. So, please, when Clara comes back, tell us your story.'

Virginia surprised Ella. She was calm, clear, and she was also right.

'You do have a personality, Virginia, and I think it may be a very nice one. You just need to get more confident,' Ella said, and smiled at her.

Clara returned with the coffee. 'So, are you going to spill?' Clara said.

'Clara, shut up. Ella will tell us in her own time,' Virginia snapped.

Clara opened her mouth to retort, but changed her mind.

'So, do you want to hear my story?' Ella said. The others nodded. 'OK, then I'll begin.' She took a drink, lit a cigarette and, watching the two anxious faces in front of her, she started talking. 'I was born Elloise Butcher. I know I changed my name but that's not all.' Ella told them of how she met Tony, agreed to marry him and how he had hit her. She told them about the last beating and Sam's rescue. As she spoke the others remained silent as they listened to her horrific story. Ella spoke as if in a trance. As she described some of the horror, Virginia had to stop herself from crying. 'One day after a nasty beating my brother came to see me.' She closed her eyes briefly, remembering the pain. 'I wouldn't let him in. I wouldn't let anyone near me. He broke down the door, saw me all battered and bruised and carried me out. I even told him I didn't want to go. God knows why. Then he started to plan revenge. Just like we're doing, only worse. He was so angry. He paid for some thugs to do to Tony what he had done to me. Only it went too far. I got a call from the hospital saying that Tony was in a coma and the hospital traced me to my parents' house. Sam and I went to the hospital. Sam said it would look suspicious if I didn't.

There were police everywhere and as I was in shock. Sam told them we'd recently split due to arguments. He said we'd had no idea that this had happened. The police said thugs broke into the club when Tony was alone in the early hours of the morning – it had been a robbery. Sam's guys had taken money to make it look that way. They said they could do nothing until Tony came round – if Tony came round. Although they didn't suspect us, Sam said I should leave rather than stay and face any music, so I did.

'Tony was lying there with all these tubes and he looked dead. I didn't feel sad – he looked the way he had made me look so many times. Sam said the guys had gone too far, but it was too late to do anything but try to get on with life. I couldn't do that there. He arranged for me to change my name, got me fake documents and sent me to London with a bit of money. You know the rest. I met my friend Jackie when I went to work for her as a waitress. I saw an article about the lack of black people in the City. I read books, got a fake degree and got my job at SFH. I wouldn't call Sam – I couldn't. I was too scared for him and for me. So I still don't know if Tony is alive or dead. I couldn't bring myself to find out. And now I don't know if I'm a fugitive or if I'm in the clear. I ran like a scared mouse. I know Sam's not in jail because I send him cheques, but that's all I know. I won't let myself call him – God knows I want to, but I can't. He saved my life and I felt that by disappearing maybe I could save his. I've messed up in a way I could never contemplate and I haven't a clue how to put my life back together. But I know that if I go anywhere near a journalist I could get into more trouble, or get Sam into trouble and I won't do that. I'll never do that.' Ella stopped, her eyes misted with tears.

They sat around the dining-table as they had so many times. But this time they didn't know what to think, say, or do. All three were feeling disbelief, even Ella: even after all this time, she could hardly believe her story.

'My God,' Clara said. For once she was lost for words.

'So you see why I can't do it,' Ella finished.

'I'll get more wine.' Clara got up and went for it via her bedroom. She felt as if she was watching one of those tacky TV shows in which a presenter, usually with a bad hairpiece, pretended to be sympathetic to guests whose lives were a mess. Clara thought her life was a mess but it was nothing compared to Ella's. She might even be wanted for murder. 'Holy shit,' Clara said to herself, as she lined up her cocaine. 'What the hell have I got myself into?'

When Clara had left the room Virginia sat still, not knowing what to say to Ella. She could hardly believe what she'd just heard. It was like a horror story and it had happened to Ella. Virginia had always thought Ella was the coldest person, but she was the one with the biggest problems and the saddest story. Clara came a close second. Virginia felt guilty about her indulgence in self-pity.

The three girls sat sipping wine in silence. The drug addict, the nobody and the fugitive. They didn't know what they were all doing there, or what would happen to them, but for some reason they began to feel that they fitted together. They didn't fit anywhere else.

Chapter Thirty

—————➤◆◄—————

'Look I know we could leave it for tonight if you want, Ella, but we still need to decide what to do about Tim,' Clara said.

'Maybe we should rethink the plan,' Virginia suggested.

'No. We've worked hard on this, and just because Clara and I have a problem facing the press, we can still do it.'

'How?' Clara asked.

'Virginia,' Ella said.

'What?' Clara and Virginia said simultaneously.

'Virginia will do it. She's got no secrets, no high-profile family and no problems fobbing them off with why she left SFH. She's perfect.' Ella smiled for the first time since she had bared her soul, Virginia turned very white and couldn't speak.

'Ella, you've fucking lost it. Look at her! She's only just learning how to have a conversation with us, let alone with a stranger who happens to be a reporter. She'd be useless.'

'Not necessarily. We'll prep her and it will do wonders for her self-confidence. She'll be fine.'

'Ella, she's a mouse. A reporter would eat her for breakfast.' Clara was furious.

'No, they won't. She'll be fine.'

'They *will*! Ella, this is crazy, it'll never work!' Clara roared.

'It fucking well will,' Ella said.

'Please, stop.' It was Virginia. The others turned to look at her. 'Clara's right. I can't do this.'

'Yes, you can. Virginia, you're our only hope.' Ella looked at her pleadingly.

'But what if they intimidate me as much as you do sometimes?'

'We do not,' Clara said.

'We'll prepare for this. Virginia, you can do it. Please,' Ella implored.

'Oh, God, I may as well call Tim and tell him all about our plan.' Clara threw her hands up in the air.

'Do you have any better ideas? Virginia can do this – she'll prove you wrong.'

'No, she'll prove *you* wrong,' Clara stated.

'She'll prove me right,' Ella said.

Virginia listened to them with mixed feelings. She was flattered that Ella thought she could do it, and felt hurt at Clara's insistence that she was useless, although part of her agreed wholeheartedly with that. And she would say all the wrong things and probably end up looking like a fool . . . But part of her wanted to do it, to prove she could.

'Christ, Ella, are you really willing to jeopardise everything by putting her in front of a hungry journalist?'

'By the time we've finished with her she'll be fine. She's not stupid, Clara, just shy. We'll prepare her so that she could win over any journalist. And, let's face it, she's the most innocent-looking one of us. No one's going to think she made it up.'

'I suppose so. But only because I don't have any other ideas. We can't send her in wearing her horrible jeans and even more horrible jumpers.' Clara sniffed.

'Um, were either of you going to talk to me about this rather than just plotting it together?' Virginia was peeved.

'Sorry, Virginia. Will you do it?' Ella asked.

'Well, I'll try. But you know how I get in front of strangers.'

'Yes, and we'll have to work on your appearance,' Clara said.

'Virginia?' Ella asked.

'I don't have much choice, do I? You helped me get Isabelle, and this is the least I can do.' Virginia felt nervous just thinking about it.

'OK. I'll find the right reporter and I'll script the story. Clara, you have to get in touch with Tim, hint you may want to see him soon, keep him hanging on. You can work on Virginia's appearance too. I mean, Virginia, there's nothing wrong with the way you look, but you should be a bit more sophisticated for this.' Ella tried to sound diplomatic.

'It's fine. I know I'm not the height of chic. And I'll do it, but please, Clara, be gentle with me.' Virginia laughed and the others did too.

'Sometimes, Virginia, I almost think you're funny,' Clara said, as she refilled the wineglasses yet again.

They kept drinking. The initial plot was set but they didn't make any move to leave. It was late, and Virginia was so nervous that she was getting more and more drunk. Ella was upset so she was drinking more than usual, and Clara was worried so she was drinking more than both of them. By the time they stopped, it was out of the question for anyone to drive. They talked more about Ella's situation. Clara was sure that Tony was alive and said that Ella should think about getting in touch with her brother. Virginia said that if her family loved her as she said they did, she should call them. After all, not everyone was lucky enough to have a family like that. Ella said she wanted to, but she was still too scared.

'We're all scared of something, aren't we?' Clara asked.

'I guess so,' Ella replied.

'So we have something else in common,' Virginia added.

'Thanks, you guys.' Ella smiled.

'What for?' Clara had never heard Ella sound so nice.

'For not judging me, for listening, for being ... well, for understanding.'

'I think that's the nicest thing you've ever said to us,' Clara said.

'Well, there you go. I have a voice and Ella has a heart. What more surprises are in store for us?' Virginia joked.

'I dread to think.' Ella laughed. Another barrier had come down.

They all stayed in Clara's flat that night. Virginia passed out from all the alcohol, Ella cried herself to sleep, and Clara took some more cocaine. She thought about Ella and felt for her. Although Tim had never hit her, the way he raped her had been violent. Clara knew that she had screwed up her life. She had been trying so hard to make her family proud of her, but they would probably disown her if they ever found out the truth. Every time she spoke to them, they wanted her to go home more, meet suitable men, get married. She had tried to tell them that she wanted more from life, but they said she was wrong. If she became Prime Minister her father would still say, 'I didn't send you to finishing school to become Prime Minister, I sent you to learn to cook.' She smiled to herself sadly as she thought how nice it would be to have their unconditional love.

They got up the next morning, still deep in thought. They agreed to think through the details of the plan and arranged to meet again on Tuesday. They were eager to get on with it before anyone changed their mind.

Chapter Thirty-one

Virginia went back to her poky flat. She didn't know which was most worrying: having to speak to a journalist or Clara's plan to make her look sophisticated. She sat in her room and tried to calm herself. It didn't work so she decided to go for a drive. On the way back she stopped at the supermarket to buy potatoes and baked beans. Since losing her job she had put herself on a tighter budget than usual. Even though she had saved money when she was working she knew that what she had wouldn't last for ever. When she reached home she picked up her mail and went into her room. She put a potato into the oven and looked at her letters. At last there was one for her parents.

She read it with a sinking feeling. They hadn't even read her letter properly. It was filled with accusations and disappointment. 'You can't even hold down a job as a sec-retary. There really is no hope for you,' read one particu-larly hurtful line. Virginia threw it away. She had tried to explain, but her parents didn't want to know. As far as they were concerned, she had messed up yet again. If only they knew what she was doing now. Not that that would make them proud. Nothing Virginia did would make them proud.

She ate her meal, feeling more alone than ever. Clara was right. She was a gutless, useless mouse. The only upside was that if she pulled off the thing with the journalist, then someone would have to show her respect for that.

Ella went home and called Jackie. She told her that Clara and Virginia knew everything now and described the new plan. Jackie said the *Sunday News* would definitely be the best paper to contact.

She spent the afternoon drafting the story. She wasn't sure if she was mad to push Virginia into this, or if she was being quite sane. She hoped it was the latter. She decided not to think about it, but to concentrate on her task.

Clara went shopping, which she hadn't done in ages, because of her love affair with cocaine. She went to Harvey Nichols, guessing that Virginia was a size ten because she was slim. She hadn't asked Virginia because she hadn't wanted to scare her — or go shopping with her.

As she browsed, she thought about what sort of outfit to buy. She didn't want to put her in a suit — if she looked too much like a serious City girl then the journalist might feel hostile towards her. If she looked slightly sexy and trendy, she might win him over. How she was going to get Virginia to look sexy was another matter.

She walked around picking up a number of things for herself before finding the perfect outfit: a below-the-knee black skirt, a pink top and a black cardigan. It was a modern look, and would make Virginia look taller, sophisticated and, hopefully, confident. She paid for the clothes, without noticing the cost. Then she went to look for shoes. When she realised she couldn't guess at Virginia's size, she pulled out her mobile.

'Virginia, it's Clara. What shoe size are you?'

'Why?'

'I'm finding you shoes, of course.' Clara was impatient.

'Five.'

'Thanks, 'bye.' Clara hung up before Virginia had a chance to ask any more questions.

She found a pair of black open-toed kitten-heeled mules. They were so pretty that she bought a pair for Virginia in a five and a pair for herself in a four.

She rewarded her good work with a drink in the bar before going home. There she called her hairdresser and booked Virginia in for the next afternoon. As it had been an exhausting day, she went back to bed.

They had agreed to meet at eleven o'clock at Clara's flat on Tuesday. Virginia was early as usual and filled with nerves. Clara decided to be nice to her for once. She gave her coffee, sat her on the sofa and made small-talk until Ella turned up.

'Hi.' Ella felt a bit sheepish now that they knew her secret.

'Are you ready to outline the plan?' Clara had felt Ella's discomfort and decided not to prolong it.

'OK. I think I've found the perfect reporter. His name is Declan Davies, although I doubt that's his real name. Anyway, he loves scandals and he seems to do more of them than anyone else. I don't know what he looks like, so I guess he keeps a low profile, and I don't know what he's like, but apparently his reputation is as the best,' Ella said.

'How do you know he's the best?' Clara asked.

'I called the *Sunday News*, told them I had a dynamite story and asked who I should speak to.'

'You made it sound like you'd found him personally,' Clara said.

'Does it matter? The fact is, we've got him. I'm going to call him and give him the outline. I'll pretend to be Virginia, fix up a meeting and then it's down to you.' Ella looked at Virginia, who began to sweat. 'It's OK, Virginia, you'll be so well prepared that nothing can go wrong. Anyway, when I speak to Declan the details of the story will be something like this: I previously worked at SFH, but was asked to leave due to a clash with my boss. This has nothing to do with my boss, so don't think it's a cheap revenge thing. Then I'll say that a senior managing director and shareholder is involved in something that would be a major scandal for the bank – I know this because I overheard a private conversation. Then I'll ask if he would like to meet. I'll also ask if they pay for things like this, which again gives a motive. If he thinks I just want to make some money, that gives more backbone to the whole thing.'

'You mean we're going to get Tim *and* get paid for it?' Clara laughed.

'Yes, I think so. Isn't that great?' Ella relaxed. 'Once I've set up the meeting you have to give Virginia details about Tim. We need her to sound convincing.'

'I think I can do this,' Virginia said, as confidently as she could.

'You bloody well better,' Clara retorted. 'Although I've just had a thought. You sound like you're from Manchester, Ella. If you call this guy and he meets Virginia who doesn't, won't he be suspicious?'

'Clara, my accent isn't strong, you know that, and people always sound a bit different on the phone. Virginia's slight Midlands accent will sound like my slight Manchester accent. I bet he doesn't even take much notice.'

'So you're from the Midlands?' Clara asked.

'Yes,' Virginia replied.

'Bloody hell, two northerners. You're the only two northerners I know.'

Ella and Virginia exchanged glances, but thought it best to keep quiet.

Ella went to Clara's bedroom to make the phone call. She got through straight away, which was a good omen. She introduced herself and outlined the story as she had told the others she would. Declan was interested.

'I can find this guy with drugs and prostitutes?'

'Well, I don't know about finding him with them, but I'm sure with the right probing he would offer to get you some cocaine and introduce you to prostitutes.' Ella felt nervous, she dreaded to think how Virginia would cope.

'So, how exactly does this work?'

'Well, of course you'll want to meet me, and I will give you more details then you make me an offer. I promise this is not a waste of time. You tell me how much money you're prepared to offer if the story is all I say it is, and we'll go from there.'

'How do I know you're not wasting my time?' Declan asked.

'Because if I was you'd know it instinctively. You're a journalist.' That did the trick. Ella set up a meeting for two days' time. She just hoped that when Virginia met him she would not behave as she normally did.

She went back into the sitting room and told the others what had happened. Virginia tried to look brave when Ella told her the meeting was the day after tomorrow.

Clara, though, was animated. 'Should I call Tim now?' she asked.

'Yes, and tell him that you think you'd like to see him, but you'll call him soon with a time and place. See what he says. And, Clara, good luck.' Ella squeezed Clara's hand. She knew it wouldn't be easy for her to speak to Tim.

Clara took a line of cocaine, counted to five then picked up the telephone. She rang his private line and prayed he would pick up. He did.

'Tim Pemberton,' the familiar voice said.

'Tim, it's Clara.' She was actually shaking.

'Clara, darling, I thought I'd never hear from you.'

'I had a lot of thinking to do,' Clara faltered.

'So you've seen sense. You want to see me.' His confidence was intact.

'Well, yes, I do. I just don't know when. Can I give you another call?'

'Why can't we arrange it now?' Tim sounded offended.

'Because, Tim, this is a big step for me, and I need to be sure that the day I see you I can handle it. Please, be patient with me, after all we've been through.'

'OK, Clara, you don't need to dredge up the past now. You'll call me soon.' It wasn't a question.

'By the end of the week.'

''Bye, Clara.' He sounded mollified, but Clara needed to be sure, she mustered all her courage.

''Bye, Timmy,' she said, in her most seductive voice, which she knew would ensure that he bought her story, hook, line and sinker.

'It's all fine,' she announced to the others. 'Virginia, I've made an appointment for you to see my hairdresser. We need to get you looking like the type of girl who would sell a story for money. At the moment you don't.'

'But isn't all this a bit drastic?' Virginia stammered.

'No. And stop stammering. You're going to *look* confident, you're going to *be* confident, and you're going to have this Declan eating out of your hand. You have to.'

'Do you want us to come to the hairdresser with you?' Ella asked kindly.

'Yes, please,' Virginia replied.

'Well, I think we'd better. If not she'll probably come away with a blue rinse,' Clara said.

'Clara, I don't think I can be someone I'm not,' Virginia pleaded.

'As we don't have the first clue who you are, I'm not sure that's possible,' Clara said firmly.

Ella smiled at Virginia again. 'It'll be fine, just you see.'

'I need the bathroom.' Virginia rushed out.

'If this goes horribly wrong, I'm going to hold you responsible,' Clara said.

'It'll be fine. I'll make sure of it. Don't worry, we will place a twenty-four-hour armed guard on Virginia. She can stay with me, if you like, until after the meeting.'

'Oh, no. I can just see the two of you screwing up. You can both stay here. As soon as she's finished at the hairdresser, you both go and collect some stuff and come back. I don't want either of you out of my sight.'

'Clara, relax. This will go just as well as the Isabelle thing, I promise.' Ella kept her cool.

'The Isabelle thing relied on the charisma of Josh, who has bags of it. This relies on the charisma of Virginia, who has none.' And with that Clara went back to her bedroom.

Chapter Thirty-two

They all set off for the hairdresser. Clara had tried to persuade Virginia to wear some of her clothes; Virginia had refused. Clara had said they probably wouldn't let her through the door of the hairdresser's looking like an Oxfam reject. Virginia had said she wouldn't go then, and Ella had to pacify them. She told Clara it didn't matter what Virginia wore now. Eventually they had set off. Clara moaned that for two people with transport it seemed ridiculous to have to get a cab. Ella said she was quite welcome to ride on the back of Virginia's scooter. Clara said that Ella's car was posy and impractical. Ella said that in that case it would suit Clara down to the ground. They were still arguing as they got into a black cab.

The hairdresser was in Knightsbridge. As soon as they got out of the taxi Virginia took one look and started walking in the other direction. Clara grabbed her. 'You'll be fine, get in.' She pushed her through the door.

Once inside Virginia was rooted to the spot. The salon was huge and white, filled with lots of people with different-coloured hair. They were the hairdressers. Most of the clients were either blonde or in the process of becoming blonde. Most of them had jewellery dripping off them; they looked expensive. As they all turned to look at Virginia, she wished that she'd taken Clara's advice and changed.

Clara marched up to the reception desk. 'Hi, darling, I've got an appointment for my friend.'

The ultra-trendy girl, with spiky pink hair and a pierced lip, looked at Virginia. She arched her eyebrows. 'Fabio is just finishing off. He'll be with you in a second, darling.' Then she looked at Ella. 'Are you all together?' she asked.

'Yes,' Clara answered, and handed over her coat. Ella sat down on one of the huge white beanbags, which she presumed were reception chairs. Virginia was still immobilised just in front of the door.

After what seemed like ages, a huge man with a blue Afro haircut and wearing a tight white T-shirt came up to Clara. 'Clara, darlin', how the hell are you?'

'I'm fab, Fabio.' Clara giggled at her appalling joke and they air-kissed. Ella rolled her eyes. Fabio was a London boy who looked like someone from another planet. Typical Clara. Virginia was now looking at Fabio, although she still hadn't moved.

'It's my friend you'll be working on today, Fabio. Meet Virginia.' Clara pulled Fabio to where she stood.

Fabio looked her over. 'I love the retro-eighties look. So, Virginia, what'll it be?' he asked.

'Huh?' Virginia said. Ella went to stand next to her, in case she fainted.

'Well, Fabio,' Clara answered for her, 'she needs transforming. You can see that. I thought maybe some colour, a trendy cut. You're the expert, though, darling.'

Fabio pulled Virginia over to a stool and pushed her down on to it. Ella and Clara followed him.

'OK. I think blonde – she'll make a good blonde. After all, her eyes are almost blue.' He stared at them. 'Well, grey, anyway. I'll give her a spiky cut, not too severe but sexy. Very sexy.' He smiled. Virginia was rigid with fear.

'Sounds divine,' Clara said.

Not for the first time Ella felt sorry for Virginia.

After that someone was summoned to take Virginia away and put her in a gown, which was more like a hospital gown than a hairdresser's gown; it reminded Ella of the way people looked before they had surgery. She and Clara sat down on two white chairs near Fabio's cutting station.

'Clara, did you have to bring her here?' Ella hissed.

'It's the best place in London,' Clara replied.

'But if we'd taken her somewhere less trendy she might not have gone into such a state of shock. This place is too trendy for anyone,' Ella continued.

'Oh, shut up. It's not too trendy for me. Anyway, Fabio's a miracle worker and she needs a miracle.'

They watched as Fabio put foils in Virginia's hair, painting it yellow. Virginia still hadn't said a word.

'You're not turning her yellow, are you?' Ella asked, horrified.

'Blonde, darlin', relax. I'm giving her a few different shades of blonde in highlights and a blonde blonde all over. By the way, did you give her Valium before you brought her here? She seems to be away with the fairies.'

'She's naturally quiet,' Clara explained, wondering how Virginia was ever going to talk to a journalist. Fabio finished painting Virginia's hair and set her under a dryer.

'I bet it'll look great,' Ella said to Virginia, who didn't respond.

'Leave her alone. Shit, Ella, if she goes into a coma in a hairdresser's she'll have no chance with the journalist,' Clara whispered.

'Well, in that case you'll have to pretend to be her and go along instead.'

'You know I can't do that. He might find out. Anyway, I'm not wasting three hundred pounds on her hair if she doesn't do it.'

'Shit *Clara*! That's a bit steep.'

'I told you, Fabio works miracles.' They scowled at each

other then sat quietly until a young man with red spiky hair took the dryer away and told Virginia he was taking her to wash her hair. Virginia didn't move, so he took her arm. She looked at him and then followed him to the white basin. The hair-washer tried to have a conversation with Virginia but she didn't even speak when he asked if the water was all right. When he'd finished, he led her back to the chair. Ella and Clara looked at the wet blonde hair and Virginia covered her eyes with her hands.

Fabio returned. 'It looks lovely don't it?' he said.

Virginia kept her hands over her eyes. 'Christ, Clara,' she moaned, 'what are you doing to me?'

Fabio started cutting. 'So, what are you up to, darlin'?' he asked Clara.

'Nothing much. I'm not working any more.'

'Always said you were too good-looking to work.' Fabio grinned.

'You sound like my father.'

'Well, you know I'd take care of you.' Fabio laughed.

'But I'm the wrong sex for you,' Clara said.

'You mean you're gay?' Ella regretted the words as soon as they left her mouth. She'd sounded like Virginia.

'Yes, darlin'. Is that a problem?' Fabio teased.

'Sorry. It's just that you don't seem, well, you know . . .' Ella stared wide-eyed at the huge man in front of her – he seemed so masculine.

'Where do you get your friends from Clara?' Fabio said, as he snipped away.

'Don't worry, Fabio, they're both northerners,' Clara said, as if that explained it.

He shrugged. 'Anyway, I'd make an exception in your case, Clara,' he said.

'Thank you, I'll keep it in mind.' Clara shot Ella a look. Fabio took out a hairdryer, plied Virginia with mousse and started drying her hair. She still hadn't removed her hands from her eyes. When he'd finished, he stepped back.

'There you go.' He beamed. Clara stood up to get a better look.

'Wow, Fabio, you're a genius,' she said. Virginia's hair looked amazing.

Ella gulped. 'Christ, she looks great.'

The colour was clever: Fabio had put different shades of gold into Virginia's hair. The cut was funky and attractive. Although they could not see her face, the hair was a definite improvement.

'Virginia, move your hands,' Clara snapped. It had no effect. Ella shrugged moving one of Virginia's hands herself; Fabio removed the other. Virginia's eyes were closed. 'Look, Virginia. Look!' Clara urged excitedly. Virginia opened one eye, then the other. She stared into the mirror and blinked. She didn't know who she was staring at but the girl in the mirror looked great.

'I knew it! I knew she was gorgeous.' Clara clapped her hands and ran to the till to pay.

'Is it me?' Virginia asked.

'Yes, it is, and you look terrific,' Ella replied. She had not imagined in her wildest dreams that Virginia could be so transformed by a haircut. She almost booked an appointment with Fabio herself.

'My God,' Virginia said.

Clara and Ella got Virginia out of the salon. She kept touching her hair. 'Is it me?' she asked again.

'Yes, it bloody well is, and I don't think it's fair that after one haircut you look like a fucking movie star,' Clara said. 'It took me much more than that.' Virginia and Ella gazed at Clara: she looked so peeved that they burst out laughing.

'It's the ugly-duck syndrome,' Clara stated, as they drove back in a cab to her flat.

'I don't think Virginia was ever ugly,' Ella said.

'No, but she looked boring. I always said she had potential, didn't I?' Clara said.

'I look so different,' Virginia said.

'Can you stop obscuring my mirror,' the cab driver asked angrily.

When they got out Ella told Virginia they were going to get their things together so they could stay at Clara's for a couple of days. 'I'll drive us,' she said, and led Virginia to her car.

On the journey Virginia didn't speak; she pulled down the sun visor and stared at herself in the mirror. Ella decided to enjoy the peace. Two days with Clara and Virginia would be anything but peaceful. They went first to Ella's, where she threw a few things in her sports bag, then to Virginia's, then headed back to Clara's.

Clara had had some more cocaine. She was a little miffed by Virginia's new look although she didn't know why. Virginia looked lovely. Clara had hoped she would drag her into the right century, but she hadn't banked on her looking quite so good. She also had not anticipated that Virginia's transformation would bother her.

When they arrived, she had a bottle of red wine waiting.

'Clara, don't tell me you've got alcohol ready.' Ella said dumping her bag by the front door and flopping down on the sofa.

'Well I thought we'd celebrate Virginia turning into an attractive young woman.' Clara said it with a hint of hostility.

'You did this to me,' Virginia retorted sensing the hostility.

'Don't forget it,' Clara hit back pouring the wine.

'I need the bathroom,' Virginia stated and ran to look at herself in the mirror. Again, she couldn't believe it. Apart from the fact she was blonde and her mousy look had gone, she did look good. She looked modern. Her eyes looked bigger and the way he had cut her hair away from her face, made her face look softer. As she smiled at herself in the mirror, she hardly recognised the girl smiling back.

'I've created a monster,' Clara said.

'Shit, Clara, anyone would think you liked her looking the way she did.'

'I didn't. I just didn't think she'd look quite so good.'

'Well it's great for us that she does. The idea was to have the journalist eating out of her hands. And looking like that, she will.'

'As long as she doesn't behave the way she did when she was at the hairdresser,' Clara said.

'We've got tonight and tomorrow to make sure she doesn't,' Ella replied.

When Virginia returned they started preparing her for the journalist. As they drank, Virginia loosened up.

'Thank you, Clara,' Virginia said.

'What for?' Clara asked.

'My hair. I know it's so I don't mess up, but thank you anyway,' Virginia replied.

'Just make sure you don't mess up,' Clara said.

She felt a new confidence. 'You know, maybe I *can* do this,' she added.

'Declan has booked lunch for you at Hush,' Ella told her. 'He insisted.'

'Who pays?' Clara asked.

'He will. We're giving him a story, after all.'

'But I'm not very good at eating in front of strangers.' Virginia's confidence had dissolved already.

'You know which knives and forks to use, don't you?' Clara asked.

'Yes, but ...'

'OK. Just order a salad and say you're on a diet. You don't have to eat much,' Clara told her helpfully.

'The food isn't important,' Ella said impatiently. 'I've written down what you have to say and I've also written down the questions I think he'll ask, with answers. Study them and we'll test you tomorrow. And, Virginia, relax. We're here for you.' Ella handed her a piece of paper.

They spent the rest of the evening trying to build Virginia's confidence. By the time they went to bed, they were exhausted.

With only one day left before the big lunch Virginia didn't sound as if she could handle it.

The following day they continued their preparations. Clara showed Virginia the outfit; Virginia said she didn't like it. Clara accused her of being deliberately difficult and ordered her to try it on. Once she did, she had to admit she felt good. She looked *very* good. It took her a while to learn how to walk in the shoes, because she had never worn heels before. Eventually she got the hang of it and she almost stopped stumbling.

'This Declan guy is going to adore you,' Ella said, trying to believe it.

'*Any* guy would adore you looking like that,' Clara conceded.

'Really?'

'Virginia, you look gorgeous,' Ella said.

By the time they went to bed, they were all tired again. Virginia was tired of all the things she had to remember. Clara had taken too much cocaine and was feeling sick.

Ella was worried – about the plan, about the effect on Virginia and Clara if it went wrong.

No one slept well that night.

Chapter Thirty-three

The following morning the flat was a hive of nerves. They had managed not to argue for one day so tempers were frayed.

Virginia felt sick – Ella practically had to push her into the shower. Afterwards Clara did her hair and put on her makeup while Ella reminded Virginia of what to say.

She insisted on driving Virginia to lunch. She thought that putting her in a cab was asking for trouble. Clara sulked because she had to wait at home, but she insisted Virginia take her mobile: if anything went wrong she could call them from the ladies'. Virginia didn't know how to use it.

'For Christ's sake Virginia, don't tell me you've never used a mobile phone.'

'I haven't,' Virginia said, shaking. It then took a while for Clara to show her, mainly because Clara was swearing constantly.

When they set off, Virginia was looking great but feeling awful.

As Ella parked the car and walked her to the restaurant, early so that she would be there first, she kissed her cheek, which she'd never done before, and wished her luck. 'You'll be fine.' She smiled encouragingly.

'Thanks.'

Virginia wobbled slightly as she walked across the cobbles

to the restaurant door. She stammered as she asked for Declan's booking. She was shown to a table, sat down, ordered a mineral water and waited. She was ten minutes early and she tried not to stare at the door, but she couldn't help it. Just as she had decided to do a runner, Declan came to the table. He was tall and blonde, he looked about forty, and his face was worn – attractively so. He was wearing a very sharp suit, which Virginia felt wouldn't have looked out of place at SFH. He stuck out his hand. 'I'm Declan. You must be Virginia. I hope you haven't been waiting long.'

Virginia took his hand and pulled herself together. 'Not at all.' She smiled.

Declan sat down. He looked at her and Virginia could feel the colour rising. She willed it away.

'Would you like something stronger than water? I thought I'd order some wine.'

'That would be nice. I prefer red.' Virginia had been told to be assertive.

'Then red it is. I hate all this waiting until we know what we're eating. I'm from the school of thought that says wine is great with anything, whatever the colour.' He was smooth and Virginia felt uneasy. On the scale of sophistication, they were at opposite ends. He summoned the waiter and ordered.

'Shall we choose some food?' Declan said, indicating the menu.

He sounded kind. Perhaps he would be nice to her, Virginia hoped, not at all the shark that Ella had said she would be eating with.

'Of course,' she said.

The wine came and Declan announced that they were ready to order. Even though she hadn't eaten the previous day, Virginia was not hungry. She opted for a salad.

'No starter?' Declan asked.

'I'm dieting.' Virginia replied, and smiled at him. She hoped it was the smile she had practised and not a moronic smile.

'You don't need to diet. Maybe I can tempt you with

dessert.' He laughed. A laugh that sounded to Virginia as if it came from a television programme. He wasn't real. She sipped her wine slowly, as Clara had told her to. He was still looking at her, examining her, making her feel uncomfortable.

'So. Tell me about this scandal.' At last Virginia could begin her rehearsed speech. 'I outlined most of it on the telephone. A managing director of SFH is very into cocaine and prostitutes. He also supplies cocaine to certain people. I've read many exposés in your paper and think this one will prove popular.'

'But when you say managing director, what does that mean?' Declan asked.

'SFH is run by twenty-one managing directors who also own the company. It's still private so he is one of the owners of Britain's oldest investment bank. They had a scandal recently, buying the wrong stock – I guess you heard that. Well, this one will rock them further,' Virginia said, keeping her voice as normal as she could.

'You've been sacked from there, haven't you? So what's your story?'

'Declan, I'm sure you already know.' Virginia attempted a giggle, which she hoped didn't sound more like a gurgle.

'Quite right. You left over a difference of opinion. That's the official line anyway.'

'I'm afraid it's the only line. I didn't like my boss; she didn't like me. Nothing more interesting than that.'

'So you didn't appeal the decision?' Virginia took a deep breath. Although she had known he would ask these questions they still made her feel uncomfortable.

'No, I didn't. I hated working there and fancied a change of scene.'

'So why come to me?'

'Because while I'm choosing this change of scene I need cash. And the information I have is worth cash. Declan, I can give you the name of this man. I can also set up a meeting where he won't be expecting you but you'll get an opportunity to talk to him. He's very impressed by money and class. You pose as a lord or something and he'll sing like a canary.' Virginia was glad she had remembered Ella's text word by word.

'Really. So we can rock the oldest bank in Britain . . . I like it. But how do I know this information is reliable?'

'It is. And I think it's worth it for you to check it out. I got my information the way you do. I overheard a conversation between the man in question and someone else. I know it's true. I also know that with the right incentive he'll talk. You just have to be the incentive.'

'How much?' Virginia was taken aback. She hadn't thought it would be so easy.

'You tell me.' She smiled and batted her eyelids at him.

'I never discuss money on an empty stomach,' Declan said, as, on cue, their food arrived.

Virginia ate as much as she could; she also drank a little more than she had planned to. But she was beginning to enjoy herself. Declan told her of how they got their stories, which was fascinating, and he told her how he thought they would do hers. She told him Tim's name; he suggested a sum of money. She looked uninterested and said it 'would do'. He laughed and said there might be more if they got any syndication for it. Virginia didn't know what that meant and didn't ask. Ella had told her not to come across as stupid. By the time the coffee arrived, the deal had been sealed.

'You call me soon with a venue. I want to do this as quickly as possible. It's too late for this week, but next week I want it in the paper. I'll do the rest. If he doesn't give me what I want on the first meeting, I'll arrange another. I'll introduce myself with a phony title, which should do the trick. If it doesn't work, you get nothing. If it does, not only do you get paid but I'll take you out to dinner.' Virginia really blushed this time: he had almost asked her on a date. As he paid the bill, she shook his hand and he held hers for a little longer than necessary. She nearly fell over when she realised a member of the opposite sex fancied her.

'Virginia, it's been a pleasure doing business with you.' He handed her a card with his private number on it and they left. She purposely walked away in the opposite direction to him. As soon as he was out of sight, she collapsed against a wall. Virginia Bateman had done it. She was a smooth operator.

After checking again that Declan had definitely gone she pulled out Clara's mobile. She dialled. Clara was on the line immediately.

'I did it,' Virginia said.

'Really?' Clara sounded unconvinced.

'We've got to call him tomorrow with a venue,' Virginia explained, hating Clara for not believing her.

'Well done. Get your arse back here.' Virginia hung up and hailed a cab. The driver looked at her approvingly. She felt good about herself and she liked the feeling.

Clara told Ella that Virginia had succeeded.

'I knew she would,' Ella said, with more conviction than she felt.

'Yeah, well, it's a bloody good thing she did.'

'Don't be such a bitch — just because you thought she'd screw up.'

'Well, come on, don't tell me you really believed she'd do it,' Clara retorted.

'You have so little faith! Of course I believed it.' Ella smiled at Clara, and they both laughed. The doorbell interrupted them.

'That can't be Virginia. She only just rang,' Clara said, as she went to open the door. It was her brother. 'James.' Clara kissed him.

'Can I come in?' he asked.

'Of course.'

He walked into the sitting room and stopped when he saw Ella. 'Hello,' he said.

'James, this is Ella,' Clara said, groaning inwardly. She hadn't planned on him meeting either Ella or Virginia.

'Hi,' Ella stammered. Clara's brother was as gorgeous as Clara was.

'James, this is a surprise.' Clara prayed that Ella wouldn't say anything to incriminate her.

'Well, you've been neglecting the parents and me. I was worried.'

'I've been busy.' Clara turned red.

James sat down next to Ella on the sofa. 'Shall I go?' she asked, feeling as if she was intruding. The vibes Clara was giving out suggested that she should.

'Yes,' Clara said.

'No, Ella, don't.' James was insistent. Clara sighed, and sat down.

'I spoke to Josh,' James announced. Both Clara and Ella groaned. 'I know about you and him and your little plots, I suppose you're involved, are you?' He turned to Ella, who shrugged.

'James, I can explain,' Clara said.

'Oh, good, I was hoping you would. Perhaps you can start by telling me how you got yourself sacked.'

Clara went white. 'He told you everything?' she whispered.

'Yes, and I wish you'd told me. Josh is worried about you and now I am too.'

'I really ought to go.' Ella stood up.

'Stay,' James and Clara said in unison.

Ella sat down again. She couldn't leave, although this family scene was the last thing she felt like being a part of.

'Jamie, I'm so sorry. I hated lying to you but I couldn't bear to think you'd be disappointed in me.'

'Clara, you're my sister and I love you. I need to know

you're all right but from what I hear you've got yourself into a huge mess.'

'I had a fling with my boss. I mean, why else would I get promoted, right? All I am is a pretty face and a pretty arse. That's what everybody thinks and they're right. So I had this fling and he sacked me when I tried to break it off.' Ella looked at Clara. Clara stared straight back at her defying her to say anything.

'Clara, that's despicable. Apart from the fact that you shouldn't have got involved with him in the first place, this guy can't go around firing people for not wanting to sleep with him. We could have claimed unfair dismissal.'

'Yes, and then as well as disgracing Tim, I would have disgraced myself. I would have been fired anyway. Don't you see? I didn't deserve my promotion – I didn't deserve anything.' Clara's eyes were full of tears.

'She was actually very good at her job, but she went quietly because of the scandal it would bring to her family. James, Clara was thinking of you.' Ella could see how much Clara admired her brother, and she could see how much this was hurting her.

'Thank you, Ella. Clara, is that true?' Clara nodded. He went over to her and took her in his arms. 'I still wish you'd told me. Is there anything I can do?'

'We're sorting it out. Did Josh tell you that? How Ella, this other girl, Virginia, and I were all sacked, and although it was kind of justified, it wasn't really. We were all victimised and we're going to make them sorry.'

'Josh told me about that woman. How you got him to sleep with her when he thought you two were going to get together. He told me you said that the only way you'd be with him would be if he did that. Then you told him to get lost. Which I don't understand. I'm not sure if I agree with this mad plan of yours for revenge, you might get into trouble. And Clara, the first one worked because you used Josh. He really cares, you know.'

'Oh, you did have a long talk with him, didn't you? Well,

Josh left me once, you know, and he would have done it again. I need the bathroom.' Clara left the room.

Ella tried hard not to look at James.

'So you're involved with this?' he asked. She nodded. 'Well, I hope you know what you're doing. Josh gave me the impression that these guys were all baddies and you were doing some sort of Robin Hood job in bringing them to justice, but I hate to think of Clara in danger.'

'We're not doing anything illegal. So far, the only person we've "brought to justice" is Isabelle, who was Virginia's boss. She was a nasty, greedy bitch who nearly destroyed Virginia. In fact, we were all nearly destroyed, including Clara. We needed to do this. If we hadn't, we wouldn't have anything left.' She still wasn't looking at him.

'So, nothing illegal? Nothing they can trace back to you?'

'No. We don't take risks like that.'

'Look, I care about Clara. When I met Josh I was furious about what was going on. Josh said Clara seemed unstable. I need to make sure she's OK.'

'What did he tell you?' Ella wondered if he knew about the cocaine.

'That she slept with her boss, was sacked, then hooked up with two other girls to get her own back. I just don't like it, Ella.'

'We would all rather this wasn't happening but it is, and we're coping. If we didn't have this, things would be worse for all three of us.' Ella looked at him and saw the concern in his eyes. Her heart broke for Sam again; it was how he used to look at her.

Clara walked back in. She had calmed down, which Ella knew was thanks to the cocaine.

'Jamie, please don't hate me,' she said.

'I'd never hate you, you know that. But what about Josh? He was serious about you, you know.'

'I don't think I can trust him yet. James, don't interfere

where he's concerned. And I didn't mean to use him, it just happened. I miss him – I really like him – but I can't cope with him at the moment, not with everything else.'

'OK. No pressure. But from now on I want you to tell me what's happening. You have to be honest with me. I'll go and make some coffee.' He went to the kitchen.

'He's going to be OK, isn't he?' Clara said.

'I think he is, but it's a bit of a shock for him. He didn't even know you were fired.'

'Um. I'm going to kill Josh if I ever see him again. Bastard.'

'He was just worried.' Ella tried to sound reasonable.

'No, he was probably trying to cause trouble for me and get his own back – I'm beginning to think the world revolves around revenge.'

'Maybe. And I don't know if that's a good thing or not. But I know that people like Tim, Isabelle and Johnny deserve to pay for what they've done. However, if everyone took revenge on everyone else, the world would be in trouble,' Ella observed.

'Could you imagine if every man I slept with tried to get their own back on me for not seeing them again?'

'Well, you should be more careful before you go break-ing hearts.'

'I think I'm going to take a vow of celibacy,' Clara said.

'I think Virginia's got more chance of getting laid than that ever happening.' The doorbell rang.

'Shit, I'd forgotten about Virginia!' Clara jumped up.

'I'll get it,' James called from the kitchen.

Clara and Ella looked at each other, then Clara ran to the door but James got there first. When Clara arrived, he was holding the door open, staring at the girl on the other side. Clara stared too: for a minute she didn't recognise her.

Virginia looked fantastic and she was smiling. 'Hi,' she said, sounding bewildered.

'James, it's just Virginia. Let her in.' She pushed him to one side.

James was still staring at Virginia. 'Sorry. Hello. Can I get you coffee?' he said. Virginia looked at Clara then nodded. Clara grabbed her and pulled her into the sitting room.

'That's my brother. He knows everything,' she hissed.

Virginia looked at her. 'God, he's sexy.' She giggled.

'Virginia, have you been drinking?' Clara asked.

'Yes, I have a bit. Oh, well, never mind, it worked.' Virginia turned pink with pleasure.

'So, tell us all about it while James is making coffee,' Ella prompted.

'Oh, yes. Well, he was a bit scary, but very charming. Then I said exactly what you told me to say and he said he thought it might be interesting and offered me five grand if it comes off. We have to call him with a time and venue where he can pounce on Tim. I have to sign some papers. Is that all right?' Virginia asked.

'Of course. We'll get them sent here and we'll check them over. Well done. I didn't think you'd do it,' Clara said.

'Neither did I.' Virginia giggled again.

'But he seemed convinced?' Ella asked again.

'Yes, and he said that when it was over he'd like to take me to dinner.'

'He asked you for a *date*?' Clara asked, goggle-eyed.

'I guess so, but I can't be sure because I've never been asked on a date before.' Virginia collapsed into giggles.

James came back with a tray of coffee, which he passed round. He couldn't take his eyes off Virginia.

'Have we met before?' he asked her.

'No,' she said.

'James, was that a line?' Clara was angry. How dare he show an interest in Virginia?

'No ... I just thought ... you know ...' he stammered.

'Anyway, why aren't you at work?' Clara asked, trying to change the subject.

'Because I needed to see you. Anyway, now I'm satisfied that you're all right. I should be getting back. Why don't I take you girls to dinner this Friday?' he offered.

'We're busy,' Clara answered, rather too quickly.

James shrugged. 'Some other time, then. I'll call you to fix it.' He kissed Clara on both cheeks and said goodbye to Ella and Virginia. His eyes lingered on Virginia, who turned fuchsia. Then he left.

'Why was he behaving like that?' Clara asked.

'Clara, I think we've got more important things to discuss. You need to call Tim to set up a meeting,' Ella said.

'Now?' she asked.

'No time like the present.' Ella got the telephone and handed it to Clara, who took it and walked into her bedroom.

'I can't have you guys listening in,' she said moodily.

'What's wrong with her?' Virginia asked.

'Her brother was flirting with you. She didn't like it,' Ella replied.

'Gosh, was he? You mean, two men in one day?' Virginia asked.

'Yes. Now, drink some more coffee because you're pissed.' Ella gave Virginia her coffee and tried to get her to stop giggling long enough to drink it.

Tim didn't answer his phone. His secretary did. 'Tim Pemberton's office.'

Clara thought fast. 'Is he there? It's his daughter's school.' It was a stupid lie, but seemed to work.

'Bear with me. I'll just see if he's available.' A minute passed. Then, 'Tim Pemberton.'

Clara breathed a sigh of relief. 'Tim, it's Clara.'

'Clara, darling, what a little fibber you are.' He sounded pleased to hear from her.

You don't know the half of it, Clara thought. 'Tim, can I see you?'

'So, you've decided to stop punishing me?'

'Yes, of course, I'm sorry I was so stubborn. When can we meet?'

'Shall we have dinner?'

'Yes. How about at your club?' The Tribor was one of Tim's favourite venues. It would be the perfect place for the journalist to seek him out.

'OK, darling, that's fine. Shall we say Friday? I'll tell my wife I have a client event.' His breathing was heavy.

'See you there at eight. 'Bye.'

They hung up. Soon he would be out of her life for ever. If all went to plan, it would take only a week. She had a line of cocaine to celebrate before she went back to the others.

'It's all set for Friday night,' Clara said, sitting down.

'We need to call Declan,' Ella said, feeling the adrenaline rush.

'*She* doesn't look in any state to talk to him.' Clara rolled her eyes towards Virginia, who had collapsed in a heap.

'I'm trying to sober her up. I'll get some more coffee.' Ella walked to the kitchen.

Eventually Virginia returned to normal. 'My head hurts,' she moaned.

'We told you not to drink,' Clara said.

'I didn't have much,' Virginia protested.

'Well, it doesn't take much for you, does it?' Clara pointed out.

'OK. Virginia, you call Declan now and tell him where he can find Tim,' Ella cut in.

'I'll write it down for you,' Clara said, and went to get the notebook. She wrote down the name and address of the club and Virginia called Declan. When she hung up, she said, 'He's fine with that. He's biking round the papers tomorrow – I gave him this address. And he wants me to send him some background information on Tim, and a photo. Have we got one?' Virginia asked.

'Actually, I have. You'd think he'd be able to get one himself, though.' Clara went into her room. She returned with a photo Tim had given her, a posed business shot used in brochures. Clara thought he looked slimy. 'I'll start writing some notes for him as well.' Clara went to the table and set to work.

Virginia left them to it and went for a lie-down.

'Clara, she did a great job, you know,' Ella said, a few minutes later.

'I know, I can't believe it. Maybe there's hope for her yet.'

'Looking like that I'm sure of it.'

'Yes, well, I'm not sure I wanted her to look quite so good.' Clara pouted.

'Clara, you should be pleased. Look how far she's come from the scowling creature who used to work for Isabelle. Honey, this is what we wanted for Virginia, for her to find out what she really could be.'

'I know, but I'm not as big-hearted as you.' Clara was jealous, and the last thing she wanted was for James to like Virginia. James was Clara's. He was all she had and she had no intention of losing him. Especially not to Virginia.

'I think we should be proud of her, that's all,' Ella said.

'Whatever.' Clara muttered.

She typed her notes so that Declan would be able to read them easily, and included details of where Tim was born, everything she knew about his career, and his personal habits. She emphasised that the one thing Tim longed for was class.

By unspoken agreement they spent the night at Clara's again. Ella cooked supper and Clara provided wine. That night they all slept soundly knowing they were over the first hurdle in the plan for revenge on Tim.

In the morning, they waited for the courier. Clara called James to let him know she loved him, and Virginia didn't have a hangover as she'd slept it off. When the courier arrived, he explained that he had been told to wait and take back the envelope. Ella read the document, found nothing wrong, so Virginia signed it. The five-thousand-pound fee would be paid on successful completion of the assignment. They handed the envelope back to the courier, shut the door and gazed at each other in relief. They were over another hurdle.

'What are you going to do with the money?' Clara asked.

'We'll split it,' Virginia said.

'No, it's yours. I don't need it. Anyway, you earned it,' Ella replied.

'I agree. Perhaps we could go shopping and get you some new clothes with it, Virginia,' Clara suggested. Ella did a double-take. Only yesterday Clara had said she wished Virginia had stayed looking boring.

'Really?' Virginia said.

'Yes, of course. We'll spend a bit on clothes for you and the rest you can save. After all, you haven't been working,' Clara said.

Clara was like Jekyll and Hyde, Ella thought. One minute she was sweet, the next a raging virago. It had to be the cocaine.

'Thanks,' Virginia said. She felt proud of herself – and for the first time she began to like herself. 'This has been really good for me, you know,' she added. The others nodded. It had been good for all of them.

Chapter Thirty-four

Tim felt good. Clara hadn't been able to resist him. She needed him, and he had known that if he waited she'd come running. Now that he'd been proved right, he felt he could do and have whatever he wanted. He had decided that it would cost him too much money to leave his wife, so having Clara as his mistress suited him fine. He would have to establish the rules, though: she would not be allowed to see anyone else and would sleep only with him. He knew that she would agree to this: she had tried and failed to live without him.

He left work with time to spare, stopping at the partners' cloakroom to check his hair. He had to admit he looked good. As he stood outside and hailed a taxi to take him to the Tribor Club, he smiled at the thought of the night ahead.

Declan was excited. He had been speaking to his editor, who had implied huge Brownie points if he pulled this off. People were getting bored with exposures of footballers and B-list celebrities. The financial world was of interest to most people who didn't understand it: they knew that everyone in it earned too much money for doing too little. SFH had always shunned journalists, keeping quiet, closing ranks, only giving the official line. It portrayed itself as a squeaky-clean organisation. It would give Declan a great deal of pleasure to blow that image apart.

After reading the information given to him by Virginia, he had worked out his approach. He hadn't needed a photograph, but he wanted to be sure that Virginia really knew the man. He had read the SFH prospectus, which was kept in the research library, and which held a photo of all the managing directors. That would be his introduction. He got his secretary to call the Tribor Club to gain him admittance as Lord William Calloway. His experience was that no one questioned titles and the receptionist had said that they would be delighted for him to visit.

He put on his tie cam carefully. It was a tiny video camera hidden his Old Etonian tie. Around his waist he wore a body-belt that contained a DVD recorder and a battery, which would allow him to record for three hours. In his trouser pocket there was a remote control so he could start and finish recording as he chose. He had selected his tie because he knew that Tim hadn't gone to Eton, or any public school. Anticipation pumped through him as he checked the camera was working then pulled on a tailored blazer. He looked in the mirror and smiled at himself. He then struck a James Bond pose, winking at his reflection. Declan was ready. The adrenaline rush he experienced when he left for the club was the reason he did his job.

Declan arrived at the Tribor at seven. He wanted it to look as if he had planned an evening there with a view to becoming a member and made himself known to everyone, including the barman. He chose a table that offered good vantage-point from which to observe the bar and sat down. A mirror hung in front of him so he could see who came in without moving his head. Declan prided himself on his attention to detail, which made him the best journalist at the *Sunday News*.

Tim walked in at a quarter to eight, but Declan was ready for him. He watched him go to the bar, order a drink, then sit at a table near his own. He studied Tim and felt he knew him, or his sort. He was expensively dressed – Savile Row, Declan guessed. His hair was neat, probably dyed; there was no evidence of grey. He looked at his watch regularly; the barman brought him another drink, which showed that he often frequented the club, and exchanged a few words with him; Tim was obviously waiting for someone.

After half an hour Tim pulled out his mobile phone and made a call; he looked irate and his voice was raised. Declan made out the word 'bitch' but nothing more. This was his opportunity.

Declan picked up his half-drunk glass of malt whisky and made his move. 'I'm going to get you, you bastard,' he said to himself, as he approached Tim's table.

'I'm terribly sorry to disturb you, but you're Tim Pemberton, aren't you?' It wasn't the most original introduction, but recognition always flattered people. Tim looked at Declan, then his eyes rested briefly on the Old Etonian tie.

'I am. And you?' Tim was hostile, but there was a flicker of interest in his eyes.

'William Calloway. Lord William Calloway.' The hostility evaporated. Declan put out his hand. Tim stood up and shook it.

'Please, sit down.' Tim motioned to the seat opposite him. 'Have we met?'

Declan laughed inside at the fake posh accent Tim was using. It wasn't as effective as *his*.

'No, we haven't. However, I've been looking at your company. SFH? I was glancing through the prospectus today, trying to decide whether to invest my money with you. It's so hard to decide, these days, with so many banks around. When you walked in, I recognised you from the photograph in the brochure. I find studying the people who work in an organisation helps me to get an idea about who I'm dealing with.' Declan put on his best smile.

'How nice. Did you make any decisions about us?' Tim raised a questioning eyebrow.

'I'm going to get my secretary to make an appointment on Monday. Can I mention your name? I'm a firm believer in the personal touch when I'm doing business.'

'Of course. Make sure you see Phillip Reid. He's the top person with the private clients. How fortunate that we met tonight.' Tim had forgotten his bad mood.

'Isn't it? I haven't spent much time in the UK over the last four years – I've been living mainly in France, but I've decided now to spend more time on British soil. I miss the old place, really, although I can't abide the weather,' Declan explained.

'Quite. It can be ghastly. Where in France?'

'St Tropez. Terribly obvious, I know, but I like the parties and the fun. It's a playboy's dream. I'll still keep my place there, but probably split my time equally between there and here.' Declan laughed and Tim joined in. 'Can I buy you a drink?'

'I'll join you in a whisky, thank you,' Tim said. He saw Calloway as a good opportunity, and although he was pissed off with Clara for standing him up, maybe he could salvage something from the evening. He summoned the barman and Declan ordered the drinks.

'Certainly, Lord Calloway,' the barman said, which pleased Declan: it gave him more credibility.

'I'm not a member yet, and I need a club in London now that I intend to spend more time here. I thought I'd have a look at this one,' Declan said.

'Well, I can recommend it. As well as pleasant surroundings and good whisky, the food is excellent,' Tim replied.

'I must try it. I have to say, I like it so far.' Declan gave Tim his best upper-class chuckle.

'You're an Old Etonian?' Tim asked.

'Yes. It was the first tie I found when dressing today, but I'm terribly old-school,' Declan laughed. 'Were you at the old place?' He knew Tim hadn't been but he seemed flattered to be asked.

'I went to a minor private school. You won't have heard of it,' Tim said. Declan knew that he had been to a comprehensive like himself and also that it would be a mistake to press the issue so he left it.

'I hear the bank is going from strength to strength,' he said.

347

'We're doing well, yes. Our management is excellent, as are our personnel.' Tim beamed with pride.

'So I've heard. My portfolio is vast, and I like to know it's in safe hands, which is why I'm thinking about moving it.'

'Who's it with at the moment?' Tim asked.

'I'd rather not say, but if all goes well I hope I shall move it to your bank. I feel it would be good to put my money in the hands of a British bank. So many Americans and Germans are taking over the financial institutions.'

'Quite,' Tim said. They sipped their drinks. Declan was just thinking about his next move when Tim spoke again. 'I was supposed to meet a business contact here but he's been unable to make it. Would you like to dine with me, Lord Calloway?'

He has no idea what he should call me, Declan thought. He almost expected Tim to bow.

'Please call me William, and I'd be delighted. I thought I'd have to rely on my own company this evening, which would have been dull.'

'I'm sure that's not true.' Tim laughed. They were becoming a mutual-appreciation society. They had another drink, and made small-talk, then Tim asked to be shown to a table. They were led to a small dining room, all leather and velvet, and seated at what was obviously the best table.

'I recommend the veal,' Tim said, with authority.

'Sounds lovely. And what wine would you go for?' Just as Declan had predicted to himself Tim picked out the most expensive one. Declan insisted on having just a salad to start, blaming French cuisine for his waistline. Tim told him he had nothing to worry about. Declan was beginning to find him annoying, a good sign: the more he disliked a person, the easier it was to trap them. Declan played his part as arrogantly as he could. Tim tried desperately to match the arrogance. To any observer they both seemed absurd.

When the food and wine arrived they were still talking business: Declan had decided that if he could convince Tim of his interest in SFH, the rest of his task would be easier. After the wine, a good meal and brandy, he was sufficiently confident of Tim's friendship to pounce. He reached into his pocket and switched on the video. He had only three hours, but his gut instinct told him it wouldn't take that long. He sat up straight to ensure that the camera was at an angle to film Tim's face. He was well practised in this and he was confident, in control of the camera. He knew how to sit and how to move so that he filmed whatever he needed to record.

'I'm so out of touch with the London scene. I don't suppose you can recommend anywhere livelier?'

'What are you after?' Tim had drunk rather more than Declan – his red cheeks betrayed him – and he was falling nicely into the trap.

'I hope I'm not talking out of turn, but I'm looking to liven myself up. If you understand.' That was a gamble, but Declan knew Tim was drunk, that he used cocaine, and that he was impressed by the phony title. There were times when Declan misjudged people and they clammed up as soon as he mentioned drugs, but he felt sure that wouldn't happen now. Declan stared straight at Tim. Tim met his eyes.

'You mean Charlie?' Tim asked quietly as he sipped his second large brandy, ordered discreetly by Declan. He wasn't yet betraying himself: he was being cautious.

'Yes. My old friend Charlie.' Declan laughed. A moment passed before Tim finally fell. 'I can get you some. One phone call and I'll have it delivered. Not just any old cocaine either, the best,' Tim boasted.

Declan smiled. 'Is this your sideline?' he joked, marvelling at Tim's loose tongue.

'Gosh, no. I only supply to good friends, if you get my meaning.' He sounded like a barrow-boy.

'How much can you get?'

'As much as you want, when you want, where you want.' He was now talking freely. 'I've got some on me that you can sample.'

Declan almost jumped for joy – the man was even talking like a dealer. Tim passed a white package under the table and Declan got up to go to the cloakroom. Once there he didn't take any but put it into his pocket as evidence. Declan glanced in the bathroom mirror and again struck his 'Bond' pose. 'Bingo,' he said to his reflection and winked at himself.

When he returned, Tim stood up. 'I need to go to the bathroom.' He winked at Declan as he said it.

'Stupid drunk fool,' Declan said to himself, and called for the bill. He was a little disappointed that Tim had been so easy. He enjoyed the chase and had almost expected to have to cultivate a longer friendship before he got what he wanted.

Tim returned as he was paying the bill in cash. 'I was going to buy dinner,' he said.

'It's the least I can do. Anyway, I seem to have rather a lot of cash on me tonight. Can't abide plastic.' Paying in cash was the only way Declan could safeguard his fake identity. He often felt he needed to explain it because most people used credit cards. 'I guess I'm just an old-fashioned man at heart.'

'I agree,' Tim said, although Declan knew he was definitely a credit-card kind of man. Big gleaming platinum ones.

'Do you know any night clubs we can go on to from here?' Declan asked.

'Actually I know a special one. And why not? Let's go.' Declan guessed the cocaine was kicking in because Tim was smiling like an idiot and behaving like an excited schoolboy.

As they made their way out, Tim felt proud and pleased with himself. William was obviously a man after his own heart. After all, the upper classes were renowned for their drug-taking. Not only was his lordship going to score him points at work but he would be good to have as a personal friend. He could imagine his wife's face at the mention of a lord at one of their dinner-parties. It would increase his social standing no end. If he played his cards right and provided William with what he wanted, which Tim guessed was drugs and girls, then Tim would be the trusted confidant of a lord. He was glad now that Clara hadn't turned up. William was far more valuable. And he could get sex anywhere.

The doorman hailed them a taxi and they both got in.

'Where is this place?' Declan asked.

'Soho, but it's very private. Strictly members and guests only. I think you'll like it. You can do what you want there. Oh, and the girls are for sale,' Tim added.

'Really? Drugs and prostitutes? It sounds just my type of place.' This was so easy. Declan loved people with huge egos; they invited his deception.

'Oh, yes. If you want any of the girls, let me know. I can arrange it easily.'

'Do you have anything to do with this club?'

'No, but I'm a good friend of the owner. I also have arrangements with several of the girls there. They come when I call. I meet them at a hotel in town – another discreet place. It's tucked away just off Piccadilly. You can rent rooms by the hour, but it's very respectable. Not like the fleapits shown on television. You only get a booking there if you know someone. Of course, any time you want one, just call me.' Tim was out of control. He seemed delighted to share all this information. Declan thought he was a huge liability for his bank, the way he spoke. And he was right: Tim often shared this information with other people – if only top clients and those he considered friends. He had already decided that William was his friend.

'Really? So you can arrange a call-girl for me?' Declan asked clearly.

'Not just one, if you get my drift. Any size, colour, age and so on. I have hotlines to all of them and, William, I would be delighted to share them with you.' Tim smiled straight into the tie cam.

They arrived at the club where, again, Tim was greeted as a

regular. It was in a cellar, not noticeable from the street. Inside it was dimly lit, with plush sofas, a small bar and lots of men draped around half-naked women. Declan scanned his tie around the room. They went to a sofa. Tim had a word with the barman, and before their drinks arrived, two girls appeared wearing gold bikinis. One was tall, blonde with a perfect figure and relatively small boobs. The other was shorter with dark hair and huge ones. They drank champagne, the girls flirted and at some point took off their tops. Tim put some money into their bikini bottoms and told them to go and powder their noses.

'You see?' Tim said, visibly excited.

Declan wasn't interested in clubs like this, perhaps because he was doing his job. He often wondered whether, if he was out socially, like Lord William Calloway, he would go for this scene. He imagined not.

'Amazing. How much are they?'

'Well, they're not cheap but they aren't your common hookers. If you look at the men around you, they're bankers, lawyers, businessmen. Lots of respectable men come here.' All Declan could see was a number of middle-aged men with young girls. They didn't look respectable. 'But I can get you anyone for five hundred pounds an hour. They usually charge a grand, but as a regular user I get a discount. I'm going to disappear with the brunette in a minute and give you time to get acquainted with Sally. If you want her, talk to me first. I'll do the negotiating.' Tim was so excited that Declan felt a bit queasy.

'So, you arrange this?' Declan asked, to be clear.

'I have an arrangement, yes. I put a lot of business their way, they repay me. I shouldn't say this but I have clients and colleagues who use these girls — and the cocaine, some of them. I like to think of myself as a fixer.' Tim beamed with pride. Declan didn't know why: he had just admitted he was a drug-dealing pimp.

'I see. It's a great place.' Declan tried to sound excited. He was pleased that he would get a chance to speak to Sally. Although he knew these people weren't kiss-and-tell types, he would get her to say something he could use. When he exposed it, this place would probably be closed down. The girls returned and Tim disappeared with the dark-haired one. Declan couldn't see where he'd gone.

He smiled at Sally and poured her more champagne. 'Where have they gone?' he asked.

'There's a booth back there were you can go for privacy. Twenty minutes at a time. Would you like to go?' Sally said.

'Not yet. I'm still enjoying the view.' Declan looked at her breasts. She was very attractive, but he didn't feel aroused. 'So, do you know my good friend Tim?'

'Yes, he's a regular. Tracy and me seem to be his favourites. We can go together if you want. It costs, but it's worth it.' She sipped the champagne.

'I bet it is. Actually, Tim was saying that.'

'Oh, Tim loves us both together. If you need a recommendation I bet he'll give you one.'

'I don't think that's necessary. I can see how exciting it would be.'

'So, you want to do it?'

'Maybe next time. I've had rather too much to drink this evening.'

Sally put her hand on his thigh. 'As you're a friend of Tim's, he'll arrange it for you whenever you want.'

'Really? Don't tell me my old mate's an organiser?' Having confirmation from the hooker as well as from Tim would be great for the story.

'Well, unofficially, yes. Actually, he sends so many men our way that we don't charge him much at all,' Sally said.

'Really? Well, lucky Tim.'

'Yeah, if he gives us cocaine and we do him for free.' Declan couldn't believe his luck. These high-class hookers were supposed to keep quiet.

'He provides you with cocaine for yourself and men for your trade?'

'Yes. He's great. I'm only saying that because you're a very attractive man. We'd like to do business with you.' Sally smiled seductively.

'Well, in that case you'll be hearing from me again. As I said, unfortunately I've had too much to drink so I'll have to go home. But I'll be in touch. Via Tim. Will you tell him I've had to go and that I'll call him?'

'Sure. See you soon.'

'Of course,' Declan said, as Sally got up and moved on to another man.

When he got back to his flat and inserted the DVD into his laptop computer Declan was shaking. As he watched the evening's events unfold in front of him he realised he had a story here that even the lawyers could not fault. The tie cam had filmed everything he needed, and the sound was clear. Thank God for small video cameras. He made copies, and as he had begun to feel turned on by the story he was about to break, he went to the bedroom to wake his obliging girlfriend.

Tim was disappointed to find that William had left, but when Sally told him he was going to call, he felt better. Sally also told him that he'd been too drunk to perform, which was why he'd gone home, but he was definitely a punter for the future.

'Well done, darling. He's a lord and could be good for all of us. Now, come to the booth with me and collect your reward.' Tim caressed Sally's nipple as he led her to the booth. 'At least *I* never let you down when I'm drunk,' he said, and pulled down his trousers to reveal a massive erection.

Chapter Thirty-five

Clara, Virginia and Ella were nervous wrecks. By Friday afternoon they were all tearing their hair out and getting in each other's way.

'I need to go out,' Ella said.

'Where?' Clara asked.

'I don't know. Anywhere.'

'You can't leave us,' Clara snapped.

'For God's sake, why do we need to spend all our time here together? I'm beginning to feel closed in,' Ella snarled.

'I know! We'll all go out and buy Virginia some clothes.'

'But I don't have any money,' Virginia said, looking scared.

'You're about to get five thousand pounds. I'll pay now and you can pay me back. At least it will give us something to do,' Clara insisted.

'But I don't get the money unless this is a success,' Virginia protested.

'It will be,' Clara said sharply.

'Do we have to?' Ella groaned. She missed her own company.

'Yes.' Clara stamped her foot.

Ella thought she was such a child sometimes, but she didn't feel up to arguing. 'I'll get my coat,' she said.

They left the flat unsure of where they were going. Virginia was wearing the outfit Clara had bought her — she resented her old clothes now. She had brought her old jeans and jumpers with her to Clara's, but now that she had transformed herself, she couldn't bring herself to wear them. Although terrified by the idea of Clara bossing her about, she wanted new clothes. For the first time ever, she was taking notice of her appearance. She had even mastered walking in heels.

'Let's go to Harvey Nichols,' Clara suggested.

'Clara, can't we go somewhere cheaper? I mean, I know I've got money coming but I need to live and pay rent,' Virginia pleaded.

Clara looked cross for a minute but then she smiled. 'We'll go to some high-street stores, then. Apparently some are quite good and they're cheap. Cheap chic, I think they call it.' She hailed a taxi.

When they got out in Oxford Street Clara led them into Top Shop.

'Wow,' Virginia said. She had never been in the store before.

'My goodness! It's amazing.' Clara had walked past it on numerous occasions but never gone inside.

'Isn't it a bit teenagerish?' Ella said, as she looked at the other shoppers.

'Apparently not. I read in a magazine that it copies all the designer stuff and it's really quite hip,' Clara replied. Ella shrugged and decided not to argue further.

Clara picked up cropped trousers, normal trousers, skirts, tops, and jackets, just about everything the store had to offer, while Virginia and Ella followed her around. Ella was weighed down with clothes, as was Virginia. They had to admit that Clara was a good shopper: she picked out the best garments and put together the best combinations. Even Virginia seemed happy with her choices. Eventually when they all had as much as they could carry, Clara led them to the changing rooms.

'You can't take all those in,' the assistant said, eyeing the bundles of clothes.

'Why on earth not?' Clara asked.

'I don't have a disc with enough numbers on it.'

'Oh, God, don't tell me you think we're shoplifters! Don't be absurd.' Clara pushed past her and the girl looked as if she was going to cry.

'Look, I promise we won't steal anything. We just need a whole wardrobe, that's all. You can keep an eye on us,' Ella explained reasonably.

'OK,' the tearful assistant agreed. This was her first day.

Ella found a seat and flopped down on it. Clara started putting things together and ordering Virginia around. As Virginia tried on the outfits, Clara decided whether they were any good or not. Under the watchful eye of the assistant she made two piles. Virginia would never have admitted it but she was enjoying herself. She tried on tops she thought were too tight but which flattered her figure. She tried on skirts she thought too short but which Clara said showed off her great legs. She tried on jeans that were infinitely more flattering than her usual ones. She felt like she was in a movie. She felt special.

The others in the changing room noticed the three girls. They were all thinking it must be some sort of fashion shoot and they fluffed their hair in case one was a model scout. Clara was oblivious to the interest she was causing as she shouted, 'Turn round. Let me see your bum. Um, nice but a bit too tarty. No, not sexy enough.' Ella had finally found some enthusiasm and was helping Clara with the decision-making. Eventually Virginia had tried on the last outfit and Clara had shouted her last order. She gave a pile of discarded clothes to the assistant and took an even bigger pile to the till.

As she paid Virginia smiled. She couldn't stop smiling. Ella smiled too: she was pleased that Virginia was happy.

'Shoes.' Clara announced, as she handed the bags to Virginia and Ella, and marched over to the shoe department. She picked out a pair of flat black shoes, which she said Virginia could wear because she was tall. She then picked up a pair of high heels in case she ever went out after dark. She picked out some trendy trainers, to replace the battered old things Virginia normally wore, and a pair of black wedge-heeled boots. Virginia tried them all on, they all met with Clara's approval and again she went to pay.

'I can't believe it. Nothing like this has ever happened to me before,' Virginia said. She felt a child in a toyshop.

'You looked great in those clothes. I have to hand it to Clara, she's a whiz with fashion.'

'Thank you,' Clara said, as she handed them the bags with the shoes. Ella and Virginia struggled up the elevator after Clara, who was empty-handed. She went outside and found a cab, pushing a businessman out of the way. He scowled as Clara beckoned to the others and they got in.

'My wardrobe isn't big enough for all this,' Virginia said.

'Your whole flat isn't big enough for it,' Clara replied.

'True. Oh, well, I'll just have to be either organised or messy.' Virginia laughed.

'I can't imagine you ever being messy,' Ella said.

'Yes, but I bet you never imagined me looking like this either.'

'God, no. But I still think you'll never be messy,' Clara finished.

When they got home they ordered pizza, and Virginia couldn't resist trying on her outfits again. Clara went to get her cocaine, which she realised was running low. She found her address book and called the dealer whose number Josh had given her. She arranged to see him the following evening. She would have to get rid of the others, or just make some excuse. She decided she quite liked having them living there and not being on her own. It made her feel safe.

✣   ✣   ✣

Their anxiety returned at seven that evening. They couldn't bring themselves to voice their fears but they all felt the same ones. When Clara's mobile rang at eight fifteen, she took a deep breath and snatched it up.

'Hello.'

'Clara, where the fuck are you?'

'Out.'

'You're meant to be with me.'

'I changed my mind.'

'What do you mean?'

'If you really thought I'd ever want to see you again after what you did to me you must be even more stupid than you look.'

'Bitch,' Tim hissed, and Clara hung up.

'Clara, that was a bit much, wasn't it?' Ella said.

'What if we need another meeting?' Virginia looked worried.

'Well, that bloody journalist of yours had better make sure we don't.' Clara shot them an evil look and went into her bedroom for more cocaine.

They sat and waited, watching the clock. They sipped wine. Clara and Ella smoked. Virginia looked at her feet. Eventually they went to bed, knowing that sleep wouldn't visit them that night.

Chapter Thirty-six

When Virginia woke on Saturday it was early and no one else was up. She took a shower and put on her new black trousers from Top Shop, with the pink top and cardigan that Clara had bought her. She dried her hair the way Clara had told her to and she even put on makeup. She loved the transformation more than she had thought possible. Serious Virginia had been more worried about economics and her career than her looks! She knew she was changing and she hoped it was for the better.

She sat down in the sitting room and put on the television quietly. Although it was only cartoons, she still liked having it on for company. She thought briefly of the last few days. Declan, James, James and James. He was so good-looking and charming. She knew he'd never be interested in her, even the new her. She got up to make coffee just as Ella emerged from her bedroom and went to the bathroom.

When Ella came back she sat on the sofa next to Virginia. 'What time are we expecting Declan's call?' she asked.

'I don't know, but he's got the number here so I hope he calls soon.'

'Perhaps he doesn't want to call too early in case you're asleep.' Ella was feeling more keyed up than ever. It had been bad enough waiting for Isabelle's downfall, but this felt even worse. Perhaps it had something to do with the fact that if this one worked, Johnny would be next.

'Maybe I should call him,' Virginia suggested.

'No. We've waited before and we'll wait now,' Ella said. She reached over and squeezed Virginia's hand. 'Virginia, you've done a bloody good job. Let's watch some kids' television and letch over the boy bands.'

Declan was at the newspaper office by seven that morning. He prided himself on being able to survive with little sleep, especially when he had a big story. The editor, Georgia Bowman, was checking through the scandals that were going to break this Sunday when Declan went to see her. He handed over the DVD, which Georgia put into the computer. They watched and listened together.

'This is dynamite,' she said.

'I've given a copy to the lawyers to check. Then I'm going to get straight to the story. I figure if they give the OK we can run it next week. I know he doesn't admit directly to being a dealer or a pimp, but the implication is strong enough.' Declan was pleased with himself.

'Fine. And if all is quiet on the celeb front it will make front page.' Georgia liked Declan because he always delivered.

'I'll get on to it now.'

'Let me have a draft as soon as you're done,' she said, as he left her office.

He was still writing when Shelby Tyler from the legal department called him and told him he had the green light. If anyone questioned anything, they had the evidence. They would also have to compile a dossier for the police. Shelby requested a draft of the article so they could check it for any possible libel claims. Declan agreed: he was a professional and he knew they had to do this. He gave a copy of the DVD to the production department for them to get pictures for his story. He finished his first draft by ten and got his secretary to e-mail a copy to his boss and to Shelby. Then he remembered he had to call Virginia.

When the telephone rang, Ella and Virginia jumped. Virginia answered. 'Hello,' she said, shakily.

'It's Declan.'

'Hi, how did it go?' She tried to sound casual but she knew she didn't.

'Fantastic. He gave me cocaine and told me he could supply it to me whenever I wanted. He took me to a private club full of hookers and offered to supply them. He sang like a canary and he bought my Lord Snooty act. Virginia, keep quiet, but it will make next Sunday's paper.' Virginia's heart was hammering.

'Thank goodness. What do I need to do now?' she asked.

'Nothing. Sit tight and make sure no one else hears of this. I don't want any of it getting to Tim. Just buy the paper next Sunday and enjoy the story. Oh, and enjoy spending the money too. I'll make sure the cheque gets posted this week.'

'Thank you,' Virginia said.

'No – thank *you*.' Declan hung up.

'Well?' Ella asked.

'It'll be in next Sunday's paper,' Virginia said.

'My God.' Ella ran over and hugged her.

'We did it,' Virginia sang.

'We did,' Ella replied, slightly embarrassed by her display of emotion.

'What did we do?' Clara, dishevelled and sleepy, came into the room.

'We got Tim,' Ella told her.

'We did?' Clara's eyes widened.

'Apparently he sang like a canary and he's going to be in next Sunday's paper,' Virginia squeaked.

'Fuck me, we're brilliant,' Clara said. 'Only one more to go.' She danced around the room singing 'Simply The Best'. Ella and Virginia joined her. They laughed, danced and sang, and any observers would have said they were drunk.

When they calmed down, they all became serious.

'We've struck twice, only one to go,' Ella said.

'Do we plan Johnny's revenge now or wait until the Tim story comes out?' Clara asked.

'Wait,' Ella answered. 'We still have to see it in print before it's finished. But I think we can celebrate tonight.'

'I can't believe how invincible I feel.' Clara laughed.

'Me too,' Virginia agreed. 'We really did it. First Isabelle, now Tim. We made this work.'

'I know. God, it feels so good to know that those lowlifes are getting what they deserve.'

'And we're going to get what *we* deserve. Just you see!' Clara said, and she hugged Ella and Virginia. They celebrated with pastries and Buck's fizz.

'I need to go to my flat. And I'm going to pop into the restaurant and see Jackie,' Ella announced.

'OK. I need to go out later too, but we'll have dinner here tonight,' Clara decided.

'I'll cook it. It'll give me something to do,' Virginia offered, wishing she had somewhere to go.

'Deal.' Ella grinned and got up to leave.

Ella took a taxi home, leaving her car at Clara's. She felt a bit merry after the Buck's fizz, and she was too excited to drive. At home she checked her answerphone for messages and found none. 'Shit, I'm popular,' she said, as she went through her mail. She opened bills, junk mail and her P45 from SFH. She threw it down. For the first time, the thought struck her that she had to decide what to do with her life. She pushed it away. She would think about it after Johnny. Not yet. She put the clothes she'd brought back from Clara's into the washing-machine and grabbed some clean ones to take back. She hated to admit it, but she liked staying there. She liked to know that she wasn't alone while she slept, and she liked the safe feeling it gave her. She tried to work out what was going on and decided to leave it to counsellor Jackie. She called her and told her she was popping by.

When she reached the restaurant, Jackie was talking to a customer. Ella waited until she'd finished and they hugged. Jackie led her to a seat. 'God, I thought I'd never see you again,' Jackie said.

'Well, it's been a bit hectic with the plans,' Ella explained apologetically.

'So tell me. My life is so dull I have to live vicariously through yours,' Jackie demanded good-naturedly.

'OK. Well, you know my plan for Tim and the newspaper. It looks as if it worked,' Ella said triumphantly.

'No! Go on.' Jackie looked eager.

Ella related the tale, ending, 'He's going to be exposed in next week's *Sunday News*. But don't tell anyone – I'm not supposed to.'

'Shit, Ella, that's amazing.'

A waitress brought over a bottle of wine and some bread. 'What do you want to eat?' Jackie asked, while the girl was still there.

'I'll have a cheeseburger,' Ella said.

'Make that two,' Jackie told the waitress, and poured the wine.

'So here's to success number two.' Jackie toasted Ella.

'I can't believe how easy it's been.'

'Well, not exactly easy. How are you all getting on?' Jackie asked.

'Not too bad. We've been staying at Clara's. At first we had to, to make sure Virginia went to this meeting, then we just stayed. I don't know why.'

'So you're becoming friends?' Jackie asked.

'Not exactly. I mean, Virginia's getting better and, God, she looks like a babe now. It's amazing what you can do with some clothes, a haircut and makeup. Anyway, sometimes Clara's quite sweet, but when she takes cocaine she turns into such a bitch. She's jealous of how Virginia looks, but then she encourages her by taking her shopping. I can't figure it out.'

'Yes, but what about you? Are you still the cold person you said you were with them, or have you thawed a bit now they know about you?'

'Well, not exactly. I'm trying to be nicer and warmer, but I still feel I should pull back.' Ella drank her wine and looked sad.

'But why? Ella, you were getting on so well with people before you got fired. You were more like the Ella I know. Why can't you do that now with those two? They know almost as much as I do.' Jackie patted Ella's hand.

'I don't know. I was making progress but when I lost my job I felt like it was because I'd let the barriers down. I know it doesn't make sense, but that's how I felt. I try with Clara and Virginia, but it's hard.'

'I do understand, but think about it, Ella,' Jackie begged.

'I will, but it's all complicated. Virginia and Clara come with their own problems.'

'This is better than a soap opera. I can't wait until you get your next victim.' Jackie rubbed her hands together.

'We are doing the right thing, aren't we?' Ella asked.

'Yes. Ella, I hear stories all the time of people getting stamped on by other people – bosses, partners, friends. You're taking a stand against that, getting the people who stamp on people. They deserve it. Also, remember you set them up but each time so far they've created their own fall. No one made Isabelle use that information. No one made Tim talk to the journalist. I think it's great.'

Virginia went to the supermarket and bought food for supper. She was so pleased that she couldn't stop smiling as she pushed the trolley round. Clara had given her a set of keys and said she might be out, so Virginia had decided that as a thank-you for letting her stay and for the shopping trip, she would clear the flat, put flowers everywhere and make it look nice. She noticed that she drew some admiring glances from male shoppers and basked in the attention. No one had paid her any attention before.

She thought about how far she'd come from the girl who was too scared to speak. Although she still said little, she had gained some confidence lately. Her performance at the lunch with Declan amazed her. She was beginning to feel as though she wasn't a failure after all.

She bought cleaning products as well as food, because although Clara insisted she had a cleaner, Virginia had seen no evidence of one. Perhaps it was an imaginary cleaner. Clara sometimes seemed mad enough to invent one. Sometimes Virginia wanted to hug her and sometimes Clara terrified her. She was warming to Ella too. After hearing her awful story Virginia understood her defensive nature and why she showed so little emotion, and she felt Ella was dropping her guard. We're all changing, Virginia thought, and by the time she got to the check-out, she was ready to change some more.

When she got back to the flat, Virginia set to work. She cleaned it from top to bottom, put flowers in the sitting room and started cooking. She imagined it was her flat, that she owned it. She was the type of person who lived there. She was so caught up in her fantasy that when the bell rang she almost jumped out of her skin. She opened the door to find James standing there.

'Hello,' she stammered.

'Have you moved in?' James asked.

'Oh, we're staying for a while,' Virginia said, as he walked into the flat. She had almost forgotten how sexy he was. He was tall with blonde hair like Clara's and the bluest eyes she'd ever seen. She tried to pull herself together. 'Clara's out.'

'Where?'

'I don't know. She just said she needed to go out. Do

you want coffee?' Virginia tried to sound casual; again, she failed.

'Sure.' James smiled at her, thinking she was cute if a little flustered.

Virginia walked into the kitchen feeling heat radiating from her face. She put the kettle on. 'You talked to Declan, you can talk to James,' she told herself, as she tried to stop herself going red. 'But that was scripted. You don't have a script now,' a voice in her head argued. She concentrated on the coffee, and made up a tray with a jug of milk and the sugar bowl. As the kettle boiled, she told herself again to keep calm.

She walked back into the room, trying hard not to tremble as she carried the tray. James stood up, took it from her and put it on the coffee table. He poured some milk and spooned two sugars into his cup. Virginia sat on the chair. She didn't dare drink her coffee for fear she would spill it.

'So, how's the plotting going?' James asked.

'Fine. I hear you don't approve,' Virginia said, tentatively.

'It's not that, I just don't like to think of Clara getting into trouble. She does seem to attract it.'

'Yes.' Virginia agreed with him. Clara did attract trouble.

'But you and Ella seem sensible. I'm hoping you'll keep her on the straight and narrow.'

'I'm not sure even we can do that.' Virginia relaxed a bit.

'So, what's happening? Did Clara's boss get his comeuppance yet?' James looked her straight in the eye. Virginia looked away to stop herself from blushing.

'Nearly. He's going to be exposed in next weekend's *Sunday News*,' she told him.

'I'll have to buy it. Look, are you sure you know what you're doing? I mean, can you get into trouble from all this?' James was evidently concerned.

'No. Ella's the sensible one and the brains behind most of this. She wouldn't let us do anything risky. It's just, well, we don't want to be victims.'

James laughed. 'You three hardly seem like victims. I wouldn't like to cross you,' he said.

'It wasn't easy. We were all really upset at being fired.'

'Of course. Actually, to show solidarity I've spoken to my father about moving our account to another investment bank.'

'Won't he want to know why?' Virginia felt worried.

'I've told him they're complacent with our money. SFH don't work for the company, it's our private money they look after, including Clara's trust fund. It'll do just as well somewhere else.'

Virginia felt uncomfortable talking about the amount of money he had. Rich people intimidated her. 'Well, that's loyal,' she said eventually.

'Or sensible. One woman's lost a fortune for the bank and her clients, thanks to you, and a partner's going to be exposed in the tabloids. SFH will take a beating over the scandal. It's probably just as well that we go elsewhere.'

Virginia didn't know what to say.

'Anyway, in the meantime I'll entrust my sister's welfare to you. And try to talk some sense into her about Josh, while you're at it. I must say, you seem quite at home here.'

'Well, I've just cleaned up and I'm cooking dinner tonight.' Virginia felt herself turn red again.

'Oh, it wasn't a criticism. I'm glad Clara has some proper friends, and not the silly giggling women she usually hangs about with. What are you having for dinner?'

'Oh, just some chicken,' Virginia replied.

'Great. What time shall I be here?' James asked.

'What?' Virginia said, horrified.

'Well, I've missed my sister and I'd quite like to see her so if you can stretch the dinner that far I thought I'd join you.'

'Oh. Well, I suppose around eight.' Virginia's heart dropped. Although she wanted him there, she knew Clara would go mad.

'I'll see you, then.' James got up. 'I can see myself out,' he added, and winked at her.

✳ ✳ ✳

Clara took a taxi to an address in Camden Town. The man she'd spoken to had sounded nice, and as the cab pulled up, she saw he lived in a massive townhouse. She got out, paid the driver, went to the door and rang the bell. She waited, heard footsteps and eventually the door opened. A flamboyant man in a Paisley smoking-jacket stood before her.

'Hello,' Clara said, thinking she must be in the wrong place.

'You must be the lovely Clara,' the man replied.

'Oliver?' Clara asked, amazed that he was a drug-dealer.

'That's me. Come in, then.' He ushered her into his house.

'So, you're Josh's girl?' he asked.

'Well, not really,' Clara answered, and followed Oliver into his living room. It was stuffed with dark wooden furniture, leather armchairs and books. She noticed as she sat down that he had the biggest television set she had ever seen; and a games machine was hooked up to it.

'So, you're not Josh's girl?' He sat down too.

'Well, we're friends, really.' Clara was at a loss for an explanation.

'Um. Well, he keeps calling me and not for the usual reasons. He keeps calling to ask if you've called me,' Oliver told her.

'Well, don't tell him, I have.' Clara was annoyed that Josh was checking up on her.

'I pride myself on client confidentiality. Just like a doctor. Which I'm not, by the way. Anyway, Josh has stopped buying cocaine lately. He said he was giving it up. Sad boy. Therefore I shan't tell him anything. Rest assured.' Oliver smiled.

'Good, then we'll get on fine. How much can you give me?' Clara asked.

'How much do you want?' He raised one very thin eyebrow.

'Four,' Clara replied.

'Oh, a heavy user, then. Sure. Wait there.' Clara was about to argue that she wasn't a heavy user, but Oliver had disappeared.

He returned and gave her a bag with some wraps in it. Then he took the money she handed him.

'You want to try some?' he asked. Clara shook her head. She wanted to leave. 'Fine. Call me any time.' Oliver stood up. Clara thanked him and left.

She walked around Camden for a while, thinking how dirty it was. She felt uncomfortable about the number of tramps who approached her holding cans of Special Brew and asking for money. As soon as she could she found a taxi and asked the driver to take her to Knightsbridge. She felt depressed. There, she went to a bar and ordered a glass of champagne. She hadn't been in there before and it was quiet. She went to the ladies' and sampled her purchase.

When she returned she sat down and spotted a man looking at her. He smiled; she smiled. He was youngish and he looked nice. Not gorgeous like Josh but pleasant. He had light brown hair and sparkly eyes. He made his way over to her table. 'Can I get you another?' he asked. His accent was foreign.

'Sure.' Clara smiled. He ordered and Clara finished her first glass. 'I'm Clara.'

'Antonio. I'm from Italy.'

Clara raised her eyebrows. He didn't look Italian, although he sounded it. 'Are you on holiday?' she asked.

'I'm visiting my girlfriend. She's English. I like English girls.'

'So where is she, then?' Clara asked.

'Shopping. I am meeting her in one hour,' he said.

'Well, you shouldn't be talking to me. She won't be pleased,' Clara teased.

'As I said, I have an hour.'

Clara shrugged and lit a cigarette.

'How much?' Antonio asked.

Clara looked at him. 'About four pounds,' she replied. How odd of him to ask her the price of cigarettes, she thought.

'I mean for you,' he explained, looking suggestively at her breasts.

The penny dropped. 'I'm not — well, I'm not cheap,' she retorted, turned on by the idea.

'I didn't think you were.'

'Five hundred.' She pulled a figure from her head, thinking he would either run or pay up.

'Where can we go?' Antonio asked.

Clara didn't know what to think or say. She was aroused by the idea, appalled too. But, then, she hadn't had sex in a while and this guy was quite tasty.

'I read somewhere that in London a girl who sits alone in a bar drinking champagne is for sale.' He smiled, and Clara vowed not to do it again.

'Follow me,' she commanded, and led him away from the table. She didn't know where to take him, but she had decided to see it through. 'Wait here.' She left him standing outside as she went into the ladies'. There was no one in there, so she put out her hand, grabbed Antonio and dragged him inside. There, she led him into a cubicle and locked the door. She took her trousers down, then her knickers. Antonio was staring at her. She yanked at his trousers. 'Do you have a condom?' she asked.

'No, but I have a very hard one.'

Clara rolled her eyes and grabbed her handbag. After scrabbling around for a while she found one. She put it on him, pushed him down on to the loo seat and straddled him. It took him only a few moments to finish, and Clara was left unsatisfied, although the idea of shagging for money in a loo had appealed to her.

'Thank you,' he said, pulling up his pants and trousers.

'It's my job,' Clara replied impassively, while she dressed herself. She unlocked the door, looked around, saw the room was empty and walked out. ''Bye, then.' She went straight out of the door to the bar.

'But your money!' Antonio shouted after her, but she'd gone. Antonio smiled. It must be his lucky day. And he still had half an hour left before his girlfriend was due to turn up.

Chapter Thirty-seven

Clara arrived home, hardly glancing at Virginia before she went to take a shower. When she came out, she looked around. 'You've cleaned up. Thanks,' she said, without sounding as if she meant it.

Virginia sighed. She knew she'd have to tell her about James and she really didn't want to. 'James called round.'

Clara looked at her sharply. 'What did he want?'

'To see you, of course.'

'Well, why couldn't he telephone? What did he say?'

'Nothing much. But he invited himself to dinner tonight.'

'What?' Clara was annoyed.

'Well, what could I do?'

'You could have bloody well told him he couldn't come, that's what. Shit, Virginia, why are you so stupid?'

'Well, I didn't think you'd mind. You always say how much you like him.'

'Of course I do, but I don't want him here with you two. Shit, Virginia, I'm not pleased about this.'

'I'm sorry,' Virginia said.

Clara paced for a few minutes. 'Well, there's nothing we can do.' She seemed to accept it.

'Where have you been?' Virginia asked, trying to make peace.

'None of your fucking business,' Clara replied, and went into her room.

'Hi,' Virginia said, as she opened the door.

'Hello. How's things?' Ella asked, bringing her bag in and walking into the sitting room.

'Hi, Ella.' Clara walked in and sat down.

'Hi,' Ella responded. Looking at Virginia's pinched face and Clara's relaxed one she guessed that all had not been well.

'James is coming for supper,' Clara told her, as if she liked the idea.

'Great,' Ella replied.

'Yes, Virginia's worked hard to get the flat tidy. What are you cooking?' Clara was sweet again.

'Mexican chicken. It's very simple,' Virginia answered, confused by Clara's *volte-face*.

'Sounds divine. I'll open some wine, shall I?' Virginia started cooking, while Ella and Clara sat in the kitchen with their glasses.

'What did you get up to today?' Ella asked Clara. Virginia got ready for the onslaught, but Clara just smiled.

'You wouldn't believe me if I told you,' she said.

'Go on, then,' Ella prompted.

'Well, I went to buy drugs, and then I went to a bar in Knightsbridge where I had a glass of champagne. This Italian man came over to join me and bought me another glass. Then he asked me how much something cost. I thought he was talking about my cigarettes, but he wanted to know how much *I* was. Gosh, it was so funny. I said I was five hundred pounds, took him into the loo and had sex with him.' Clara looked triumphant and Virginia dropped a saucepan.

'You made that up.' Ella couldn't believe what she had heard.

'I did not. It really happened.' Clara pouted.

'You had sex in a toilet for *money*?' Virginia asked, trying to retrieve the vegetables from the floor.

'I forgot to take the money.' Clara giggled.

'That's disgusting,' Virginia said, shocked.

'It's dangerous.' Ella was staring at Clara.

'Not really. We used a condom. Anyway, I told you I was a sex addict. This proves it.'

'Clara, it's not funny.' Virginia was getting angry.

'Anyway, I was thinking, Virginia needs money so she could go on the game.' Clara giggled again.

'Clara, shut up.' Ella had seen Virginia's expression.

'No, really. If it's that easy she can. I could be her madam, or whatever they call it nowadays.' Clara began laughing hysterically.

'Clara, *shut up*. If James knows what you get up to, you'll be in serious trouble. Leave Virginia alone and stop behaving like a cheap slut. Christ, you could have been arrested. He might have been a cop. And you put yourself in danger – he might have been a murderer or anything.'

'Of course he wasn't a murderer. He was just some randy man who wanted sex. Anyway, I *like* danger,' Clara said defensively.

'No, you don't. You take too much cocaine, you drink too much and you convince yourself you're a sex addict. I don't think it's sex you're addicted to.' Ella's voice was raised.

'Well, what is it, then?' Clara yelled.

'Drugs, Clara, that's what. You're a fucking cokehead.' Ella was angrier than she'd been in a long while.

'I am *not* a drug addict. I'm not, I'm *not*,' Clara shouted, then burst into tears. She sat at the kitchen counter heaving with sobs, and Ella reached over to hug her.

'OK, calm down. But, Clara, you are not behaving like this any more. I won't allow it. If you don't promise to stop we won't let you out on your own.' Ella's voice was soothing.

'I'm not a drug addict.' Clara sniffed, but she allowed

Ella to hold her. 'I need a bath,' she said, and went to her bathroom.

Virginia was stirring the sauce for the chicken. She felt physically sick because of what she had heard. Especially as James had said they must look after Clara. 'What *are* we going to do?' she asked Ella.

'I don't know. God, Virginia, she's a mess. We can't let her carry on like this.'

'Why does she do it? She's beautiful, she's rich, her brother adores her, and men like Josh fall over themselves to be with her. Why behave like this?' Virginia was lost.

'She's all those things, but she's bloody insecure too. She's sweet and kind when she's normal, but when she takes cocaine she turn into a monster. One minute she acts as if she wants us around, the next she's being nasty. She has the lowest self-esteem of all of us,' Ella said.

'I still can't understand. If I was like her I'd be really confident,' Virginia said.

'I know, but we don't know what it's like to be her. I don't know what it's like being you and you don't know what it's like being me. We all act like we're in control but none of us is.'

'I never act like I'm in control.'

'Virginia, you are more in control than Clara is. Believe me.'

'We need to help her.'

'But how?'

'What you said. From now on we spend all our time with her and we don't let her out on her own,' Virginia suggested.

'How the hell did we get into this situation?' Ella asked.

'We got fired,' Virginia said simply.

'Yes, we bloody did. And I thought that was the hard part.'

'This is worse, isn't it?' Virginia asked.

'Yes. Oh, God. What are we going to do?' Ella sat still while Virginia carried on with the dinner. Neither knew the answer.

*   *   *

Clara returned as Ella was setting the table. 'You won't tell James, will you?' she pleaded.

'No. But you have to think long and hard about your behaviour.' Ella sounded like a schoolteacher.

'I have been. You're right. I shouldn't do the things I do. I'm going to give up the coke,' Clara announced.

'Really?' Ella asked, disbelieving her.

'I promise,' Clara replied, not meaning a word of it.

'And men?'

'I'll try, but you have to trust me. I need you to trust me.'

'We'll do our best,' Ella said, as Clara walked into the kitchen where she had the same conversation with Virginia. She believed her because she needed to believe her.

James arrived at eight with four bottles of wine. He hugged Clara, who clung to him for longer than was necessary.

'What's that for?' he asked.

'I'm just pleased to see you,' she said.

Virginia served dinner, and James and Clara kept them all entertained with stories of their childhood. James had been the golden boy, Clara said. Clara was always in trouble, James said. They told stories with affection that ripped at Ella's heart. Although her life and theirs were a million miles apart, she knew they shared what she and Sam had shared. They enjoyed the meal, and Virginia was pleased. She started to contribute to the conversation. Ella noticed that James stared at her constantly, but Clara seemed oblivious to this, as did Virginia.

After dinner, James insisted on loading the dishwasher and making coffee. Clara didn't pop into her bedroom at all, although she drank even more than usual. Virginia was so happy that she smiled and laughed all evening, and Ella was busy trying to figure everything out.

'I should be off. Thank you for a delicious meal and wonderful company,' James said eventually.

'You're such a charmer,' Clara teased, hugging him again.

'Well, if I always get a reception like that I'll visit more often.' James kissed Ella on both cheeks then Virginia, lingering with her.

'I'm going to be better,' Clara told them. 'I'm going to see someone.'

'Who?' Virginia asked.

'One of those counsellor people. Someone who can help. You were right. I need to sort myself out. I'm really going to do it.'

'Good.' Ella was still not convinced.

'I'll start next week.' Clara continued, thinking that that would buy her time away from the others. 'And I would appreciate it if you'd help me through it. If you stay with me, I'll get better more quickly.'

Ella and Virginia exchanged glances.

'Of course we will. Clara, I'm really pleased,' Virginia said.

Clara had a plan. She wasn't going to see a counsellor but she was going to prove her sanity. She would prove she wasn't addicted to cocaine. She would set up the plan for Johnny all by herself. The others would be so proud of her they'd forget all this telling-off and see that she was perfectly in control. She would show them that Clara Hart was not an addict, that she was capable of more than they realised. That night, she dreamt about her plan.

Chapter Thirty-eight

Late the following Saturday night Ella and Virginia set out to buy the early editions of the Sunday newspapers. They found a vendor at a tube station and bought three copies of the *Sunday News*. Tim had made the front page. 'SFH Director In Cocaine and Prostitute Scandal,' the headline screamed. There was a picture of Tim with a half-naked girl, next to the picture of him that Clara had sent to Declan. The story read like a dream.

'We'd better get this to Clara,' Virginia said.

Clara was pacing the flat. She had told them to go so that she could make an important telephone call and take some cocaine. They had stopped guarding her so closely now: she had told them she had been to see her counsellor three times that week but she hadn't. She'd been hatching a plan. A plan that was working well. She had managed to hide her cocaine-taking by not being mean to either Ella or Virginia. She was so sweet to them that they fell for it. 'Suckers,' Clara hissed, as she put more white powder up her nose.

Virginia let them in with the keys she had. They found Clara sitting on the sofa, smoking. Virginia handed her a paper. Clara's eyes widened as she read the story. It had Tim's background, his career history and his position. It had a transcript of a conversation in which he had said he could get cocaine and girls for the reporter he thought was a lord. Clara couldn't believe her eyes. The second headline read: 'Will Seymour Forbes Hunt, Britain's oldest investment bank, withstand the scandal that one of its shareholders and a prominent member of its management team is not only a cocaine and prostitute user but also offered to supply both to our undercover reporter?' It was fantastic.

'This is *amazing*.' Clara was thrilled.

'He'll be ruined.' Ella laughed.

'I'll drink to that,' Clara shrieked, and went to get champagne.

Tim always had the *Sunday News* delivered along with the *Sunday Times* and the *Sunday Telegraph*. This week the delivery boy had left two copies of the *Sunday News*. When Tim picked it up the colour drained from his face. His wife had brought him breakfast in bed with all the newspapers. She hadn't said anything. He read the story and the penny dropped. 'Lord William Calloway' had been a reporter. He tried to think what to do. He couldn't sue because, as he knew, the story was true. He picked up the rest of the paper and tore it in half. Then he noticed that his wife had left a note on his breakfast tray. 'Get out, you bastard,' it read. Tim panicked. The telephone rang, and he knew instinctively who it would be. Someone to tell him he was finished at SFH.

As he left the house, his wife refused to look at or talk to him. He took his passport and wallet but no clothes. He picked up the keys to his Bentley and left the house. He thought fleetingly of Clara: she must have set him up. At first he thought he would kill her, but that would be fruitless. Then he tried to convince himself that it hadn't been her, that it was just bad luck. But he knew he had underestimated her. Now he was ruined. He drove to the airport, went to the BA desk and asked for a first-class ticket to New York. He didn't know what he'd do there, but he knew he needed to leave the country. Tim had misjudged everything, especially his own infallibility.

A second emergency managing directors' meeting was called at SFH, this time on a Sunday. Men were pulled away from their families and hauled off the golf course; some even had to get last-minute flights so they could meet at the office that night. The head of PR had also been called in. They were all upset at the press revelations. The bank had had to fight hard to retain some of its clients after the Isabelle Holland incident; this was bound to shake them further. SFH had had an impeccable record, yet now it had faced two onslaughts from the press caused by two members of staff. They knew they must issue a statement quickly.

They worked overnight to ensure that the following state-ment was with every newspaper, ready for Monday's editions.

SFH condemns wholeheartedly the behaviour of Tim Pemberton. We, as an institution and as a management team, knew nothing of his outside activities. Mr Pemberton is no longer a part of SFH and his shares in the company are being transferred. He will no longer play any part in the running or ownership of the bank.

We would like to reiterate our commitment to our clients at this time. We will continue to work hard to ensure that their interests are met to the highest standard. One man does not make or break an investment bank with a history such as ours. We will continue to be successful, and promise further vigilance to ensure that a situation like this does not occur again.

We would also like to offer our co-operation to the police in any investigation. SFH has nothing to hide, so our doors will be held open for them. Again we express regret at this situation, and offer our assurances that it has been dealt with.

Chapter Thirty-nine

Until the story broke, Virginia and Ella had been too concerned about Clara's behaviour to think about Johnny. Now they were ready to plan again. Two successes had made them sure that their objectives were right. Ella worried briefly that Tim might come after Clara, but then she rationalised that he would be too concerned with getting away. He wouldn't have time for revenge. Anyway, he was in enough trouble as it was. And if he did try anything Ella would make sure that he didn't get close to Clara.

On Sunday morning, she woke late, showered, and found Virginia cooking breakfast. 'God, you're an angel,' Ella said.

'No, I'm just hung over again. I need food,' Virginia replied, dishing up breakfast for the two of them.

'No sign of the princess?' Ella asked.

'You know Clara. She can sleep for England.' They sat at the counter eating.

'We should start thinking about Johnny,' Ella suggested.

'We should. I think his plan should be very different from the other two. I can't help but feel we sailed a bit close to the wind with Tim,' Virginia responded.

'I was thinking the same. I mean, Isabelle would have no idea we set her up, but Tim was supposed to be meeting Clara. He'll know.'

'Yeah. I hope he doesn't do anything.'

'He won't. Don't ask me how I know, I just do. He's going to be in no frame of mind to do anything. My guess is that we'll never hear from him again.'

'So what about Johnny? Any ideas?' Virginia asked.

'No. You?' Ella replied. Virginia shook her head.

When Clara emerged she said she didn't want breakfast. She poured herself a cup of coffee and sat down.

'We were just talking about Johnny,' Virginia said.

'Have you got any ideas for a plan?' Ella asked.

'Actually I have. But I can't tell you yet. Give me a couple of days, will you?' Ella and Virginia exchanged glances.

'Can't you give us some idea?' Ella asked.

'No. It's still in the planning stages, and as I said, I'll tell you in a couple of days.' Clara picked up her coffee and went to her room.

She laughed when she thought of what she had done. No one had even noticed. So much for them putting her under guard. They let her do exactly as she wanted. Clara had told them that the only appointments she could get with her counsellor were in the evening. She had also told them that she paid for three hours of intensive counselling so she had a certain amount of freedom. She refused all offers to go with her because 'I need to do this on my own.' And they had fallen for it. Clara doubted that counsellors even worked evenings.

Clara's plan had started with Liam, Ella's ex-colleague. She had rung him and told him she needed to talk to him. They met when Clara was supposed to be at her first counselling appointment. Liam had recognised Clara from work, but Clara hadn't recognised him. Liam had looked approvingly at her, then proceeded to talk about Ella. Clara said that she would try to get Ella to call him, but he had to be patient. She also told him that in the meantime he could help her with something. She said that if he helped her she would help him. She took a gamble, but it paid off. She told Liam that she was going to take revenge on Johnny for what he had done to Ella. Liam was thrilled, and told her how much everyone hated Johnny. The plan was simple. Clara would meet Liam at a bar; he'd invite Johnny then leave them together. She told Liam that she couldn't tell him the details but that he could trust her. Liam said he wanted to see Johnny burn in hell.

The first meeting had been a success. They had met in a wine bar not too far from work, but far enough for Clara not to bump into anyone else from SFH. She almost felt sick as she saw Johnny, all pimples and greasy hair, but she knew she had to go through with it. She made it look like a chance meeting — he had never seen her at SFH and had no idea she had worked there so she told him she was in PR. Which, for now, she was. Liam left, saying he'd forgotten something and had to go back to the office, and for the next two hours Clara charmed Johnny. When she announced she had to leave, she gave Johnny her mobile number and asked him to call her. She kissed his spotty cheek and hailed a cab.

He called her the following day, and she met him when she was meant to be at her second counselling appointment. This time she told him she found him attractive and she kissed him properly. He was practically drooling. Kissing him was as unpleasant as it had been to kiss Tim, but that was OK. She was working.

By the third meeting, she despised him. However, he obviously felt that she was besotted with him and he revealed his confidence in himself: he kept telling her how important he was, how respected in the office, how he was probably the best trader they had. He talked about himself all the time, and only stopped when Clara put her tongue in his mouth. She didn't have sex with him and always left early, telling him she had work to do. He never asked about her work so that was easy. She took his telephone number and told him she really liked him, and as soon as she had finished her big project, they would have a night out together properly. He saw the implication and told her he would wait. What she hated about him, apart from his looks and sweaty hands, was the way he treated her. He patronised her. He acted as if she was lucky to be with him. And his self-importance was higher even than Tim's had been. He was a shit too. He told her that girls threw themselves at him. Clara knew this would only be true if he stood near a bridge and they were trying to drown themselves. He also hinted at what he'd done to Ella, saying, 'Nobody gets in my way.' Clara knew he would tell her about Ella soon. He would do it in his boastful way and expect her to be impressed. She felt sad that he had ruined Ella's career when he was a nobody.

Clara had opened up a line of communication with Liam. She called him on his mobile to give him updates and he did the same. He told her how Johnny had been boasting about a 'hot, horny chick' he'd been seeing. Clara told him she was hot to kill Johnny, nothing more. Liam said that if there was anything he could do she should let him know.

Last night, when Ella and Virginia had been scouring London for the newspapers, she had called Johnny and woken him up. She told him she couldn't stop thinking about him and she wanted him. He offered to come over but she told him it would be better if they waited. She arranged to meet him on Sunday night. She needed to get rid of Virginia and Ella so that after she had had dinner with him in the Atlantic Bar, she could bring him back to her flat.

She still hadn't worked out what her plan would be, but she knew she would get some inspiration soon. She was determined that the others would only be told when things were finalised. She took a shower, got dressed and walked into the sitting room to find Virginia and Ella on the sofa watching a black-and-white movie on television.

She took a deep breath. 'You guys have been really good staying with me this week, but tonight I need to be on my own.'

Ella and Virginia exchanged glances.

'I don't think that's a good idea,' Ella said, although she relished the thought of an evening with Jackie.

'But my counsellor said it would be good for me to do it. She thinks I'm ready.' Clara lied.

'Really?' Virginia asked.

'Yes, and you need to show me trust. That's what she said too.' Clara was firm. Virginia hated the thought of going back to her horrible flat, but she could see that Clara was not going to budge. 'Look, Virginia, just for tonight. Tomorrow you can both come round and check to see if I'm still in one piece.'

'OK,' Ella conceded. She stood up and pulled out her mobile to call Jackie. Jackie said that she'd take the evening off work and they'd have a good chat at Ella's flat. Ella left at six and drove home.

Virginia lingered, and Clara didn't know what to do with her. Eventually she said, 'I'm going out to meet a girlfriend for dinner, just like Ella. I have to go now, so you can let yourself out.' Clara needed to get away from Virginia, who was making her feel guilty.

'I thought you wanted to be on your own,' Virginia said accusingly.

'I do. Well, I want to sleep on my own — not that I sleep with you but I have to get my life back to normal and I haven't seen anyone but you and Ella for ages. I'm having an early dinner, then I'll come home and have an early night. I'll see you tomorrow.' Clara picked up her jacket and bag, and prayed that Virginia wouldn't be there when she got home.

'I'm just going to clear up, then I'll go,' Virginia said.

'See you tomorrow?' Clara asked.

'Sure. Have a nice time.' Virginia watched her go.

Virginia started to clear up. She cursed Clara and Ella for having other people to see when, she still had no one. Just as she had picked up some clothes and put them in her backpack, the doorbell rang. Virginia answered it. James was standing there. Her heart missed a beat.

'We must stop meeting like this,' James said, with a grin.

'Clara's not here,' Virginia said, a little too quickly.

'Well, you can make me coffee, then,' James teased.

'I was just leaving, actually.'

'Where are you going?'

'Home,' she answered simply.

'Where's that?'

'Maida Vale.'

'OK, I'll drive you. It's practically on my way.'

'On your way where?'

'Home.' James was still teasing her.

'But you live in Chelsea.'

'It's the scenic route. Come on.' James grabbed her bag and her hand, and led her out of the flat.

Virginia nearly fainted when she saw James's car. It was a red Ferrari and it looked brand new. 'Nice,' she said.

'I use it to impress all the girls.' Virginia looked at him with hurt in her eyes. 'I'm teasing,' James said hurriedly. 'I love cars and I love this one.' He opened the door for Virginia and she got in.

'How come you're going home?' James asked.

'Oh, you know, I need to every now and again.' Virginia smiled weakly.

'What about the plotting?' James asked.

'Clara's got something up her sleeve but she hasn't told us what,' Virginia said.

'And then it'll be three.'

'What?'

'Three victims, darling. Your work will be done.'

'I suppose so.' This thought did nothing to cheer her up.

'What are you doing this evening?' James asked.

'Nothing,' Virginia responded, wishing it wasn't true.

'Then I'm taking you to dinner. I'll drop you home, wait while you change and then we'll go somewhere swanky.'

'Really?' Virginia asked, and regretted the question as soon as it left her mouth.

'Really. And I won't take no for an answer.'

Virginia directed him to her flat and began to get out of the car.

'Aren't you going to invite me in?' he asked.

She couldn't let him see her poky room! 'No. I won't be long. Do you mind waiting in the car?' Virginia asked, trying not to sound panicked.

'Not at all,' James replied. He watched her open her door and wondered what it was about her that he liked. She was good-looking, but she was so timid and she seemed terrified of him. And she could be quite strange. She intrigued him ... and he really quite liked to be intrigued.

As she ran up the stairs and into her room Virginia tried to slow her breathing. She kicked aside the mail that sat on her doormat and unpacked her bag. She looked at the few clothes she had brought back with her and felt relieved that she had a skirt and a nice top. She also had her kitten-heeled shoes. She applied some lip-gloss and mascara and pushed back her hair, grabbed her handbag and left. 'I do have something tonight,' she sang to herself, as she walked into the street where James and his Ferrari were waiting for her.

They went to Quo Vadis in Soho. James asked Virginia if she'd been there before and she shook her head. She almost told him she'd never been anywhere before.

'Champagne?' he asked, and ordered a bottle from the hovering waiter before she had a chance to reply.

'Thank you.' When it arrived, she drank quickly because she was nervous.

'Are you going to tell me your story?' James asked.

'What story?' Virginia replied.

'Your life story, of course,' he said, looking into her eyes. Virginia told him everything. She told him about her disappointed parents, her numerous failures, her job at SFH, the Private Clients job and Isabelle. It was a long story.

'Goodness. You've had a tough time, haven't you?' James said softly, and stroked her cheek. Virginia felt electricity course through her veins. 'Shall we order? I'm starving,' he said, and removed his hand. Virginia nodded and took another gulp of champagne. They ordered but Virginia didn't notice the food. She couldn't believe she was here with him. He was so nice, kind and tender, and she was falling hopelessly in love. Over coffee, James lit a cigarette.

'I haven't seen you smoke before,' Virginia said.

'Oh, I only do it occasionally. Normally just after sex,' James teased. Virginia went red. 'Sorry, I wasn't suggesting anything,' he added hastily, sensing her discomfort.

Part of Virginia wished he was. She didn't know she had a libido, but something in her was out of control. 'Don't apologise,' she said, and smiled.

'God, are you flirting with me?' he asked.

'No. Maybe. Yes.' Virginia giggled.

'Christ, and I thought you were immune to my charms,' James said, leant over the table and kissed her. Virginia nearly fell off her chair. She couldn't believe her luck. He really *did* like her.

James called the waiter and asked for the bill. He paid it, and took Virginia's hand. 'I'm driving you home,' he announced.

Virginia didn't know whose home he meant: his or hers. 'Haven't you had too much to drink?' she asked.

'No, but you have. Which is why I'm driving you to your place and, like a gentleman, I will see you to your door and go home myself.'

Virginia felt disappointment flood her. 'Oh,' she said.

James led her out of the restaurant and to his car. He opened the door for her and she got in. When he started the engine, he looked at her. 'Can I see you again?' he asked.

'Really?' Virginia said, cursing again.

'Yes, really. Can I?' He leant over and kissed her lightly.

'Yes, I think so.' Then she remembered who he was. 'Oh, God. We can't tell Clara,' she said.

'Why on earth not? I think she'll be pleased that her brother and her friend are dating.'

'No, I don't think so. Please, James, not yet. I don't want her to know.'

'Whatever you say. But I like you, Virginia, and that isn't going to go away.'

'Really?' Virginia asked, feeling breathless and as if she was floating into space.

'Yes, really.' James laughed and drove her home. As he dropped her off he handed her a card with his telephone numbers on it and she clutched it to her chest.

As she watched him drive off, Virginia wondered if she was dreaming. She pinched her arm, yelped in pain, and thought that if she had been it would have been the most heavenly dream ever.

Ella sat in her sitting room with Jackie. They were about to watch a video and they were eating popcorn and drinking lager.

'Clara's up to something,' Ella said.

'What makes you say that?' Jackie asked.

'She says she's given up cocaine, she's acting like a saint and she says she's seeing a counsellor,' Ella explained.

'And isn't she?' Jackie asked.

'She keeps asking us to trust her, but I just can't. Apart from anything else, she sees this counsellor in the evenings for three hours at a stretch. Now, I know that Clara has enough money to buy anyone at any time, but I don't think that that happens.'

'You're probably right. What are you going to do?'

'I feel like running. Letting her get on with it.'

'She's playing you both for fools,' Jackie said.

'So what should we do?'

'I don't know, honey, but there will be a time when she needs you and I know you'll do the right thing then.'

'Maybe, but I don't know if I have the strength. It's tiring being with them, you know.'

'Yeah, but you'll do it. Don't forget it's nearly over.'

'And then what the hell am I going to do?'

'I don't know that either.'

'Jackie, you're useless.' Ella hit her with a cushion then went to put the video on.

Clara walked around Piccadilly Circus waiting for seven thirty when she had arranged to meet Johnny. She cursed Virginia for not leaving her flat earlier, but when she rang her number she was pleased that no one answered. All she needed was to take Johnny home and find Virginia there. She went to the restaurant, smiled at the doorman, walked in and up to the woman who was looking after the reservations.

'Rupfin, I think. Table for two?'

'Here you go. The gentleman is here already.'

Clara found Johnny at the bar drinking what looked like whisky. 'Hi,' she said.

'Hello yourself. You look nice tonight.' Johnny stood up and kissed her on both cheeks. As the *maitre d'* led them to their table, he looked at Clara, who saw surprise in his eyes. He probably couldn't believe that a girl like her was with such a loser.

'So, what would you like to drink?' Johnny asked.

'Champagne, of course.'

'How silly of me.' He beckoned to the waiter by waving his arms around, which horrified Clara. It was almost as bad as if he'd snapped his fingers. 'A bottle of your finest champagne,' he requested. When the waiter poured it, he looked at Clara with so much sympathy she almost giggled.

'Here's to us.' Clara raised her glass and Johnny clinked it.

They drank their champagne while they looked over the menu. Johnny kept suggesting what Clara should eat, which annoyed her, but she listened to him patiently. He chose the wine too. Clara just smiled in agreement. When they had ordered, Johnny started talking about himself and Clara lit a cigarette.

'Do you have to smoke? I find it common in a woman to smoke,' Johnny said.

'I do apologise, but I'm addicted,' Clara answered, and seethed inside.

'Well, if we're going to have a future I think you should give up,' Johnny said seriously.

'I'll book an appointment with a hypnotist. In the meantime, I'll have to keep smoking. I'm sure you can put up with it just for the moment.' She smiled seductively.

'I suppose,' Johnny said sulkily, then carried on talking about himself. He managed to stop for just long enough to eat, but he was still talking when the waiter took away their empty main course plates. He was also drinking a lot.

'You see, Clara, in order to be as successful as I am, you need to be clever. I don't let anyone get in my way.' Johnny paused for effect.

This was Clara's opportunity to get him to talk about Ella. 'What do you mean?' she asked sweetly.

'Well, when I started working at SFH, I was given this awful woman as a boss. Now, I don't work for women. I don't believe that women should be in the financial world. It's a man's world. You work in PR, which is a girl's thing, but finance, well, you're better off keeping away. Anyway, this woman was not only a woman but she was northern and common. You could tell. I think she only got the job because she was black. Unfortunately banks are becoming so politically correct nowadays that things like that happen. Anyway, she thought she was better than I was and, of course, she wasn't. We had a couple of rows, she tried to humiliate me, so I did the same to her.' Johnny smirked.

'Go on.' Clara urged, seething inside.

'Well, I got my father's secretary to dig into her background. I just knew there was something dodgy about her. I was right. She'd faked her university degree certificate. She never even went to university. God, she was a lying bitch.' As Johnny told the story Clara had to try hard to resist slapping him. As she smiled at him she felt contempt build up inside.

'Wow, you really are a hero,' Clara said, as Johnny finished his talk. Ella had been right. He was a cock-sucker.

They ordered coffee and brandy, and Johnny lit a cigar.

'I thought you didn't like smoking,' Clara said.

'I don't like *women* smoking,' Johnny replied.

Clara was astounded. Johnny didn't seem to like women full stop. After he paid the bill, she knew what she had to do. 'Are you going to come back to my place?' she asked.

'I think so,' he replied, full of confidence. Johnny hailed a taxi and when they got in Clara put her hand on his crotch, praying that she would think of a way to finish him soon.

When they got to her flat she opened the door and walked in. Virginia had tidied up and she was glad about that. She had a feeling Johnny didn't like mess. She knew the sex would be brief – she could spot premature ejaculators a mile off. She kissed him and pulled herself out of her top at the same time, her best trick. Johnny fumbled with her bra, which took him a while. Then Clara pulled at his shirt and chinos. Before long they were naked.

'Where's the bedroom?' Johnny said breathlessly. Clara led him through. He pushed her on to the bed and climbed on top of her. It was over in seconds.

'Was that good for you?' Johnny asked, as he climbed off her.

Clara didn't know what to say. It took her longer to blink. 'Fantastic,' she replied.

Johnny stroked her hair, kissed her and then did something she had not expected. 'I'd better go,' he said.

'You're leaving?'

'I like to sleep in my own bed. That's just the way I am.' He walked into the lounge. Clara couldn't believe her luck. She stood in the sitting room, naked, and watched him pull on his clothes.

'It doesn't bode well for getting married,' Clara joked.

'Clara, I don't think we're nearly at the stage to talk about marriage.'

'I was only joking,' she said, trying not to laugh.

'Girls never joke about marriage,' Johnny replied, pompously. 'I'll call you tomorrow,' he said, and kissed her goodbye. Then he left and Clara was free.

Chapter Forty

Clara woke the next morning and had a line of cocaine. She needed to get her head round the plan. She also needed more coke. Her supply was practically out. She washed and dressed, then called Virginia and Ella. She told them she had a counsellor's appointment that afternoon and asked Virginia to let Ella in. She said she would be back as soon as she could. She assured them she was fine, then hung up. She needed to tell them something soon; she needed to finalise the plan. She felt frustrated that even after sleeping with Johnny she was no closer to doing that.

She called Oliver, who said she could go over when she wanted. She said she would see him later. She knew she would sort things out. She had to. She had some more cocaine and then she left.

She took a cab to Camden Town and rang the bell. When the door opened it wasn't Oliver who stood there but a stunning girl.

'Hello,' Clara said.

'Hi,' the girl replied, and showed her in.

'Where's Oliver?' Clara asked, following her into Oliver's living room.

'He'll be down in a minute.' Just then Oliver walked in. 'Clara darling, I see you've met Gavin.'

Clara looked at Oliver in amazement. 'Gavin,' she repeated.
'Yes darling, Gavin. He's a man,' Oliver laughed.

'What?' The person Clara was looking at wasn't a man, he
didn't even sound like a man.

'Oh sweetie, don't look so confused. I'm just dressed as a
woman,' Gavin explained lighting a cigarette.

'Are you a drag queen?' Clara asked. They both laughed.

'No, he's not Clara. Gavin is a male prostitute. For men
only. He has clients who like him to dress like a woman,' Oliver
explained.

'But fuck like a man,' Gavin added.

'But you're gorgeous,' Clara said.

'Thank you darling. God Ollie, she's such a sweetie.'

'Cocaine, anyone?' Oliver asked, and pulled out a mirror. He
handed Clara a rolled-up note. 'Proper ladies first,' he said.

Clara watched as Gavin took his line, then handed the
mirror to Oliver. She was still intrigued by him and a plan
was forming.

'So, Clara, what brings you here? Not just my company,
I take it.'

'You know why I'm here. Can I have five this time?'
she asked.

'Of course. I need to go and sort it out. I'll leave you two
to get better acquainted.' Oliver blew them a kiss and walked
out of the room.

'What do you do?' Gavin asked.

'Nothing much at the moment. Do you enjoy being a
prostitute?' Clara was over her initial shock, she was intrigued.

'It's a job and I so need the money. You must know that
white powder doesn't come cheap,' he smiled.

'But do you like dressing up?' Clara persisted.

'Not really. High heels are bloody uncomfortable and I
have to shave everything,' he giggled, 'well nearly everything.
And I'm not really comfortable wearing makeup, although I
like the way I look.'

'You look very convincing,' Clara said.

'Thank you darling girl. It's hilarious that you really thought I was a woman.'

'It's hard to believe you're not,' Clara added.

'I'm a little bit girly even when I'm not dressed like this. The only thing I really can't do is butch. But I need the money so if a client wanted butch I'd do my best.'

Clara's mind was working overtime. Excitement welled inside her. She had no idea how but she thought that Gavin was the answer to her prayers.

'How about if I came up with a way for you to earn a bit more money?' Clara suggested.

'Do tell,' Gavin said.

'Well, it's like this. I need to take revenge on a man. It's a long story and I'm not going to tell you now, but I know I could use you. And I'd pay.' Clara still didn't have the details.

Oliver came back. 'What are you girls talking about?' he asked.

'Clara was saying I could help her take revenge on a man,' Gavin replied.

'What fun. Let's have some more cocaine. What's it all about, Clara?' Oliver looked excited.

Clara took a line and started telling them all about Johnny.

'But how could Gavin help? Is this guy gay?' Oliver asked.

'I don't think so. He's dating me,' Clara said.

'Yes, but, darling, I think you could turn most men straight,' Gavin said.

'Well, he was very quick in bed. He's sexist and horrible. But he'd think Gavin was a woman, wouldn't he?'

'You did,' Oliver answered.

'A very attractive woman,' Clara mused. The three sat deep in thought.

'I have an idea.' Clara's eyes widened. She had another line of cocaine, then continued, 'We set them up together. He thinks Gavin is a woman and he goes back to her place.

We set up a video in Gavin's place and record the whole thing.'

'I'm not being funny, but wouldn't he notice that Gavin's a guy when he drops his skirt?' Oliver said.

'Yes, but that's why we need to think of something before that.' Clara sighed.

'I know,' Gavin said. 'We drug him.'

'Brilliant.' Oliver clapped his hands.

'I'm not sure ...' Clara hesitated.

'It's perfect. We set up a video camera – hidden, of course. I assume money is no object for you, darling. Anyway, then you arrange to meet him and stand him up. Gavin works his charm – which, believe me, is very, very charming. He gets him back to his place, slips some sleeping stuff in his drink. I can provide that. When he's asleep, Gavin will remove his clothes and turn the video on. Although they won't be doing anything, we can ensure the video shows that Gavin has a dick and he'll be in bed with this man. No sex involved.' Oliver was excited.

'But what happens when he wakes up? He'll call the police.' Clara was worried.

'No, he won't. Gavin will be fully clothed again and he'll tell him he passed out. He won't know anything until we send the video to his colleagues.'

'My God, you're a genius,' Clara said. The cocaine had made her head a bit fuzzy, but this made sense.

'How much?' Gavin asked.

'How much what?' Clara asked, still thinking.

'How much will you pay me?'

Clara thought for a minute. She had no idea what the rate for this sort of thing was. 'Five thousand pounds?' she offered.

'My God,' Oliver said. 'You must really hate him.'

'I do,' Clara replied.

They continued planning. Gavin was almost falling over himself to be involved. He wasn't sure how he'd do it, but for that money he'd make anything work.

'I'll need you to meet the others,' Clara said.

'What others?' Gavin looked nervous.

'My two friends. We're in this together. But don't worry, they'll be thrilled.' Clara really thought they would.

'You must keep me updated,' Oliver interjected.

'Gavin, give me your number. I'll call you, and perhaps you can come round tomorrow.' Clara was getting excited.

'Here.' Gavin found some paper and wrote down his number. 'I'm working tomorrow, but I could come round first. I need to be free by seven.'

'Perfect.' Clara tucked the piece of paper into her bra along with the five grams of cocaine. She paid Oliver, kissed them both and left.

As the door closed behind her Clara realised she needed the loo. She didn't want to go back so she made her way into the nearest pub. On her way out of the ladies', she walked straight into someone. Her bag dropped and its contents fell out. As she reached down to pick everything up, so did the person she had bumped into. A policeman. She almost died again as he picked up a wrap of cocaine that was sitting at his feet. She hadn't known she had any in her bag. As the policeman informed her she was under arrest she panicked as she remembered the other five wraps in her bra.

Chapter Forty-one

Virginia arrived at Clara's flat at five in the evening. She hadn't been able to think about anything but James all day. After the initial euphoria of last night had worn off, reality sank in. When it did, Virginia was terrified. There was a man she really liked, and he was Clara's brother. She was staying with Clara and she didn't know what to do. She knew she had to call him because he couldn't call her. Virginia didn't have much confidence and in the man-calling line she had no experience at all. She couldn't help but think that this was not real. Why would someone like James want to date a loser like her? She tried to feel upset by everything, but she couldn't. A fifty-foot smile was plastered across her face.

Ella turned up at half past five and smiled at the doorman, with whom she was on first-names terms now. She rang the bell and Virginia opened the door. 'Hi.' She walked in.

'Clara's not here,' Virginia said.

'Well, she said she'd be out,' Ella replied.

'Yes, but I'm nervous.'

'Me too,' Ella agreed, and sat down. They sat and waited, discussing Johnny but not getting far. They were aware that Clara had a plan and they were infuriated that they knew nothing about it. Then the telephone rang.

'Should we get that?' Virginia asked.

'It might be Clara,' Ella said, and picked it up.

'Hello.'

'Ella, it's me,' Clara said.

'Where are you?' Ella asked.

'At the police station.'

'*What?*' Ella screeched, and Virginia leapt to her feat.

'I've been arrested,' Clara replied, quite calmly.

'What for, Clara?' Ella asked.

'Possession. A wrap of coke I didn't even know I had fell out of my bag.'

'Your coke fell out of your bag?' Ella repeated. Virginia's face drained of colour.

'I bumped into a policeman and dropped my bag. Can you come and get me?' Clara said.

'Clara, hang on. I don't understand. What the hell? Oh, God.'

'Shut up and listen. Ella, my coke fell out of my bag. I didn't know I had any. I haven't taken any. The policeman arrested me and they charged me with possession. I promised I didn't usually do this and I just bought the stuff from someone on the street. OK? They're giving me a caution. I need you to come and get me because I don't have any money and I don't know how to get out of here.' Suddenly Clara was sounding hysterical.

'Where are you?' Ella asked.

'Kentish Town police station. It's on Holmes Road, NW5. Do you know it?' Clara said.

'No, but I'll find it. Fuck, Clara,' Ella replied.

'Just get here. 'Bye.' Clara hung up.

'Come on. We've got to go and get her,' Ella said.

'But . . .' Virginia started.

'I'll explain on the way, but I'll be fucked if I understand.' Ella grabbed her bag and ran out of the door.

After about ten minutes they hailed a taxi. 'Kentish Town police station,' Ella said.

'This is too much for me,' Virginia said, as she sat down.

'Pull yourself together,' Ella retorted sharply, then explained what little she knew while ignoring the interested glances of the cab driver.

'Clara's a liability,' Virginia said.

'I know,' Ella concurred.

'What are we going to do?'

'We are going to finish what we've started,' Ella replied, as calmly as she could.

'Right.'

'Then we're putting Clara into rehab.'

'Right.'

'Then we're going to therapy.'

'Right.'

'I know a good therapist,' the cab driver offered, and was met with dagger looks. God, he thought, those two look like they need a good seeing-to, never mind therapy. But he kept quiet and he kept driving.

They pulled up at the police station and saw Clara flirting with a policeman on the steps.

'Can you wait?' Ella asked.

'Sure,' the cab driver replied. This was better than a film.

If Clara was stricken by her experience she didn't show it. She was smoking a cigarette and waiting. As soon as she saw Ella and Virginia, she waved. 'My friends are here,' she said to the policeman.

'Sorry, Officer,' Virginia said, immediately hating herself for it, and Ella rolled her eyes.

'It's such a disgrace you don't give us criminals a lift home.' Clara simpered at him. Ella grabbed her, dragged her to the cab and they got in.

'What the *fuck* are you doing?' Ella asked, angry again.

'I told you, it's a mistake,' Clara said innocently.

'What were you doing here?' Ella asked. 'You told us your counsellor was in Mayfair.'

'So I lied. I was working on my plan for Johnny,' Clara said defensively.

'OK. Then tell us about it,' Ella commanded.

'I'll explain tomorrow.' Clara folded her arms defiantly.

'Fine. But you'd better have come up with a good one,' Ella said.

'Oh, I have.' Clara smiled.

When they got home, Ella paid off the cab driver, ignoring his smirks. They walked inside in silence.

'Thank you again for rescuing me.' Clara giggled.

'Clara, just shut up. You're in a lot of trouble,' Ella roared.

'Really? I'm scared.'

'You are still taking drugs,' Ella accused her.

'Well, tomorrow you'll be glad I am. Now I'm going to bed.' Clara slammed the door of her room, although it was barely seven o'clock.

'What do you make of it?' Virginia asked.

'She's been lying to us. There's no counsellor, no plan, just a drug-dealer,' Ella answered simply.

'So what do we do?' Virginia asked.

'Virginia, I do not have all the answers.' Ella was sharp again.

'Well, I do. We wait until tomorrow and see if she has anything. Otherwise, we make our own plan. We've done it twice we can do it again.'

Virginia had raised her voice and Ella was surprised. 'OK. Sorry,' she said.

'That's fine. Let's try to get along,' Virginia suggested.

'Shit, what happened to you?' Ella asked.

'I can't tell you,' Virginia said, again thinking of James.

'Have you met someone?' Ella asked.

'Maybe, but I won't tell you yet. OK?'

'OK,' Ella replied, and settled down on the sofa.

They avoided proper conversation and watched television. They went to bed and woke the next day feeling unsettled.

Chapter Forty-two

Virginia was up first, and Ella found her cleaning the kitchen.

'Morning,' Ella said, trying to sound more cheerful than she felt.

'Morning,' Virginia replied. They looked at each other awkwardly.

Ella put the kettle on and made coffee. She handed a cup to Virginia.

'Thanks.' They lapsed back into silence.

Soon afterwards, Clara appeared. 'Hi,' she said, looking ashamed.

'Well, hello,' Ella replied.

'I'm sorry,' Clara announced.

'What for?' Ella asked.

'For last night,' Clara replied.

'Oh. You mean for being arrested and acting like a total moron?'

'Leave it,' Virginia said.

'Why?' Both Ella and Clara asked it at the same time.

'Because this isn't getting us anywhere.'

'The oracle has spoken,' Clara said sarcastically.

'Shut the hell up,' Virginia shouted. 'Clara, we know you're still taking coke. We don't believe any of this counsellor shit. And don't ask us to trust you because you've never given us a reason to. Ella, stop pushing. Either we leave each other now or we carry on. That's our choice, the only choice we can make.' Virginia stopped, and the others just looked at her.

'Well, you've certainly found your voice,' Clara said.

'Yes, I bloody well have, thanks to you. God, you guys snipe at each other all the time and usually I cower, but not now. Never again. If you don't start to behave then I'm out,' Virginia said angrily.

The other two were shocked. Virginia had never stood up to them before.

'Clara, have you been using cocaine?' Virginia asked.

'Yes, but later you'll see that I'm not an addict,' Clara answered.

'Right. You're a bloody fool then,' Virginia snapped.

Clara looked impressed. 'Gosh, you've sworn twice in one day. That must be a record,' she said.

'Fuck you, Clara. At least I wasn't arrested. At least I didn't risk everything we've worked for. You're a bloody liability,' Virginia barked.

'I said I was sorry. I'm not what you think. I've worked out the Johnny plan, I promise. I'll tell you tonight,' Clara pleaded.

'You'd better not let us down,' Virginia said sternly.

'You can be quite scary when you're riled,' Ella said.

'Yes, I can, can't I?' Virginia replied, and they all collapsed into giggles.

They spent the day sitting around trying to be nice to each other. At one point Clara went off to call Gavin. She told him to be there at five that evening. She received a call from Johnny. With raised eyebrows from the other two, she went into her room and told him she missed him but was working hard. He asked for her work number. She told him to call her mobile as she was never at her desk; he seemed pacified. She said she would see him later that week and he said he might be available. 'Of course you'll be available, you sad fuck,' Clara said to herself.

*   *   *

Virginia was sitting on the sofa, looking and feeling awkward, Ella slumped in an armchair while Clara was pacing the room maniacally. She had sneaked a couple of lines of cocaine, and although the others had noticed, no one said anything. Ella was unsure what to do. She was angry with Clara, but she knew that Clara was not easily convinced of her wrongdoing. She decided that she would wait and watch and hope that a miracle intervened. Clara was excited about her plan and feeling very clever. It was time to fill the others in.

'OK. We've had two successful results. You masterminded the last two attempts, although I know I helped. You see, I really only had a little bit of involvement, and then I was arrested and you two are worried about me. But you don't need to worry, I'm fine. Just a little keen on the old recreational drug, but that's nothing, really, and I've got to say thank you for Tim, which was better than I ever imagined. And, well, you guys did a great job, and Isabelle, although that wasn't my personal vendetta, I still feel very happy she got what she deserved, so now I've planned the last one myself to say thank you.' At last Clara stopped to draw breath.

'Clara, we're in this together, we all contributed, and we think it works because we all put forward different ideas.' Ella could see that Clara was out of control.

'Yes. I think it might be better if we all think this through together,' Virginia said in support.

'Don't be silly. Anyway, I have Johnny's revenge all worked out. It's so great and you'll be so pleased with me.' Clara resumed the pacing.

'Well, are you going to share it with us?' Ella asked.

'Of course. I found a man who looks like a woman. Well he does when he dresses like one. Which he does sometimes because he's a prostitute. And he's gay. But he's really stunning and I thought he was a woman, gosh I was so shocked when

I found out he was a man. He even sounds like a woman. So we are going to get him to seduce Johnny and videotape them together. We'll send the tape to your old desk, Ella, and he'll never be able to show his face again. Or anything else.' Clara shrieked with laughter.

Virginia and Ella did not.

'That is the dumbest idea I've ever heard. How on earth is Johnny going to let himself be seduced by a man and how on earth are you going to video them? This is ridiculous,' Ella said, and Virginia was speechless.

'Ella, you're such a drag. Of course it'll work. All Gavin — that's his name — has to do is meet Johnny in a bar and chat him up. You said he was egotistical so he's bound to fall for it. Then all he has to do is to take him home and put some sleeping stuff into his drink, undress them both and video them in bed together.' Clara was still smiling. The others weren't.

'That's date rape. Christ, Clara, that's illegal. So far we haven't broken the law and we have not used drugs and rape. My God, I feel sick at the thought.' Ella was furious.

'It's not rape because nothing will happen. It's just that it will look like it has on the videotape, two men sleeping side by side. That's all. He's not going to actually do it. There's nothing illegal at all. I don't see what all the fuss is about.'

'Drugging someone is illegal. What happens when it all blows up? If Johnny goes to the police, says he was kidnapped and drugged, your Gavin will blow the whistle on us and we'll be done for. I do *not* want to take that risk. I'm not doing it.' Ella was furious.

'Nor me,' Virginia agreed.

'Oh, God. Here I am with two little Miss Perfects. Listen. When Johnny wakes up Gavin will be wearing girl's clothes and will tell him he passed out. Johnny won't suspect a thing until he sees the videotape. What do you mean date rape? That won't stand up in court.' Clara was furious that they weren't grateful.

'Clara, this is the worst idea I've *ever* heard,' Ella said, and Virginia nodded in agreement.

'Ella, this is *exactly* what it's about. We set out to destroy the lives of the people who tried to destroy ours. We did it with the other two and we're going to do this now. My way. Even if you two don't agree, this is going ahead and it's going to be the best. But, of course, why should you trust me? No one else does. Everyone expects me to mess up — my parents, Tim, now you two. And I thought we were beginning to trust each other. I thought we were all we had. But you just think I'm useless, like everyone else in my life. Thanks, girls, thanks a lot.' Clara stormed off.

'She's mad,' Virginia exclaimed. 'What *are* we going to do?'

Just then the doorbell rang. Ella answered it and found herself staring at an attractive woman.

'I'm Gavin,' the 'woman' said. Ella let him in, lost for words.

Clara had returned from her bedroom. 'Gavin darling, how are you?' she gushed, and kissed Gavin's rouged cheek.

'Fine, darling. Have you told them?' he asked, looking at Virginia and Ella.

'Yes, but they're a bit worried about it,' Clara replied.

'Why?' Gavin asked.

'Oh, they think he'll go to the police and try to pin date rape on you,' Clara explained apologetically.

'Well, that won't work, will it? I'll say nothing happened,' Gavin giggled, 'and he passed out as soon as he got to my flat. I'd defy him to prove otherwise.'

'That's exactly what I said. Drink, Gavin?' Clara asked, and left the room.

'You don't look like a man,' Virginia said.

'Do you want to see my penis?' Gavin offered.

'No,' Virginia said quickly.

'We're just worried about the legalities,' Ella said.

'And I'm worried about the money. Do you want me to do it or not?' Gavin enquired, stroppy now.

'Yes,' Clara said, as she returned.

'How do we get them together?' Ella asked reasonably.

'That's easy. I've been seeing him,' Clara replied, pouring wine for everyone.

'You've *what?*' Ella was appalled.

'Look, I know I told you I was seeing a counsellor, but I wasn't. I was seeing Johnny.'

'How *could* you?' Virginia asked.

'Because we had to get him, and to get him we needed to know where he was and what he was doing. I was doing you a favour.'

'Clara, tell me you haven't slept with him,' Ella said, her head in her hands.

'I screwed him. It was brief and horrid and I did it for you,' Clara screeched.

Gavin looked on with interest.

'I'd *never* ask you to do that,' Ella said, horrified.

'Well, I bloody did,' Clara replied.

'So am I going to do it or not?' Gavin asked calmly.

'*No,*' Virginia and Ella said.

'Yes,' Clara shouted.

'Well, which is it to be?'

'Gavin, I said we would do this and we will. Please excuse my ungrateful friends. I'll call you tomorrow to set it up,' Clara said. 'How do you get your boobs to look so real?'

'I've had this thing for ages. It's a bra with built in squigy things, like water really or silicon. Do you want a feel?'

'No,' Virginia and Ella shouted in unison.

'I do.' Clara got up to inspect them. Virginia buried her head in her hands and Ella stared in silence. 'Gosh, they feel real as well. How clever. Oh Gavin, what name do you use when you're being a woman?'

'Crystal,' Gavin said proudly. Virginia groaned from behind her hands. Ella shook her head.

'Crystal. What a perfect name.' Clara sat down again.

'Anyway darling, I must go to work now, I'll wait to hear.' Gavin kissed Clara, scowled at Virginia and Ella, and left.

'We can't do this,' Virginia said, after he'd gone.

'We're doing it,' Clara replied.

'It's madness,' Ella said.

'No, it's not, it makes perfect sense.'

'It makes *no* sense,' Ella said tightly.

'I'm sick of people not trusting me!' Clara shouted.

'Clara, calm down and think this through,' Ella begged.

'I fucking well am calm and I'm going to do this. I'm doing it for you, Ella, and if you don't agree then that makes me sad.' Clara burst into tears.

'Oh, God.' Virginia rolled her eyes.

'Oh hell, Clara, I'm sorry.' Ella was not ready to tip her over the edge.

'Please, *please* let me do this,' Clara implored.

Virginia and Ella looked at each other. They knew it was a bad idea, but they had no alternative to offer.

'OK,' Ella conceded.

'I can really do it?' Clara asked, her eyes glistening.

'If it goes wrong—' Virginia started.

'I promise it won't.' Clara hugged them both, and went to have a bath.

Ella looked at Virginia. 'What do you think?' she asked.

'I think it's the worst idea I've ever heard and that this is going to get us into trouble.'

'Me too. But I don't know how to head her off. What *are* we going to do about her?' Ella was lost.

'I don't know. But I'm scared. Christ, we *have* to stop her.'

'But I'm not sure that's possible. Every time we question her she just goes mad or bursts into tears.'

'I know.' Suddenly Virginia thought of James. 'I need to make a call,' she said.

'Who to?' Ella asked.

'Just someone,' Virginia replied, picked up the telephone and walked out of the room.

Ella shuddered as she realised that everything was totally out of control.

She was shaking as she dialled the number. After the fifth ring, James answered. 'Hello.'

'It's Virginia.'

'God, how are you?'

'I've been better. You?' Virginia needed him.

'I'm fine. Are you around?' he asked.

'I'm at Clara's,' she replied.

'Is she all right?' James asked quickly.

Virginia crossed her fingers. 'She's fine.'

'Can I see you?' James asked.

Virginia thanked God. 'I could come round,' Virginia suggested.

'Shall I come and collect you?' James asked.

'No. I'll get a cab. Give me your address.'

She went back into the living room and put the phone back on the charger. 'I have to go out,' she said to Ella.

Ella sat up straight. 'Where to?' she asked.

'Just out. Please don't ask me,' Virginia replied. She couldn't find words to tell her – and she didn't want to.

'Fine. So you leave me with little Miss Cokehead, who we also can't question, and you go free. Fine, Virginia,' Ella said crossly.

'I'm sorry,' Virginia said, although for the first time in her life she wasn't.

'Oh, what the hell? You go and I'll try to talk her out of this stupid plan.' Ella's life was becoming a nightmare.

'I'll be back tomorrow morning,' she said, as she picked up her coat. Ella watched her and knew instinctively where she was going. The sly cow is seeing Clara's brother, Ella thought. Then she went to check on Clara.

Virginia hailed a taxi easily. After the madness of the past two days James seemed to represent comfort and safety. She tried to feel guilty about leaving Ella to deal with things, but she didn't. Clara had promised them she would get help to get off cocaine. She'd lied, and she'd come up with this crazy plan. Virginia was angry with her. Clara needed help, and she knew how much trouble they might face if the revenge on Johnny went wrong. She couldn't tell James about any of this, and she felt trapped. Ella felt the same, she knew. They were trapped by the revenge plans – and by loyalty to each other. They were trapped by loneliness too. As she sat in the cab on the way to see a gorgeous rich man Virginia knew that she was only in this position because of Clara and Ella. The loneliness that bound her to them had also turned her life round. She was so confused.

James answered the door wearing jogging bottoms and a T-shirt. 'God, what a sight for sore eyes,' he said, grabbed Virginia and kissed her. They broke apart and went into the house. James had a gorgeous cottage in Chelsea and Virginia fell in love with it the minute she entered it. Although it was sparsely furnished and very clean, it was also cute. Real wooden beams jutted out from the ceiling. Virginia loved it even more than she loved Clara's flat.

'So, what brings you here?' James asked.

'You,' Virginia answered. She had made a decision on the way over. She had decided she wanted to lose her virginity.

'Really?' James said mockingly.

'Yes really.' Virginia hugged James and immediately felt better.

'Can I get you a drink?' he asked as he held her.

Virginia was nervous. She did want him but part of her

was still scared. A drink would help. 'Have you got any wine?' she asked.

'Only red I'm afraid, is that OK?'

'Fine,' she smiled.

Virginia sat down on the sofa and waited for James. When he returned with two glasses of wine he sat next to her.

'Have you been playing hard to get?' he asked.

'Why?' Virginia didn't understand.

'It's been ages. I thought you'd call before. I missed you.'

'I missed you too. I'm sorry, but things have been crazy.'

'Virginia, I'm not sure I want to talk about these plans of yours.'

'Well I certainly don't,' Virginia said sipping her wine.

Although James was next to her, she was unsure of what she should do. Before she had a chance to dwell on this, he leaned over and kissed her tenderly. When they finally broke apart, James looked at her. 'Do you want to come to bed?'

Unable to speak, Virginia nodded. As he led her to his bedroom she tried to quash her nerves. She decided to let James take control.

He kissed her, then undressed her. As he caressed her she felt both self-conscious and heavenly at the same time. James was an expert and he lowered Virginia on to the bed, kissing, licking and touching her. Virginia groaned with a pleasure she had never experienced. James took this as a sign to take his clothes off. Virginia's eyes widened at the sight of him. He guided her hand downwards and she started stroking. Although she felt unsure of herself, she gained confidence by James' groans of satisfaction. He was still kissing her all over when he suddenly stopped.

He reached into his bedside table and pulled out a condom. He stared at her as he put it on; he then pushed her down to a lying position before climbing on top. Virginia bit hard on her lip so she didn't cry out. She was in pain, but it was a good pain.

'Are you all right?' he asked and she nodded. He kissed her again. Virginia finally realised she had been missing out. When James climaxed, Virginia was really enjoying herself. James lay next to her holding her in his arms.

'Do you want to get under the covers?' he asked tenderly.

'Yes,' Virginia said, suddenly feeling cold without his body warming her up. He moved her gently then he gasped.

'What?' Virginia said feeling worried.

'Virginia, you bled.' James looked at her. 'You were a virgin?' he asked disbelieving.

'Yes,' Virginia admitted, feeling stupid.

'Why didn't you tell me?' James asked.

'Why should I?' Virginia said defensively.

'Because, darling, I would have been more gentle. God, I'm sorry.'

'You were gentle. Anyway, I was too embarrassed. A virgin at my age.' Virginia felt stupid again.

'Virginia, you're full of surprises. You know I really like you, don't you?'

'Do you?'

'You're very special. And now, well, I feel privileged. But I wish you'd told me.'

'What difference would it have made?' Virginia felt insecure.

'None to how much I wanted you, but I hate to think I wasn't considerate enough.' James pulled her close.

'You were gentle enough to make me want to do it again,' Virginia said boldly. She didn't know where the words were coming from, but they kept coming.

'Oh, yes? Well, then, I should oblige you.'

'You'd better. I mean, I need to make sure it's as good as I thought it was the first time.'

James caressed her. 'I promise you it'll be better.'

They made love twice more before they fell asleep in each other's arms. Virginia slept properly for the first time in ages.

In the morning, James woke her. 'I've got to go to work,' he said, kissing her ear.

'I'd better get back to Clara's,' Virginia replied.

'Are you going to tell her now?'

'Not just yet. Please, James, not yet.'

'So am I just a one-night-stand?'

'Do you want to be?'

'No, I bloody don't. Will you call?' he said.

'Of course, but I've got to finish this business. Can you be patient with me?' Virginia looked at him.

'Of course, but promise you'll call.' Virginia couldn't believe this was happening to her. How could he want *her*? But he said he did so he must.

'I'll call,' she said, kissing him.

James went to the shower and Virginia put on her clothes. She still couldn't believe she'd done it. She had seduced a man. A gorgeous man. A man who said he liked her. A man with whom she was falling rapidly in love. She waited until he was dressed and they left at the same time. He dropped her off near Clara's flat but on the main road. They kissed, and Virginia watched as he drove away.

Chapter Forty-three

Ella woke early. She had had a horrible night with Clara demanding to know where Virginia was. Ella had said that Virginia was in shock over the Gavin thing, which made Clara launch into a tirade about how naïve Virginia was. Then she had taken Ella's presence as a sign that she was on her side. They had sat up for ages arguing over the plan. Ella had kept telling Clara that it was the worst idea she had ever heard, which prompted tears and tantrums. Clara argued that it would work. In the end, she had agreed just to get her to shut up. Ella missed Virginia desperately.

It was only six in the morning, but she got up and showered. Then she made coffee, sat in the kitchen, and tried to think rationally. Her head was pounding from lack of sleep. Her eyes were sore. She was feeling sick and panicked.

At eight she heard the front door open and Virginia walked in.

'So you're back,' Ella said.

'Yes.' Virginia looked shy.

'I told Clara you'd gone home. You were with James, weren't you?' Ella's voice was cold.

'Please, Ella, don't tell her,' Virginia begged.

'I won't. But only because things are bad enough already.

Last night was hell. Hours of Clara going on about how brilliant her plan is.'

Virginia giggled. 'She didn't convince you, then?' She was too happy to be fazed by Ella's mood.

'Shit. You had sex,' Ella said.

'I know.' Virginia giggled again.

'Is it serious?' Ella asked, mellowing.

'It might be.'

'God, you're full of surprises, aren't you?' Ella said.

'Ella, this whole thing is a mess. Even James and me. When Clara finds out, I don't know what she'll do.'

'I'm not even ready to think about that,' Ella agreed. Virginia made some coffee and passed Ella a cup. 'What *are* we going to do about this plan of hers?'

'Let her do it,' Ella replied.

'*What?*' Virginia exclaimed.

'Well, unless you think you can stop her, or come up with a better one, I don't see that we've got any choice.'

'Ella we can't,' Virginia argued.

'Listen Virginia, I can't talk her out of it, and I have tried. All bleeding night. That failed, so I guess we just let her go ahead.'

'Ella, don't you care any more?' Virginia asked.

Suddenly Ella felt very angry. She wanted her head to stop pounding; she wanted to stop feeling sick. The room seemed to close in on her. 'Actually I don't. And as you had a night off, I'm going home. *You* can deal with her ladyship today.' Ella grabbed her bag from the sitting room and stormed out. Virginia tried to look indignant as she watched her go, but she couldn't wipe the smile from her face.

Ella drove home, cursing the rush-hour. Sitting in the traffic, she remembered that she had no job and no future. After the latest débâcle with Clara, she knew it was time to face facts. She needed to move on. Without the other two. But she cared about what happened to them. And caring had not been a part of her plan.

She parked her car and walked up to her flat. Tears streamed down her face as she moved from room to room, not feeling at home, not feeling as if she had a home. Loneliness engulfed her, along with the anger and other feelings she couldn't identify. 'It was not meant to be like this,' Ella shouted to herself, as she looked in the mirror and saw only a stranger. Before she knew what she was doing, she pulled her suits out of her wardrobe. Designer labels everywhere. Pinstripes. More pinstripes. She felt hot with anger. She went calmly to the kitchen, found a pair of scissors, walked back to her bedroom and began to cut up her suits until she was surrounded by tiny pieces of fabric. Then she sat on the floor, the tears took over and she rocked herself back and forth.

At eleven Clara emerged from her room and found Virginia in the sitting room. 'You decided to come back,' she said huffily.

'I just needed time to think.'

'What about?' Clara said.

'Lots of things.'

'Where's Ella?'

'She went home. Actually, she stormed out.'

'Why?'

'I'm not sure. One minute she was fine, the next she said she didn't care about anything any more and she left.'

'Virginia, didn't you try to stop her?'

'Well, you know she can be determined,' Virginia said, as she realised that she should have done so.

'Um. But aren't you worried?' Clara asked.

'Why? I needed my space last night. She needs hers today.'

'Right. If you say so, I, on the other hand, am worried. I'm going to call her.'

Virginia immediately felt guilty. 'But, Clara, she just went home, you know what Ella's like,' she protested.

'Yes, I do know, but I can feel that something's wrong. Don't ask me how, but she wouldn't have gone like that if there wasn't something. You should have stopped her,' Clara snapped.

'I'm sorry, I didn't think,' she said.

'No, I'm sorry. I shouldn't have snapped. I just have a feeling, that's all. It's nothing I can put my finger on but, still, I think I'll call anyway.' She walked to the telephone and dialled Ella's number. It rang and rang and then the answerphone switched on. Clara shouted, 'Pick the fucking phone up, Ella.' It didn't work. She slammed the phone down in frustration.

'Oh, my God. What have I done?' Virginia asked.

'It's not your fault. We still don't know if anything's wrong.' Clara was being reasonable.

'You're right. She seemed off-balance. Oh, God.' Virginia turned pale.

'Have you got her friend's number? You know the girl she stayed with for a while after the sacking.' Clara asked.

'Yes, yes I have. Her name's Jackie.' Virgina ran to her bag and pulled out her address book. She found the number and gave it to Clara.

'We're going round to Ella's,' Clara said.

'Are you sure we should?' Virginia asked.

'I'm not sure about anything but I know something isn't right.'

Clara dialled the number. 'Hello, is that Jackie?' she asked.

'Yes. Who's this?'

'Well, you don't know me, but I'm Clara, a sort of friend of Ella's.'

'Hi Clara.' Jackie sounded friendly.

'We're worried about Ella. She was out of sorts this morning and she said she was going home. But she's not answering her phone and we're a bit worried. Do you have a key to her flat?'

'I do, actually. What do you mean out of sorts?'

'I didn't see her but Virginia did. Apparently she was fine one minute and stormed off the next.'

'Do you have her address?' Jackie said.

'Yes.' Clara said.

'Meet me there. I need to get dressed so if I'm not outside the building wait for me.'

'We will. Thank you.' Clara hung up and ran to put her clothes on, leaving Virginia to berate herself for having been so wrapped up in what had happened to her last night. Otherwise she might have seen that Ella was upset.

As they pulled up outside Ella's apartment block, they saw a girl with jet-black hair about to enter the building.

'Are you, Jackie?' Clara called.

'Yes. Clara and Virginia?' They all smiled weakly. 'I tried pushing the buzzer but there's no answer. Shall we just go in?' The others nodded.

They went up in the lift to Ella's floor. Jackie opened the door of the flat and they went inside. Everything looked normal. Virginia made for the kitchen, Clara went to the end of the hall, and Jackie to Ella's bedroom.

'Holy shit,' they heard her say, and ran to join her.

The three of them stood still as they saw Ella surrounded by scraps of suit material rocking herself and crying.

'Oh, my God,' Virginia said.

Jackie knelt down beside Ella. 'Honey, it's ok, we're here now.' Jackie took her in her arms. Ella looked at them without seeing; she kept rocking.

'I think we should call a doctor,' Virginia suggested.

'I hardly think she'd want that,' Clara said.

'Shut up and let me think,' Jackie said, still holding Ella.

'One of you go and find some brandy. We'll try that. If it doesn't work we'll call a doctor,' Jackie said.

Virginia dashed off and soon returned with a glass.

Jackie held it to Ella's lips and managed to persuade her

to sip some. After a while Ella stopped rocking and threw up everywhere. Virginia ran to the bathroom and found a towel. She came back and tried to mop up the mess. No one spoke.

'I'm going to put her in the bath,' Jackie said finally. She and Clara carried Ella to the bathroom leaving Virginia to clear up the vomit.

As Jackie ran the bath she said, 'Maybe Virginia's right and we should call a doctor.'

'Jackie, I know you and Ella are close, so I don't mean to be rude, but she really wouldn't want that, think about it,' Clara answered.

'I know she wouldn't. I'm just not sure we have any choice.' Between them they lifted Ella fully clothed into the bath.

'Why the bath?' Clara asked.

'I don't know. You got any better ideas?' Jackie snapped.

They splashed Ella with water to rinse off the vomit. She had finally stopped crying.

Virginia came in and stood beside the door. After what seemed like ages, Ella blinked and looked at them all. 'What am I doing?' she asked.

'Thank God,' Jackie said.

'Jackie?' Ella asked.

'Honey, we were worried. You didn't answer your phone, so we came round.'

'I remember driving home. I don't remember what happened after that.'

'You cut up your suits. We found you in the bedroom,' Clara said.

'I did?' Ella stammered. Then she looked at Jackie. 'Can you help me?'

Virginia took Clara's arm and led her out.

'Why did you do that?' Clara asked.

'I think they should be alone,' Virginia said. 'Ella's known Jackie for ages and she feels more comfortable with her than with us.'

'I can't believe she cracked up,' Clara said.

'Well, if I were putting money on which of us it would be, I'd have put it on you or me,' Virginia agreed.

'Thanks a bunch,' Clara said, but they squeezed each other's hands to show they understood.

A bit later Jackie came out of the bathroom. 'She's just getting undressed and drying off. But, listen, I'm taking her away,' Jackie told them.

'Where?' Clara asked.

'I'm not sure. I'll find somewhere in the country and just let her have some space and air.'

'What about our plan?' Clara said.

'It'll survive without Ella for a few days. Look, she's been strong for you both through all of this and she needs a break.' Jackie was firm.

'You will call us and let us know what's happening, won't you?' Clara asked.

'Of course. I'll bring her back to you and she'll be fine. But do one thing for me.'

'What?'

'While she's away get Johnny. Let her come back to the knowledge that the weasel who did this to her is finished.'

'Don't worry, Jackie, we will,' Clara promised, and felt a new strength. She would take charge now. She had always thought Ella was the strong, clever, resourceful one, but now Clara would step into her shoes.

Chapter Forty-four

As soon as they got back, Clara sprang into action. She called Gavin and they decided that Thursday would be a good night: Oliver had given her the phone number of someone who could install the video equipment, so Clara rang it and made an arrangement. Then she called Gavin again to tell her when it would be fitted. Gavin asked when she would get her money. When they had the tape, Clara told her.

'What money?' Virginia asked, as Clara put the telephone down.

'You don't think he's doing this out of the goodness of his heart, do you?' Clara said.

'I suppose not. But how much?'

'It doesn't matter. It's on me.'

'I wish I could contribute,' Virginia said.

'You have. You did the Declan thing when Ella and I couldn't. You did a fantastic job, so it's my turn.' Clara smiled.

'But you've done more than any of us for this one,' Virginia protested, still thinking that Clara had done too much.

'We've all done our bit. And I'd better call Liam now.'

'Liam? Why?'

'We're going to need him to make sure everyone sees the videotape, and I've got to put him on standby.' Clara went to make the call, leaving Virginia alone. She missed Ella, and didn't know how she would cope without her.

'Liam, it's Clara.'

'Hang on, I need to move away from my desk.' Liam took his mobile into a quiet corner. 'OK, we're clear.'

'Liam, something's happening on Thursday night. On Friday you'll receive a videotape and I need you to make sure that everyone sees it. I can't tell you what's on it but I'll have it delivered to you.'

'Clara, you know we only have a few conference rooms with video-recorders in them and people will be stuck at their desks. Can't you send it on e-mail?'

'E-mail?'

'You know what e-mail is don't you?'

'Of course I do. How do I get a video on to e-mail?'

'I'll get you the number of a man I know who's a computer whiz. He owes me a favour. He'll help you. But if you've got something everyone should see I can e-mail it to the whole floor. Have you got a computer?'

'I'll buy one from your man. We can really do this with e-mail?'

'Yes. But what about sound? Most of us don't have a sound facility, do we need it for this?'

'It's visual.'

'OK. Well, send me a videotape as back-up.'

'Liam, won't you get into trouble e-mailing whatever I have to everyone?'

'Clara, I'm not a total idiot. I'll do it from Johnny's computer.'

'God, that's a fantastic idea! Liam, you're a hero.'

'Well, whatever I'm doing it's for Ella – no, for all of us. If we don't get rid of Johnny soon, we'll all go fucking mad. Just make sure Ella knows that. I'll call you back with that number.'

With Ella out of the way, Clara took charge. This meant

that she barked orders at Virginia. While Clara called Johnny to ask him out on Thursday, Virginia had been told to make coffee. The date was arranged. The coffee was made. Later, after Liam had called again, she outlined to Virginia the e-mail idea, called Liam's contact and arranged for him to bring a computer round to her flat.

When Clara had finished organising, they sat down together.

'Do you really think this is going to work?' Virginia asked.

'Of course,' Clara said indignantly, although she was beginning to have doubts.

'I miss Ella,' Virginia said.

'So do I.'

'What's happening to us, Clara? We all seem so fragile, you, Ella and me. I sometimes feel we're all teetering on the brink and I'm scared we'll fall off.'

'We might fall off, Virginia, but we'll get back up. This won't destroy us.'

Virginia hoped she was right.

That night, as they were paging listlessly though some magazines, Clara asked suddenly, 'Virginia, what's your story?'

'What story?'

'Your life story. We know Ella's, which is freaky, but we don't know yours.'

'Maybe I'm too boring to have a story.'

'Maybe it's because you have a story that you're boring.'

'What's got into you? First you fall apart and promise to give up the coke, then you tell us you're seeing a counsellor, then we find out you lied and you get arrested and now you've gone all nice and interested and even intuitive.'

'I don't know, really,' Clara answered truthfully.

'OK. Virginia Bateman has been a huge disappointment to

her parents on every level. When I was little they sent me to ballet, piano lessons and Brownies. I had no co-ordination for ballet and the teacher told my parents I had no ear for music. The piano teacher told them that too. I didn't get as many badges in the Brownies as my mother's friend's daughter, and the shame she had to endure every time I failed to become a pack leader has never left her. My parents pushed me. "Be the best, Virginia," they always said. But I never was. I was just average. Average at school, with average looks. I was never good enough. My lower-middle-class parents from middle England couldn't bear that I wasn't a superstar. Even though neither of them was a high achiever that didn't excuse me. I was told so many times I was a failure that I started to believe it. Then I went to university and started hanging around with the bright people — well, the people who were interested in economics rather than beer. I met Noël, who was average-looking, probably below-average in personality. I let him dominate me until we left. I got a below-average degree and only managed to get a job as a secretary. Nothing was the way my parents wanted it, but then nothing was the way I wanted it either. I didn't *know* what I wanted. When I nearly got that job as a salesperson I was so proud of myself. I was almost a different person. It really hurt when it was snatched away.'

'Virginia Bateman, you are *not* average. I know I always call you boring but you're not. You're very nice. I think you'll do something special.'

'I hope so.' Virginia tried to smile.

'My life was the opposite of yours. My parents had no expectations of me — well, apart from finding myself a husband and learning to cook. Neither of which I have managed. James was the one they pushed. I was just a girl. My parents wanted me to become my mother. She is very thin with a huge collection of Chanel suits, matching shoes and handbags and expensive jewellery. She was beautiful, she still is, but she's so dull. She sits and listens to my father talking and she doesn't understand a word he's saying. She does charity things, she has lunch, she goes to the hairdresser. Apparently that and being a wife is a full-time job. So when I protested that I had a brain and a personality, they pretty much ignored me. My father always says to me, "I didn't send you to finishing school so you could get a job. I sent you there so you could learn to cook." He says it nearly every time we meet.'

'Parents have a lot to answer for.'

'Yours put all their ambitions on to you when they should just have loved you. They gave you low self-esteem. Mine did the same by belittling everything I did. I do love James but I'm as jealous as hell of him.'

'I don't have anyone else.'

'You do now. I know it's not much but you have me.'

The new Clara went to bed and slept well; the new Virginia lay awake thinking about James and sex.

Chapter Forty-five

When Virginia woke up Clara informed her she was going out.

'Where?'

'I've got to meet this video guy at Gavin flat,' Clara said.

'Do you want me to come?' Virginia asked.

'Well, you don't exactly approve of the plan or him . . .'

'I'd like to come.'

Gavin lived in Highgate, in a large white flat.

'God, darling, I wouldn't have thought this was your type of place,' Clara said, looking about her. Its plainness didn't suit Gavin, somehow.

'It's not mine. I look after it for a friend.' Clara decided not to ask any more questions. Virginia stayed quiet: Gavin was scowling at her, which made her nervous.

'Gavin, why are you dressed as a woman now?' Clara asked.

'Because sweetie, I'm getting into character.'

'I thought you always wore women's clothes,' Virginia said.

Gavin rolled his eyes. 'Darling, I only dress like this when someone's paying.'

'Where's this guy?' Clara asked. 'He was supposed to be here ages ago.'

'He'll be here, darling,' Gavin said, and went to make iced tea.

When Mr Spyman, as Clara called him, finally turned up, they were sitting on white cushions on Gavin's floor drinking the iced tea. Clara and Gavin were smoking.

'Hello Mr Spyman,' Clara said, shaking his hand. The big fat black haired man that stood in front of her was so mesmerised by the sight of three lovely women he didn't even bother to correct his name.

'So what can I do for you lovely ladies?' he asked. Virginia groaned inwardly, but Gavin and Clara giggled.

'We need a hidden camera in here, facing the bed.' Clara took him into the bedroom.

'The wardrobe's the best place. We'll have it set up in no time.' Mr Spyman laughed.

'It doesn't sound very technical,' Clara said.

'It's only a bleeding video love, you find these in many bedrooms these days. I'd like to know what you're using it for. Some lesbian stuff is it?' Mr Spyman was getting a little sweaty.

'No it isn't,' Virginia shouted a little too loudly.

'Suit yourselves. I'll be about half an hour. When it's done, I'll call you and we can test it.'

They waited in the other room. Gavin and Clara giggled together, but Virginia kept quiet. Eventually the man shouted to them and they went in. He told Clara and Gavin to go and lie on the bed then gave Gavin a tiny remote-control button. 'Press this when you want to turn it on. It's a VHS videotape as requested, and it'll run for three hours. 'I'll be here on Friday at two to collect the equipment.'

When he had gone, Clara said, 'Right. Phase one complete. Now, Gavin, you bloody better make sure you know how to turn that video camera on. Now, I don't have a photo of Johnny but

he's short and spotty and he'll be the only short spetty boy in
the bar. Make sure you talk to him as soon as you see him. And
ask him his name to be doubly sure. He thinks he's meeting me
at eight. When you're sure the tape has everything on it, call
me and I'll come and collect it. You have to get this right.'

'I know I do, I need the money.'

'What are you going to wear on Thursday?' Clara asked.

'Sugar, I hadn't thought. I'm going to Frontline which is
trendy. I don't have any trendy women's clothes. Oh God.'
Gavin looked stricken.

'Don't panic. Let's go and look.' Clara went to his wardrobe.

'It's utterly hopeless, I have nothing,' Gavin wailed. Virginia
shook her head.

'Shush darling,' Clara said as she rummaged through the
clothes. 'I've got it.' She pulled out a short, plain black dress.

'You think?' Gavin asked.

'Put it on,' Clara commanded. Virginia sat on the bed and
stared at the wall intently.

Gavin put the dress on. It was low cut but not obscenely
so and it fell just above the knee. Clara then pulled out a cream
cashmere cardigan and she ordered him into.

'It's a bit boring isn't it?' Gavin asked.

'No. Johnny thinks he's classy. He prefers the understated
look. Now wear some black heels and some jewelry and you'll
look lovely,' Clara smiled, kindly.

'What about my handbag? Is my handbag ok?'

As Clara put the finishing touches to Gavin's outfit Virginia
longed for Ella. She was in an absurd situation and she had no
idea how to handle it. Gavin was behaving more like a woman
than any woman Virginia knew and Clara was behaving as if
dressing a man in female clothing was the most natural thing in
the world.

'You look stunning darling.' Clara stood back and admired her handiwork.

'Thanks sweetie. Gavin kissed her cheek.

'Virginia, we've got to go and buy a video-recorder.'

'But you've got one.'

'I have to make two copies of the tape, so I need another machine and some leads. Come on.'

Outside Clara hailed a cab. 'Peter Jones in Sloane Square,' she instructed the driver, and they got in. 'This is just like an espionage movie,' she said to Virginia.

'What? Going to Peter Jones?'

'You know what I mean.'

In the shop Virginia followed Clara to the electrical department where, she grabbed a salesman. 'I need a video-recorder,' she said.

The young man smiled. 'What sort, madam?'

'How should I know? One that plays videos,' Clara snapped.

'Well, we have an extensive range,' he said.

'We'll take the cheapest,' Virginia put in.

'You'd be better off going for one of our top-of-the-range models, madam.'

'She said we'd have the cheapest, and I'm in a hurry. Please just give me the cheapest one and some leads. Oh, and some blank tapes. About four.' The salesman hurried off.

'Phase two all but complete,' Clara said, smiling.

When the computer man showed up that evening, Virginia was setting up the video-recorders. She was proving to be a bit of a technical whiz.

When the bell rang Clara opened the door and saw only a stack of boxes on legs. 'I'm Peter,' a muffled voice said. Clara led him through to the sitting room.

'I've got more in the car,' he continued, putting his burden on the table.

'Oh, Virginia will help you.' Virginia glared at her and followed Peter out.

'You need to tell me what you want. Clara wasn't very clear on the telephone so I brought everything I could think of.'

'Well, we need to get a video on to an e-mail format and e-mail it,' Virginia explained.

'That should be easy. Does either of you know how to use a computer?'

'Up to a point, of course. But probably not to achieve this.'

'Fine. I owe Liam a favour so I'll teach you.' Peter smiled at her. He was about thirty with long hair. They finished getting the boxes out of the car and went back inside.

'Let me set up the computer first, then I'll go through everything.'

'Would you like a drink?' Clara asked.

'Cup of tea, please. Milk, two sugars.'

'Virginia be an angel,' Clara said. Virginia glared at her again but went to the kitchen anyway.

Peter set up a computer and a number of other pieces of equipment that Clara didn't recognise. By the time he had started to explain how everything worked, she had lost interest and was watching television.

'Are you going to hook us up to the Internet?' Virginia asked.

'Of course — otherwise you can't do this. I've brought this Internet Explorer CD. I'll set up your address. Who should I register it to?'

'Clara Hart,' Virginia said.

'No,' Clara said. They looked at her. 'We don't want this e-mail traced back to me. Can't we make up a name?'

'Sure.' Peter had no idea what they were up to, but he'd promised Liam he'd do this.

He got them connected quickly, then hooked up a number of leads and showed Virginia how to get the video from the tape on to the web. Eventually he was ready to leave. 'Are you sure you understand?' he asked Virginia.

'Yes. Actually, it's quite straightforward. I think I'll be fine.'

'Well, you've got my number if you need me.' And with that he saw himself out. They were on their own.

'Christ, it all sounds very complicated,' Clara said.

'No, it's fine, I'll be fine,' Virginia replied. 'Did you need to buy all this equipment, couldn't we just hire it?'

'It's about time we got into the computer age anyway,' Clara said, showing absolutely no interest in it. Virginia spent the rest of the evening experimenting with the equipment until she was satisfied she could do it.

By Thursday the nerves had returned. Clara had taken some cocaine to calm herself but it was having the opposite effect. She called Johnny again to confirm their meeting, she called Gavin, she called Oliver and she called Liam. Liam told her he had primed Johnny's computer ready for tomorrow. He had also found the e-mail addresses of Johnny's father and his uncle an extra insurance in the destruction of Johnny's life. They were ready to go.

'Virginia, here's the *Yellow Pages*. Find a courier firm and book a bike for first thing tomorrow morning. Actually, book two. They pick up here and deliver two tapes. One to Liam Rice at SFH, and one to Johnny Rupfin at SFH. I want them delivered separately.'

Then, while Clara had her second bath of the day, Virginia took the telephone into her room and called James. 'Can I speak to James, please?' she asked the female voice. Her heart was thumping.

'May I say who's calling?'

'Virginia Bateman,' she replied. She was put on hold and had to endure some awful music for what seemed like for ever, until James was on the line.

'I thought you might have called before now,' he said accusingly.

'James, things have been manic. Ella's ill and she's gone away for a break. We're about to finish the plans. The last one's tonight. I wanted to call you before but—'

'Good. So when do I see you?'

'I don't know. I can't leave Clara until Ella's back. But I do want to.'

'All right. But as soon as this is over we're telling Clara. I don't want to have to wait for you to call me and I don't like never seeing you. It's not the best way to start a relationship.'

'*What?*'

'Well, I had hoped we were having a relationship.'

'Really?'

'Virginia, would you stop saying that? Yes, really.'

By Thursday evening, Clara and Virginia were watching television, drinking coffee and waiting.

'Perhaps we should go to the bar,' Clara suggested.

'Are you *mad?*'

'Well, at least that way we could see if it was working. I'm fed up with waiting. We waited for Isabelle, we waited for Tim, and now we're waiting again.'

'Clara, don't you think Johnny would notice if we turned up?'

'We could go in disguise.'

'What as, for heaven's sake?' Virginia was incredulous.

'Oh, I don't know?'

'We'll wait,' Virginia said firmly.

'I suppose we have to,' Clara replied, defeated.

Chapter Forty-six

Johnny was a few minutes late, but that didn't worry him. He'd had a bad day at work: instead of giving him the respect he deserved the other traders were still giving him a hard time. Liam was the worst and the rest of the desk weren't much better. Johnny resolved to go and talk to Jeff. They all needed to be put in their places, to know with whom they were dealing.

He walked into Frontline, noting that it was very trendy. He liked the fact that Clara knew where to go in London. He walked up to the bar to order a drink.

He didn't notice a woman watching him from the other end of the bar. Gavin had known he was Johnny as soon as he walked in. He was exactly as Clara had described.

'He's hideous,' Gavin thought to himself as he watched Johnny take a bottle of beer from the barman and hand over his credit card. It was a good job he was getting paid handsomely.

Gavin watched him for about ten minutes. He kept glancing at the door and then at his watch. After a while he pulled out his mobile phone, dialled a number and waited. His call went unanswered and Johnny looked annoyed. It was time for Gavin to go to work.

'Are you alone?' he asked as he went to stand next to Johnny.

'Yes, I'm supposed to be meeting a work contact. I don't know where they could be,' Johnny lied.

'Well, I'll keep you company until they turn up.' Gavin smiled seductively.

'I'm Crystal,' Gavin said, stretching out a perfectly manicured hand.

'Johnny. Pleased to meet you.' Johnny took Gavin's hand gently and looked him up and down.

'Well Johnny, are you going to buy me a drink?'

'I could,' he replied with a wink. Then he turned to the barman. 'Another Becks and a glass of champagne for the lady.'

By half past eight, Johnny had had three beers. Gavin had two glasses of champagne. Johnny had told him he was an important trader in the City. He said he didn't really want to meet the boring person who was obviously not coming, and again he emphasised how important he was.

When Gavin spotted a free table he suggested that they should sit down. As Johnny carried the drinks, Gavin positioned himself so Johnny had a good view of his long legs, and he slumped down a little to show off his fake cleavage.

'Thank you Johnny, you're a true gentleman,' Gavin said taking his drink. After a few minutes of listening to Johnny's ramblings, he excused himself.

'Darling, I must go and powder my nose.' As he stood up, he gave Johnny his best seductive smile.

As he entered the ladies', he decided he would make his move soon. Johnny was a bore and Gavin hated bores. He reapplied his lipstick and thought of the money as he made his way back to the table. Seeing Johnny as five thousand pounds made him look a lot more attractive.

'You have nice legs,' Johnny said.

'Thank you. There are lots of nice things about me.' Gavin giggled. He wished he could smoke, but Clara had told him not to.

'When you're as important as I am, you get a lot of girls wanting to show off their nice bits,' Johnny slurred.

'I bet you do. But it's not your importance I'm after.'

'Really?' Johnny was swaying slightly.

'No, I'm after your cock.' Gavin always liked the direct approach. He also wanted to get this business finished before he lost his nerve.

'Would you like to come back to my flat?' Johnny asked, as he felt himself go hard.

Gavin laid his hand in his crotch. 'No, darling, but I'd like you to come back to mine.'

'OK.' Johnny stood up, swaying slightly.

Gavin got the door attendant to hail him a cab. Outside Johnny was propped against the wall. At this rate, Gavin thought, he wouldn't need any sleeping pills, he'd just pass out.

They got into the taxi and started kissing. Gavin was an expert and could see that Johnny was aroused. When they arrived in Highgate, he had guessed something that Clara had missed. This will be the easiest money I've ever made, he said to himself, as he let them into the flat and led Johnny to the bedroom. Something had been bugging him all evening and now he knew what it was. Johnny was gay – or, if not gay, bisexual. Gavin knew the signs and he could have kicked himself for not realising it sooner. He had a sixth sense when it came to sexuality and he had never been wrong before. He would have put all of the five thousand pounds on Johnny being a closet homosexual.

When they got to the bedroom he kissed him again, and flicked on the video camera. He decided that if this worked he would ask Clara for another couple of grand. After all, he was actually going to have sex with him. The idea turned him on.

'Sit here a minute,' Gavin commanded, pushing Johnny on to the bed in full view of the camera. 'There's something I need to tell you.'

'What?' Johnny asked impatiently, making a grab for him.

He ducked out of his grasp. He was wiggling around near him as he spoke, making sure that he became increasingly aroused. It was a gamble, but he knew he could afford to take it.

'Well, I've brought you here on false pretences. You see, oh, God, I'm sorry, but I so fancy you.'

'And I fancy you,' Johnny said, pulling at her cardigan.

Gavin pulled away. 'Johnny, I'm a man.'

Johnny laughed. 'Don't be absurd.'

'Let me show you.' Gavin stood in front of Johnny, just a little to the side so that he was still visible to the camera. Seductively he took off all his clothes to reveal his penis. Johnny stared. While most men would have been filled with revulsion and bolted out the flat, Gavin could see that Johnny wasn't one of them. He had guessed correctly.

'I was right about you, wasn't I?' Gavin said.

Johnny reached out his hand and started to stroke his penis with one hand and his chest with the other.

'If you mean will I have sex with you, then yes, I will. I love sex with men.' Johnny was breathless with desire.

'My God, Johnny, I knew it. I'm you're perfect creature.'

Gavin thought he might start working in porno movies — he was so good on camera angles. He pulled out a condom and they had sex. All the time he made sure that Johnny's face was as visible to the camera as what they were doing. He was all over him.

Afterwards he kissed him and held him in his arms. Gavin had really enjoyed it. 'Johnny, are you gay?' he asked.

'Of course not — not in *my* profession.'

Gavin felt a bit sorry for him. He had to pretend to be straight. No wonder he hadn't managed to service Clara properly. For a minute he felt bad about what he was about to do, then he told himself that he needed the money and Johnny was a self-important prick. He waited until he was asleep before he turned off the camera.

He smiled as he thought about what he was giving them. They would be so shocked! Clara had only wanted it to look like they'd slept together. Instead, she was getting the real thing. Gavin took the tape out of the machine quietly and went to the sitting room. He called Clara, who said she would be over in about half an hour. Gavin said the price had gone up, and asked for seven thousand pounds. He told Clara that he had actually slept with Johnny and that he had consented to it verbally on the tape.

Clara nearly screamed. She said immediately that she would bring a cheque with her.

When the cab arrived Virginia and Clara saw Gavin watching for them out of the window. He ran down to the street and gave Clara the tape in return for the cheque.

'You're the best,' Clara said, hugging him.

'Actually, I quite enjoyed it. He's not bad in the sack.'

'Maybe not with men but he was crap with me.'

'Oh, God,' Virginia said.

The taxi driver thought they were on a drug run, but he knew better than to ask questions.

When they got home, Clara put the tape into the machine.

'I'm not watching.' Virginia shuddered.

'Don't then.' The tape was better than Clara could ever have hoped for. She couldn't wait for Liam to see it. Johnny would never be able to show his face at SFH again.

Virginia stood staring out of the window. She could hear what was happening, but she still couldn't bring herself to watch it.

'Clara, this is not good,' she said.

'What do you mean? It's fucking fantastic.'

'I feel like a pornographer.'

'Well, *we* didn't stand in the wardrobe taping it, did we?'

They made the copies, and Virginia was forced to see some

of it. She felt sick and her legs buckled. Then Virginia put one into Liam's envelope, another into Johnny's.

'This is for Ella,' Clara said, as she sealed the envelopes. 'Now, what about the e-mail?'

'Shit, I don't know. How much should we put on it? I mean, I don't think we should send the bit with them actually having sex.'

'OK, just put the first bit on, up to where they're both naked and kissing. That should be enough,' Clara replied. Virginia got to work following her notes and although it took a while she succeeded. They checked it by sending an e-mail to themselves, as Peter had shown her, and it worked.

'Christ, you're a genius,' Clara said, patting her on the back.

'This is for Ella,' Virginia said, and e-mailed the evidence to Johnny and Liam.

Chapter Forty-seven

The couriers had been ordered for seven the next morning. Virginia got up at six and waited. She had thought about it last night and the weirdness of the situation baffled her. How had Gavin known? What if Johnny had run? She was relieved it was over — she had been so worried about it. But Clara had pulled it off.

When the courier came, Virginia handed him the packages, then closed the door. She knew now they would have to wait again. This time until Liam called.

Liam was in the office earlier than usual. He went to Johnny's computer and got into his mail box. He opened it and watched as it showed a sequence of events that made his hair curl. He quickly sent a 'to all' e-mail to ensure that everyone on the floor received a copy. He also e-mailed it to Johnny's family. He was shaking.

A bit later one of the trading assistants came over with a package for Liam and one for Johnny. Liam opened his. 'Trevor. Keep watch for me, I'm just going into conference room four,' he said.

'What for?' Trevor asked.

'I'll tell you in a minute. Just don't let anyone else come in.'

Trevor sighed. Liam was such an idiot sometimes. He stood by the conference-room door, glad that the markets were quiet so Liam could play his games.

Liam put the tape in the video-recorder and pressed play. He sat down in disbelief and, finally, disgust at what he saw. 'Christ,' he said. This was even more explicit than the e-mail had been. He rewound the tape, pulled it out of the player and left the room.

Already it seemed that everyone on the floor had seen the e-mail.

'Liam, you've got to look at this,' John called, as soon as he saw him. The office was in overdrive as everyone was discussing it.

'Let me see,' Trevor said, going over to the computer.

'I think you'll find everyone's got one.' Liam laughed.

'Well, who sent it? Johnny isn't even here,' Trevor asked, watching with a mixture of fascination and revulsion.

'Maybe he sent it then legged it,' Liam suggested. 'And look, someone's sent me the whole show.'

'Well, let's watch. I can't wait to see Johnny.' John guffawed.

All the men on Johnny's trading desk went into the conference room and Liam pressed play.

'Oh, my God.'

'Holy shit!'

'Fuck!' The men all watched in amazement.

Liam only played a few seconds of the tape. 'Johnny Rupfin shags men. Either that or it's a real porno movie. Johnny Rupfin is a porn star.' Liam laughed and the others did too.

'First the e-mail then this. Christ.' Trevor was in shock.

They returned to the desk, which was surrounded by people demanding to know why Johnny had sent everyone an e-mail of himself naked, kissing a man. Liam faked as much curiosity as everyone else. Then Jeff walked over and everyone dispersed.

'Have you seen that e-mail?' he asked.

'Yes, boss, unfortunately we did,' Liam replied.

'What *is* he playing at? Christ, this is unacceptable behaviour. What he does in his spare time is his business, but to send it round in an e-mail!'

'Well, there's always the possibility that he didn't send it,' Trevor pointed out.

'Who else did? It came from his computer. As soon as you see him, you'd better tell him to get into my office.' Jeff was furious. What SFH needed at the moment was not another scandal. The press would have a field day.

Johnny had woken up to find that Gavin had disappeared. He looked at his Rolex. He was late. He pulled on his clothes without showering and ran outside. He hailed a cab and asked the driver to take him to work.

Total silence greeted him as he walked on to the trading floor. Everyone was staring at him. He wondered if he was wearing the wrong clothes, but he looked at his suit and saw it couldn't be that. He walked to his desk and sat down. Then he picked up a package addressed to him.

'So, you like to shag men,' Liam said. The whole desk roared with laughter.

'What?' Johnny said, colour draining from his face.

'Your extra-curricular activities are the subject of the video in your package. For some reason I got one too. And not only that but you seem to have sent us all an e-mail with little snippets of the tape in it. The whole floor got it, including Jeff. Johnny, we don't care about what you get up to in your personal life, but I don't think you had to send us the highlights of your sex life. Jeff wants to see you by the way.'

'I don't believe you,' Johnny said, clicking on his e-mail. The whole desk watched as his face turned white, red, purple, then green.

'Oh, no,' Johnny roared, and he ran off the trading floor faster than he'd ever run before.

Liam called Clara. 'I'm not sure how you did that, but he's gone.'

'Trade secret,' Clara told him.

'Well done. The bastard will never be back here.'

'Good. Liam, let me tell Ella, then I promise I'll ask her to call you.'

'Do that. Tell her I want to buy her a slap-up meal to celebrate.'

Plan three was complete.

Chapter Forty-eight

They tried to call Ella, but her mobile was switched off. Clara was frustrated, and so was Virginia.

'We should drink champagne like we did with the others,' Clara said.

'But it seems wrong without Ella,' Virginia replied.

'We were the Three Musketeers, but not without Ella,' Clara said. 'Or Charlie's angels.'

'We don't have a Charlie,' Virginia pointed out.

'I have Charlie, loads of it.'

Virginia gave her a look. 'Clara, when you told us you'd give it up, when you asked us to trust you, you lied.'

'But I was dealing with Johnny. And I did it well. I was trying to prove a point. If I was a drug addict I would never have been able to put such a good plan into action.'

'Clara, it was a mad plan and we were lucky. If it hadn't been that Johnny is that way inclined, we could all have ended up in jail.'

'But we didn't, and Johnny will never work in the City again. Just like the other two.'

'How can you be so sure?'

'The grapevine. Remember when we worked at SFH and the guys all got pulled up for Internet porn? E-mails went round the City like wildfire and I know that the same will happen here. Besides, his father and his uncle will probably disown him. They're very traditional men from what I know of them. Johnny Rupfin's life is over.'

'You don't think it's a bit harsh?'

'Not after what he did to Ella, and not after spending time with him myself. We've achieved what we set out to do. Doesn't that mean something to you?'

'It means I'm not the failure I thought I was.'

'Good girl, because that's exactly what it means to me.'

They succumbed to the champagne anyway, although the victory was not as sweet without Ella.

'Virginia, I've been thinking. Why don't you move in here?' Clara said.

'What?' Virginia asked.

'You've been practically living here for the last few weeks anyway, and it's such a big flat. Your place ... Well, really, your place is horrid. I'd like the company. You don't need to pay rent, just keep it clean. I seem to have lost my cleaner so I need that and, actually, we almost get on well. What I'm trying to say is that I like you and I like having your company.'

Virginia coloured. 'You really like me?'

'Yes I do, actually.'

'But you used to hate me.'

'I also hated Ella. And, well, you hated me.'

'We did.'

'So, friends?' Clara said.

'Friends,' Virginia answered, with tears in her eyes.

'Flatmates?' Clara asked.

'Oh, yes, please,' Virginia said. She pushed to the back of her mind that she would be thrown out when Clara found out about James. Now, though, she basked in the joy of having friends — excellent friends too.

Ella was feeling better. She had talked everything through with Jackie and now she knew that as she no longer had her job to hide behind, she no longer had the façade she had created for herself. She had faced up to the Tony situation and grasped that with no job, no obvious future, it was time for her to address the past.

As soon as she felt strong enough she was going to call Sam. The thought of hearing his voice made her feel happier. She would find out what had happened to Tony. If he was dead, she would not mourn. How could she mourn the man who had nearly destroyed her? If he was alive she would just ensure that she never saw him again. After all, he hadn't found her in London, which had been one of her fears in her early days there. The chances were that he was either dead or not interested in her. She could deal with both those options.

The next issue she discussed with Jackie was that of Johnny. The plans for Isabelle and Tim had been wonderful. They had worked better than anyone could have imagined or hoped. Although Ella acknowledged that they had both been set up, they had still created their own downfalls. They had used the worst aspects of each person's character to lure them into a trap. Both Isabelle and Tim had allowed themselves to be trapped. But the plan with Johnny was not only illegal but idiotic. Jackie had agreed with Ella then told her that when she had spoken to Clara before they had left, she had asked her to get Johnny. If the plan was activated in Ella's absence, she would be absolved from any consequences. If they hadn't done anything, Ella would be in a stronger position to deal with it when she got back.

The last issue was one that Ella had been refusing to face: her relationship with Virginia and Clara.

'Despite your flagrant attempts not to like them, you do and they like you. Without knowing it, you're all friends now.'

'Jackie, those two girls are not my friends. We were together only to make a plan, and we've done, or almost done, just that. We've spent a lot of time together but as soon as this is all over that's it.'

'I don't believe that, and neither do you. Why do you think they called me the other day? They were worried about you, and it was a good job they were. You said that Virginia is nice now that she's found a bit of confidence and Clara's sweet when she's not off her head. I think you should face up to the fact that you all care about each other.'

'Yes, but I still think it's only because of the firing thing. If we'd been fired separately, I would never have met them. Sometimes I think it would have been better if I hadn't.'

'You know when I told you to go through with the revenge thing? Well, that was because I believe everything in life happens for a reason. When I was fifteen and living with the pervert, I now know that although he almost finished me off, I needed to go through that. It was because of him I got the restaurant and my house, and now I'm able to go to college. You were meant to meet Clara and Virginia, you all needed each other and you still do. If it hadn't been for them, you wouldn't have worked through all this. God, Ella, I've known you for nearly four years and this is the first time you've been able to put the past behind you. That's down to those two "losers".'

'You're not going all religious on me.'

'Just fatalistic. You've been healed and Virginia has had sex, which probably means she'll be strong enough to face the future.'

'I'm not sure sex can do that for a person.'

'No, but being wanted can. You said that Virginia has no friends, her family sound like terrible people, and she's never had anyone show any interest in her. Having this guy want her, Clara's brother, who sounds like a complete babe, will give her the confidence to move on.'

'Do you always have to be right?'

'Yes, I do. Now, that leaves Clara.'

'Yes, Clara.'

'You're going to get her off the cocaine.'

'I am?'

'You and Virginia. Don't ask me how, but you will. And then she'll be ready for the future and to face her life.'

'God, it's all so corny. We're complete fuck-ups and then we aren't. Will we all live happily ever after?'

'Of course not. You know life isn't that kind. But you'll live, which I think at the moment is good enough.'

'And you?'

'Well, I'm going to get a degree and then I'm going to write your story and become a wealthy author.'

'You dare!' Ella laughed.

'Oh, well, just an idea. What if I change all the names?'

'No way.'

'I guess no one would believe it anyway.'

By Friday, they had taken the decision to go home on Sunday. Ella wanted to start putting things back into place. She didn't even care about Johnny any more. After all that, she didn't need revenge. They had all thought they needed it, but in fact they had just needed to do something. Revenge had been like a disguise and for a while it had proved effective. Ella no longer wanted or needed a disguise. She called Clara from her hotel room.

'Hello,' Clara said.

'It's Ella.'

'Ella, where the fuck have you been? Why didn't you call? We tried your mobile but it was switched off.'

'I left it at home. Clara, you know I had things to work out. Is everything all right?'

'All right? It's fantastic. Since you've been working things out, we got Johnny.'

'My God. You mean you went through with it?'

'Yes, and you can thank me later. Listen . . .' and Clara told her the whole story. When Clara finally finished. Ella turned white.

'Ella, are you still there?' she said.

'Yes,' Ella squeaked.

'Well, we didn't distribute the full sex show, just enough to humiliate Johnny. Liam said he left the building and no one's seen him since. I wish I knew what his father said.'

'Clara, is this all true?'

'Of course.'

'But Liam?'

'Oh, God, you didn't know. Well, I'd been talking to Liam for a while. He really likes you. He keeps saying you have to call him. I think he's got a thing for you. Anyway, without him we couldn't have done it. After, Virginia, my web expert e-mailed the thing to Johnny, Liam sent it all round the office. The best thing was that he sent it from Johnny's e-mail. Liam was a star. We couldn't have done it without him.'

'Clara, I don't know what to say. I can't believe you pulled it off.'

'Well, I told you I would. Mind you, I have to admit it was more luck than judgement.'

'I just don't know what to say.'

'Say you're coming back soon so we can celebrate properly. Virginia's fine but she's addicted to the Internet now and I think I need someone to help me stop her turning into a nerd again.'

'Send her my love. And my thanks. I'll be back on Sunday, so I'll come straight over.'

'Ella, are you better?'

'I am now. 'Bye.'

Ella put the telephone down and went to tell Jackie what had happened. She could not believe it. The plan had worked well and, true to form, Johnny had helped in his own downfall. And now she knew for sure that she really did care about Clara and Virginia.

Chapter Forty-nine

On Saturday Virginia moved her belongings into Clara's flat. Clara had even gone with her to help. She didn't have much so it only took one taxi journey. She was giving notice to her landlord first thing on Monday morning.

Then they got ready for Ella's arrival. Clara made sure they had enough champagne and Virginia was in charge of food. They were behaving like girls without a care in the world. Although Virginia knew they still had problems.

Although she no longer had to pay rent and she had the money from the newspaper story, she needed to go out and earn some. She had no idea what she was going to do. She also knew that Clara, despite her protestations, was still a heavy cocaine user. James was also a consideration: he had called the day before. Luckily Virginia had picked up the telephone and had begged him to leave it until Ella was back. Also, she had started to face the fact that since they had disposed of Isabelle, Tim and Johnny, their own situations hadn't changed. Virginia was still out of work, Ella was still out of work and Clara was still a drug addict. They had come a long way, but they hadn't come far enough.

When Ella arrived she was smiling and bearing gifts, champagne, chocolates and flowers.

'It's so good to see you,' Virginia said, through tears.

'I never thought I'd hear either of you say that.' Ella laughed.

'Well, are you pleased to see us?' Clara asked.

'Yes, I have to admit I am. Jackie dropped me off here – I haven't even unpacked yet, that's how much I wanted to see you. And to thank you.'

'For what?' Virginia asked.

'For the way you saved me the other day. Shit, I really lost it.'

'But are you OK now?' Virginia asked.

'Yes, I am. I'm calling Sam tomorrow. I need to speak to him and I need to be alone when I do. Then I'm putting my flat on the market and selling my car. I'm going to live with Jackie. She's going back to college, and I think I am too.'

'Christ, you've made all those decisions in the last couple of days,' Clara said.

'I want to put the past behind me and I need to do something. Apparently I can do an access course, get to college, and take a proper degree. With the money from my flat, I think I'll be all right.'

'So we've got something to thank SFH for after all.' Clara giggled.

'And you. If it hadn't been for that day we met and got drunk in the pub I don't think I'd have found the strength to do anything,' Ella said.

'Let's not get too corny,' Clara said, as she went to open the champagne.

'Does she know about James?' Ella asked, when Clara was out of the room.

'No. And I've moved in here, so I don't want her to know yet.'

'When are you going to tell her?' Ella hissed.

'I don't know. I was thinking never sounds good.'

'You have to.'

'But she'll throw me out, Ella. I've never lived anywhere as lovely as here. I really want to stay and I don't want to lose the friendship.'

Clara returned with three glasses of champagne. 'Here's to us.'

'To us,' they all chanted.

'Ella, there's something you left off your list of things to do,' she said.

'What?' Ella asked.

'Call Liam. He only helped because I promised you'd have dinner with him.'

'I don't believe that for a minute.'

'Well, it's true, so you have to.'

Clara smiled, Virginia smiled and Ella smiled.

'I will, but I've only got his work number.'

'*Voilà*. A mobile number.' Clara found it and passed it to her.

'OK, but let me have a drink first.'

'Well, there's nothing left to do now but to get Virginia laid,' Clara said. Virginia went red. 'I'm going to find you a man. That'll be my next project.'

'Leave it,' Ella commanded.

'I will not. You're sorted. Virginia is living with me, and I have a strictly no-virgin rule about who I live with.'

'What about you? You need to sort things out with Josh and give up cocaine,' Virginia shot back.

'Josh? I don't think so, and you know now that I'm not a drug addict. I proved that.'

'Leave it, Virginia,' Ella said.

'After all this time we still fight,' Clara said.

'I think it's part of the charm,' Virginia answered, and laughed.

Ella called Liam. He insisted they have dinner that week. Ella agreed to meet him on Tuesday. Monday was for Sam.

Virginia spoke to James and promised she was thinking of him, although he was getting impatient.

Clara took cocaine. They were so near, yet they were still so far.

PART SIX

The Aftermath

Chapter Fifty

Ella's hands shook as she dialled the number. As soon as she heard his voice she burst into tears.

'Elloise, is that you?' Sam said.

'Yes,' she squeaked.

'Fucking hell! Where? What? How?'

Ella took a deep breath and began to explain.

After she had finished, Sam was silent for a few moments. Then he said, 'Ella, he lived. I wanted to tell you but I couldn't. I even tried to get your bank to pass on a message but they thought I was a stalker or something. Anyway, he lived and he believed it was a robbery. He came round once to find out where you were but I made it plain that he'd never see you again. He's married now and probably battering his wife.'

'What about Mum and Dad?'

'They haven't changed. They still miss you. I'm so angry.'

'Sam, you said you'd understand.'

'I do, but I missed you. I do love you so much.'

'I love you too.'

'I'm getting married.'

'No way! Who to?'

'She's called Natalie and she's put me on the straight and narrow. I love her and we're getting married later this year. I prayed that you'd be there.'

'Well, I will.'

'You mean it? You'll come home?'

'To visit, yes. This is my home now.'

'There's so much I want to say to you, I don't know where to start.'

'Me too.' Ella burst into tears again.

The call lasted for four hours. It was filled with tears and eventually laughter. Ella came off the telephone emotionally drained, but stronger than she had been in a long time.

She called Virginia, Clara and Jackie to tell them, and said she would be out of action that week; she needed to get everything else sorted out. Then she called an estate agent, and nearly fainted when he told her how much her flat was worth. As she'd been sensible and had paid off most of the mortgage, she was going to be rich. Well, rich to her. She put an advert in *Loot* for her car – she was really getting somewhere, she thought. She felt guilty fleetingly about Virginia and Clara, but she called them frequently and now the plans were finished there was no need for her to be with them so much.

Before she knew it, it was time for dinner with Liam. Ella smiled as she thought about how far she'd come. When the estate agent had measured her flat, Ella felt nothing. She was ready to say goodbye to 'City Ella,' just as she'd said goodbye to Elloise.

Liam had booked a table at the Ivy and even came round in a taxi to pick her up.

'You look gorgeous,' he said, as soon as he saw her. Ella had put on a blue dress, which fell to just below her knees, and a cashmere shawl was wrapped around her shoulders.

'I see you haven't lost your charm,' she replied, as she kissed his cheek. She looked at Liam, all smart in his suit with his hair neatly cut short, and saw for the first time that he was quite cute. They went into the restaurant and sat down.

'Your friend Clara's a bit mad, isn't she?' Liam said.

'I know. Thank you for your help with Johnny.'

'I still can't believe you all came up with such a mad plan.'

'Believe me, it was all Clara's idea. I went away while she implemented it.'

'Why?'

'I had things to sort out. Anyway, I was convinced it wouldn't work. I still can't believe it did.'

'It was fantastic. Although I think Jeff's losing his hair.'

'Liam, I really miss the office.'

'We miss you. I know you faked your degree. Are you going to tell me why?'

'Maybe one day.'

'I see. It isn't a first-date sort of story?'

'So this is a date, is it?' Ella smiled.

'I hope so.'

They ordered dinner and talked the whole way through. Ella was enjoying herself and Liam was becoming increasingly attractive to her. After he had paid the bill, they got up to leave. 'Are you going to invite me back for coffee?' he asked cheekily.

'I'm going to invite you back for more than coffee,' Ella said, and they got a taxi home.

The next day, Ella smiled all day and sold her car. A number of people came to look round her flat. It was all happening so fast. Liam called and they arranged to meet again the following night. He was cooking her dinner at his place. Ella held out little hope for good food, but she knew she'd get good company and good sex. She called Clara and Virginia and told them what was happening, and they asked her to go round that evening, but Ella needed to phone her parents. She was still working through her list.

The rest of the week passed in a blur for her. By Friday morning she was basking in the afterglow of another fantastic evening with Liam and thinking they might have a future. The estate agent called: he'd received three offers on her flat. She celebrated with a cup of coffee as she read the prospectus she'd been sent by the London college. She felt as though she was finally putting her life back on track.

Chapter Fifty-one

Virginia told Clara she was going to register with some temp agencies. Clara said it was a waste of her talents to go back into secretarial work, but she didn't have any ideas for alternatives. She still didn't know what she would do. They both missed Ella.

The revenge was finished and they felt empty. Clara went to see Oliver and came back with more cocaine, which she devoured. Virginia sneaked out to see James a couple of times. He was increasingly insistent that they tell Clara, but Virginia still didn't feel ready. She wished she could do what Ella had done: Ella had seemed to put everything behind her so easily, and in a way Virginia wished they still had more plans to make so that she wouldn't have to face the future. Her working future. She had been using the Internet increasingly often, and had begun to think she wanted to do something with it. She just didn't know what.

One night Clara went out with an old boyfriend and slept with him, which left her angry with herself and unsatisfied. She buried her nose in more cocaine. She was also upset that Ella had seemed to put her and Virginia behind her so easily. Although she had called, she hadn't been round all week.

On Friday morning, while Virginia was out job-hunting, Clara had a visitor. It was James.

'Jamie, how are you?' Clara hugged him.

'I'm fine, darling, but I need to talk to you.'

'What about?' Clara sat down on the sofa.

'Virginia.'

'Virginia? What on earth for?'

'I like her, Clara.'

'So do I. I asked her to move in and everything. She's lovely.'

'I agree, but I like her a bit more than that. We've ... well, we've had a couple of dates.'

'When?'

'That doesn't matter. What matters is that she thinks you'll disapprove and she doesn't want you to know. She thinks that you'll throw her out, stop being her friend. I told her you weren't like that and you'd be happy for us.'

'Right.' Clara felt cold.

'You don't mind, do you?' James asked.

Clara thought for a minute, then smiled. 'Of course not, Jamie.'

After James left, Clara went to get more cocaine. She was so angry. How dare Virginia get James? How dare he get Virginia? She knew it would only be a matter of time before they forgot her, as everyone else forgot her. As Ella had forgotten her. And Virginia had lied to her; James had lied to her. Everyone she loved and trusted lied to her and left her. She took more cocaine, more than she'd ever taken in her life. She walked into the lounge and started throwing things around. She broke everything she could find, she ripped the cushions off the sofa, she hit the walls with her fists, she drank half a bottle of vodka. When the anger and the tears had subsided, she called Ella and begged her to come round.

That Friday afternoon, when Ella hung up, she wondered why Clara had summoned her. She had sounded on edge but she wouldn't say anything on the telephone. Ella felt guilty about keeping away, but she tried to brush that aside. She had called them every day and things had seemed fine, but she couldn't shake the feeling that something was wrong, and she couldn't shake her guilt.

When she rang Clara's doorbell, as she had so many times, she was hoping against all hope that everything was OK.

'Come in,' Clara said.

'Hi,' Ella said, then stopped and gasped at the sight before her. Clara looked awful. Her pupils were so dilated that Ella wondered if she had gone mad. Her hair was wild and so was was the flat: it looked as if she'd been burgled.

'What the hell's going on?' she asked.

'You'll see,' was the reply from the mad girl who seemed to be Clara, but a Clara she'd never seen before. Ella sat down and lit a cigarette, for want of something to do. She vowed again that she'd give up, but this was obviously not the right time. Why did she feel so nervous? They'd had all the bad times, hadn't they? After a while she heard a key in the lock and Virginia walked in.

'Oh, God,' Virginia said, as she stared into the same mad, staring eyes that had greeted Ella. 'I've been job-hunting. What's going on?' she asked.

'What's wrong? Has something gone wrong?' Ella asked as she looked from Virginia to Clara.

'She knows,' Clara hissed, waving a hand at Virginia. She lunged toward her, stumbled and tried to regain her balance.

'Clara, you're on drugs,' Virginia said, stating the obvious but seeming calm. She had the upper hand for once. She knew what had caused this. She knew and she was scared for Clara, but at least she understood.

'You bitch,' spat Clara, once again losing her footing and grabbing the back of a chair to steady herself.

Ella realised that this was the final phase. It was time to help Clara.

'Tell me,' she commanded.

'Our little virginal friend has been sleeping with my brother,' Clara snarled.

Ella wondered why this should reduce her to such a state. Clara moved forward and grabbed a vodka bottle. White powder was scattered over the coffee table; Ella realised that she had been on a major bender.

'Yes, my fucking brother. The stupid slut's got my brother or he's got her.' Clara burst into tears.

'God, Clara! I didn't think you'd mind this much. I've only been on a couple of dates with him.' Virginia was afraid.

'Why? Why did you have to have *him*? Why did he get you? He's got *everything*, always has had, and now you! You were *my* friend, not his, and now you're with him, and I'm alone and I've got no one and you've got James or he's got you and I've got no one and that's the way it's always been.' Clara fell over.

Ella went to her. 'How much have you had?' she asked, worried that this time Clara had gone too far.

'Fuck off, bitch, bitches, bitch. How could you? I did this for you. I got you out of your messes and your sad lives, and you take my brother, and you're my friend and now you're his, like everything else in my pitiful life.' She grabbed the vodka bottle and threw it across the room. It hit the wall. Then she went mad, hitting the walls and screaming, 'Bitch,' repeatedly.

Virginia stopped looking scared. 'You're right about one thing,' she said. 'Your life is pitiful. Christ, you stupid cow. James loves you, he's the first man who's been nice to me, and we could all be friends, but you have to try to kill yourself because I'm dating your brother. Well, I'm seeing him again and I hoped you'd be happy.'

'Calm down,' Ella screamed at them. 'Virginia, go and get black coffee for all of us.'

Virginia scurried off and Ella crossed to where Clara was sitting on the floor.

Despite her resolve, she knew none of this was finished.

Would it ever be finished? Because as she had learnt the hard way, through her work, through getting even and with her quest to sort her own life out, none of this was over until it really was over.

She hugged Clara, who had clearly had too much – she couldn't even vent her rage properly. 'Clara, why can't Virginia see James?'

'I hated you both at first, you cold, her boring, but now I don't because you're all I have and with you I felt I was going to be OK. Virginia my new housemate, you my friend, we were invincible. But now you've gone, we haven't seen you all week, and Virginia will be with James so I lose all three of you. You, Virginia and James.'

She was childlike as she wept, and Ella encased her in her arms as a mother would, stroking her hair, wiping her tears, holding her as close as she could. She blamed herself for walking away. Clara and Virginia had helped her when she needed them and she had known that Clara would fall at some stage. She shouldn't have left them. Clara and Virginia, the unlikely girls who had worked with her to take their revenge on their bosses, who had helped her confront her demons and stop fearing Tony. And although she had thought she could walk away, she now realised she couldn't, because they still needed each other, and that was the way it was. 'It's not over yet, it's just not over,' Ella said to herself.

Virginia returned, tear-stained, with the coffee. She sat down too, and hugged Clara. 'I really like James, but only because he's so like you. You're my friend first, and if you want me to stop seeing him, I will,' Virginia whispered.

'No, no, I don't want that. I just want – I just want help.' It was the first time that Clara had asked for help. It was not the first time she had fallen apart, but it was only now that Virginia and Ella were being given a chance to put her back together again.

An hour later Clara got the shakes. She looked at them both with her big blue eyes. 'I need more,' she said.

Ella shook her head. 'Listen to me. If you can get through tonight with us both here, then you can get through tomorrow and the next day. We're going to help you, and, God, we'll help you.' Clara lay shaking in Ella's arms as Virginia went to get a blanket.

'When I was little and couldn't sleep, my brother used to make up stories for me about princesses and princes and they always made me feel safe.' Clara glanced at her, still a little unfocused. 'Tell me a story now,' she asked.

'There once was a beautiful princess and she was called Clara . . .'

Chapter Fifty-two

As day broke the three girls sat huddled together. Clara had stopped shaking about two hours earlier and Virginia had made more coffee to keep them awake. Ella had never seen anyone look so fragile and she knew that they had been given one last chance to do something.

A phonecall, a packed bag and James was all it took. Ella couldn't help noticing the look in Virginia's eyes when the handsome heir to Clara's family fortune walked in. He hugged her, hugged Ella and took Clara in his arms. 'Tell me what happened,' he said.

'It's cocaine,' Virginia said.

'You knew about this? You knew and you didn't tell me?' James shouted at her. After what they had been through last night, Virginia burst into tears. She was exhausted, they were all exhausted.

Ella said firmly, 'James, a word in the kitchen. Virginia, stay with Clara.' She grabbed his arm and marched him out of the room.

'We couldn't tell you. Clara promised us it was over; she kept saying it was under control. You are the last person we'd tell because she loves you more than life itself and she feels ashamed of herself. If we'd got you involved before she let us she would have shut us all out and she probably would have died. Now Virginia has been in pieces about you, about Clara and about the drugs. We would never have let her get like this if we could have done anything to stop it. The reason she tipped over the edge was because you told her about Virginia and you. It ate her up with jealousy. So don't blame us. You saw her as we did. You couldn't tell that she was off her head and neither could we. We tried, James, and when we couldn't do any more we called you.'

'I'm sorry. I don't blame you, I blame myself. I should have seen she was in trouble.'

'Then fix her, James.' They walked back into the sitting room.

'Sis, I love you, darling, don't kill yourself.' They saw the tears in his eyes.

As he carried her to the car, Ella and Virginia trailed behind him with her bag. 'I'll take care of her, don't worry, and I'll call you,' he said. Ella kissed Clara's cheek, and Virginia did the same.

'Thank you,' Clara whispered, as James put her into his car.

Chapter Fifty-three

It seemed a long time ago that they had witnessed Clara being taken away, and although they had spoken to her, this was the first time they had been allowed to visit. The first time she'd been allowed to phone she had begged them to go and get her. On the second she had told them she hated them. On the third, she had apologised, and on the last she had asked them to visit.

They drove up in Ella's little Peugeot, which she had bought to replace the TVR.

'A bit of a come-down,' Virginia had joked, as she got in.

'Yeah, but when you're going to be a student you need the money. I could probably live for a year off the money I got for my TVR,' Ella laughed, 'and of course, it would hardly have fitted with the lifestyle. If I went to college in that they'd probably throw me out. And no one is going to get the chance to throw me out.' They smiled conspiratorially.

Ella had been accepted on an access course. She planned to study economics – she still loved it. Everyone, including Liam who was now a big part of her life, had encouraged her. She had moved in with Jackie and she saw Virginia all the time. She had been building bridges with her family; she had started to laugh again; she felt happy with who she was. She still called herself Ella: she had decided to leave Elloise buried in Manchester.

✳   ✳   ✳

Virginia and James had been comforting each other, and were becoming close, as friends and lovers. James was helping Virginia with her future. He had coaxed out of her that she wanted to do something with the Internet, and put her on a course to learn more about it. They had both been working out her next move. She was drawing up a business plan and had ideas that she hoped would become reality. She was going to work with Clara; she was also going to work with James. Even Ella had been roped in to help set things up.

She had sent a change-of-address card to her parents. At first, she wrote a letter, pouring out exactly how she felt about them. It was filled with accusations, all the things she'd told Clara, Ella and James. Then she ripped it up. She knew they wouldn't suddenly change and apologise. She knew they wouldn't understand. So she sent the card with her new address and nothing else. They knew where she was if they wanted to write to her but she didn't need them any more. She had also started e-mailing Susie again. Their relationship had changed beyond belief and it comforted Virginia to see how it was she who was different, not Susie. She wasn't going to let Susie go, though: she had been her only friend for so long that the friendship would endure.

Virginia and Ella approached a building that looked more like a palace than a rehab centre. It was called Manor Park, which made Ella laugh.

'I feel like I'm in a Jane Austen novel,' she joked. They parked and walked to the entrance, feeling a little nervous of what lay ahead. The inside didn't reflect the glory of the outside as they made their way to Reception. It was cold, grey and more than a little scary. Virginia thought it was just how she imagined prison to be. She glanced at Ella, who squeezed her hand. They had to be strong for Clara. They were led to a 'visitors' room', where an ageing sofa and a chair were the only furnishings.

They sat waiting for what seemed like for ever, when the door opened and in walked Clara.

Ella hoped that her sharp intake of breath hadn't been noticed. Clara stood before them in a baggy navy blue jogging suit, her hair scraped back from her face, which was devoid of makeup. She looked unwell, her skin was grey and she had lost weight. When she saw them she burst into tears.

They hugged, kissed and hugged some more. Then they sat down.

'Are you all right?' Virginia asked, feeling horribly inadequate.

'My name is Clara and I'm a drug addict.' Clara smiled at her feeble joke.

'Shit, is that all? God, we thought it was something serious.' Ella giggled.

'Apparently I'm not addicted to sex at all; it was just the coke. After all, I've managed to resist the advances of all the sex addicts in here so I'm OK on that front. Mind you, the way I look doesn't get me the admiring glances I'm used to.'

'What about shopping?' Virginia asked.

'Well, I can't test that out in here either. There's nothing to buy. But I think an addiction to shopping might be OK.'

'Alcohol?' Ella asked.

'I know I drank too much, but I was never an alcoholic. In here, they encourage you to give up everything, but I know that the cocaine and the alcohol weren't linked. I'm not giving up drink – I only drank too much with the cocaine. I can't imagine never having champagne again, or wine, or vodka. But if I ever start drinking in the morning, I'll be back here. Do you think I'm right? Do you think I can still drink?'

'Clara, I think that as long as you don't replace cocaine with drink you'll be OK,' Ella said.

'It's been awful, really awful. I've had withdrawal, which I don't even want to tell you about, and counselling, and I seem to be really good at crying in front of strangers. And I've learnt all about my problems – which, of course, in true Freudian style all stem from my parents. I told my father he was responsible because he's always made me feel inadequate and he said, "I didn't send you to finishing-school so you'd end up in rehab, I sent you to finishing-school to learn to cook." Which just about sums it up. Mummy's terribly pleased I'm in here. Apparently it gives her more in common with all her friends whose daughters have already gone through rehab. I'm a late starter. But at least James is helping me to cope with everything. Speaking of which?' She smiled at Virginia, who blushed.

'He's lovely,' she mumbled.

'Christ, I wouldn't have chosen you for my sister-in-law, but, then, I wouldn't have chosen you two as my friends.'

'Having me as your sister-in-law can't be that bad,' Virginia said, and they all laughed.

'Please tell me you're not marrying my brother.' Clara grinned.

'No, but, well, I really like him.'

'Then you have my blessing.'

'Ella's going to college,' Virginia said, to change the subject.

'That's fantastic. What about Liam?'

'We're getting along. Shit, this sounds like *The* fucking *Waltons*. I like Liam and we have a dynamite sex life. I'd almost forgotten what sex could be like. And Sam and I are still talking every day. I'm going up there soon for his wedding, so everything's great. For once. And I owe it all to you.' Ella's eyes misted.

'That's a bit over the top, Ella. You saved my life.'

'And you gave me one,' Virginia said.

'Bloody hell, now we really do sound like a soap opera,' Ella said, in mock-exasperation.

'A crap one at that. Who'd have thought we'd be friends? I couldn't stand either of you.' Clara laughed.

'Believe me, the feeling was shared by all. You were such a bitch and Virginia was so prim, but I guess it was inevitable we'd become friends.'

'Why?' Virginia asked.

'Because we all hated ourselves,' Ella replied.

'By the way, Josh has been here,' Clara said.

'Really?' Ella asked.

'Yes, and he said he still fancied me even in this get-up. I told him I needed time but when I get out maybe we could meet up. He told me he'd wait, and he even told me he loved me.'

'Thank God you've seen sense,' Virginia said.

'What do you mean?' Clara asked.

'He's one of the sexiest guys in the world. And he's lovely, kind, sweet and funny. In fact, he's just about perfect,' Ella finished.

'I know. I'm such a stupid cow. It's not him telling me he loves me that's the problem, it's me believing it. Until I can value myself no one else can be in my life. You see, I need to stop feeling so inferior and undeserving before I'm ready for him to love me. That's a direct quote from therapy.'

'When will they let you out?' Virginia asked.

'Two weeks. I'm counting the hours.'

'No more cocaine?' Ella asked.

'Never. I nearly let it kill me and I won't do that again.'

The walls of the room were bare, the friendship unlikely, the sight a strange one.

'What are you going to do?' Clara asked Virginia.

'I'm glad you asked. I'm going to start my own business. Well, with a partner. It's an Internet company. While you've been in here I've been doing my homework. I did a course and James is going to help me find financing. I've almost got it all sorted.'

'What?' Clara asked.

'It's a sort of information site. People subscribe for information. People pay to advertise. I'll give you a business plan as soon as I've finished it. I'm really quite excited. James thinks we can make a lot of money although it'll be hard work.'

'Who's your partner?' Clara asked.

'You.'

'*Me?* But I'm rubbish at stuff like that. I don't even know how to use the Internet properly.'

'No, you're not. At SFH your clients loved you. You'll have

your new ones, eating out of your hand, and with my business acumen, or organising skills, we'll make a winning team.'

'I guess I can invest money in it,' Clara offered unsurely.

'It's not your money I want. It's your people skill and your PR skill. We're going to do this on our own, and if we fail we fail, but if we succeed we'll have done it ourselves.'

After a brief pause, Ella asked, 'Are you sure you're allowed to drink?'

'Bloody hell, yes. I told you, I might have drunk too much but I know I wasn't an alcoholic.'

'But you drank a huge amount,' Virginia pointed out.

'Well maybe, but we did a lot of moping and a lot of celebrating.'

'Well, if we get caught, I'll be shot, but look what I brought.' Ella pulled a flask out of her bag.

'Tea?' Clara asked.

'Champagne,' Ella announced triumphantly.

'Oh, Ella, imagine putting champagne in a flask!'

'It's the only way I thought I'd be able to smuggle it in.'

'Ella! You can't bring that in here!' Virginia reproved her.

'You're still the same Miss Tight-knickers.' Clara said.

'Actually, my knickers are a bit looser, these days. If we get caught, we'll *all* be shot. Fancy bringing alcohol into a rehab place.'

'Ella, I love you,' Clara said, as Ella opened the flask.

'It might be a bit flat,' she apologised.

'Who cares?'

Ella pulled out three paper cups and handed them to Virginia. When each of them had a cup of champagne in her hand, Ella raised hers. 'I propose a toast. To us for getting the bad guys and living to tell the tale. To Clara for beating her addiction. To Virginia for losing her virginity, and to me for finally being able to put away the pinstripes.'

'To the pinstripes,' they said, as they drank the champagne.

'No. To life after pinstripes,' Virginia said, and they all drank to that.